THE INDIGO KING

Written and illustrated by

James A. Owen

D1396143

SIMON AND SCHUSTER, LONDON

For Sophie

SIMON AND SCHUSTER
First published in Great Britain by Simon & Schuster UK Ltd, 2009
A CBS COMPANY

Published in the USA in 2008 by Simon & Schuster Books
for Young Readers, an imprint of Simon & Schuster
Children's Division, New York

Copyright © by James A. Owen, 2008
Book design by Christopher Grassi and James A. Owen
The text for this book is set in Adobe Jansen Pro, and the illustrations
are rendered in pencil, pen and ink

1 3 5 7 9 10 8 6 4 2

Simon & Schuster UK Ltd
1st Floor,
222 Gray's Inn Road
London WC1X 8HB

A CIP catalogue record for this book is
available from the British Library

ISBN 978-1-84738-267-2

This book is a work of fiction. Any reference to historical events,
real people, or real locales is used fictitiously. Other names, characters,
places and incidents are the product of the author's imagination,
and any resemblance to actual people, living or dead, events
or locales is entirely coincidental.

Pr...

Contents

Contents

List of Illustrations

Acknowledgements

The Indigo King was the book that I most looked forward to writing, the book I dreaded writing, the book that was the hardest to write, and my favourite book so far. And it would not be the book that it is without the hard work and dedication of my editors.

David Gale is exceptionally patient and knows how to persuade rather than push a writer. He gave me support when I needed it, and room when I needed *that*. Navah Wolfe, whom I got to know as an online friend prior to her employment at Simon & Schuster, is an excellent editorial assistant for David and is as first-class as they come where this author is concerned. She is smart, and caring, and she kept me on my game. Dorothy Gribbin remains an editorial rock in my world. I've often rethought certain passages just because I knew she'd question them. And it's always been for the better. And Valerie Shea is a rock star. I sometimes feel like she's been more exacting with details than I am, and that fact both impresses and humbles me.

My legal team added a new name, Erik Hyman, who is both deft and witty, and as reliable as his Loeb & Loeb compatriot Craig Emanuel. Both have been invaluable supporters of my work, as have my managers at the Gotham Group: Julie, Ellen, and Lindsay. Ben Smith at ICM remains the agent's agent, and I am grateful to them all.

My senior apprentice, Mary McCray, stepped to the forefront of the work on this book by turning all of my thumbnail sketches into full-size layouts. Lon Saline, apprentice emeritus, added his skilled touch to several pages, and Jeremy Owen kept all of the trains running on time at the Coppervale Studio while also doing a smashing colouring job on the cover.

Joe Pruett of Desperado Publishing helped me to jump-start a few projects that have languished for far too long and in the process gave us another vehicle for promoting the novels.

Justin Chanda, publisher of Simon & Schuster Books for Young Readers, opened a door into our mutual future – and I am lucky to have him on my side. Also on that front, my publicists Kate Smyth and Paul Crichton have done a stunningly good job of promoting me and my work, organizing my tours, troubleshooting, and in general just taking good care of this author. And my art directors, Lizzy Bromley, Chlöe Foglia, and Laurent Linn, continue to make the books look better than I'd dreamed.

Joe LeFavi brought me together with Jason Lust, Lisa Henson, and Brian Henson, all of whom have become my friends and among the biggest supporters of my ambitions.

Stephenson Crossley deserved to be acknowledged in the first two books, as none of them would exist if he hadn't fed, housed, and encouraged me while I was trying to sell the first book – but his girlfriend, Karen, said if I didn't wait until at least the third book, he'd be impossible to live with.

And not least among my influences, I want to thank Jimmy

Swihart, my first business partner, who has recently come back into my life and brought with him some great memories.

The greatest of my influences, however, is my wife, Cindy. Without her, I would not have lived the life I have, had the family we're raising, and created the work that I love. And I am forever thankful for her love and support.

Prologue

In the centuries that would pass, the spacious stone room known as Solitude would fill with an accumulation of culture; not by design, but because those who would eventually come to seek the occupant's skills would feel the obligation to bring something, anything, as gifts, or perhaps tribute. But that was in a time yet to come. In the present moment, it was empty save for the items he'd brought with him: a torn robe, an empty scabbard, a quill and half-filled bottle of ink, and as many rolls of parchment as he could carry.

When he entered, the door had swung shut behind him. He knew without touching it that it had locked, and also, with less assurance, that it would probably not be opened again for many years.

He had once had a name – several names, in fact – all of which were irrelevant now. In his youth he had aspired to be a great man, and had been afforded many opportunities to fulfill that destiny; but far too late, he learned that it was perhaps better to be a good man, who nevertheless aspires to do great things. The distinction had never mattered to him much before.

Solitude had not been created for him, but he took possession of it with the reluctant ease of an heir who receives an unexpected and unwanted inheritance. He laid the robe in one corner, and the scabbard in another, then sat cross-legged in the centre of Solitude to examine the rolls of parchment.

Some of them contained drawings and notations; a few, directions that may or may not have been accurate, to places that may or may not have existed. They were maps, more or less, and at one time it had been his driven purpose to create them. But that was before, when his sight was clearer and his motives more pure. Somehow, somewhen, he had lost his way – and in the process, ended up on a path that had brought him here, to Solitude.

Still, he could not help but wonder: Was it the first step on that path, or the last, that had proven to be his undoing? He looked down at the maps. The oldest had been made by his hand more than a millennium before; but the newest of them had been begun, then abandoned, a century ago. He examined it more closely and saw that the delicate lines were obscured by blood – the same that marked the cloak and scabbard as symbols of his shame.

Some things cannot be undone. But someone who is lost might still return to the proper path, if they only have something to show them the way.

Taking the quill in hand, he dipped the point into the bottle. Whether the place he drew existed then didn't matter – it would, eventually. All that mattered now was that he was, at long last, finding his purpose again. Would that he had done so a day earlier. Just one day.

As he began to draw, tears streamed from his eyes, dropping to the parchment, where they mingled freely with the ink and blood in equal measure. The man in Solitude was a mapmaker once more.

PART ONE

The Mythopoeia

. . . he looked down at his watch, checking his progress . . .

CHAPTER ONE
The Booke of Dayes

Hurrying along one of the tree-lined paths at Magdalen College in Oxford, John glanced up at the cloud-clotted sky and decided that he rather liked the English weather. Constant clouds made for soft light; soft light that cast no shadows. And John liked to avoid shadows as much as possible.

As he passed through the elaborate gate that marked the entrance to Addison's Walk, he looked down at his watch, checking his progress, then looked again. The watch had stopped, and not for the first time. It had been a gift from his youngest child, his only daughter, and while her love in the gift was evident, the selection had been made from a child's point of view and was therefore more aesthetic than practical. The case was burnished gold (although it was most certainly gold-coloured tin), the face was painted with spring flowers, and on the back was the embossed image of a frog wearing a bonnet.

John had absentmindedly pulled it out of his pocket during one of the frequent gatherings of his friends at Magdalen, much to their amusement. Barfield in particular loved to approach him now at inopportune moments just to ask the time – and hopefully embarrass John in the process.

John sighed and tucked the watch back in his pocket, then pulled his collar tighter and hurried on. He was probably already late for the dinner he'd been invited to at the college, and although he had always been punctual (mostly), events of recent years had made him much more aware of the consequences tardiness can bring.

Five years earlier, after a sudden and unexpected journey to the Archipelago of Dreams, he'd found himself a half hour late for an evening with visiting friends that had been planned by his wife. Even had he not taken an oath of secrecy regarding the Archipelago, he would scarcely have been able to explain that he was late because he'd been saving Peter Pan's granddaughter and thousands of other children from the Pied Piper, and had only just returned via a magic wardrobe in Sir James Barrie's house, and so had still needed to drive home from London.

His wife, however, still made the occasional remark about his having been late for the party. So John had since resolved to be as punctual as possible in every circumstance. And tonight he was certain that Jack would not want to be on his own for long, even if the third member of their dinner meeting was their good and trusted friend, Hugo Dyson.

Hugo had become part of a loose association of like-minded fellows, centred around Jack and John, who gathered together to read, discuss, and debate literature, Romanticism, and the nature of the universe, among other things. The group had evolved from an informal club at Oxford that John had called the Coalbiters, which was mostly concerned with the history and mythology of the Northern lands. One of the members of the current gathering referred to them jokingly as the "not-so-secret secret society," but where John and Jack were concerned, the name was more ironic than funny. They frequently held other meetings attended only by themselves and their friend Charles, as often as he could justify the trip from London to Oxford, in which they discussed matters that their colleagues would find impossible to believe. For rather than discussing the meaning of metaphor in ancient texts of fable and fairy tale, what was discussed in this *actually* secret secret society were the fables and fairy tales themselves . . . which were *real*. And existed in another world just beyond reach of our own. A world called the Archipelago of Dreams.

John, Jack, and Charles had been recruited to be Caretakers of the *Imaginarium Geographica*, the great atlas of the Archipelago. Accepting the job brought with it many other responsibilities, including the welfare of the Archipelago itself and the peoples within it. The history of the atlas and its Caretakers amounted to a secret history of the world, and sometimes each of them felt the full weight of that burden; for events in the Archipelago are often mirrored in the natural world, and what happens in one can affect the other.

In the fourteen years since they first became Caretakers, all three men had become distinguished as both scholars and writers in and around Oxford, as had been the tradition with other Caretakers across the ages. There were probably many other creative men and women in other parts of the world who might have had the aptitude for it, but the pattern had been set centuries earlier by Roger Bacon, who was himself an Oxford scholar and one of the great compilers of the Histories of the Archipelago.

The very nature of the *Geographica* and the accompanying Histories meant that discussing them or the Archipelago with anyone in the natural world was verboten. At various points in history, certain Caretakers-in-training had disagreed with this doctrine and had been removed from their positions. Some, like Harry Houdini and Arthur Conan Doyle, were nearly eaten by the dragons that guarded the Frontier, the barrier between the world and the Archipelago, before giving up the job. Others, like the adventurer Sir Richard Burton, were cast aside in a less dramatic fashion but had become more dangerous in the years that followed.

In fact, Burton had nearly cost them their victory in their second conflict with the Winter King – with his shadow, to be more precise – and had ended up escaping with one of the great Dragonships. He had not been seen since. But John suspected he was out there somewhere, watching and waiting.

Burton himself may have been the best argument for Caretaker secrecy. The knowledge of the Archipelago bore with it the potential for great destruction, but Burton was blind to the danger, believing that knowledge was neither good nor evil – only the uses to which it was put could be. It was the trait that made him a great explorer, and an unsuitable Caretaker.

Because of the oath of secrecy, there was no one on Earth with whom the three Caretakers could discuss the Archipelago, save for their mentor Bert, who was in actuality H. G. Wells, and on occasion, James Barrie. But Barrie, called Jamie by the others, was the rare exception to Burton's example: He was a Caretaker who gave up the job willingly. And as such, John had realized early on that the occasional visit to reminisce was fine – but Jamie wanted no part of anything of substance that dealt with the Archipelago.

What made keeping the secret difficult was that John, Jack, and Charles had found a level of comfortable intellectualism within their academic and writing careers. A pleasant camaraderie had developed among their peers at the colleges, and it became more and more tempting to share the secret knowledge that was theirs as Caretakers. John had even suspected that Jack may have already said something to his closest friend, his brother Warnie – but he could hardly fault him for that. Warnie could be trusted, and he had actually seen the girl Laura Glue, when she'd crashed into his and Jack's garden, wings askew, five years earlier, asking about the Caretakers.

But privately, each of them had wondered if one of their friends at Oxford might not be inducted into their circle as an apprentice, or Caretaker-in-training of sorts. After all, that was how Bert and his predecessor, Jules Verne, had recruited their successors. In fact, Bert still maintained files of study on potential Caretakers, young and old, for his three protégés to observe from afar. Within the circle at Oxford, there were at least two among their friends who would qualify in matters of knowledge and creative thinking: Owen Barfield and Hugo Dyson. John expected that sometime in the future, he, Jack, and Charles would likely summon one (or both) colleagues for a long discussion of myth, and history, and languages, and then, after a hearty dinner and good drink, they would unveil the *Imaginarium Geographica* with a flourish, and thus induct their fellow or fellows into the ranks of the Caretakers. Other candidates might be better qualified than the Oxford dons, but familiarity begat comfort, and comfort begat trust. And in a Caretaker, trust was one of the most important qualities of all.

But none of them had anticipated having such a meeting as a matter of necessity, under circumstances that might have mortal consequences for one of their friends. Among them, Jack especially was wary of this. He had lost friends in two worlds and was reluctant to put another at risk if he could help it.

He had requested that all three of them meet for dinner with Hugo Dyson on the upcoming Saturday rather than their usual Thursday gathering time, but as it turned out, Charles was doing research for a novel in the catacombs beneath Paris and could not be reached. He'd been expected back that very day, but as they had heard nothing from him, and he had not yet appeared back in London, John and Jack decided that the meeting was too important to delay, and they confirmed the appointment with Hugo for that evening. It was agreed that the best place for it was in Jack's rooms at Magdalen. They met there often, and so no one observing them would find anything amiss; but the rooms also afforded a degree of privacy they could not get in the open dining halls or local taverns, should the discussion turn to matters best kept secret.

This was almost inevitable, John realized with a shudder of trepidation, given the nature of the matter he and Jack needed to broach with Hugo. Oddly enough, it was actually Charles who was responsible for setting the events in motion, or rather, a small package that had been addressed to him and that he'd subsequently forwarded to Jack at Magdalen. Charles worked at the Oxford University Press, which was based in London, and very few people knew of his connection to Jack at all – much less knew enough to address the parcel, "Mr Charles Williams, Caretaker." Charles sent it to Jack, with the instruction that he open it together with John – and Hugo Dyson.

Invoking the title of Caretaker meant that the parcel involved the Archipelago. And Charles's request that Hugo be invited meant that whether their colleague was ready for it or not, it might be time to reveal the *Geographica* to him.

When they were not adding notations – or more rarely, new maps – John kept the atlas in his private study, inside an iron box bound with locks of silver and stamped with the seal of the High King of the Archipelago, the Caretakers, and the mark of the extraordinary man who created it, who was called the Cartographer of Lost Places. In that box it was the most secure book in all the world, but now it was wrapped in oilcloth and tucked under John's left arm as he walked through Magdalen College. Still safe, if not secure.

John shivered and hunched his shoulders as he approached the building where Jack's rooms were, then took the steps with a single bound and opened the front door.

The rooms were spare but afforded a degree of elegance by the large quantity of rare and unusual books, which reflected a wealth of selection rather than accumulation. A number of volumes in varying sizes were neatly stacked in all the corners of the rooms and along the tops of the low shelves that were common in Oxford, which all the dons hated. Jack commented frequently that they'd probably been manufactured by dwarves, just to irritate the taller men who'd end up using them.

As John had feared, Hugo was already there, sitting on a big Chesterfield sofa in the centre of the sitting room. He was being poured a second cup of Darjeeling tea by their host, who looked wryly at John as he came in.

"The frog in a bonnet set you back again, dear fellow?" said Jack.

"I'm afraid so," John replied. "The dratted thing just won't stay wound."

"Hah!" chortled Hugo. "Time for a new watch, I'd say. Time. For a watch. Hah! Get it?"

Jack rolled his eyes, but John gave a polite chuckle and took a seat in a shabby but comfortable armchair opposite Hugo. The man was a scholar, but he wore the perpetual expression of someone who anticipates winning a carnival prize: anxious but cheerily hopeful. That, combined with his deep academic knowledge of English and his love of truth in all forms, made him a friend both John and Jack valued. Whether he was suited for the calling of Caretaker, however, was yet to be determined.

The three men finished their tea and then ate a sumptuous meal of roast beef, new potatoes, and a dark Irish bread, topped off with sweet biscuits and coffee. John noted that Jack then brought out the rum – much sooner than usual, and with a lesser hesitation than when Warnie was with them – and with the rum, the parcel that had been sent to Charles.

"Ah, yes," said Hugo. "The great mystery that has brought us all together." He leaned forward and examined the writing on the package. "Hmm. This wouldn't be Charles Williams the writer, would it?"

Jack and John looked at each other in surprise. Few of their associates in Oxford knew of Charles, but then again, Charles did have his own reputation in London as an editor, essayist, and poet. His first novel, *War in Heaven*, had come out only the year before, and it was not particularly well known.

"Yes, it is," said John. "Have you read his work?"

"Not much of it, I'm afraid," Hugo replied. "But I've had my own work declined by the press, so I might find I like his writing more if my good character prevails when I do read it.

"I'm familiar with his book," continued Hugo, "because the central object in the story is the Holy Grail."

"The cup of Christ, from the Last Supper," said John.

"Either that, or the vessel used to catch his blood as he hung on the cross," answered Hugo, "depending on which version of the story you believe is more credible as a historian."

"Or as a Christian," said John, "although the Grail lore certainly blurs the line between history and myth."

"It's very interesting that you feel that way," Jack said, unwrapping the parcel and casting a sideways glance at John, "because the line between history and myth is about to be wiped away entirely."

Inside the brown wrapper was a book, about three inches thick and nearly ten inches square. It was bound in ancient leather, and the pages were brown with age. The upper left-hand side of the first few pages had been torn, and the rest bore several deep gashes. Otherwise, the book was intact. The cover itself was filled with ancient writing, and in the centre was a detailed impression of the sacred cup itself: the Holy Grail.

Hugo stood to better take in the sight. "Impressive! Is it authentic?"

Jack examined the book in silence for a few minutes, then nodded. "It is. Sixth century, as closely as I can estimate."

Hugo gave him an admiring look. "I didn't realize you were an expert in this sort of historical matter."

"I have some knowledgeable associates," said Jack. He turned to John. "Can you read it?"

John dusted off the cover with a napkin. "Absolutely. The forms are Anglo-Saxon, but the writing itself is Gothic."

"Gothic!" Hugo exclaimed. "No one's used Gothic since . . ."

"Since the sixth century," said John. "But it was one of my favourite languages to play with when I was younger."

"That's what makes him a genius," Hugo said to Jack. "It's all play to him."

The two men refilled their glasses (this time adding a bit of hot water to the rum) and stood back to let John work through the translation. After a few minutes had passed, John turned to Jack and grinned.

"It bears closer study," he said. "If I can refine the actual letter-forms, I might even be able to compare it to some of the Histories and narrow down who the author might be. If I didn't know better, I'd say it *is* one of the Histories."

"The author?" Hugo exclaimed. "Surely you're having a joke at my expense, my dear fellow. Narrowing down the century would be impressive enough, but I doubt the author signed his work. Not in those days."

"You'd be surprised," said Jack. "In a way, that's why I asked you to come, Hugo."

"It's quite exceptional, really," John exclaimed. "It purports to be a historical accounting of the lineage of the kings of England. And that history is intertwined with the mythology of the Holy Grail. Except . . ."

"What?" blurted Hugo.

"Except," John finished, "it starts at least five centuries before the birth of Christ."

"So, pure mythology rather than history," said Jack.

"That's debatable," said Hugo, "but you yourself said this would wipe away the line between history and myth."

"Indeed," Jack said, turning to John. "Was Charles's note correct? About the writing?"

John nodded. "The cover text is relevant, but it's the first page that really has me baffled, the same as it did Charles." He lifted the cover. "And for that page, there's no need for me to translate."

Instead of the Gothic writing on the cover, the words on the first page were written in a reddish brown ink in modern English. The page had been torn crosswise from left to right, but the message was largely intact:

> The Cartographer
> He who seeks the means to
> the islands of the Archipelago
> will follow the true Grail and
> Blood will be saved, by willing choice
> that time be restored for the future's sake.
> And in God's name, don't close the door!
> —Hugo Dyson

Hugo clapped them both on the shoulders. "I knew it! Well done, you old scalawags! An excellent joke! Oh, this will be a tale to dine out on! But tell me this: Who is the Cartographer?"

The door was sitting slightly askew within the arch.

Chapter Two
The Door in the Wood

"It isn't a joke, Hugo," said Jack. "You can't tell anyone of this. That isn't ink. And you should take a closer look at the handwriting."

Hugo did so, and his astonished gasp confirmed what Jack had suspected and John had just realized: The writing was in Hugo's own hand.

"Mmm," said John, examining the writing for himself. "You're right, Jack. This *is* quite the mystery. I wonder if that's actually Hugo's blood?"

"Hard to say for certain," said Jack. "It's nearly fourteen centuries old, so there's probably no way to tell."

"My blood?" exclaimed Hugo. "Really now, this is carrying things on a bit past the edge, don't you think?"

"Oh, don't be so squeamish, Hugo," said John. "It's dried, after all."

Jack sat on the sofa and leaned back, his hands behind his neck. "Let's assume this is what it appears to be. Hugo and Charles have never met. So why would this have been sent to Charles?"

"And not only that," John interjected, "but to him in his capacity as a Caretaker."

"A Caretaker of what?" said Hugo. "And who is the Cartographer?"

"I think," John said, reaching for the oilcloth-wrapped book he'd brought with him, "that it's time we explained a few things to you, my baffled friend. Beginning with this."

On top of the table, John unwrapped the *Imaginarium Geographica*.

"We're going to need more rum," said Jack.

As Hugo sat in stunned silence, John and Jack took turns telling him a slightly abridged version of all the adventures they had experienced as Caretakers of the *Imaginarium Geographica*. When they were finished, a completely discombobulated and still slightly sceptical Hugo Dyson squinted one eye and looked them over.

"This is all completely on the level, then?"

"As level as it's possible to get," said John. "And as you can see, the *Geographica* itself is fairly compelling evidence."

"Indeed," said Hugo, rising to look at the atlas. "It is extraordinary, I'll give you that. Extraordinary. And you say this Cartographer of Lost Places created all these maps?"

"Yes," Jack said, nodding.

"So who is he, really?"

"I don't think anyone really knows," said John. "Bert might have his ideas. Samaranth as well. But I've never come across any mention of him in any of the Histories. What we know of him is all there *is* to know."

"Perhaps he's the one who sent it," Hugo suggested. "After all, the note I, uh, wrote seems to be for his benefit."

John shook his head. "It wouldn't have come by post. He'd have sent Bert, or a dragon, or a postal owl or something."

"A postal *owl?*" said Jack.

"I was just giving a 'for instance,'" said John. "I don't think it was really delivered by an owl. Everyone knows swallows are more suited for that sort of thing, anyway."

"That's even worse," said Jack. "At least a good-size owl would have a shot at lifting a heavy book. You'd need *several* swallows to match that."

"He has a point," said Hugo.

"Whatever," said John, irritated. "What I mean is that it was sent by someone in this world, not someone in the Archipelago."

"But who here knows that we're the Caretakers?" asked Jack. "And why not just contact us directly?"

"Maybe they couldn't," offered Hugo. "Perhaps whoever sent the book was prevented from bringing it themselves."

"I think that the reason it was addressed to Charles is obvious," said John. "His novel proves his interest in Grail lore, and as a Caretaker he has resources other scholars wouldn't."

"Fair enough," said Jack. "But what initiated Hugo's involvement in all this?" They both turned to their friend, who gulped and grinned sheepishly.

"I'm just trying to keep up, honestly," said Hugo. "As I said, I was familiar with Charles's work, but my interest was in what I *hoped* the novel was, not what it is.

"I'm doing a lot of reading in Arthurian legends, and so of course I'm taking detours into Grail stories. I thought Charles's book might be a nice diversion, but it was rather disappointing to discover it's wholly contemporary. To him the Grail is an object, a device, if you will, to allow him to tell a story of the supernatural. And that wasn't what I was looking for at all."

"I see," said John. "We'll have to speak further about the Arthur legends. I think we can help you there" – he winked at Jack – "particularly with the material about his descendants."

"You can show me the actual Histories?" Hugo exclaimed.

"Better," said Jack. "We can show you the actual *descendants*."

"We're the last one's godfathers," John explained.

"Good Lord," said Hugo.

"What I want to know is the connection between the Grail and the Cartographer," said Jack. "How are they linked, I wonder?"

"Arthur again," said John. "Remember, the seal of the High King is what keeps the door locked in the Keep. There must be a connection there."

Jack snapped his fingers. "Right. I'd forgotten. So what do we do?"

"Let's do this," said John, rising. "Tomorrow I'll use the Compass Rose to summon one of the Dragonships from the Archipelago, and we'll go ask the Cartographer himself. We can answer all these questions in a matter of days."

"You said the, uh, fortress . . . ," began Hugo.

"The Keep," said Jack.

"Yes, the Keep of, uh, Time, was almost destroyed. Will we be able to get to him?"

John and Jack looked at each other, thinking the same thing: They were glad, in this moment, that Charles was not in the room. Despite the fact that his actions had once saved their lives, he was nevertheless responsible for the Keep being set ablaze and would have been embarrassed to discuss the matter in front of Hugo.

"Yes," said Jack. "It's difficult, but still possible. The fire is long extinguished, but the tower itself continues to crumble. We've had to spend more and more time doing damage control with the various Time Storms that have formed as a result, but just going there to speak to him shouldn't be a problem."

"Hmm," said John. "I wonder if a Time Storm might not be the genesis of this book. After all, there has to be some explanation for how Hugo's writing got on it fourteen centuries ago."

"I've never seen a Time Storm here, in our world," said Jack. "Just in the Archipelago."

"There have been crossovers," John pointed out. "The Bermuda Triangle, for one. And of course, the whole business with the *Red Dragon*."

"*Red Dragon?*" asked Hugo.

"You'd know it better as the *Argo*," said Jack.

"Ah," said Hugo. He got to his feet with a visible wobble. "I think I need some air. Anyone fancy a walk?"

"Excellent idea," agreed John.

After rewrapping the Grail book and the *Geographica* (in the unlikely event that one of Jack's students or the college "scout" responsible for tidying up the rooms should wander in and find them), John, Jack, and Hugo left the New Building and headed down the direction from which John had come earlier. Addison's Walk was a favourite stroll of theirs; it made a circuit around Magdalen from one side of the college, leading to Dover Pier, and then around to the other side along the Cherwell. It was lined with trees and grassy meadows and offered beautiful views of Magdalen Tower and the Magdalen Bridge. It was an eminently peaceful path to walk alone or with companions, and all three of them had followed it often.

The night was pleasant for mid-September, and it was perfect weather for contemplating the universe. The only thing that made the stroll disquieting was the occasional shadows cast by the lamps they passed. Jack tried not to look like he was avoiding them, and he hoped John wouldn't notice.

Hugo walked ahead of the other two, hands clasped behind his back, deep in thought. Occasionally he would stop and begin to utter some half-formed thought, then reconsider and keep walking. Finally he fell back with the others.

"So," Hugo asked, "according to your experiences, all myths are real, and they happened someplace within the Archipelago?"

"That's an awfully general statement," said Jack. "I think it's more reasonable to say that much of what we have believed to be myth and legend in our world here was actually derived from real events in the Archipelago. We've been at this Caretaking business for a number of years now, and we're still just getting our feet wet."

"Indeed," said John, who was rustling around in the brush for a walking stick. "Fact and fiction do not fall into the clear patterns they once did."

"So taken as a whole, mythology, or some of it at least, might actually be real history?"

"We're still trying to figure that out ourselves," replied Jack, "although I must admit it's quite a relief to be able to discuss a lot of this openly with you, Hugo. It's sometimes been very difficult to restrain myself during conversations with Owen Barfield, for example."

"I'd imagine," said John.

Seeing Hugo's puzzled look, Jack explained. "In recent years Barfield has made the argument that mythology, speech, and literature all have a common source, a common origin. In the dawn of prehistory, men did not make distinctions between the literal and the metaphorical. They were one and the same."

"The word and the thing were identical," said Hugo.

"Exactly," said Jack. "That can be described best as the mythological meaning – somewhere between reality and metaphor. When we translate a word, we make distinctions based on context, but early speakers didn't.

"Barfield used the Latin word 'spiritus' as an example," Jack continued. "To early man, it meant something like 'spirit-breath-wind.' When the wind blew, it was not 'like' the breath of a god. It *was* the breath of a god. And when it referred to a speaker's self, his own spirit, he meant it literally as the 'breath of life.'

"What made this compelling was that I had already had several discussions along the same lines with John, Charles, and Ordo Maas in the Archipelago."

"The shipbuilder you told me about?" asked Hugo.

"The same." Jack nodded. "It began with the discussion of the similarities between himself, as Deucalion, and the Biblical Noah, and the fact that stories of the flood and great arks go back well before Gilgamesh."

"But some are real, and others are myths based on the realities?"

"There are different kinds of reality," said Jack. "Barfield said mythological stories are metaphors in narrative form – but that makes them no less real."

Hugo shook his head. "Language gives us the ability to make metaphors, but really, that's all myths are, whether or not they were created around real happenings. Pretty them up all you like, but myths are essentially lies, and therefore worthless."

John and Jack stopped and looked directly at Hugo. "No," John said emphatically. "They are *not* lies."

At that moment there was a rush of wind through the trees that pushed past the three friends and swirled down the shallow hill beyond. It burst upon them so suddenly and forcefully from the still, warm night that it sent a cacophony of leaves raining down from the branches, and it was nearly a full minute before the patter subsided and the walk was quiet once more.

They held their breath, standing still on the path.

"What was that all about?" exclaimed Hugo.

"Quiet," said Jack. "Something's changed."

And he was right. Something *had* changed. There was another presence there with them, somewhere among the trees.

Unmoving, the three men looked about, but nothing seemed amiss. The streams burbled, the trees stood, sombre, and the night was as quiet as it had been moments before. And then . . .

Something fell.

"Here," John said, pointing off to the right. "It came from this small clearing."

Cautiously the three scholars stepped away from the path and walked down the gentle slope, threading their way among the beeches and poplars to a small meadow that overlooked one of the streams. In the meadow, standing resolutely in the grass as if it belonged there, was a door. Not a building, just a door. It was plain, made of oak, and set into an arch of crumbling stones. A few feet away lay one of the stones – presumably the one they had heard tumble down from the frame.

All three of them noticed something else that was obviously meant for them to see: Painted across the face of the door in the same reddish brown colour as the writing on the book was the image of the Grail.

Hugo turned slightly green. "If that's more blood, I think I might lose my dinner."

Jack let out a low whistle. He recognized the door right away. It was unmistakably one of the doors from the Keep of Time.

"But how can it possibly be here?" John said, answering Jack's unspoken question. "And what's the meaning of the Grail?"

"It's not a coincidence," said Jack. "It's here because we are. I sense a trap."

"That's a bit cloak-and-dagger," said Hugo, who was recovering from his initial surprise. "It's just a door, isn't it?"

"A door into some other time," stated Jack, who was examining the door, albeit from a safe distance, "and from a place far from here."

"Remember what the Cartographer told us," John said. "The doorways were focal points, not actually the pathways themselves."

"You say that like you know what it means," said Jack, "when really, we have no clue how the Keep or the doorways worked."

"I think you're both getting all hot and bothered over a piffle," said Hugo. "Besides, look." He pointed with the toe of his shoe. "It's already open."

Hugo was right. The door was sitting slightly askew within the arch. Not open enough to really see through to the other side, but enough to realize it could be pulled open farther – and so Hugo reached out, and did.

"Hold on!" Jack yelled as he and John both grabbed at Hugo. "You don't know what's on the other side!"

"What can it hurt to open the door?" Hugo reasoned.

"You've obviously never been to Loch Ness," said John.

"What does that mean?"

"Never mind," said Jack. "Hugo may be right. Look."

The door had swung open to reveal . . . nothing.

It was just meadow on the other side.

"See?" said Hugo with a chuckle. "It's just a set dressing, perhaps meant to scare us. Or maybe you're taking a practical joke to unprecedented heights. Either way, I think it's harmless."

And then, as if to prove his point, Hugo walked through the doorway, and half a dozen paces on the other side. Then he turned and spread his hands, smiling. "Gentlemen?"

John and Jack both relaxed visibly.

"I was really quite concerned for a moment," said Jack, as he crouched to sit down in the grass. "I—" He suddenly stopped talking, and his brow furrowed.

"What?" said John.

Jack didn't answer but started moving his head side to side, looking at Hugo. Then his eyes widened and he jumped to his feet.

"Hugo!" he exclaimed. "Come back through the doorway, quickly! Hurry, man!"

Hugo chuckled again. "Jack, you sound like a mother hen. How much rum did you have, anyroad?"

John was looking around, anxious and worried. His Caretaker instincts had gone hyperactive – of them both, Jack wasn't the one to panic easily – and he realized something was wrong.

Jack grabbed him and pulled him two feet to the left of the doorway. As John watched, Hugo vanished.

"Shades!" John hissed. "Hugo! Are you there?" He stepped back. Hugo reappeared.

"Have you both gone round the bend?" asked Hugo. "I'm right here."

He was – but only if they were looking straight through the open doorway. If they moved to either side, and looked around the arch, he disappeared.

"Hugo," said John, "we'll explain in a moment, but for now just walk slowly towards me and through the door."

But Hugo was having nothing of it. "This has gone far enough, I think. It's been a grand joke you two have arranged, but I think it's time to go."

He walked forward and then, whether by happenstance or in defiance of his friends' urgent pleading, he stepped over a fallen stone, and then around the frame rather than through it. And just like that, in a trice . . .

. . . Hugo Dyson was *gone*.

. . . hanging from every available surface were badgers . . .

CHAPTER THREE

The Royal Animal Rescue Squad

It took several moments for John and Jack to realize what had happened – and when they did, they realized that there was very little they could actually do.

"Hugo!" John shouted. "Hugo, can you hear me?" But there was no response.

"The scenes we could view through the doorways in the Keep were static, remember?" said Jack.

"Until someone crossed the threshold," said John. "I think Hugo put it into motion."

"But we can see right through it!" protested Jack. "How can he have disappeared so completely?"

"It *is* another time," said John, walking a wide circuit around the door. "He's just moved out of earshot. He's still here. He's just . . . Elsewhen."

"I really wish Charles were here," said Jack. "This is more his forte than ours."

"We'll make do," said John, hefting his walking stick with both hands. "Listen, I'm going to step inside, but I'm going to keep hold of this stick. I want you to remain here and hold on to the other end. That way, whatever happens, you can pull me back through."

"What do you plan to do?"

"I'm going to look around the corner and yell at that idiot to come back through," said John. "With any luck, he's stayed here in the meadow and is wondering where in Hades we got to."

Gingerly Jack took hold of one end of the stick, and with a deep breath, John stepped through the door.

"So far so good," he said, looking over his shoulder. "It really doesn't look any different over here.

"Now," he continued, "I'm going to move around the corner and see if I can spot Hugo."

Keeping the stick firmly grasped in his left hand, John cautiously turned and moved to his right, around the arch, where he found himself looking directly . . .

. . . at *Jack*.

"Jack," said John.

"John," said Jack.

"I don't think it worked. Why isn't it working?"

"Maybe it's because you're holding on to the stick," Jack suggested. "It's keeping you anchored here, to this side."

John made a noise of frustration, and then more on impulse than out of reason, let go of the stick. He leaned sideways and saw Jack leaning on the stick opposite the door.

He walked around to Jack, touching his shoulder to make sure it was not some sort of illusion, then went back through the doorway. Still nothing. Whatever it was that had happened to Hugo was not happening to John.

They tried reversing the process, this time with Jack playing the part of the canary, but with the same result.

Hugo was gone, and they were helpless to do anything about it.

◆   ◆   ◆

The two Caretakers sat under a poplar about twenty feet from the door and stared at it, trying to decide what had just happened.

"This is bad," said John.

"I know," said Jack.

"This is very, very bad," John said again.

"I know!" Jack shot back. "We've just lost a colleague!"

"More like we misplaced him, really," said John. "After all, we do know *where* he is – it's *when* that's the problem."

Jack scrambled to his feet. "Regardless, we haven't the time to sit here moaning about it. We need to get to the Compass Rose and summon some help."

"Who should we call?" asked John, standing and brushing the dry grass from his trousers. "Bert? Or perhaps Artus?"

"Whoever can get here the fastest – probably Stephen, with one of his new airships."

"That's right," said John. "The magic feathers. Perhaps there's even a ship not too far from England. It could ferry us to the Cartographer, and we can get to the bottom of all this."

"You make it sound like getting some help is as easy as snapping your fingers," said Jack, snapping his fingers. "If only—"

As if on cue, a ferocious rattling and roaring sound echoed across the fields, and a curious shape appeared on the other side of the Magdalen Bridge. In seconds it had moved swiftly into view.

It was a metallic conflagration of wheels, gears, levers, and belching smoke. It moved with the lurching fluidity of a caterpillar fleeing a swallow, and with the same urgency. It had a vague resemblance to the vehicle driven by their friend, the badger Tummeler, but only in the same way that an elephant and a goat were both mammals.

"Dear Lord," declared John. "That contraption looks as if it was built by some fiend with his own three hands in the basement of a third-rate workhouse."

"It probably was," Jack said, "but it's a welcome sight all the same."

As the vehicle came closer, they could better see its makeup. It was essentially a truck, but it seemed to have unfulfilled aspirations of becoming a train. Or a fire engine. Or both. And hanging from every available surface were badgers.

In a cloud of dust and smoke, the motorized monstrosity screeched to a halt on the path above John and Jack, and a dozen badgers in emergency gear leaped to the ground. They moved into a loose formation, then saluted. After a moment (and suppressing grins), John and Jack saluted back.

The tallest of the badgers (and the one who had been driving) stepped forward and offered its paw.

John shook the animal's paw. "I'm guessing you're looking for us."

"We are," said the badger. "The Royal Animal Rescue Squad, at y'r service. Have I th' honour of addressing Scowler Charles?"

"No, I'm John."

"Ah," the badger said, turning to Jack. "Then you must be . . ."

"I'm Jack."

"Oh," said the badger, craning his neck to look around the clearing. "Then Scowler Charles is . . ."

"In France," said John.

As one, all the animals immediately slumped in disappointment and began fidgeting.

"Oh," the apparent leader of the Squad said again. "We're

happy to meet you, too, but if Scowler Charles isn't here, then p'rhaps we wasn't needed after all."

"How did you know we were here to begin with?" asked John. "What brought you looking for us?"

"We wuz told that on this particular Saturday, Scowler Charles would be in trouble an' needin' our help. We've been waiting for this day f'r as long as I can remember."

"That's all well and good," said Jack, "but he isn't here. We're awfully glad to see you, though."

The badger waved over one of the others, who pulled out a book that they both began examining with great fervour.

"That binding looks very familiar," said Jack. "What is that book, anyway?"

"Th' Little Whatsit," answered the smaller badger. "It's our guidebook of everything that's anything."

"Sort of like the Great Whatsit back on Paralon?" asked John.

"No," said the first badger, "*exactly* the Great Whatsit. Just portable-like, so we have what we need to know when we needs it. Um, what year is this, anyway?"

"It's 1931," replied John.

"It's the right date," the badger said. "Maybe we're in th' wrong place! Oh dear, oh dear!"

All of the badgers' eyes widened in shock, and the bigger ones started smacking themselves in the heads with their paws.

"But, Father—," said the little one.

"Not now," the first badger said, shushing him.

"Here now," said John. "What's going on?"

"We've failed," said the first badger. "We've failed the great Scowler Charles!"

"I assure you," Jack said soothingly, "Charles is fine. He's nowhere near here. But our friend Hugo is in trouble, and you are, ah, exactly what we needed."

"Really?" the badger said hopefully. He saluted again, and the others followed suit. "The Royal Animal Rescue Squad, at y'r service."

"Thanks," said John. "Say, none of you would happen to be related to our friend Tummeler, would you?"

The first badger nodded enthusiastically. "I is indeed! I am the son of Tummeler, and this," he added, pulling the smaller badger with the book alongside him, "is the son of the son of Tummeler."

"Well met!" said Jack. "And how are you properly addressed?"

"Charles Montgolfier Hargreaves-Heald," said the badger, "but everyone calls me Uncas."

"And you?" John asked, looking at the other, slightly smaller animal. "What's your name?"

"Uh, Fred," said the badger.

"Fred?" said John.

Uncas shrugged. "Badgers named Charles Mongolfier Hargreaves-Heald name their children Fred."

"Why not follow the tale completely and call him Chingach-gook?" asked Jack.

The badgers wrinkled their snouts in distaste. "That's a very strange name," said Uncas. "Why would I call him that?"

"Didn't you get *your* name from the Cooper story?"

"The who what?" said Uncas, shaking his head. "I was once in a play called *The Last of th' Phoenicians*," the badger explained proudly. "It was written by my father. He gots th' name from there, an' it stuck t' me."

"My mistake," said Jack.

• • •

"What can we do for you, Master Scowlers?" asked Uncas.

John and Jack explained what had happened with the Grail book, and the evening stroll, and the door in the wood, and Hugo's disappearance. All the while they were speaking, the badgers listened with great attentiveness.

"Well," said Uncas when they had finished, "we really had expected to be rescuin' Scowler Charles, but seein' as we're already here, an your friend Hobo—"

"Hugo," John corrected.

"Right, Hugo," said Uncas. "Since he's in trouble, we'll see what we can do."

The badgers swarmed around their vehicle – which Fred explained was called the Howling Improbable – apparently preparing for whatever it was that a Royal Animal Rescue Squad did, while John and Jack watched in patient amusement.

"Do you think Charles is aware of the hero worship being spread around the animal community in the Archipelago?" asked Jack.

"Probably," said John, "but if he isn't, I'm not going to be the one who tells him."

Jack gestured at the badger called Fred, who approached the men with a mixture of shyness and awe. "Yes, Master Scowlers?"

"Tell us about your book," said John, crouching down to meet Fred's eyes. "This 'Little Whatsit.'"

"The prince, Stephen," said Fred. "It was his idea, really. He thought it was impractical to have to go back and forth to Paralon every time he needed to look something up in the Histories. So he set Solomon Kaw and the other crows to work compiling important information and distilling it into a single volume.

"It doesn't have everything about anything," Fred concluded, "but . . ."

"It has something about everything," Jack finished for him. "Brilliant."

"I think so too," Fred agreed. "I never go anywhere without mine. Grandfather Tummeler published it, like he did with the *Geographica*. It's only been printed once, but Grandfather says something like this takes time to find an audience."

"Pardon my asking," said John, "but you don't seem to talk in quite the same way as your father and grandfather. You're a bit more . . ."

"Educated?" guessed Fred.

"I was going to say 'articulate,'" said John, "but yes, educated will do."

Fred looked over his shoulder to where Uncas was co-ordinating some sort of effort involving coiled wires under the chassis of the Howling Improbable.

"I studied with Stephen under Charys, and Solomon Kaw, and even Samaranth himself," said Fred. "I always thought that maybe, just maybe, if an animal could make himself learn everything it was possible to learn, then I could make my grandfather proud of me. I even hoped . . . I thought maybe . . ."

"Maybe what, Fred?" Jack asked.

The little mammal shifted his feet and would have blushed, if not for his fur. "I thought it might be possible that if I could become a good enough scholar, I might even be able to become a Caretaker myself. Like Charles. Like you."

John and Jack looked at each other, then smiled at Fred. "I think you'd make a very good Caretaker," Jack told the badger. "A very good one indeed."

+ + +

"We've formulated a plan," Uncas announced finally.

"Excellent," said John. "What is it?"

"We're goin' back t' the Archipelago and getting more help," said the badger.

"What!" exclaimed John and Jack together.

"You've been doing . . . *things* around your vehicle for an hour," said John. "And after all this, the best you can manage is to give up?"

"We're not giving up," huffed Uncas. "But an animal has to know the difference between fight an' flight. And we wasn't prepared to handle something like this."

"What do you usually do?"

"Well, t' be honest," Uncas said sheepishly, "this be th' first time we ever went out on a job."

"The first time?" exclaimed Jack.

"Yes," said Uncas. "In truth, the whole reason the squad was formed was for this one night, and after fourteen years, we're, uh . . . we're really not sure what t' do."

The little animal looked as if it might burst into tears at any second. Jack sighed heavily and sat down next to him.

"Fourteen years," said John. "You've really been waiting fourteen years for this mission, tonight?"

"Yes," said Uncas. "The Prime Caretaker is going to be very disappointed."

"The what?" asked John.

"Th' Prime Caretaker," said Uncas.

"I'm the Caretaker Principia," John said.

"Not the Caretaker Principia," said Uncas, "the Prime Caretaker."

"Do you mean Bert?"

"The Far Traveller? No. He is a friend to us all, but he is not the Prime Caretaker. The Frenchman is."

"Frenchman?" asked John. "Do you mean . . ."

"Never mind who arranged for you to be here," said Jack. "You are still exactly what we'd hoped for. If you appeared here, in Oxford, you must have a means of crossing the Frontier."

"We does indeed," said Uncas. "Every principle in the service of th' New Republic is equipped with a Dragon's Feather." He gestured at the cab of the Howling Improbable, where a bright silver case was fastened above the steering mechanism.

"Well then," said Jack, "let's get back to Paralon, posthaste. We can consult with Aven and Artus, and then go together to see the Cartographer. Between us all, we should be able to sort this all out and rescue Hugo from wherever – whenever – he is."

The badgers all let out a whoop and a cheer. "Rescue Squad!" Uncas shouted joyfully. "Clear the site! We're going home!"

As the animals rejoiced, John and Jack gave a last look at the doorway.

"We should go back to my rooms," said Jack. "We need to pick up the *Geographica*, and I'm sure Artus would like to have a look at the Grail book."

"Agreed."

"Fred," Uncas said, "give me a paw with this, will you?"

It took a moment for the Caretakers to realize what the two badgers were doing, and that was one moment too long.

"No!" yelled Jack. "Don't close the—"

But it was too late. John and Jack both jumped for the door just as Uncas and Fred were closing it, and as the four of them touched it, they heard the gentle but unmistakable click of stone meeting wood. In that instant, the door vanished as if it had never been there.

And that wasn't all.

The Howling Improbable and all the other badgers in the Royal Animal Rescue Squad were also gone.

So was Magdalen Tower. And from what they could see, most of the buildings of the college.

The sky had turned dark, the air chill, and a pall settled over the entire landscape. It was deathly quiet. The trees, what remained of them, were scrawny and barren of leaves. Where there had been soft grass and flowers underfoot, there was now only hard, packed earth.

The stench of decay and rot hung thickly in the air, and for a moment, it seemed to John and Jack as if they'd forgotten to breathe.

"Uh-oh," said Fred.

"Mistakes were made," said Uncas.

And the badger was right, thought John, but the mistakes had all been his.

He was the Caretaker Principia. He was the one who was trained, and experienced, and always, always prepared. And all the signs had been there, all the clues he needed. But he'd grown careless and cocksure. His success in the academic world had given him confidence, and the years of relative peace in both the natural world and the Archipelago had made him sloppy. It was bad enough that Hugo was paying a price for that imprecision, but now, now . . .

With a mounting pressure inside his head, the gravity of their situation was becoming more and more evident.

The doorway *had* been a trap. Jack had even said as much. And up until a moment ago, all John had to do to escape it was to listen to the warning he'd already been given by Hugo himself:

And in God's name, don't close the door!

The thing that followed them resembled a motorcar . . .

CHAPTER FOUR
The Unhistory

The moon rose, and the wan glow it cast over the desolation gave an eerie bas-relief quality to everything the companions saw.

What had been the gently pastoral countryside and beautiful city of Oxford only a minute before was gone. In their place was a cold, bloodless terrain that had been drained of life. No, worse, John thought – it seemed to have been drained of the *will* to live. The trees were scrawny and leafless, and the Cherwell and its many streams were reduced to foul-smelling trickles that were little more than open sewers.

John, Jack, and the badgers cautiously moved onto the walking path above the river and scanned the horizon for any recognizable landmarks. There were none. This was no longer England – or at least, the England they knew.

"It's painful just to look at anything," Fred complained, rubbing at his eyes. "My headbone hurts."

Uncas sniffed the air and wrinkled his snout in disgust. "Death. It smells like death all round, Master Scowlers." The little animal shivered and pulled his son close. "I don't like it a'tall."

John took Jack by the elbow and pointed downriver. "What do you make of that?"

It was a tower, obscured partially by cloud and fog. They'd only just noticed it in the increasing moonlight. It seemed to suck in light, to blend with the night sky. It was, Jack estimated, almost four hundred feet tall. At the top, a reddish glow emanated from a strange crown of stones that looked more like a lidded eye than parapets.

"I couldn't say," Jack replied. "It's not Magdalen Tower, but it's the only thing I can see that seems to have been the work of a civilized mind."

"That's what I was thinking," agreed John. "Until we discern just what's happened to us, we ought to get out of the open – and except for *that*" – he jabbed his thumb at the tower – "it's *all* open."

"Fine," said Jack. "But what do we do with Uncas and Fred? We certainly couldn't take them with us into Magdalen."

"This *isn't* Magdalen," said John. "I don't know what it is. But I think that somehow, Hugo changed the past when he went through that door, and we're seeing the result."

"Hugo vanished an hour before this happened," said Jack. "Why do you think it was he who caused this?"

"Because of how the doors worked in the Keep of Time," said John. "The times we viewed through them only became kinetic when the threshold was crossed. I think Hugo set into motion whatever 'past' that door led to when he stepped through. The doorway, while open, kept it in flux and connected to our 'now.' But when the door closed . . ."

"Awwooooooo . . . ," Fred howled softly, putting his head in his paws. "I'm so sorry, Scowler John, Scowler Jack."

"There now," Uncas said, trying to comfort his son. "I'm in charge of the squad. It be my fault, not yours."

"It be – I mean, it is no one's fault," said John, as forcefully as he thought he could sound without rattling the badgers even further. "We shouldn't place blame. But now we have to work together to find a way out of this mess. Are you with us?"

The badgers girded themselves up, wiping tears away with one paw while saluting with the other. "Th' Royal Animal Rescue . . . uh, Team, is ready to serve, Master Scowlers."

"Fine," John said, turning to Jack. "The badgers stay with us."

They made a quick accounting of what they had with them, and the list was scanty. Uncas had a coil of rope, a small hatchet, and a box of oyster crackers ("For real emergencies," he said), while Fred had a remarkably large key ring, festooned with keys of all shapes and sizes, and his copy of the Little Whatsit. John had his Frog-in-a-Bonnet pocket watch and a small penknife. Jack had only an embroidered handkerchief and a few coins.

"So, other than the crackers, we've no food," said John.

"What did you expect?" Jack exclaimed. "We were taking a walk on the college grounds within shouting distance of my own rooms. Why would I have laden my pockets with anything else, especially food?"

"Don't worry about it," John told him. "You're right. There's no way for us to have known. I just hate feeling so . . . so . . . *unprepared*."

"At least we have the crackers," said Jack.

"Um," said Uncas, quickly brushing the crumbs out of his whiskers, "we *did*."

"I thought those were for an emergency," John exclaimed.

Uncas spread his paws and tipped his head back and forth in

a matter-of-fact manner. "Seems t' me this *is* an emergency."

"We really should have some sort of Boy Scout kit," said John. "An emergency preparedness sort of thing, for use just in case there's a power outage, or an earthquake, or when one of our friends changes history and makes all the shops vanish."

"I'm thinking I wish I'd brought a pie," said Fred.

"I'm thinking I wish I'd brought more crackers," said Uncas.

"I'm thinking I wish I'd brought the rum," said Jack.

Carefully, and trying to stay alert to their surroundings, they began to make their way towards the dark tower, picking their way along the better maintained, passable parts of the path.

John and Jack each had the same thought: Apart from the eerie resemblance to the Shadowed Lands they had once freed, this tableaux was not entirely unfamiliar in another way. They had both seen – and smelt – places very similar, during their days as soldiers in the Great War. Uncas was right – the smell of death was everywhere.

Several hundred yards on, the path broadened out into an avenue that looked to be even more difficult to traverse, because of a large amount of debris that obstructed the roadway. Broken wheels, discarded carts, and half-burned boxes were scattered in large piles, nearly obscuring the fact that it was an intersection. On closer examination, Jack noted that there were great spider-webs strewn across the piles, clumped in some places, but completely clear of it in others.

"We sh-should go round, Master Jack," said Uncas, the fear in his voice making him stutter.

"Agreed," said Jack.

"No cars," John observed. "Nothing modern whatsoever. No electricity, as far as I can tell. No automobiles. Not even gas lamps. And those wheels and wagons are archaic. I wonder how far back Hugo went, to have caused this."

"Sixth century," said Jack. "The message on the Grail book had to have been written when he went back. And he knew something bad would happen – that's why he told us not to close the door."

"Don't remind me," said John. "My only consolation is that Charles isn't here to see this too."

"I wish Scowler Charles *was* here," said Uncas. "He'd have set things aright already, I thinks."

"And entirely by accident, knowing Charles," said Jack.

"Which still saved you, more than once," Fred pointed out. "Uh, sir."

"You're probably right," John said, as he scratched the little animal affectionately on the head. "He does have a knack for doing the right thing at the right moment – whether he knows it or not."

The tower stood in what should have been the centre of Oxford, and was ringed with walls of sturdier construction than anything else they had passed. They were several dozen yards high, and unlike the tower they encircled, the walls shone brightly in the moonlight.

"That's a hopeful sign," Jack commented. "At least whoever is in charge around here keeps the outer walls clean."

"Hmm," said John. "Now that's odd. For a fortification, anyway."

He was looking at the great iron and wood doors that were

set into the wall, just to their left. Massive, they were obviously intended to withstand a hefty assault – but the crossbeams and braces were on the exterior, rather than inside.

"Odd isn't the word," said Jack. "That's just stupid engineering. With all the braces out here, it wouldn't keep anyone out at all. It'd be better for keeping people . . ." His voice trailed off as he realized the conclusion he'd drawn.

"Back up," John said, looking around with a growing unease. "Back up slowly, Jack."

The badgers, for their part, had gone no closer, but stood clutching each other, trembling.

"Uncas?" Jack said, concerned. "Fred? What is it?"

"Headbones," Fred whispered. "Lots of suffering."

"Are you hurt?" asked John.

"Not ours," said Uncas. "Human bean headbones."

The little mammal pointed with a shaking paw at the walls, and they suddenly realized why the walls shone. They weren't clean, so much as *bleached*.

It was interesting to realize, John thought, just how neatly skulls could be stacked, and with such precision.

Suddenly a booming cough came from behind the fortified walls, followed by another, and another, and then something of tremendous mass threw itself against the great doors. The doors shook violently, but held. The creature was tall enough that they could see its hairy bulk rising above the crest of the walls as it – they – paced back and forth, testing the doors with another blow now and again.

"Do you think they know we're here?" John whispered. "Jack – did we wake something up?"

"I'm not going to wait around to ask," Jack began, before he was cut off by another cough, which was followed by an even more chilling sound.

"Jaaack . . ."

Jack froze. So did the others.

"Jaaaack . . . We hear you, Jaaack. . ."

It was the great creatures inside the walls. Even from that distance, they could hear the companions whispering.

"Who are you?" said John.

"Sssss . . . Weee are the children of Polyphemus . . . ," the creature said. "Be ye alive, or be ye dead . . . we'll grind your bones to make our bread. . ."

"Giants!" Jack hissed. "What are giants doing in Oxford?"

"This isn't Oxford," John said irritably. "But if these are giants . . . Perhaps we could use the Binding? From the *Geographica*? Maybe . . ."

"Is that even possible to do without royal blood?" Jack whispered back. "Who'd be crazy enough to try?"

There was a chuffing noise from behind the walls of bone, and after a moment the companions realized that the giants were laughing at them.

"Foolish mansss . . . ," the giant said. "Nnooo Bindings on the sons of Polyphemus . . . not like before . . ."

"Before?" said Jack. "Someone *has* tried to Bind them."

"Yess!" rasped the giant. "You, Jaaack . . . you have tried . . . Jaaack, Jaaack, the Giant-Killer . . ."

"Oh Lord," Jack said under his breath, before he remembered they could hear him anyway. "You've got me confused with someone else," he called more loudly. "It wasn't me!"

There was a pause, almost as if denying it was persuasion enough. And then . . .

"*Jaack Giant-Killer . . . Caretaker Jaack, Companion of John . . .*"

It was a strange moment for Jack, as John looked at him with something akin to astonishment, while the badgers looked at him in unabashed admiration.

"*Achaemenides!*" the giant bellowed. "*Achaemenides! Loooose usss! Loose us to seize the slayer of our father!*"

With an impact that shook the ground, the giants – four of them, the companions could now see – pressed against the walls, and one began pounding on the gate. The giants were tall enough that the tops of their heads rose above the walls, and the companions could see that below the scraggly tufts of hair and rough foreheads, their eyes had been sewn shut.

"They're blind," said Jack. "At least they can't see us."

"*Nnooo . . . ,*" said the first giant, a triumphant purr settling into his voice, "*but weee can* hearrr *youuuu. . .*"

"That's it," John exclaimed, grabbing each of the badgers by their collars. "Run, Jack! Run!"

With the calls of the giants echoing in the air behind them, the four companions ran as fast as they could, John carrying Uncas and Jack carrying Fred. There may have been some slight breach of etiquette or decorum in simply carrying the small animals like cabbages – but at the moment, none of them cared. All that mattered, literally, was getting out of earshot of the giants.

John was more than happy to let Jack take the lead again. Of the two of them, Jack was the quicker thinker in situations like this.

Jack led them back to the intersection where the great spiderwebs were, then took the road leading to the right, keeping them at a dead run.

The direction they were running took them to an area that was pockmarked with structures. Most of them were on stilts and stood ten feet or more off the ground. The ones that weren't on stilts were either in a bad state of disrepair, or burned past usability. The road itself was in better condition, and there were fewer obstructions to slow them down. There were still no lights or fires visible, but as they passed, John imagined he could feel someone watching them from the shadows.

When they had finally gone a far enough distance that the badgers could run for themselves, John and Jack lowered them to the ground and slowed to a brisk trot. As they jogged along, Jack realized that he was still the object of intense admiration.

"Did you really kill a giant, Scowler Jack?" Uncas asked. "They sure seemed t' know *you*."

Jack sighed. "I'm sure if I had, I'd remember it, and if I was the Giant-Killing type, I probably wouldn't be as afraid of that lot as I actually am."

"Oh," the badger said, deflating slightly. "But," he added, brightening, "y' did speak t' them very boldly."

"That he did," Fred agreed. "Very boldly indeed."

"Oh, for heaven's sake," Jack said, sitting heavily on a softlooking patch of dirt. "I think we've run far enough. And I'm knackered at any rate."

John scanned the horizon in the direction from which they'd come. "I think we're okay for the moment. But I think our plan of approaching whoever is in charge of the tower is right out."

Jack pulled off one of his shoes and examined his foot. "Bugger this for a lark. I've got a blister. I hope it doesn't get infected."

"A blister?" John snorted. "I've seen you take cudgel blows that nearly took your arm off, you've been stabbed by swords, and even shot with an arrow – and you're complaining about a blister?"

"It's a really *big* blister," said Jack.

"Here," Fred said, hopping forward. "I can help with that."

The little badger started flipping through pages in the Little Whatsit, humming to himself as he did so. Then he seemed to settle on the page he wanted, scanned it twice, then replaced the book in his coat.

"I'm going to need the penknife, please, Scowler John, and Scowler Jack, tell me – are any of your coins silver?"

"One of them," Jack said as John handed over the knife. "What are you going to do?"

"This'll sting a little, and I'm sorry for that," said Fred, "but I can keep it from getting infected."

Jack removed his stocking and let the animal examine his blistered foot. Fred clucked and purred over it a moment, then swiftly lanced the blister with the knife. As it drained into the cloth Jack pressed against it, Fred used the knife to scrape tiny slivers of silver from the coin, which he then ground to a fine dust between two stones. Finally satisfied with the powdered silver, he pressed it to the wound, then bound the foot tightly with a strip of cloth from his coat. Standing back, he handed the coin to Uncas and told Jack he could replace his stocking and shoe.

"It'll sting a bit, there's no helping that," Fred repeated, "but it'll be healed in a few hours, and it won't get infected."

"Amazing," said Jack. "How is it you learned this?"

Fred patted the book in his pocket. "The Little Whatsit," he said proudly. "I told you – it has something about everything in it."

"Handy, that," said John. "I'd like to take a look at it – but later. I think someone's followed us."

There was a bulky shape moving along the road some distance back, coming straight towards them. It was too small to be one of the giants, but large enough to be worth hiding from.

Jack led them under one of the stilt-houses and under the fallen archway of a house that had been burned. With any luck, they'd blend in with the protruding ribs of the frame that were sticking out of the rubble.

"I think something must have died," Jack whispered, wrinkling his nose and checking his shoes. "It smells horrid over here."

"Uh, that would be me," Uncas admitted sheepishly. "I stepped in a puddle. Sorry."

"Wet badger fur," Jack groaned, nodding. "Charles never told me it was this bad."

"Quiet," said John, hunkering down. "It's coming."

The thing that followed them resembled a motorcar, but it had no engine. Instead it was drawn by two skeletal-looking horses with bandaged heads. With horror, the companions realized that these were dehorned unicorns. And the appearance of the carriage's driver gave the impression that he'd happily have done it himself, and then used the horns as toothpicks just for spite. He stepped down from the carriage and looked about, eyes narrowed. From their concealment, the companions could see he wore a great grey trench coat and a matching top hat. His beard was full and black, he was all of eight feet tall, and he wore a blue rose on his lapel. A Cossack, out on the town.

Then he opened his coat.

Where his torso should have been was a great wicker cage, and through the weave they could just make out the shapes of small creatures moving about inside. At first John thought they might be monkeys, but then the large man stopped and opened his chest to let them out, and the true horror was laid bare in the chalky moonlight.

They were children.

Little boys, perhaps ten but certainly not as old as twelve, and thin as bamboo. They were filthy, and dressed in rags. Each had a thick iron ring fastened around its neck, which was connected to a leash held by the man. The dozen or so boys who emerged from him spread out at his feet, sniffing the ground.

"Ah, my little Sweeps, my precious Sweeps. Finds us the man-flesh. Finds us it, and make Papa happy."

"Yes, Papa," the children answered in unison.

As the companions watched from their hiding place, the Sweeps began a revoltingly fascinating transformation. They bent low, walking on all fours and sniffing the ground. And as they went, they began murmuring phrases that at first seemed like nonsense.

"I love my vegetables," said one.

"I stabbed my sister in the eye," said another.

"My farts smell like flowers," said a third.

And as the boys voiced these obvious lies, their noses began to grow. Some grew longer than others, but all of them soon had noses of extraordinary length, and their search picked up the pace accordingly.

"Good, good, my precious Sweeps," purred their "papa". "Finds us the man-flesh. Finds it now, for your papa and the King."

The man and his Sweeps were looking around the stilt-houses on the opposite side of the road, far from where the companions were hiding. For a brief instant, John and Jack both harboured the notion that they could sneak away, but then one of the Sweeps stood stock still, like a chipmunk. It sniffed the air several times, and then turned and looked directly at the companions.

The Sweep ran to its master and whispered to him, and the great man and his hideous children all turned around and began to move across the road.

Suddenly a ball of flame erupted in the centre of the road, throwing a blazing light over the whole area. For a moment the Sweeps' master locked fury-filled eyes with John, but he retreated from the fire, pulling all the children back inside himself. Mounting the carriage, he wheeled the unicorns about and disappeared over the hill.

"That was lucky as all Hades," John said, rising from where he'd been crouching. "Very lucky."

"It weren't luck, really," came a muffled voice from above. "The Sweeps can withstand a lot, but the Wicker Men hate fire more than anything."

A thin, limber man dressed in tattered clothes dropped down from the stilt-house to the left of them. His face was wrapped in cloth save for his eyes, and his arms were bandaged to the fingertips. From the blackened cloth, they could tell he'd been badly singed in saving them.

"Naw," he said, waving off their concern. "I's been burned worse, see?"

He unwrapped the cloth from his face to reveal old scars along his right cheek and chin. The companions all gasped in shock – but not because of the scars.

It was Charles.

"Scowler Charles!" Uncas said joyfully. "Of course it be you who rescued us! Of course!"

"Who's Charles?" said the man, eyeing the badger suspiciously. "I only helped you out 'cause I hate the Wicker Men. It weren't to save you lot of idiots a'tall."

"These are scowlers . . . uh, scholars, not idiots," Fred said defiantly, "and they are two of the greatest men in all the world."

"It doesn't matter why," Jack said, offering a hand that was studiously ignored. "Ah, I mean, there's no one in England I'd be happier to see right now."

"England?" the man asked. "What's an 'England'?"

"What kind of question is that?" John spluttered, spreading his arms. "*This* is England. This country, where we live. England. Great Britain. Home."

The man looked puzzled. "I don't know where you blokes come from, but this is Albion. Always has been, as long as anyone can remember. There are some what call it otherwise, but not aloud, not unless they be brave, or foolish. The king's minions, like that one what just run off, have seen to that. I shouldn't even be sayin' as much as I have."

"Either way," John said, "we are truly grateful for your help. I'm John." As Jack had done, John stuck out his hand, which the man finally shook.

"Strange, stupid travellers from afar, you can call me Chaz," he said hesitantly. "Welcome to the Winterland."

PART TWO

Fractured Albion

"*Whatever it is you've come about, Chaz, I want no part of it . . .*"

CHAPTER FIVE

Tatterdemalion

The fishermen had wondered about the cart, and the scrawny horse that pulled it, and the solitary driver who had waited with it by the river's edge for nearly three hours. He was unshaven and unkempt, but wore robes of great quality and worth. His cart was battered and poorly kept but could withstand such treatment because its builders had been masters of their craft. And the steed was thin, but its bearing was noble. This driver was, despite the appearances, a great dignitary, or even possibly a king who sat in his cart next to the river.

The wild-eyed look he wore, coupled with the fact that he seemed to converse only with himself, encouraged them to leave him be. The fishermen moved their nets farther down the river and left him to his own devices.

The king (for that was, in fact, what he was) had been lured to the riverside by a promise. All he need do was wait for the man depicted in an illumination he'd been given, then deliver him to the distant tournament that had already commenced. And for this, the king would be given his heart's desire – or at least, the fulfillment of the family obsession. It never occurred to him to wonder how his benefactor had discovered the location of the

Questing Beast, but the promise itself was enough, and made it worth his effort to try.

When it was nearly dusk, the autumn light had faded to a haze that painted the belly of the clouds gold and crimson. As the sky grew dimmer, the king's patience finally found itself rewarded when a shortish, slightly discombobulated man came staggering up the embankment.

He was more dishevelled than in the illumination, but the manner of dress was the same, and he was here, in the appointed spot, at (almost) the appointed time. The king lowered himself from the cart with a grunt and a groan and bowed his head in greeting.

The odd man he'd been sent to retrieve spoke strangely, almost unintelligibly. Perhaps he was an idiot. Either way, the king reasoned, he needed to communicate his intention. With a series of half phrases and pantomimed gestures, it became evident to the man that the king was there to offer transport. He clambered into the cart, sitting next to the king, and stuck out his hand in greeting. The king looked at it oddly for a moment, then gripped the man's wrist, as if looking for a concealed weapon.

The man laughed uproariously at this and said something the king finally realized was his name: "Dyson. Hugo Dyson. Pleased to make your acquaintance."

The king loosed his wrist and nodded. "Pellinor," he said, tapping his chest. "Pellinor." With that he grasped the reins and clucked his tongue at the horse. They were three days late and still had a long way to go.

Following their familiar-yet-still-a-stranger liberator gave John and Jack time to observe and evaluate him. He was, for all that their senses could accrue, Charles. But at the same time he was, as he insisted repeatedly, not.

Some of the scars he bore were fresh, but others were years old. He had not come here in a trice, as they and the badgers had done. It was possible he had gone through one of the doorways, as their hapless colleague had earlier, and found himself thrust backwards in time – but that wouldn't explain why he didn't recognize them, or worse, why it seemed as if he had no memory of the Charles they knew at all.

Chaz was obviously uneducated, and he spoke with worse grammar than Uncas. He bore some of Charles's mannerisms, and certain speech patterns were familiar, the cadences, the tone. . . But both the scholarly rationalism and playful inquisitiveness were gone. What remained was the shape of Charles, his outline, but it was filled with fear, and distrust, and overwhelmingly, the basest of instincts: to survive at all costs. This was made clear right away.

"Get rid of the animals," Chaz had said, to the badgers' great dismay.

"We're not getting rid of anyone," John stated firmly, backed by incredulous nodding from Jack. "They're with us, period."

Chaz shrugged. "Have it your way. But they smell, and that means death here."

"You aren't a garden of roses yourself," Fred pointed out.

"Fred!" Uncas exclaimed. "Mind your tongue! This be Scowler Charles you be addressin'!"

"There you go with that 'Charles' business again," Chaz said, irritated. "My name is Chaz, not that it matters to you. And you owe me a life-debt."

"For what?" asked Jack.

"Saving you from the Sweeps," said Chaz, "but I'll consider it paid if you give me the fat badger to roast."

Uncas couldn't decide whether to be offended at being called fat, or horrified at the idea of being eaten. Fred just bared his teeth and stepped in front of his father.

"You must be joking," said Jack. "These aren't merely animals – they're our friends!"

"Thank you," said Uncas. "I think."

"Where we're from, Chaz, we don't eat our friends," John explained.

"I thinks you're *here* now, not where you're from," Chaz replied. "But I'm not really that hungry anyway." With a last look at the badgers, he turned and trotted off. About twenty yards away, he turned around, a silhouette against the hillside. "Well? Are you idiots coming or not?"

There had been little choice. And as obscured as it was by strangeness, the voice that beckoned to them was their friend's voice. So they – all four of them – followed.

Chaz set a pace that was swift, but not impossible to keep, even for the badgers. They were slowed only by bewilderment, remorse, and no small amount of fear. It wasn't a scholar who had looked at them, but a predator. And it ran contrary to animal sense to follow a predator into its own lair.

A short distance farther on, John unconsciously checked the time on his watch, noted the fixed hands, then smiled ruefully and put it back in his pocket.

"Why don't you carry one that works," suggested Jack, "and

keep that one in another pocket to show Priscilla when she asks about it?"

"I can't quite manage the deception," John admitted. "It seems like a small thing, to be sure – but when I tried it, I found myself fussing about with them and worrying about which one was draped on the waistcoat and which was hidden . . . and then I forgot, and Pris saw the other one, and the hurt in her eyes was excruciating. So it's the Frog-in-a-Bonnet time or none at all, I'm afraid."

"Perhaps you could ask Father Christmas to give her a good watch this Christmas, to be passed on to you," Jack said, grinning.

"That's not a half-bad idea," John said. "I'll have to ask him about it the next time we're in the Archipelago."

Jack turned his head, but not swiftly enough for John to catch the look of doubt that crossed his features. Bantering about home and family was one thing. But mentioning the Archipelago brought them both back to the present dilemma, and the creeping despair that was becoming impossible to push away.

It took longer for the companions to get to the small village where Chaz lived than it might have if John or Jack had been in the lead. The entire area seemed deserted, and the only other structures they saw were more of the odd stilt-houses that pockmarked the roads. But Chaz had insisted on taking a circuitous route that roamed back and forth across the entire countryside.

"It's because of the Wicker Man," he finally explained when the others pressed for his reasons. "He was out looking for you lot in partic'lar, and there's no telling how many more are doing the same. Their Sweeps follow your scent, an' so it's best to leave a trail that'll confuse 'em before they finds you."

"How many more *what* might be out looking?" asked Jack.

"Wicker Men," Chaz replied without turning around, "and their Sweeps. That wasn't the only one, you know. And there are other creatures too. Some better. Most worse."

"We saw the giants," John said. "Should we be talking aloud, with them lurking somewhere back there?"

"Oh, the giants is no worry," Chaz said breezily. "They can't be loosed until they been summoned, an' . . ."

He stopped as if he'd said too much, then scowled at John. "Be that as it may, mayhap we shouldn't ought t' be talking aloud, anyroad."

After another hour of Möbius loops, Chaz finally brought them to his strange abode. Unlike the dozen or so stilt-houses that clustered nearby, it was set into the side of a hill. It had a round door that was lightly camouflaged and heavily fortified. Through the doorway, they could see that the ceilings were low, but it seemed a good enough place, if not really one suited to guests.

The area itself was more intriguing to Jack. It was disconcertingly familiar. The trees, what remained of them, were bare, but the soil itself, the reddish hues, the texture . . . It was all the same, along with the spot nearby where the quarry should be. . .

And then he knew.

It was the Kilns, Jack suddenly realized. Home. *His* home, at any rate. His and Warnie's, and Jamie's. Chaz had brought them to the one place Jack most wanted to be, except it wasn't that place at all – it was a place that looked like home but was really in some hellish otherworld in which they were trapped, perhaps permanently.

"So how have you managed to survive on your own?" Jack asked.

"I makes do," Chaz said after a moment. "I scavenge, mostly, and trade a little of this, a little of that. But I gets what I needs."

"I think I need some sustenance," said John, "if you have anything you can spare, Chaz."

"My stores is scanty, save for roots and a bone or two," said Chaz, eyeing the badgers while trying to look as if he wasn't, "but it may be enough for a thin soup, since we have nothing else t' put in the pot."

"Soup – thin or not – sounds fine to me," Jack said, folding his arms and standing protectively in front of the badgers. "I just wish we had Bert's magic stone to help it along."

"Ah yes," said John. "His Stone Soup. Meal fit for, well, a king. Or a group of lost scholars."

"Who's Bert?" Chaz said without looking up from his dinner preparations. "Not that I really care, but talking passes the time."

"Are you sure he's not Charles?" Jack whispered to John.

"Heh," said John. "Bert's our mentor, Chaz. A great man. And I really wish he were here."

"Maybe he is," offered Fred. "If Scowler Char – uh, I mean, if Mister Chaz is here, and he's almost like Scowler Charles, than perhaps others we know are here too."

"Everything here is upside down and sideways anyway," Jack said, indicating their reluctant host. "Perhaps Bert goes by Herb or Herbert or George or some such."

Uncas nodded sagely. "Th' Far Traveller can be knowed by many names."

For the first time it seemed as if the conversation had engaged

Chaz's full attention. He stood abruptly, ladle in hand. "Far Traveller? This Bert fellow is also called the Far Traveller?"

"Does that make a difference?" asked John.

"It does if I knows a 'Far Traveller' and not a 'Bert,'" Chaz replied, suddenly animated. "Is he really a friend of yours?"

"Friend and teacher," said John. "I think what we need is to get some food and rest, then get our bearings in the morning and see if Bert really is somewhere hereabouts."

Chaz dropped the bowl of roots he'd been pulling out of a cupboard and turned to them, incredulous. "Are you mad?" he exclaimed. "Why would you possibly go about during the day?"

"Why would that be a worse plan than traipsing about at night?" asked Jack. "What with giants and Sweeps and Wicker Men roaming around."

"There are worse things than them what serves the king," Chaz said slowly, "an' they go about when the sun is high."

The fear in his voice was enough to convince them. The companions ate the meal he prepared, then stretched out on the dirt floor as the sun began to rise, to sleep until dusk. And so none of them saw the raven Chaz kept in the cage in the rear of the house, or the name he wrote on the note he tied to its leg before he turned it loose into the harsh Albion daylight, closing the door behind it.

When the sun had finally dropped to just a sliver of blood-tinted light on the horizon, Chaz finally opened the door again, and they began the journey to find the Far Traveller.

Chaz led them south and west, to the channel that was the nearest access to open waters in that part of Albion. As they journeyed they could see more towers in the distance. None were close enough for the companions to worry about being seen, but they kept watchful eyes all around, just to be safe.

It was still fully night when they reached their destination, a small hamlet Chaz called Trevena. It consisted of fewer structures than the village that had been the Kilns, but all here were on the strange stilts. The largest of them, made of stone, was at the edge of the beach, surrounded by a courtyard. A wooden bridge ran up at a slope to the front door, which was open.

The courtyard was bare rather than clean; and the shack simple rather than orderly. Spareness might resemble cleanliness, but it cannot disguise the bleak dreariness underneath.

Chaz passed over the bridge and through the shack with a proprietor's ease and opened the door at the rear of the building. "He'll be out this way, on the pier," he said, gesturing. "Follow me close-like."

The pier, which was itself a generous description, was high off the ground, but short. The beach dropped away sharply, since there was no longer any water flowing underneath, and the sand stretched out into the darkness.

"Must be low tide," John observed, "but the beach seems awfully parched."

Chaz chuckled. "'Tis, 'tis," he said in agreement. "Been low tide for almost two hundred years, as I heard it said. The ocean's still out there, somewheres, but no souls alive has seen it."

"Strange pier," Jack said. "If there's no water, where do you moor the boats?"

"Hsst!" Chaz hissed, looking behind them. "You can't just go round sayin' words like that. Words kill, you know."

"Sorry," said Jack.

"Is that him?" John asked, pointing.

At the end of the pier, a shadow stood against a piling. A shadow with a very familiar shape.

John began to move closer, but Chaz motioned for him to hold back. Instead Chaz stepped to the far right side of the pier, where he could be seen in the dim light – but without getting too close to the figure at the end of the pier.

The shadow raised its head in alarm, then lowered it in resignation.

"Whatever it is you've come about, Chaz, I want no part of it. Go back to your game-playing with the Wicker Men, or better yet, go play some pipes outside the bone towers, and let the giants have some fun with you. I don't care either way – just leave me be."

"Weren't my call to come seeking you either, you old goat," Chaz retorted, "but I run into some fellows who says they knows you. Calls you 'Bert' or summat."

At this the shadow stood upright, startled. "Bert? There's no one else still alive who would use that name, not in *this* world, not unless . . ."

He pushed away from the piling where he'd been braced, and hobbled out into the hazy light. For everyone but Chaz, there was a shock of recognition, and for John and Jack, a further shock of seeing nightmares made real.

It was indeed Bert. But he had been *changed*.

The cheerily ruffled tatterdemalion of their first meeting was barely in evidence here. The clothes and hat were the same, but threadbare and shabby. He was thin, nearly emaciated, and his face haggard and drawn. There was no spark in his eyes, no twinkle. Neither of them had ever seen him without the twinkle, even in the grimmest of circumstances. But then again, neither of them had seem him without all his limbs, either.

Bert supported himself by gripping a small ash walking stick with his left hand – his only hand. His other sleeve was folded and pinned just below his elbow. And in place of his right leg, fastened just under the knee was a piece of wood wrapped in leather, which ended with a crude wooden foot inside his shoe.

Before John or Jack could say anything, Bert threw aside his stick and hobbled forward, grabbing John by the lapels. Weakly, but driven by surprise and rage, his hand shook as the younger man tried to steady him. Bert pressed close, eyes wild, and all but screamed at John.

"Where have you been? Where ... have ... you ... *been?!*"

On it sat a skull, a scroll, and a small box of a unique design.

Chapter Six
The Serendipity Box

"*Bert!*" John said in choked astonishment. "You know us? You really know us?"

"Of course I know you, John," the ragged old man said, finally letting go of John's coat and brushing him away. "I gave you the *Geographica*. I helped the three of you learn your roles in the great clockwork mechanism of things that are. I stood by you against a great evil, and we saved the world, once. And then you let it degrade to . . . to . . . this," he spat, gesturing with his good arm. "Here, you. Badger. Give me my stick."

Fred jumped forward and retrieved the short ash staff, handing it to the old man. Neither he nor Uncas understood what was taking place, and so they remained quiet while the humans played out the drama.

Bert stood a few feet from John and Jack, forming a rough triangle, but he refused to look at either of them – not directly. Chaz stood farther back, observing.

"Fourteen years," Bert wheezed. "We came here fourteen years ago, to . . . heh . . . *SAVE* you . . . to *HELP* you . . ."

"You said 'we,' Bert," Jack said, interrupting. "Who else came with you? Surely not Aven?"

"No, not Aven," Bert replied. "Your pretty ladylove stayed in the Archipelago, where she needed to be. She doesn't love you, you know," he added, almost conspiratorially. "Never did. Didn't love the potboy, either. No, Nemo was her companion, but you fixed that, didn't you, Jack?"

In earlier years Jack would have reddened at this and become flustered. But he'd matured a great deal in the intervening time, and could face his own shortcomings and mistakes foursquare, as a man is supposed to do.

"I stopped feeling responsible for that a long time ago, Bert," he said calmly. "James Barrie told me things about Nemo, and you, and . . ." He stopped. "Verne. You came here with Jules Verne."

Bert sighed heavily and turned his back to them before answering. "Yes," he said finally. "Jules and I came here together. We came . . . *here*. . . ."

Without warning, the old man suddenly burst into tears. "Why did you have to bring her up, Jack? Why did you have to mention Aven, now that I'd finally nearly forgotten about her?"

Jack started to reply, but John silenced him with a gesture. Bert was speaking from a long, deep pain, and perhaps they might learn something of what was happening.

"If she'd been killed in battle, I might have been able to live with it," Bert sobbed. "But here, after what's happened, it's as if she never existed! She is worse than dead!"

"The Lady Aven is not dead," came a soft voice. "I saw her myself just yesterday."

Fred was standing nearby, head bowed and paws folded respectfully, but when he spoke his voice was firm with conviction. "She is alive. Maybe not here, where we are, but somewheres. She is. And when Scowler John and Scowler Jack, and, uh, Mister Chaz help us t' get back there, maybe you can come with us and see for yourself."

At first Bert reacted in rage, raising the ash stick to strike at the little creature. But Fred didn't move. He barely flinched, and closed his eyes to receive the blow.

Seeing this, Bert lowered the stick, then fell to his knees and grasped the badger, pulling Fred to his chest. "I'm sorry, I'm sorry, little child of the Earth," Bert said through muffled sobs. "I will not strike you. I won't. It's just . . . It's been so long. . . ."

Fred hugged the old traveller, and after a moment, Uncas moved in to do so as well. "It be all right," said Uncas gently.

"Animal logic," Jack said to John. "Loyalty is all, and all things may be forgiven."

"We should go inside," said Chaz. "The sun will be coming up soon."

"Yes," Bert agreed, rising and wiping his eyes. "We have a great deal to discuss."

With the badgers supporting him on either side, Bert moved down the pier to the bridge that connected it to the house. John followed behind, but Jack pulled Chaz aside.

"If this is indeed 'our' Bert," Jack whispered, "how has he survived? *You* knew just where to find him. Wouldn't the king have killed him long before now?"

"He has, in years past, proved himself to be a friend to the king," Chaz replied, "or at least, wise enough to seem as such."

"And this," Jack said, indicating the damaged man walking ahead of them, "is how the king treats his friends?"

Chaz shrugged. "Someone asked him that once. And th' king laughed an' said, 'A friend this valuable you can't eat all at once.'"

Bert took them all inside the little shack, where he lit two candles, which he placed at opposite ends of the cramped quarters. For a single person, the accommodations were tight; for four men and two badgers, it was practically claustrophobic. There was a table and only one chair, which Bert took. The others sat on the floor, except for Chaz, who remained standing nervously in the doorway.

"You'll have to forgive my lack of hospitality," Bert told the others. "I'd offer you tea, but I haven't any tea. I'd offer you brandy, but I haven't any brandy. In fact, I don't even have any crackers to give you."

"We did," said Uncas, "but there was an emergency."

"There still is," said Jack.

"That's a shame," said Bert, "to run out of crackers before you've run out of emergency. And in Albion, it's always an emergency."

"The king, whoever he is, sounds like an utter despot," John observed.

"Well said, John," said Bert, "for he is just that. A despot. A petty, cruel dictator who hates himself and takes it out on everyone else. He suffers, and so makes the world suffer too."

"That sounds awfully familiar," said Jack.

"More than you know," said Bert. "You've met him. Killed him, actually, more or less."

"That's impossible," said John.

"Improbable, but clearly not impossible," Bert corrected. "In the world you came from, the Winter King fell to his death in the year 1917. But here it is the one thousand four hundred and fourth year of the reign of our Lord and King, Imperius Rex, Mordred the First."

It took some time for the reunited friends to explain what had been happening to them, and Bert listened to their accounting of the situation with Hugo Dyson without comment. When they at last had finished explaining, he nodded sadly.

"I begin to understand, at long last," he said, still unwilling to look at any of them directly. "If Hugo went back to the sixth century, then he changed history. And everything proceeded apace from there to what we see now, today. Something that happened in the past gave Mordred the means to conquer and rule and emerge victorious against all opposition – if there ever was any."

"Why do you still know us, Bert?" asked Jack. "Chaz is obviously what Charles became in this timeline where he never knew us – but you're still our Bert."

"Jules and I left Paralon right after the War of the Winter King," said Bert. "He had come across a passage in a future history that mentioned the re-emergence of Mordred, and so we returned here to England to warn you. When we arrived, we found things as you see them now, and we were trapped."

"We've seen you since then," said Jack. "Many, many times, in fact. How is that possible if you've been here all these years?"

"Where *is* here?" Bert asked. "'Here' wasn't created until Hugo went through the door. And once that happened, everything forward changed."

"I still don't see how that would affect your return to England," said John. "Our past hasn't changed. Why did yours?"

"Jules and I travel via means that take us outside of time and space," said Bert. "If we'd simply come back on one of the Dragonships, we'd never have noticed a difference. Jules has always kept his own counsel, though, and insisted that we needed to travel by his usual method, so we did."

"You've mentioned time travel before, Bert," John said, "but you've never gone into detail about how you really do it. It never came up as a factor in our roles as Caretakers until the problems with the Keep of Time, so I never asked about it."

"And those problems are the very ones that caused this, aren't they?" Bert said, his voice harsh. "If you'd paid closer attention to your responsibilities, then maybe we wouldn't be here now."

"That's hardly fair, Bert," Jack exclaimed. "You were there with us when Charles led us out of the Keep, before Mordred set it aflame."

"Don't bring *me* into this," put in Chaz, "even if it's the other me."

"Jack's right," said John. "There were things you and Verne could have told us – about time travel, for example – that might have prevented this. But you always seemed to be playing your own cards close, Bert."

"You weren't ready yet," the old man replied. "At least, in Jules's estimation you weren't. We had focused on you, John, as the one with the most potential to learn about the intricacies of time as well as space. But then we realized it might be Jack who possessed the greater capacity. We were wrong on both counts, it seems. No offence."

"I can't be offended," Jack said, "when I don't even understand what you're talking about."

"So you get my point," said Bert. "Excellent. No, we realized it was Charles who had a bent for not only time travel, but also for interdimensionality. So we came back to England specifically to warn *him*."

"Same with th' Royal Animal Rescue Squad," Uncas put in. "We were given our instructions by th' Prime Caretaker fourteen years ago."

"That's what I find intriguing," said John. "Verne obviously knew more than he was telling you, Bert, to set a plan into motion that involved a rescue effort on the very day that these events would be set into motion in your own future."

Bert stood and hobbled his way over to the mantel of the small tumbledown fireplace at the far side of the shack. On it sat a skull, a scroll, and a small box of a unique design.

Bert removed the box and set it in the centre of his small table. The box wasn't polished, but it was shiny with age; great, great age. The wood it was constructed of was pale, and there were cuneiform-like markings carved into the top and sides. Across the bottom were signs of scorching, as if it had been held to a flame. Jack reached out to lift the lid, but Bert slapped down his hand with the ash staff.

"Not so quickly, lad," the old man said. "No telling what'll come out of the Serendipity Box. Don't want to let anything out that's best kept in, for now."

"What is a Serendipity Box?" Jack asked as he rubbed his knuckles. "Some sort of Pandora's Kettle?"

"Not so dire as that," said Bert. "It was your mentor, Stellan, who actually named it, John. What it was called before that, I can't say.

"As the legend goes, it was given to Seth, the third son of Adam and Eve, who passed it to his own son, Enos. Where it went after that is mostly lost to the mists of antiquity. But sometime in the past, it came into the possession of Jules Verne, and it was he who explained its workings to myself and Stellan.

"Adam explained to his son that the box could be used but once, and it was his choice alone when to do so. It would give whoever opened it whatever they most needed, and so the old Patriarch advised Seth that he should save it for a crisis, for a time of great peril, and only then open the box."

"What did Seth use it for?" asked John, who still had not decided whether he even wanted to touch the Serendipity Box, much less open it. "I've never heard of it."

"It was too long ago, and there are too many versions of the stories to know for sure," Bert replied. "Some say that he was given a knife with which to avenge his brother, Abel. Others, that it contained three seeds from the Tree of Life, one of which he placed under Adam's tongue when he died, the second of which he planted in a hollow at the centre of the Earth, and the last of which he saved. One story even says that his wife, whom some called Idyl, sprang forth fully formed from the box, like Athena from the forehead of Zeus, and that she was not a Daughter of Eve at all.

"There is a fragment of scripture that claimed Enoch and Methuselah both used the box, and another that claimed it had been used by Moses to part the Red Sea. An entirely apocryphal account says that it was the Serendipity Box that held the thirty pieces of silver given to Judas Iscariot. But no historians I know of believed it."

"Why is that?" asked John.

"Because," said Bert, "according to the story, it was Jesus Christ himself who gave Judas the box."

"Who had it between then and now?"

Bert shrugged, then rubbed absentmindedly at the stump of his right arm. "Jules and Stellan had some theories, and we read through the Histories at Paralon for clues, but apparently miracle boxes that are only good for a single use aren't worth writing about."

"Jules never said where he got it?"

"Here," Bert said, rising and taking the skull from the mantel. He tossed the skull to John, who jumped up and caught it against his chest. "Ask him yourself. And let me know if he answers – I've been talking to him for years now, and he hasn't said a word."

The companions were speechless, except for Chaz, who watched with mild interest. "Kept it, did you, old-timer?" he said blithely as he walked to the window to pull back the curtain and peer outside. "I suppose the king wouldn't notice one more or less in his tower walls."

"This is Jules Verne?" John asked, flabbergasted. "He's dead?"

"The world we knew thought he died in 1905 anyway," said Bert, "and he may well have. But he had a lot of travelling around to do, in time as well as in space, and he had the bad fortune to end up here, with me, in this dismal place."

"What happened?"

"Mordred was waiting for us," said Bert. "He knew we were coming, somehow, some way. And before we could gird ourselves up to work out what had happened to us – hell's bells, to the whole bloody *world* – Jules was killed."

"There was no way to contact the Archipelago for help?" Jack asked, taking the skull from John and hefting it in one hand. "Samaranth, or Ordo Maas? Anyone?"

Bert shook his head and looked at Jack intensely. "You still don't get it, do you, boy? In this place, there is no Archipelago! Mordred destroyed it all centuries ago, and then set about destroying this world as well! The only creatures or lands who survived were those who joined him, like the giants and the trolls! Everything and everyone else – dragons, elves, dwarves, humans . . . all gone! There was no way to contact anyone, and no one to hear the call if there had been a way!"

"Could you have used the Serendipity Box?" asked Jack.

"I did use it," Bert said, sitting again. "And as Jules had said it would, it gave me what I needed. At least," he added, "I hope it did. Only time shall tell."

"I don't know what all the fuss is about," said Uncas. "There's nothing but crackers in here, anyway."

The others turned back to the table to see the box, top flung wide, spilling over with oyster crackers. Uncas was happily shoving them into his mouth with both paws, while Fred stood a few feet away with a horrified expression on his face.

John took a bowl from a cupboard and emptied the box into it, then closed the box and replaced it on the mantel, higher than a badger's reach.

"Oh, great," Jack groaned. "We have one chance each to get something miraculous from that box, and Uncas wastes it on crackers."

"It doesn't work like that," Bert said with a chuckle. "It isn't a magic genie's bottle that you rub to get three wishes. It gives you, and you alone, one time, what it is that you need the most. So," he finished, rubbing Uncas on the head, "it's likely that it doesn't matter when or where or how Uncas opened the box. It would probably have been full of oyster crackers just the same."

"Forry," said Uncas through a mouthful of crackers. "I juff willy wike 'em."

"I think you might be correct," Bert mused, turning to John. "I think perhaps Jules had planned ahead for something only he was privy to. Something that's happening right now."

"Hold on, you old goat," Chaz said, still glancing out the window and fidgeting nervously. "Don't go gettin' any ideas. . ."

"But don't you see?" Bert exclaimed. "If all of this was foretold – was anticipated – by Jules, then that changes everything!"

"What are you talking about?" asked John.

"The Serendipity Box was left for you, John. Jules left it for you, and Jack, and Charles. He said you'd come for it. I just never imagined it would take fourteen years."

"I'm surprised Mordred didn't take it for himself," said Jack.

"He did," Chaz answered, gesturing to his face. "He opened it, then flew into a rage at whatever it was he saw inside. Then he tried to burn it, but I managed to steal it back. That was the day I got these scars."

"Mordred didn't know the box can't be destroyed," said Bert. "I've kept it here since, waiting."

"He does have a habit of trying to burn things that can't be burned," said Jack, clapping Chaz on the back. "Well done, old boy."

"We met," Bert said, indicating Chaz, "using the same logic you used to come here. I went looking for you, as you came looking for me. For better or worse, I found *him*."

Chaz made an obscene gesture and looked out the window again. "Sky's brightening. Sun'll be up, soonish."

"We're together again, is what matters," said Jack. "Any reunion of friends is a good happening."

But John was not nearly so pleased. He was putting together parts of the puzzle that made more sense to him than he liked, and he was slowly realizing that as safe as they felt at that moment, they might in fact be in greater danger than ever. There was a connection of some kind between Chaz and Mordred that had not been revealed. But there was one question on his mind that was even more terrible.

"Bert," John intoned dully, "why were *you* spared? Why was Verne killed, and not you?"

Bert closed his eyes and sat silently for a long moment before answering.

"Because," he finally said, "it was what had to happen."

"Practicality," said Chaz. "You did what you had to do."

John stood up and backed towards the door. "What did you do, Bert?"

"What I was destined to do," Bert replied, his face gone cold. "I just never got thirty pieces of silver."

"You sold him," Jack whispered. "You sold Verne to Mordred, to save yourself."

"I won't argue that on the face of it," Bert said plaintively, "but I take exception to your implication. I did what I had to do to survive to this point in time – but it was not of my own volition, and I compromised myself greatly to do so. I've made many more compromises since, all to make certain that we would be here, tonight, to have this very conversation. So were my actions virtuous, or shameful?"

"That," an icy voice said from just outside the door, "depends entirely on one's point of view."

"Please, come inside," said Reynard.

CHAPTER SEVEN
Noble's Isle

All of them save for Uncas and Fred recognized the voice immediately.

"May I come in?" it said, in a tone that made it sound more like a statement than a query.

Bert sighed heavily. "Enter freely and of your own will, Mordred."

The door opened, and silhouetted against the rising sun they saw the imposing figure of the man they had known as the Winter King. The man they had caused to be killed. The man who, more than once, had tried to kill *them*. And their most trusted ally had just invited him into his house.

Mordred was not significantly different from when they had seen him in their own world. He seemed perhaps more aged, more weathered here. He was stouter, and slightly round-shouldered, but his arms were corded with muscle, and his hair cascaded down his back in a mane. He was dressed in royal colours and had the bearing and manner of a king.

He was in appearance, John realized with a shock, everything one would expect a king to look like, to emanate. And he suddenly understood how a man could be a tyrant and still rule: It was a question of the ability to command, to draw respect, even in the wake of evil acts.

Immediately John and Jack took defensive stances in front of Bert and the badgers, but Mordred ignored them, leaning casually against the door frame and addressing Bert.

"My old friend, the Far Traveller," the king said. "We meet again."

Bert glared at him. "Nothing going on here concerns you, Mordred," he said, gripping the staff so tightly his knuckles turned white. "You needn't have come."

"Oh, but everything in my kingdom concerns me, *Bert*," Mordred replied. John and Jack, still facing their enemy, didn't notice the blood drain from Bert's face at the mention of his name. "The citizens who walk my streets, as well as the Children of the Earth who live beneath them."

This last he said to Uncas and Fred, who both hissed at him in reply. They did not need to have seen him before in the flesh to realize they were facing the greatest adversary of legend, whom Tummeler had told them about.

For his part, Bert simply slumped in the chair, his chin resting on his chest. He seemed already defeated in a game where the stakes had not even been named. "Why are you here, Mordred?"

"Why?" Mordred replied in mock surprise. "I have simply come to meet the two new friends I have waited to meet for so very, very long."

Waited to meet? John thought. Had Bert given them up as well? John looked at his mentor, but the old man simply continued staring at the king.

"That's very bold, to come here alone," Jack said to Mordred, taking the lead in the game being played out in the shack. "Maybe you don't have any memory of it, but we have all clashed before and seen you bested in battle."

"Is that so?" Mordred purred condescendingly. "What battles were these?"

"I beat you on the ocean, with a ship called the *Yellow Dragon* in the Archipelago of Dreams, and he," Jack said, gesturing at John, "beat you in a swordfight."

Technically, everything Jack said was true – although there had been luck and allies aiding him in the sea battle, and John had not precisely won the swordfight. Either way, the bravado didn't faze the king.

"I think not," Mordred said, smiling. "At any rate, the loss of a battle is not the loss of a war – or its victory, either."

"You've certainly learned a few things," John said. "There's no disputing that. It's a shame it didn't make you a better ruler."

"Whether I am a better ruler than others might have been is not for you to judge. There is only one man who ever lived who was fit to judge me, and he—"

Mordred stopped, almost violently, as if he had spoken too openly. "All that is important to a ruler," he continued, "is strength, and mine has been more than sufficient for a very, very long time."

"Bold words, given the odds," said Jack. "I count four to one."

"Five, if you stack the badgers," said John.

"I count far fewer than that," said Mordred. "The Far Traveller – Bert, is it? – really only counts for half, don't you think? And the animals are even less to me. So that makes it even, doesn't it, Chaz?"

Uncas and Fred let out small howls of dismay, and Bert's head dropped farther to his chest.

John looked at Chaz, astonished. "Don't tell me you're taking his side."

Chaz refused to respond – which was response enough.

"Of course," Jack spat, clenching his fists. "He's like the Wicker Men – a lackey and a traitor. He was going to sell us out to the Winter King all along."

It was Bert's turn to be surprised. "Chaz!" he exclaimed in shock. "Why? Why would you do that?"

"You've always known how I gets by," Chaz shot back. "It never bothered y' before."

"It always bothered me, Chaz," said Bert. "I know you're better than this. I always have."

"That wasn't me you knowed," said Chaz. "That was some other bloke called Charles. Not me."

"But . . . but . . . ," Bert spluttered, "you knew I was looking for them. Why would you sell them out to Mordred, only to bring them . . ." His voice trailed off, and he let out a despairing breath. "You gave him my name too, didn't you, Chaz?"

"Actually," put in Mordred, "a little bird told me. Hugin. Or Munin. I forget which. Ravens all look alike to me."

"What's in a name?" Jack said, breaking through the pall that had settled over the room. "Calling Chaz 'Charles' wouldn't make him less of a traitor, so why does it matter whether or not Mordred knows *your* name?"

"True names are imbued with power – and knowing some-one's true name gives you some of that power yourself," Mordred said in response. "Enough, at least, to do what must be done. Am I correct, Far Traveller Bert?"

"That's what you did," John said to his old mentor. "You told him Verne's name, and somehow Mordred used it against him."

Bert seemed caught somewhere between lashing out in anger and bursting into tears. He sat, trembling, and glared at Mordred and Chaz.

Mordred chuckled and turned around, his hands clasped behind his back. "That was it, and that was all, and it was enough . . . ah, what did you say your name was again, child?"

"That be Scowler John y' be addressin'!" Uncas exclaimed.

"Uncas, no!" Jack shouted before realizing he'd just made the same unwitting mistake by blurting out the badger's name. "Oh, damnation," he muttered. "Sorry, John, Uncas."

Mordred chuckled again and raised his left hand to his mouth. He bit into his thumb, hard. Blood welled into the torn flesh and he turned around, eyes glittering.

"Don't apologize t' me," said Uncas, who clearly was the only one in the room who did not realize what was transpiring. "A king might talk t' Fred an' I like that, but he should respect men like you, Scowler Jack."

John slapped his forehead in resignation. The Winter King now had all their names. And the hapless Caretaker already anticipated what was coming next.

Before any of them could react, Mordred moved, almost faster than they could follow, first to Jack, then, surprisingly, to Chaz, then John, then the others. He marked them each on the forehead with the blood from his thumb, and as he did so, he called them by name: "Jack and Chaz, John and Bert, Uncas and Fred – I am Mordred the First, thy king."

Then, he began to recite words John did not realize Mordred knew:

By right and rule
For need of might
I thus bind thee
I thus bind thee

By blood bound
By honour given
I thus bind thee
I thus bind thee

For strength and speed and heaven's power
By ancient claim in this dark hour
I thus bind thee
I thus bind thee.

The instant Mordred began speaking, all the companions found themselves unable to move; their arms felt bolted to their sides, their jaws fixed and unmoving. All, that is, save for one.

Mordred finished the Binding and once more looked at each of them in turn. He was triumphant, but there was a trace – the merest trace, John thought – of melancholy in his expression.

Of regret.

"Long ago there was a prophecy," Mordred began, "that mentioned someone called the Winter King. It was said that he would bring darkness to two worlds, and that . . ." He paused, considering, then continued. "It said that three scholars, three men of imagination and learning from this world, would bring about his downfall.

"It was more than a thousand years before some among my people began to call me by that name – and only then did I remember the old prophecy.

"The prophet never mentioned the Far Traveller, but when he and his companion first came here fourteen years ago, it rekindled the possibility that the prophecy was true. And so since then I have waited patiently for the three scholars it spoke of to arrive: John, Jack, and *Charles*."

This last he said with a wink at Chaz. "Not precisely what had been prophesied, but when the Far Traveller sought you out, I saw a possible connection and decided not to take chances. And when you sent word that you'd found these two, your own fate was sealed.

"My Shadow-Born will attend to you all shortly. We shall not meet again."

Mordred spun about as if to leave, then thought better of it and stepped slowly back to where Jack was standing.

"I was not always as you see me, child," he whispered. "I *was* different, once. . ."

Frozen in place, Jack could not respond, and after a moment Mordred took a step backwards, turned, and opened the door. They heard him striding across the bridge, then nothing. He was gone.

The Binding was absolute. There was no way to move or speak. But it was not so complete that it did not allow tears to flow, and Bert wept. So did Jack, but more from frustration than sorrow. Chaz was still too stunned to weep; and John's mind was racing too fast to stop and worry over the desperate situation they were in. Even without the Binding, Fred would have been petrified by fear. A blood marking was a potent thing, and even more so among animals than men. Combined with the Binding spell, it was impossible to overcome. And so none of them were able to turn around to see what was making the crunching noises under the table.

"Oh, bother," Uncas said. "That's all the crackers, gone. If I'd known we were going to become prisoners, I'd have saved some of the soup, so as not t' die on an empty stummick."

Uncas was unfrozen. The Binding had not affected him at all. He continued complaining, all the while rubbing worriedly at the small silver coin he'd had in his pocket.

Of course, John thought. *Bindings may be broken by silver! Uncas must have been touching the coin, and so he wasn't frozen. There might still be a way out of this after all!*

John's initial rise of hope quickly dropped as he realized that Uncas being free might not be such a big advantage. The badger still had not realized that the rest of them could not move.

"Y'think he's gone?" Uncas asked, peering over the bottom of the windowsill. "What d'you think that blood-marking business was about, anyhow?"

When no one replied, Uncas scurried over to his son, finally realizing that something was amiss. "Fred? What is it? What is it, son?" he asked. "Fred? Can't you answer?"

Fred couldn't, and didn't, and the reality of what had occurred finally dawned on Uncas. And then he did the only thing he could think of, and consulted the Little Whatsit.

"Hmmm hm hm hm hmm," Uncas hummed as he flipped through the pages. John had just enough range in his field of vision to see the pages below. The badger seemed to be following some arcane indexing system based on keywords.

"Spells, curses," Uncas murmured, chewing absently on the coin, "also see: Bindings, counterspells, blood-oaths, and . . . ah, yes, here we go. It's under the section on blood. You know, it be a fascinatin' thing . . . I never would have made th' connection to lycanthropy, but . . ."

Uncas blinked, then looked at the coin. "Well, pluck my feathers," he said. "Silver's good for lots o' stuff."

He repeated the process Fred had performed earlier, grinding the coin to a fine powder. Then, apologizing for the presumption, he sliced five shards of wood from the ash staff, moistened them with his tongue, then rolled them in the silver dust.

"Let's try this with you first, Fred," he said to his son. "If it works, y' can help with th' others."

Uncas closed his eyes and murmured a badger's prayer under his breath, then plunged the ash and silver dart into Fred's forearm.

It worked.

"Ow!" Fred yelped, rubbing at his arm. "Good show! The Royal Animal Rescue Squad, trained an' true!"

The remedy worked equally well on the men. "Sort of a reverse Balder, eh, Jack?" John asked, examining the dart. But Jack wasn't listening. The second he was freed, he had Chaz pinned to the wall.

"Why did you do it, Chaz?" Jack shouted, livid. "Was it really worth selling out your friends for a few lights?"

"You in't my friends!" Chaz howled in reply. "Besides, he froze me the same as you!"

"No time! There's no time for this!" Bert exclaimed. "Mordred's minions are everywhere, and the news we've escaped may reach him any moment – and then we'll all be lost!"

"Where can we go that he won't find us?" John said. "We have nothing to fight him with – not even his true name."

"Yes, you do have something," said Bert. "You have the prophecy. And you have this." He took the rolled parchment from the mantel. "This is what Jules was given when he opened the Serendipity Box. It was then that he said I must give him to Mordred, and then wait for you. He died so that you could have this chance."

"Well, let's have a look at it," Jack began.

"No time, no time," Bert said. "Just know this: It's a map, to the last island in the Archipelago. The only map left, which has been hidden from Mordred all these years. The only one that was made by the Cartographer, but by covenant, never bound into the *Geographica*."

Hearing this, Uncas and Fred exchanged questioning glances, but said nothing.

"Here," Bert said, stuffing the parchment, the box, and Jules Verne's skull into a bag. "Take these, and let's get you on your way."

"How does y' plan t' do that?" said Chaz.

For the first time, John and Jack saw the old familiar glitter in Bert's eyes. "Easy," he said as he opened the back door. "I'm going to use what the Serendipity Box gave to *me*."

The old man hobbled his way out to the far end of the dock. Looking westward, the companions could see nothing but dust. It was, in all ways, a desert.

"Are we going to walk to this island?" Jack asked. "I've already got a blister going."

"Shush," said John. "I think Bert's got better than that in mind."

"Oh yes." Bert nodded. "I do have something good up my, er, sleeve, as it were."

He reached into his pocket and pulled out a brooch. It was an Egyptian scarab beetle, set in a bronze fitting, and the shell of the beetle was translucent blue. It also seemed to be in motion. Bert turned it over. "Recognize the writings, John?"

"Egyptian, obviously, and..." He peered closer. "Is that Hebrew and..." John's eyes grew wide. "Is this what I think it is?"

Bert nodded. "From Aaron's hand to mine. His brother didn't part anything. The Red Sea was taken up, whole, and put away for safekeeping. And since the Good Lord saw fit to give it to me, I'm sure he won't mind that I've moved it a few thousand miles west."

Bert drew back his arm, and with surprising strength hurled the brooch high into the sky.

It arced high, higher, then plunged downwards, hitting the ground some hundred yards away.

"Now what?" asked Chaz.

Suddenly the earth underneath the brooch fissured and split, and it fell into the ground, out of view. A low rumbling sound shook the air, and the pier began to tremble. Then, where the brooch had fallen, a fountain burst into the sky from the centre of the fissure, then another, and another.

In seconds it was as if a reverse thunderstorm had exploded out of the dry earth, filling the sky with water, which fell back to ground and began pooling in greater and greater volume.

As the flood gushed up, rain clouds began to form, and almost immediately a downpour started. The water met in the middle with such force that the winds nearly swept the small group off the dock. And then, as quickly as it had started, the storm subsided, and the clouds began to settle, and the companions found themselves looking out upon an ocean restored.

That was not the end of the surprises: In the distance, perhaps a few miles out, they saw a ship.

A *Dragonship.*

"I thought Mordred would have destroyed them all," said John, "all the Dragonships, along with all the lands in the Archipelago."

"Not this ship, and not this island," said Bert. "There *were* no other Dragonships when this timeline changed. And there were reasons this island was never included in the original *Geographica.* This is one of them."

And so it was with mingled wonder and awe, and no small surprise, that the companions watched as the *Red Dragon* glided smoothly through the water and alongside the dock.

"But why, Bert?" John asked as the companions climbed aboard the ship. "If you had the brooch and could do this at any time, why did you wait so long?"

"For you," Bert said simply. "We had faith in you. Jules trusted in your destiny, and so did I. It was hard, terribly so at times. And I regret to say I am not the same, in many ways. I'm worn thin, John. But I'm heartened by your arrival. And overall, considering what Jules sacrificed, I really shouldn't complain."

"Well, you waited long enough," said Jack, offering a hand. "Step aboard, and let's get the hell away from here."

But Bert didn't move. Instead he simply looked at them all

with sorrowful eyes, then patted the *Red Dragon*'s hull. "I'm sorry, lads. I won't be going."

"Why not?"

"Because," Chaz called from the far side of the deck, "someone's got t' stay behind, t' make sure we in't followed."

"I nominate you, traitor," said Jack. "Better you than Bert."

"No," Bert said. "My time is past. This is your destiny to fulfill, the three of you – not mine."

"But he's not Charles!" exclaimed Jack. "Don't do this, Bert!"

The old man was not swayed. "Whatever's going on, Jack, is for you to work through. All things happen for a reason. You have to find out what the reason is, and fix what's been broken."

He tapped the hull again, and, as if a signal had been given, the *Red Dragon* came about and headed for open waters.

Sadly, the companions gathered at the aft railing to wave goodbye to their friend and mentor, but he had already left the dock and returned to the shack, closing the door behind him.

For the first few hours, John and Jack had kept watch, fearing pursuit.

Chaz sat at the fore of the ship, sulking. The badgers busied themselves with examining the ship itself and basically trying not to get in the way.

"That's really some book you have, that Little Whatsit," John said to Fred. "It's been pretty handy so far, anyway."

"Sure," said Jack, "except we had only the one silver coin. What happens when we need more?"

"Not everything in th' Whatsit involves silver," Uncas explained. "Some got t' do with gold, f'r instance."

"Hey," Jack said brightly. "We might have a use for your watch, John."

"Funny scowler," said John. "Here now, let's have a look at this map, shall we?"

The map had been drawn on the same parchment and was of the same dimensions as most of the maps they were accustomed to seeing in the *Imaginarium Geographica*, and it had been created by the familiar hand of the Cartographer of Lost Places.

"'Noble's Isle,' it says it's called," said John. "It's a volcanic island, and looks to be in the south. The markings are clear, though, and in classical Latin, so we shouldn't have any problem navigating there."

"The animals have another name for it," said Fred, peering underneath John's arm. "We call it Sanctuary."

"Sanctuary?" asked Jack. "From what?"

"From the world," said Fred. "Both literal and otherwise.

"When Ordo Maas took us into the Archipelago, he gave us many gifts – but they were things unearned. We wanted to grow up, to have a place that was ours, and no others. A place to do our own work, and to learn to be better than we are. And so the animals went sailing through the Archipelago with Nemo's great-great-great-umpteen-grandfather, Sinbad, and he found this uncharted island. He named it Noble's Isle, but we called it Sanctuary. And when the map was made, we asked that it be kept secret, private-like. Only the High King ever had a copy of it."

"And it was the one thing Jules Verne most needed when he opened the Serendipity Box," John mused. "Interesting. Let's hope that when we get there, more of these mysteries become clear."

◆   ◆   ◆

Bert had spoken true – all the other islands, everywhere, were gone. There was no frontier to cross, no boundary. And the *Red Dragon* never wavered in its course. The only island left in the natural world, or in the Archipelago itself, was Noble's Isle.

"Impossible," said John. "He can't have destroyed them all. He's not that powerful, is he?"

"The king may not be," Chaz said from the rear, "but she is." He was pointing to the deepening sky, where the moon was beginning to rise. "Before the seas went dry, there was a great flood. . ."

"Of Biblical proportions?" Jack said wryly, leaning over the rail and dipping his hand into the waves. "What the good Lord giveth, he also taketh away. Then he puts it back again."

It took only a few hours for the ship to reach Noble's Isle. "Land ho!" Uncas called out from his perch high atop the mast. "Sanctuary, straight ahead!"

The island was covered with palm trees that thinned out closer to the centre as more cultivated gardens took over. The beaches were shallow, of dull grey sand, and offered no easy access for the *Red Dragon*.

Here Uncas took charge and steered the ship (in a more expert fashion than even Fred was expecting) to a narrow inlet on the southernmost tip. The waterway led to a deepwater dock that was both well lit in the approaching twilight, and well cared for.

The companions tied down the ship and stepped onto the sturdy dock, where they were greeted very smartly by a large fox, who bowed deeply at their approach.

He was walking on his hind legs, as the badgers did, and was dressed similarly in a waistcoat, blazer with tails, and trousers.

"I am Reynard," he said in greeting. "Welcome to Noble's Isle, Children of the Earth and Sons of Adam."

The companions returned the bow and, at Reynard's prompting, followed him off the dock to an awaiting principle. It was large and elegant and hummed like a cat. They clambered aboard, and Reynard pulled onto a paved lane that led directly to the centre of the island.

The inlet had lain between two ridges, which flattened out as they passed upwards along the road. To one side was a foul-smelling swamp, and to the other, they saw various cultivated gardens, which were punctuated here and there with greenhouses and outbuildings.

As they drove, Reynard kept up an amiable chatter with Uncas, who talked with the fox as if they were long-lost war veterans who'd been separated for a lifetime and had only an hour to catch up. In less than ten minutes, however, the road widened into a circular drive, which was surrounded by a cluster of buildings. These, Reynard explained, were the main dwellings of Sanctuary, and he'd been instructed to bring the visitors there.

"Instructed by whom?" John asked as they climbed out of the principle.

"By the Prime Caretaker, of course," said Reynard, gesturing towards the main house, "and at the request of Ordo Maas himself. Otherwise you would not have been allowed to set foot on this island."

Reynard bowed again as he spoke, but the companions realized that as respectful as he was, he was not altogether pleased that they were there.

"Please, come inside," said Reynard. "The show is about to begin."

CHAPTER EIGHT
The Infernal Device

The main houses of Sanctuary were familiar in an unfamiliar way. It was as if Oxford had been built for use by scholars three to four feet tall, who may or may not have had prehensile tails. The construction, decor, and layout were practically Edwardian, but allowances were made for those who were actually in residence.

The hallways were lined with doorways far too small for the companions to use. Possums, groundhogs, hedgehogs, and squirrels, all dressed nattily, were scurrying back and forth, seemingly absorbed in the business of the evening. Few if any gave more than a single startled glance to the strange visitors before going on about their business.

There were other doorways, much larger, that would have easily admitted John, Jack, or Chaz, but Reynard discreetly closed these as they passed.

Uncas and Fred were right at home, quite literally, and strode along behind Reynard with an assurance Jack and John had seldom seen in the badgers. It occurred to them that this might be how they had appeared to their students at the colleges. They were all permitted to be there; but some were more permitted than others.

There . . . sat an unusual if not extraordinary device.

Jack was abuzz with a thousand questions, all of which Reynard answered patiently. Despite the flashes of reluctance he showed at having them on Sanctuary, he was an exceptional and gracious host.

John asked fewer questions, if only because he was still trying to process everything that was happening.

Only Chaz had remained completely silent since their arrival on the island, which everyone else attributed to sulking. Only after they'd passed a number of animals in the corridors did John realize the truth: The man was terrified.

Another creature, a ferret wearing a pince-nez, paused and squinted at the companions before snorting huffily and scampering off in the other direction.

"It's odd that we aren't attracting more attention," noted Jack, "seeing as there are seldom any humans admitted on the island."

"It's not a matter of inattention," Reynard said blithely. "More an excess of it. We've been preparing for you a long while."

"That's our understanding," said John, who was carrying the bag Bert had given them and could feel the slight pressure of Verne's skull against his hip. "What can you tell us about Jules Verne, Reynard?"

"The Prime Caretaker?" said Reynard. "What would you like to know?"

"For one thing," Jack answered, "why he's called the Prime Caretaker."

The fox stopped and looked at Jack as if he'd asked why water was wet. "Because that is what he is," Reynard said. "He is the Caretaker of us all. Is he not, even now, guiding your path to do what must be done?"

"Guiding or manipulating," said John. "I can't decide which."

Reynard nodded. "We had similar concerns, when he first came to us. Had it not been for the blessing of Ordo Maas, his coming here would not have been allowed."

"Fourteen years ago?" asked Jack.

Reynard gave him another look. "Fourteen centuries ago, give or take. As I said, we've been preparing for you a long time."

"It is a remarkable place you have here," John said. "Very civilized. More so than the rest of Albion, that's for sure."

Reynard shuddered. "The Winterland, yes. When he who calls himself the king began to sweep across the world, we closed ourselves off, even from the Archipelago. And when we again ventured outside, we realized we were all that was left."

"The animals?" John asked.

"The Children of the Earth, yes, but we here on Sanctuary were also all who were left to oppose him," said Reynard. "The king had either slaughtered or enslaved the Sons of Adam and the Daughters of Eve, and when they ran in short supply, he turned his attention to us.

"There was a great rebellion, and there were many terrible battles. All the larger creatures were slain. Many more of us smaller animals were lost as well. Some, to our great sorrow, chose to side with him – and in doing so, became truly beasts. These he shaped through his dark arts into terrible, terrible creatures."

Reynard shuddered with the thought, then went on. "Those who could escape him, even temporarily, fled to the edges of the Earth. But even there, in those havens, they will eventually be found, and used – although it took him centuries to realize our fiercest warriors were those closest to the earth."

"The houses," Jack said, snapping his fingers. "That's why most of the houses were on stilts, to raise them up off the ground."

"Human arrogance," Reynard said, nodding, "to think that we are limited to crawling on our bellies in the dirt. To do otherwise was among the first things taught to us by Ordo Maas."

In unison, the fox and two badgers stood at attention and began to recite:

> "Not to go on all fours, not to suck up drink; not
> to eat flesh or fish; not to claw the bark of trees;
> not to chase other creatures, to willingly cause
> them harm. For all those of the earth are bright
> and beautiful; all creatures, great and small; all
> beasts are wise and wonderful; for the Lord God
> made them all."

"Coleridge?" Jack asked.

"Cecil Alexander," said John. "Mostly, anyway. Coleridge may have been a Caretaker, but he was never that sentimental, or poetic."

"Pardon," said Reynard. "A Caretaker of what?"

"The *Imaginarium Geographica*, of course," said Uncas. "The great book, with all the maps of . . ."

He stopped, and his eyes widened in realization as the fox looked at them all with a blank expression. The rest of them realized it too.

In this place, in this timeline, there *was* no *Geographica*. There had been no Caretakers, no Coleridge. All that existed was a single map, one that had never been a part of the atlas to begin with – and the sole Caretaker who had been known by that name was only a skull in John's bag.

"Never mind," said John, patting Uncas comfortingly. "We'll fix that soon enough."

Reynard led them to an ornate hallway, which ended in a great carved door. It was elaborately decorated with sculpted cherubs and angels and, reassuringly, dragons. Inset at the centre of the door, on a shield held within a dragon's claws, was the symbol π – the mark of the Caretaker Principia. John's mark.

Jack caressed the surface of the door and exhaled heavily. "As happy as I was to see the Dragonship," he said with a broad grin, "I'm almost happier to see this. It tells me we're on the right path. I don't recognize the dragon, though."

This was the first remark any of them had made that seemed to rattle Reynard. "You actually know a dragon?" the fox said, mouth agape. "Really and truly?"

"We know many dragons," said Jack. "I'm surprised you don't know them yourself."

The fox shook his head. "Not in many, many centuries. They were the guardians of the Archipelago, but something happened to them when the Winter King ascended. After that, there was no one left who could appoint them."

"Appoint them?" John said in surprise. "Isn't a dragon simply a dragon?"

Reynard looked puzzled for a moment, then brightened. "Oh, I see. You misunderstand. No, a dragon isn't the name of the creature – although most of them were the great sky-serpents you're thinking of. 'Dragon' is the name of the office they hold, and it is a title given only by appointment.

"Now," he said, turning back to the door before the companions could ask more questions, "which among you has the Golden Ticket?"

"The what?" said John.

"Golden Ticket," Reynard replied. "This room has been locked for almost fifteen hundred years. Only my distant ancestors, who helped to build it, and the Prime Caretaker himself have ever been inside. And the door can only be opened here," he said, indicating a slit beneath the mark on the shield, "by inserting a Golden Ticket."

John sighed. "I'm sorry, Reynard, we don't—"

"But we might," Jack interrupted. "You've forgotten the box."

They opened the bag John had been carrying and removed the Serendipity Box, careful to keep it out of Uncas's reach.

"Could it be that simple?" John said, turning the box over and over in his hands.

"It can't hurt to find out," said Jack. "At worst, we'll end up with more crackers."

"I only get to open it once," said John. "Do we really want to risk it to gain a ticket? What if we need something more pressing in the future? What if someone's life may depend on when we choose to use it?"

"I think someone's does," Chaz blurted out. He glanced meaningfully down at Verne's skull and gulped hard.

"Good enough," John said. He closed his eyes and lifted the lid.

"Darn," said Uncas. "I was really hopin' f'r crackers."

◆   ◆   ◆

The ticket slid smoothly into the slot and engaged a mechanism
inside the door that whirred and clicked and hummed like one of
the principles the animals drove. Finally a series of bolts slid back
inside the door frame, and the door slowly swung open.

Inside was a postcard-perfect Victorian theatre in miniature.
There were two dozen lushly appointed chairs upholstered in red
velvet, and elegant gas lamps placed artfully along walls embroidered with elaborate patterns. The ceiling was pressed tin and
reflected the light evenly throughout the room. At the front, a
curtained stage extended from one side to the other, and in the
rear was a small booth, also curtained, and a table.

The table was the only anomaly in the room. It was metallic
and round and slightly concave. On it was a golden ring four inches
or so in diameter, and a note written on the cream-coloured paper
that seemed to be favoured by all the Caretakers. It read, simply,
Spin me.

"You're the Caretaker Principia," Jack said, gently shoving
John towards the table. "*You* spin it."

John picked up the ring and examined it, then chuckled and
gave it a twirl on top of the table.

The ring spun about in a blur – but instead of slowing down
and losing momentum, it began to spin faster, circling the rim
of the table in increasingly smaller circuits. When it reached the
centre, a voice projected from the ring, loud enough for all of
them to hear it clearly.

"This is Jules Verne speaking.

"If you three – John, Jack, and Charles – are hearing this
recording, then I am in all likelihood dead, or worse."

"Worse than dead?" Chaz snorted. "He's loopy, he is."

"Shush," said John. "We need to hear this."

"What has been closed, may be opened again," the voice continued. "What has been written, may be rewritten. You have already been given warning of your adversary – now I give you the means to defeat him.

"I have become learned in many means of travel through time and space. And I have found that certain boundaries must not be crossed – not if we are to emerge victorious against our enemies."

"Enemies, plural?" Jack groaned. "Great. Just great."

"I have left you the means to the end you must reach," Verne's voice went on, "through the use of what our friend Bert called the 'Infernal Device.' It is the most specific of the devices I use, and also the most fragile.

"You must discover our adversary's name. His *true* name.

"I have left you five slides for use in the Lanterna Magica. Each corresponds to a key moment in his history, and each will afford the three of you the chance to find him. Each slide may be used only once, and the portals they create will remain open for only twenty-four hours, and no more. If you do not return to Noble's Isle within that time, you will be trapped there, and all our efforts will be for naught.

"Only thus, by seeking him out, naming him, and Binding him, may he be defeated. But remember: Our adversary may not be whom you expect. Be wary. Be watchful. And remember your training. All things come about, in time.

"Answer the question unanswered for more than two millennia, and perhaps you may yet restore the world."

The golden ring began to slow, and with a soft clattering, it fell still and silent on the table.

◆　◆　◆

The companions tried to spin the ring again, to see if there was any further information to be gleaned, but it simply repeated what they had heard the first time.

"Let's have a look at this lantern, then," Jack said. "In for a penny, in for fifty pounds."

"It's here," said Reynard, gesturing to the small booth near the table. There on a small platform sat an unusual if not extraordinary device.

"To leave a message, he can use a magic ring," said Jack, "but for time travel, we need an antique projector. Splendid."

John ignored his friend's sarcasm and set about examining the machine. The slides were already set into a rotating frame in the centre, and where the original gas lamp had been in the back there was an incandescent bulb. Below it an electric cord snaked down and across the floor to an outlet.

"Not entirely antique," John said appraisingly. "Shall we give it a go?"

"Not yet," Jack replied, turning to face Chaz. "You're going to stay here, where you won't cause any trouble."

"Fine by me," Chaz said, plopping himself heavily into one of the chairs. "Nothing to do with me, anyroad."

"Wrong," said John. "Verne said all three of us were meant to do this. And even Mordred himself said in the prophecy that we three—"

"Not we three," Chaz shot back. "You, him, and some bloke called Charles, who I in't. I won't be going anywheres with you lot. I'm fine right where I be."

"Oh, for heaven's sake," John said. "Uncas! Stop that!"

While the humans were arguing, the badgers had switched on

the Lanterna Magica and were using the light projected through one of the empty frames to make shadow puppets on the wall.

"Look!" said Uncas. "It's a rooster."

"Quit playing with the time machine," John said sternly. "Remember what happened with the door."

"Sorry," said Uncas.

"Since it's already on," John said as Jack continued glaring at Chaz, "we might as well see what we're in for."

At his signal, Fred scurried over to the Lanterna Magica and rotated the disk that held the five slides. The first frame had been empty and simply projected a pool of light against the curtains. But the next contained a slide – a landscape of some kind. And as they looked, it seemed that the images projected through the stationary slide . . .

. . . were *moving*.

"Here," Reynard said, pulling on the draw for the curtains. "Perhaps this will help."

Instead of a screen or sheet, behind the curtains were layers of a gossamer substance, very much like theatrical backdrops. The image from the projector passed through some layers, but not others. It was like watching a film painted on smoke.

The landscape in the projection was unmistakably Greek. There were temples and great statues of ancient gods visible, all entwined with grapevines and at the bases, olive trees. Farther back, they could see a large group of people gathered in a small amphitheatre, listening to a man who stood in the centre. The details were sharp and clear, and to the companions it seemed as if they could reach in and touch one of the stately columns.

Then there was a gust of wind in the projection, and one of

the grape leaves twisted off its vine and twirled through the air to land in the room at Reynard's feet.

"Dear God," John breathed. "It does work. It will work. Just like the doors."

"But with a time limit, remember," said Jack.

Just then a rumble of thunder shook the room, and the projection wobbled. Reynard looked visibly alarmed, and with no comment, hurried from the room.

"A storm must have come up," said Jack. "Funny. It was clear out before."

"That's not thunder," said John. "That's an impact tremor. Something massive just stepped onto the island."

They looked at one another in alarm. It could only be the giants. Mordred had discovered their escape from Bert's shack and had sent his largest servants to reclaim them.

"Oh, that's capital," groaned Jack. He turned to Chaz, teeth clenched and his temper rising. "You had something to do with this, didn't you?"

Chaz stood up defensively. "I been with you the whole time! And I got no loyalty to him! Not now!"

"You mean after he betrayed you the way you betrayed us?" snapped Jack.

"I'm sorry!" Chaz said. "I . . . I didn't know."

Reynard ran back into the room as another footfall rattled the island. "The giants have come, friends of the Caretaker. And it is time for you to leave."

"What about you?" Jack said. "We can't abandon you!"

The fox shook his head. "We have an understanding with the giants. They only want you. If you are not here, they will leave us be. It doesn't matter where else you go, or," he said, gesturing suggestively at the projection, "when."

Uncas and Fred both agreed with Reynard – they would be safe. So John grabbed the bag with their scanty supplies and stepped quickly between the chairs to the screen, gesturing to the others as he did so. "Jack! Charles! No time to debate! Let's go!"

"I am *not* Charles!" Chaz exclaimed over the din. "I shouldn't be allowed!"

Jack merely shook his head in disgust and stepped into the projection. John turned around and faced Chaz.

"Perhaps not in this place," he said through the crashing sounds that were now all around them, "but in another place, another dimension, you *are* our friend Charles, and I would not think of leaving you behind."

He reached out his hand, imploring the confused man to take it.

"Chaz!" John beckoned. "Come with us! Now!"

With both hands, Chaz took John's outstretched arm and stepped into the picture.

PART THREE

After the Age of Fable

The attention ... was focused on the young man in the centre ...

CHAPTER NINE
The Storyteller

This Pellinor, Hugo decided, was the most loquacious fellow he'd ever met, even if he seemed mostly to be conversing with himself. The fact that Hugo had more than a passing fluency with Anglo-Saxon made little difference: King Pellinor was in his own realm, and Hugo was merely an interested observer and infrequent participant.

That was fine with Hugo, who had at first determined that he was at the centre of the greatest, most elaborate practical joke ever devised by an Oxford don. Jack was probably the instigator, but John had certainly played his part, and played it well. That they had both disappeared along with the door he'd passed through could be attributed to some sort of stage illusion; but the fact that they'd made Magdalen, and in fact, all of Oxford itself disappear could only be explained by the idea that he'd been hypnotized, or transmogrified, or whatever it was that the illusionists did to people that made them think they were the Queen or a chicken or some such. But as the hours passed, Hugo began to realize that it was no illusion, and certainly no joke.

The strange old king produced the crumpled photograph of Hugo that had been taken at the University of Reading, where he taught English, but he remained closemouthed as to who had given it to him and why.

They travelled southwards throughout the night, their path lit only by the small lamp Pellinor had attached to the side of the cart. The king kept up a rambling monologue (or more precisely, a solo dialogue) for most of the way, only occasionally interrupting the flow of words to incorporate an answer to one of Hugo's queries. Most of the tales the king told seemed to involve his personal genealogy, and an ancestor who had been shamed at Alexandria, but Hugo couldn't really be sure.

With the coming of daylight, Hugo was better able to take in Pellinor's unusual appearance. The clothing was as authentic as any Hugo had ever seen in museums – but so were the scars that laced the old man's arms and neck. There was even a deep gash along his cheek, which had long since healed.

The old king dismissed queries about the wounds with a laugh and a story about the mythical Questing Beast. And after noticing the weapons and armour still reddened with blood in the back of the cart, Hugo stopped asking questions and just listened to Pellinor ramble.

As the light came up, Hugo could make out other carts and horsemen off in the distance all around them, all headed in the same direction.

He asked Pellinor about them, and the old king answered with an uncommon gravity. "They are going to the same place that we journey to," he said, eyes fixed on Hugo. "To the tournament. To the great Debate."

"Debate?" asked Hugo. "What kind of debate requires horsemen and swordplay?"

"The kind that determines the future of the land," said Pellinor. "The kind that may only be held in a sacred place. A place of death and rebirth."

"And where is that?" asked Hugo.

Pellinor answered, but the accent made it difficult to understand.

"Camazotz?" Hugo said.

Pellinor laughed. "Close enough, my odd friend."

"Camelot," the king said. "We are going to Camelot."

Once John, Jack, and Chaz were through the portal, all the din and clamour of the giants' assault upon Sanctuary ceased. It had opened along the wall of a tall building and was framed by pillars and grapevines. Looking back, they could see the faint impressions of the room they had left behind, lit by the glare of the projector. Reynard was near the door of the room, barking instructions to someone in the hallway, and both badgers were giving a relieved thumbs-up to the companions, who would be visible now inside the projection. There was no doubt – Verne's Infernal Device had worked.

The building formations within the plaza where they had emerged were familiar to John and Jack, who had seen similar structures in the islands of the Underneath in the Archipelago. The main difference was that these were clean and undamaged. This architecture was that of a vital, living city.

Chaz couldn't understand the words being spoken by the storyteller in the amphitheatre, but John and Jack were both adept at speaking the language and identified it immediately.

"Extraordinary," marvelled Jack. "We've actually gone back in time."

"And, ah, across in space," added John. "We're in Greece . . . or perhaps Turkey."

Jack nodded. "The structures are Ionian, definitely. But it must be prior to the Persian conquest," he said, glancing about, "given the manner of dress we're seeing. So what time do you think it is, anyway?"

On impulse, John reached into his pocket and pulled out his pocket watch. He had it open for a few seconds before chuckling mirthlessly and hastily putting it back.

"Force of habit," he said, shrugging and hoping no one had noticed the strange device he'd just held.

Jack voiced a similar concern. "We're not going to accomplish much dressed like this." He gestured at their modern English outfits. "We're going to need to, um, borrow something more suitable."

A robed figure appeared at their side and proffered two robes to them. "Here, take these."

It was Chaz.

"How did you get these?" exclaimed Jack. "We've only just walked through the portal!"

"I'm a thief, remember?" Chaz said drolly. "Just doin' what comes natural."

"Oh, I'm not . . . ," Jack started to protest, as John took both robes and pressed one on him.

"Don't argue, Jack," he said. "We were about to do the same thing – you just resent that it was Chaz who acquired them for us."

Jack grumbled under his breath but put on the robe. With their sleeves and trousers sticking out, they looked more akin to travellers from the east or south than native Greeks, but the disguises would work well enough.

No one was looking at them, anyway. The attention of everyone in the plaza and amphitheatre was focused on the young man in the centre, who was telling stories. And for good reason – he was positively magnetic.

The man exuded a natural charisma that came with the confidence of knowing that the audience was completely caught up in the tale being told.

Chaz looked bewildered; he clearly could not understand anything being said. John leaned close to him to translate.

"He's telling a story about a great warrior," he whispered, "who came to this land at the behest of a king called Minos, to defeat a giant called Asterius. The giant had horns and six arms and could not be beaten by a display of strength or prowess, but only by a game of logic."

"Six arms," Chaz replied. "Who ever heard of a giant with six arms?"

"He's got the number of arms right," Jack put in, "but if Asterius is a giant, I'm Sir Walter Scott."

Chaz, scowling, continued watching the storyteller. He'd survived in the Winterland by being aware of everything in his environment. And here he was watching with the eyes of a predator; not looking for prey, but trying to spot the competition. And in a trice, he realized that was exactly what he was seeing: another predator.

"The teller," Chaz said, moving closer to the others and speaking in a hushed whisper. "Look closely at the teller."

There *was* something familiar about the young man. The tilt of his head, perhaps; maybe the tone of his voice, even disguised as it was by the rhythms of ancient Greek speech. Even his gestures seemed . . .

"That's it," breathed Jack. "My God, Chaz, you're right. It's how he moves, his body language. It's definitely familiar. Could this boy actually be a young Mordred? Is he the one we've come to find?"

"Possibly," John replied. "This is the place that Verne's machine sent us. It can't be coincidence that the fellow who's the centre of attention seems so familiar to us."

The young man was just finishing his tale of Asterius, much to the delight of his audience, who responded with laughter and applause.

"Tomorrow," the storyteller said, "I will tell you a tale of the giant Polyphemus, who was blinded by the great Odysseus, the sacker-of-cities, and then killed by the slayer-of-giants called Jack."

John looked accusingly at Jack, who sighed heavily and rolled his eyes.

"What?" said Chaz, who had caught Jack's name among the gibberish. "What did you do?"

"Don't look at *me*!" Jack whispered. "I don't have the slightest idea what all this 'Giant-Killer' business is all about. It's got to be coincidence, that's all."

"Except the giants back in Albion recognized your voice, didn't they?" asked Chaz. "How do you explain *that*?"

"I can't," Jack said hotly. "But until I actually kill a giant, I'm not taking the blame, whatever rumours have gone around."

"Look at it this way," offered John. "At least you know that whenever it does take place, the outcome is assured."

"Easy for you to say," said Jack. "You're not the one who's going to feel the pressure of centuries of expectations."

"Far easier to do summat about this boy teller," Chaz reasoned, moving around Jack with his eyes fixed on the man at the front of the amphitheatre. "We ought t' just kill him here and be done wi' it."

"We can't!" John hissed, grabbing his arm. "We are only supposed to learn his true name and Bind him, remember?"

"And who's t' do th' Binding?" asked Chaz. "You?"

He was right. John and Jack might know the words, but they didn't have the authority to speak the Binding. Only one of the royal bloodline could – and there wasn't anyone left who qualified back in Albion.

"Drat," said Jack. "Maybe we *should* just kill him."

"And risk really wrecking history?" said John. "I don't think so. Look at how much trouble Hugo caused – and he only went back six centuries. We've gone considerably further than that. If we change something now, the repercussions could be disastrous."

"On t' other hand," said Chaz, "there'd be no King Mordred t' trample an' piss all over everything. Might be worth the trade."

John looked down at the possible Mordred, who was conversing with the crowd as they left the amphitheatre. "No," he said, shaking his head. "We were given instructions by Verne to discover Mordred's true name, then return to Noble's Isle. And that's what I intend to do."

Jack and Chaz looked at each other, debating. "You're the Caretaker Principia," Jack said. "I'll defer to you."

"Fine," said John. "Chaz?"

Chaz shrugged. "Whatever you say. I'm not even supposed t' be here, remember?"

As they spoke, a short, solidly built man who had been watching them from across the plaza approached, and before any of them could move, he had pointed a small dagger at John's stomach.

"My name is Anaximander," the man said, smiling politely, "and you do not belong here. Please state your business, or I will slay you where you stand."

Chaz and Jack both tensed for a fight, but John answered first, holding out his hands placatingly. "We are travellers, strangers to your land," he said in fluent Greek. "We've come here seeking knowledge of that man, there."

Anaximander's eyes darted along the line John's arm made to the young storyteller, who was still accepting farewells from his listeners. "Is that so?" he said. "That's very interesting, as I happen to be his teacher. How is it that you know of him at all, that you come seeking to know more?"

"We've got a history with him," Jack said, "so to speak."

"I don't believe you," Anaximander said, pressing closer with the blade. "Tell me something truthful, or your friend will pay the price, and you after."

"Oh, for heaven's sake," Jack said to John. "Mordred's almost as much trouble here and now as he was in the Archipelago."

Jack had switched to English, but Anaximander recognized the word "Archipelago," and it startled him. He lowered the dagger and looked at the three companions appraisingly.

"Perhaps you speak truth after all," he said finally. "You mean him no harm?"

Jack started to reply, but John cut him off. "We just want to speak with him," he said testily. "That's all. And then we plan to, ah, return to our homeland."

"Fair enough," Anaximander said. "We'll be meeting later, at my home. Please, come with me." With that, he turned and strode away. The companions had little choice but to follow.

The home of Anaximander was only a short distance away, but Chaz kept an eye on the streets they traversed so as not to forget where the portal was located. Of the three of them, he was the one most aware that they had a time limit.

Anaximander's home consisted of three low bungalows connected by a courtyard where he could teach small groups of students. A few minutes before, he'd threatened the companions with violence, but now he was acting the perfect host. He offered them wine and a platter of cold figs, which they consumed with great vigour.

"You seem quite hungry," Anaximander commented. "Did you not bring provisions for your journey? You seem ill-equipped for a long voyage."

"We're staying nearby," Jack said, not exactly lying. "Everything we need is there."

"You said you were a teacher," said John. "What do you teach, if I might ask?"

Anaximander bowed his head at the question. "I am a philosopher of the school of my master, Thales, and I teach what I am still seeking the answers to myself: the origin of all things. I call it Aperion."

"Wait now," said Jack. "I've heard of that. It means 'Infinite Beginning,' does it not?"

"Not precisely," said Anaximander. "More 'Infinite Perpetuity.' There is no beginning or ending, but merely an endlessly repeating process of beginnings *and* endings. Thus, an infinity of all things in space . . . and time."

Jack nearly spit out his wine.

"Amazing," said John, and translated for Chaz. "That's a rather all-encompassing subject."

"Indeed," the teacher said. "Presently I am working on a new theory, which I call 'multiple worlds.' Essentially, I believe that our own world is but one of an infinite number that may appear and disappear at any given moment. Some find solidity and remain, while others flounder and disappear."

Jack raised an intrigued eyebrow and looked at John. What Anaximander was describing was the very time paradox that Hugo Dyson had caused: The world they knew had vanished and been replaced by the Albion of the Winter King.

They both had the same thought: Was this Greek scholar in some way involved in what had taken place, or was his theory merely another coincidence?

A few more hours of discussion with Anaximander confirmed the answers to many of the questions that John and Jack had wondered about. The city was Miletus, on the Ionian coast of what they knew as Turkey. And as close as they could estimate from their fellow scholar's calculations, the date was sometime around 580 BC.

The companions held off discussing the specifics of how and when they'd come to be in Miletus until their host had excused himself to fetch some more refreshments.

"Twenty-five hundred years!" Jack exclaimed, slumping back in his chair, "and then some. What was Verne thinking? What can we possibly solve by going back this far?"

"Remember what Bert said," John reminded him. "Whatever

it was that Hugo caused to happen in the past – uh, future – well, whenever he went – was anticipated by Verne. And we know who our adversary is. I think before we can do anything about Hugo, we've got to defeat Mordred, just like the prophecy said."

"We already did that," Jack huffed. "What if it was *that* defeat the prophecy referred to?"

John shook his head. "But we didn't. Not in this timeline, remember? That would have happened after Hugo went through the door."

"Drat," Jack said. "I keep forgetting."

Anaximander came back into the courtyard accompanied by a young man who appeared to be a student of his, given the way he responded to the older man's instructions – not with abject obedience like a servant, but more deferentially than a son or nephew would have done.

"Come, Pythagoras," Anaximander said, indicating the low table adjacent to John. "Just set the tray here. That will be fine."

The boy deftly set the tray, laden as it was with bread, cheese, and grapes, on the table and then left.

"I see I've allowed the teacher in me to supplant the good host," Anaximander commented, moving to the centre of the courtyard. "You didn't come here to ask about my philosophies; you wanted to know about my student. I assumed it was because of the legend that has sprung up around the stories that have been told."

"What stories?" asked Jack.

"You are familiar with our great storyteller Homer?" Anaximander asked. "He of the *Iliad*, and the *Odyssey*?"

"Of course."

"Not long ago," the philosopher went on, "a rumour began

to spread throughout the land that the gods had allowed Homer
to be reborn as a youth, to reawaken the Greek people's belief in
wonder and mystery. From town to town and city to city, stories
were being told in exchange for room and board. Stories the like of
which have not been heard for centuries.

"Great, adventurous tales of fantastic creatures – centaurs and
Cyclopes; talking pigs, beautiful sirens, and many, many more.
And among these tales were scattered references to the place where
they all were supposed to have happened – the Archipelago."

John and Jack couldn't resist the impulse to sit up straighter at
this. "Your reborn Homer," John said, "has he actually been to the
Archipelago?"

"Better than that, if the stories are to be believed as truth, and
not fabrication," Anaximander replied. "They were *born* there."

"I beg your pardon," said Jack. "Did you say 'they'?"

Anaximander merely smiled and rose to his feet. He crossed
the courtyard and disappeared through one of the doors. The companions heard a muffled exchange of voices, and a moment later the
philosopher reappeared, this time accompanied by two young men.

The first was not so much handsome as striking, which came
across mostly through the intensity of his eyes. He was swarthy,
muscular, and very, very confident.

The second young man was practically identical to the first.
He was only negligibly shorter, and a bit more stocky. His com-
plexion was slightly more pale, as if he spent more time indoors
than his brother. But it was evident, John realized, that these were
not only brothers, but twins.

"Gentle scholars," said Anaximander, "may I introduce my
two prize students – Myrddyn and Madoc."

♦ ♦ ♦

Chaz squinted and peered at the twins as if he'd been conked on the head and couldn't quite register what he was seeing. "*Two* of 'em?" he said to John. "*Two* Mordreds? I think we just went from th' kettle directly inta th' flames."

John and Jack both stood to receive the visitors, but they were nearly as stunned as Chaz. Myrddyn and Madoc took each of their arms in greeting, and the companions realized that if pressed, they would not be able to say which of them had been the storyteller.

"It depends on the day," Anaximander said in response to their unasked question. "That's what has made the rumours of Homer's return both credible and compelling. The 'single' storyteller has at times been reported in two cities on the same night, and has on occasion held an amphitheatre full of citizens in thrall for several days with no apparent pause for sleep. These miracles are only possible, of course, because the single storyteller is, in fact, two."

The twins took some fruit and goblets of wine from the table and settled into the chairs opposite the companions. As Myrddyn and Madoc recounted the events of the day with their teacher, John took the opportunity to examine them more closely. Myrddyn was the more outgoing of the two, and John was nearly certain that it was he whom they had seen in the amphitheatre earlier. But then again, Madoc, while less forthcoming than his brother, nevertheless was compellingly familiar. Every gesture, every expression, bore some trace of the man they'd come seeking.

"This is impossible," Jack whispered, leaning in close to John. "I can't tell them apart. If they traded chairs, I might not even lose the thread of the conversation."

"I know what you mean," John whispered back. "Verne never mentioned this particular problem."

"You do realize," Myrddyn said, addressing the companions, "that our teacher is very protective of us and rarely speaks of our secret with anyone."

"You mean your names?" asked Jack.

A flash of something indescribable crossed the young man's eyes. "I meant the secret that we were born not here, in this world, but in the Archipelago."

"Almost no one in the Greek empire knows of its existence," said Madoc. "There are legends and stories, of course, but few who know the reality of it, as you seem to."

"We've been there often," Jack said before John could stop him, "and have many friends among its peoples."

"Really?" Myrddyn said, leaning forward. "Such as who?"

John groaned inwardly, as did Jack, albeit a moment too late. He'd forgotten – they were centuries removed from the time that they knew, and their own journeys in the Archipelago of Dreams. Nemo was not yet born, or Tummeler, or Charys the centaur, or . . .

"Ordo Maas," John said suddenly. "We are friends of Ordo Maas."

The only reaction from the young men was a polite stare. The name meant nothing to them.

"Deucalion," put in Jack. "He is also known as Deucalion."

This brought about an entirely different reaction: Surprise and delight – and was that an expression of triumph John saw? – registered on Myrddyn and Madoc's faces, and even Anaximander's eyes widened in astonishment.

"The Master of Ships?" he said, his voice cracking. "Surely you jest with us."

"Not at all," John replied. "Do you know him?"

"Indirectly," said Myrddyn. "He is our – mine and Madoc's – direct ancestor."

John and Jack looked at each other, bewildered. This was an unexpected complication. If one of these young men was indeed destined to become Mordred, that meant their greatest enemy was actually a blood relative of one of their strongest allies. But surely Deucalion would have known of this connection, wouldn't he?

"How direct?" Jack asked slowly. "What *is* your exact lineage, if I may ask?"

Myrddyn nodded genially. "Of course. That is, in fact, what we have come here to discuss. Our ancestry is tied to both this world and the Archipelago.

"Deucalion, the son of Prometheus, was our ancestor six generations removed from our father, who went on a great voyage through the Archipelago in a ship given to him by *his* father. Near the end of his voyage, when all his companions had perished, his ship ran aground on an island where he spent seven years, before finally leaving in a small craft he built in secret.

"He left behind the ship of his father, Laertes; our mother, Calypso; and myself and Madoc, his sons."

John was speechless, as was Jack. Only Chaz, who was barely following the conversation, remained unaffected. "What is it?" he asked John. "What did he just say?"

"Calypso, Laertes . . . ," John said to Jack. "Is it possible . . . ?"

Myrddyn smiled. "We were born in the Archipelago, but we have always known our destiny would lie here, in the land of our father – Odysseus."

"The ship ran aground . . . crashing violently against the rocks . . ."

Chapter Ten
The Shipwreck

"Nearly a year ago I was sailing with a small crew on a diplomatic mission to establish a colony at Apollonia," Anaximander began, "when we lost our way and fell far off course. We were caught up in a terrible wind and found ourselves run aground on an island that seemed divided in half by a great line of storms."

"Like Avalon," Jack murmured. "Interesting."

"While we repaired our own vessel," the philosopher continued, "we saw another ship being tossed about by the waves, nearly to its destruction.

"The ship ran aground on the coast, crashing violently against the rocks, and I was the first to come to the wreckage. It was still being battered by the surf, but the two passengers aboard had been thrown clear. Before they could drown, I pulled the two of them from the water and brought them here."

"Is it still there?" John asked. "The ship? Can you take us to the wreck?"

Anaximander shook his head. "The island is too far to travel to safely and quickly, and even were we to go, the ship isn't there any longer anyway.

"As they recovered from their injuries, they both cried out for the ship in their fever dreams," he explained, "concerned for the safety of their father's vessel. But when I went back with several men to help me pull it aground, it was gone. An old fisherman who appeared near the rocks at the shore claimed to have seen it pulled back out to sea by seven scarlet and silver cranes."

John looked at Jack. He recognized the description of the scarlet and silver cranes – the sons of Ordo Maas.

"After my duties at Apollonia were discharged," Anaximander went on, "I offered to bring them here to become my students. But it turned out that I became their student as well – for they have told me many extraordinary things. Things unexpected from men of such youth."

"And many tales of the Archipelago, I'd imagine," said John.

"Yes." The philosopher nodded. "Especially those."

"Why are you sharing all of this with us?" asked Jack. "If you are from the Archipelago, the sons of Odysseus himself even, what can we possibly tell you about it that you don't already know?"

Madoc leaned forward, eyes glittering. "You can tell us the most important thing," he said, his face flushed and earnest. "You can tell us how to go *back*."

At once, John and Jack remembered just *when* they were in history. There *were* no Dragonships yet. Ordo Maas had not yet built them. His own vessel, the great ark, had only passed through the Frontier because it carried the Flame of Prometheus, the mark of divinity. And so the only other passages between worlds, like the journey of Odysseus, and Myrddyn and Madoc's voyage back, were achieved through pure chance.

"We waited a long time to be able to come here, to the land of our father," Myrddyn said, giving his brother an oddly disapproving look, "but we would like to be able to return home, to the island of our birth. And we would be willing to pay a great price to any man who might assist us in doing so."

During the course of the discussion, Chaz had begun to pick up enough of the language to at least follow the thread of what was being discussed, and he brightened visibly when he realized there was an exchange of value being proposed.

John translated the words Chaz had missed as the others waited patiently.

"That's an easy answer," Chaz said when John was done. "We should just figure out a way t' get that Dragonship of yours through the portal, and let *it* take them where they want t' go."

Jack slapped his head in dismay. Chaz had just blurted out several things they'd planned to keep to themselves – the ship, the portal . . . They were lucky that he'd spoken in English, so the philosopher and his students wouldn't know what had been said.

John and Jack were so focused on Chaz at that moment that they did not see the shadow of fear that passed over the twins' faces at the mention of the word "dragon". But the philosopher did see.

Before John and Jack had time to respond further to Chaz, Anaximander pointedly cleared his throat, and Myrddyn and Madoc rose to their feet. "You must forgive us," Myrddyn said, bowing. "We have enjoyed this meeting a great deal, but we have some responsibilities to attend to. May we continue this discourse in a short while? Perhaps in the morning?"

"Of course," John said, also rising. "We have much more to discuss, I think. But please be aware," he added with a glance at Jack and Chaz, "that we are merely passing through and cannot stay past tomorrow afternoon."

While Anaximander saw the two young men out, John and Jack had an opportunity to quickly relate to Chaz everything else that had been said.

"It's all beyond me," he said, shrugging. "I don't know what any of that whose-father-sailed-what-ship stuff has t' do with our job."

"It helps us understand what's at stake," John told him, "and gives us clues to figure out what to do."

Chaz took on a disdainful expression. "Easy-peasy," he said. "We go back to Sanctuary and try both names – Myrddyn and Madoc – on th' Winter King. Whichever one works, well, that'll Bind him, right?"

"I don't think it'll be as easy as all that," John replied. "Not when there may be a blood rite, and the speaking of the Binding itself – if we can find someone who's able. It's too much time to risk on fifty-fifty odds."

"So we have to find out for certain which of them will become a tyrannical despot in the future," Jack was saying as Anaximander returned to the courtyard. "Great."

"Hey," said Chaz, "how do I ask where the, uh, facilities are?"

"Facilities for what?" asked John.

"I have t' pee."

"Oh," John said. He repeated the query in Greek to Anaximander, who seemed not to understand.

"He wants to go to the room where we make water?" the philosopher asked. "We don't have a 'room' for that, but we do have pots in some of the larger buildings. I have one myself, if your friend would like to make use of it."

John translated, and Chaz screwed up his face in disgust. "I'd just as soon not be sharing a chamber pot, t'anks," he said. "Isn't there a nice, clean hollow log somewheres?"

Again John translated, and Anaximander answered.

"He says most everyone just uses the street," John said apologetically. "Welcome to ancient Greece."

Grumbling, Chaz exited the same way the twins had left, and Anaximander moved over to take his chair.

"What do you think of my students?" the philosopher said, sitting between John and Jack. "Impressive, are they not?"

"Do you believe them?" Jack asked. "Do you really think they are the sons of Odysseus?"

"It's impossible to know for certain," Anaximander admitted, "but their tale rings true. We know from our own histories that Odysseus had children with both the witch Circe and the nymph Calypso, but little was known of what became of them, until last year, when I found Myrddyn and Madoc and learned of their parentage. They know more about the details of Odysseus's journeys than any scholar, more than has been recorded in any history. And so I must give credence to their claims, however outrageous they might seem."

"I don't know what we can do to help," John said plaintively. "We've told you all we can."

"Ah, but I think this is not the case," Anaximander replied. "No – don't be alarmed. I'm not irritated that you have chosen to keep things to yourselves – especially in front of an unknown audience. Am I correct?"

Their uncomfortable silence told him he was.

"Well then," the philosopher said, "it seems I must make the first gesture of trust." He stood and walked to the far side of the courtyard, motioning for them to follow. "I have been developing a new science, based on the idea that there are places in the world that cannot be travelled to except by following a very specific and detailed route," he said as he opened a large, stout door.

"The place where Myrddyn and Madoc were born, the Archipelago, is of our world, and not, all at once. And so I reasoned that the only way to discover the location of an unknown place would be to create a means to represent all the places that *are* known." Anaximander lit one of the lamps in the darkened room, and it suddenly blazed with light. "I call it a *map*."

The two Caretakers stepped into the room and looked around in mute astonishment. Maps. The entire chamber was filled with maps. There were also globes, whole and in pieces, and crude sextants, and even a construction that resembled the solar system, hanging from a thin wire in a corner of the room.

"Cartography," John said, his voice trembling with the realization, as he gripped Jack by the shoulder. "Anaximander is teaching them to make maps."

"Better than that," Jack replied. He was also shaking. "He's making maps to unknown lands. To lost places."

"Are . . . are you the Cartographer?" John asked.

Anaximander bowed deeply. "I am what I am," he said simply. "Now, let us speak of the Archipelago, shall we?"

The problem with trying to relieve oneself in ancient Greece, Chaz decided, was that everywhere he went, there was some kind of statue or carving or bas-relief with a face on it – which meant that every time he stopped to pee, something was watching him.

And it was flat-out impossible to loosen one's bladder when one was being watched.

Finally he managed to find a decent spot in between a tall, stout olive tree and a great cistern. The shadow underneath afforded just enough privacy to do what needed doing, as long as not too many people passed by.

Chaz had unbuckled his trousers and was just preparing to relax and let loose the torrent, when he heard familiar voices. He pulled up his trousers and leaned back to peer around the cistern.

It was Myrddyn and Madoc. They were at the other end of the alley, having a heated if hushed exchange.

Chaz moved closer to listen. He still could not understand most of what they were saying – but he could *remember*. And he was catching just enough – words like "ship" and "dragon" – that he knew it might be important to remember it all.

"And what happens if we're found out?" Madoc was saying. "They claim to know Deucalion – that means they could discover the truth: that we were exiled from the Archipelago."

"No one needs to know that!" Myrddyn hissed, grabbing his twin by the collar. "Least of all Anaximander! Only Deucalion, the Pandora, and the Dragons themselves know what really took place before we came here. And that's the way it will stay until we can return!

"No," he said, finally releasing his grip on Madoc's tunic, "we'll use them for whatever information we can glean, and then we'll dispose of them, as we have the others. He's already prepared the wine, as he has before."

"You know I'm uncomfortable with that, Myrddyn," Madoc said, his voice low. "We could have trusted some of them, I think."

Myrddyn shook his head. "It's too great a risk," he said blithely. "The knowledge of the Archipelago is rare, and it must remain so. The fewer who know anything of it, or of us and our real reasons for returning, the better. Do you want to get father's ship back or not?"

After a moment, Madoc nodded, still reluctant. Then together the brothers turned and walked back towards the amphitheatre.

When he was certain they had gone, Chaz emerged from the shadow of the cistern where he had been watching them and stood in the alleyway, breathing heavily and trying to reason out what he believed he had heard.

For a long moment, Chaz considered his options, looking hard in the direction of the philosopher's house. Then, abruptly, he spun about and began walking towards the amphitheatre and the plaza . . . and the portal back to Sanctuary.

Of any scholars of the ancient world who made maps, only Anaximander had conceived of one depicting the entire world.

The maps he showed to John and Jack were crude by their standards, but revolutionary for the philosopher's time. And they were good enough for a beginning. Some, John suspected, might even be *in* the *Imaginarium Geographica*.

Anaximander had already sussed out the fact that John and Jack were versed in the reading and function of maps, and so he proposed that they help him in indexing the ones he and the twins had already made, to see if they could add details to their growing store of knowledge about the Archipelago.

With unspoken reservations, and keeping their objective in mind, the two Caretakers agreed – but while they worked, the same concern played out in both of their heads.

To return home, Myrddyn and Madoc needed two things: first, something to guide them – the maps, which would eventually form the basis for the *Imaginarium Geographica*; and second, a vessel touched by divinity, as Odysseus's ship had been once, able to make the journey and traverse the Frontier.

They could not help with those things, but they could provide a lot of information about the Archipelago itself. Too much, in fact. In their own time, when they'd first met each other, it had been Mordred's objective to seize the *Geographica* in order to conquer the Archipelago. And that was after he'd only been back in the Archipelago for twenty years.

Giving him, whichever of the twins he was, the means to return twenty-five centuries earlier could devastate the world more than Hugo's mishap had. So they would organize, but not contribute to, the philosopher's work.

A not-too-casual mention by Anaximander that he was fascinated by the concept of time was enough of a prompt for John to pull out his gold pocket watch and proudly show it off. He explained the mechanism and workings of the watch, but much to Jack's amusement and Anaximander's confusion, the watch, as usual, didn't work.

"So it's like my gnomon," the philosopher concluded. "A stationary vertical rod set on a horizontal plane. But," he added, still puzzled, "what is the transparent dome for? It seems it would work better if the rods were more vertically inclined."

"Oh never mind," John said, setting the watch on the table and glaring at it. "It's really best as a paperweight."

"It's an excellent paperweight," said Anaximander.

Twice as they worked, the philosopher's younger student,

Pythagoras, brought food and drink. The second time, Anaximander left the companions for a moment to give more instructions to the boy.

"John," whispered Jack, moving around the table so Anaximander would not overhear them, "Chaz went out a *long* time ago. I don't think he's coming ba—"

"*I know*," John whispered back, his voice bitter. "I know, Jack. We still have time. Let's just do what we can here, and hope . . ."

John let the sentence trail off without finishing and resumed work on the maps.

Chaz made it to within twenty feet of the portal, where he paced through the entire night. He couldn't decide whether to go through or pee, so he merely paced, and argued with himself.

He had paced through the night and into morning before the pressure became too bad, and he finally was forced to relieve himself on the broad wall next to the plaza entrance.

"Aw, geez, Mister Chaz," came a small voice from behind him. "D'you hafta do that out here, where everyone can see? What, were you raised in a barn?"

Startled, Chaz turned around to see who had spoken. It was Fred, tapping his foot and trying not to watch as the human splashed urine all across the wall.

"Fred!" Chaz exclaimed, with a chagrined, half-embarrassed look. "Have you been watching me pee?"

"No," replied Fred, "we've been watching you pace. We thought you must have been sent back t' stand guard. You only just *started* t' pee."

Chaz looked around worriedly. It might be a strange land,

but he suspected a talking badger wouldn't go unnoticed for very long. "What are you doing here? Why did y' come through th' portal?"

The small mammal held up an hourglass. "Th' time limit!" he exclaimed. "It's almost up. You and Scowler John and Scowler Jack must return, right now!"

The badger was right. There was only a thin layer of sand left inside the upper globe of the hourglass. Could it really have been twenty-four hours already? Chaz wondered. Regardless, he wasn't about to be trapped in a place where he couldn't speak or understand the language without getting a headache.

"Okay," he said, heading for the portal.

"Wait!" Fred cried, pulling on the man's shirt. "What about Scowler Jack and Scowler John?"

Chaz sighed and rolled his eyes, then looked from the portal to Fred, and back again.

"This way," he said finally, fastening up the buckle on his trousers. "We'll have to hurry."

By midday Anaximander's entire map room was sorted and indexed, John and Jack were completely exhausted, and they were not one inch closer to discovering which of the twins was destined to become Mordred.

"This would have been easier if he already had the hook," Jack grumbled, yawning.

"At the Ring of Power, when Artus and I were fighting Mordred, he said he was nearly as old as Ordo Maas," John said, rubbing his chin. "I thought it was just bluff and bluster at the time, but the flood that took Ordo Maas to the Archipelago happened at the beginning of the Bronze Age, and the timing is right for the genealogy to work."

"That's still almost a thousand years earlier than we've come," Jack countered. "But I suppose it isn't inconceivable that they both lived a long time, maybe centuries, in the Archipelago before coming here."

Before they could continue the discussion, the door burst open and Chaz and Fred rushed inside.

"Where the *hell* have you been?" Jack exclaimed. "We thought you—"

"Wasn't coming back?" Chaz shot back. "Hah. Fat chance of that, eh, Fred?"

The little badger looked up, surprised, then gave Chaz a thumbs-up and a grin.

"Where have you—," John started to say.

"No time," Chaz cut in. "You have to hear what I overheard last night, an' then" – he pointed to Fred's hourglass – "we got t' go."

Chaz quickly recounted the whole argument he'd witnessed between Myrddyn and Madoc, repeating the strange Greek words as best he could. When he was finished, Jack snorted.

"You don't *speak* ancient Greek, Chaz," he said mockingly. "I think you're making things up out of your head."

"I'm picking up more than you know," Chaz retorted. "An' I didn't need t' understand it all t' *remember* it."

"I don't know, Chaz." John said doubtfully. "It all fits, but Jack does have a point. We don't know you heard what you think you heard."

"If it wasn't me," Chaz asked, glancing down at Fred, "if it was *him*, th' other me, would you trust me?"

"You mean Charles?" said Jack. "Of course."

"Then trust him," Chaz said to John. "Somewhere I'm him, you say. Well, last night he was me. Trust him. I mean, me. Trust me, John."

John looked questioningly at each of the others in turn. Fred nodded immediately, and finally, more reluctantly, so did Jack.

"They want to get Odysseus's ship back, do they?" John began. "He got it from his father, Laertes, who was one of the original Argonauts," he said, rubbing his chin. "Do you suppose the ship Anaximander saw was . . . ?"

"The *Red Dragon*!" Jack said excitedly. "They came here from the Archipelago in the *Red Dragon*!"

"Mmm, no," said Chaz. "They called it something else . . . the 'Aragorn' or some such."

"The *Argo*," said John. "Jason's ship. That means that Ordo Maas, or at least his sons, had gone to the island to take the wreck of the *Argo* back into the Archipelago, in order to transform it into the first of the Dragonships – the *Red Dragon*."

"Exiled, eh?" said Jack. "I bet that's the reason they were shipwrecked, and why the ship was taken back once they were here."

"One or t' other has t' be Mordred," said Chaz, "but if the other is anything like th' first, then wouldn't he still be somewhere in the future, too?"

Jack's jaw dropped. "That's brilliant, Chaz."

"We already *have* met both of them!" John said. "One of them is the Winter King – and his twin is the Cartographer of Lost Places! It's the only answer that makes any sense!"

"But which is which?" said Jack.

Fred tugged on Chaz's shirt and tapped the nearly empty hourglass.

"The twenty-four hours!" Chaz said. "It's almost up! We have to go, else we'll be trapped here!"

"You've laboured long and hard," a voice said from the doorway. "I've brought you more refreshments."

Anaximander entered carrying a tray with a flagon of wine and two goblets. He started when he saw Chaz, and he studiously ignored Fred. "I'm sorry," the philosopher said, awkwardly balancing the tray. "I'll fetch another goblet."

"Where's Pythagoras?" Jack asked. "Doesn't he usually fetch the wine?"

"I, er, sent him home," Anaximander said. "I thought as a show of gratitude I would serve you the morning wine myself."

"No!" yelled Fred, leaping up to the table and knocking the tray from the philosopher's hands.

"Fred!" Jack began, but he stopped short as they all looked down at the spilled wine, which sizzled and bubbled on the stone floor.

"Animal instincts," said Fred, "and a good nose."

"Right," Chaz said. His left fist snapped up, and he struck Anaximander brutally in the jaw. The philosopher went down hard, falling in a sprawl at the man's feet. "Y' unnerstand *that?*"

The truth of what was happening slowly sank into John and Jack as Chaz and Fred headed out the door. "You didn't make any of these maps, did you, Anaximander? One of your students did."

"The desire is there, but I have not the skill," the philosopher admitted, teeth clenched. "It was that boy, that *child*. . . He had such a hand, and such a clear mind for detail. . . I had saved his life, after all. Wasn't I entitled to benefit from that? Wasn't I?"

Jack cursed in English, then switched back to Greek. "We don't care about that!" he said harshly. "We just want to know which of them it was!"

"Jack! John!" Chaz shouted from the courtyard. "Now!"

"Anaximander! Please!" John called as he backed out of the map room. "We have to know! We need to know! Tell us, please!

"Who is the Cartographer?"

But no answer was forthcoming. John and Jack raced out of the philosopher's home as he collapsed in a wreck of tears and regret.

Chaz, with Fred trailing behind, already had a good lead, and the streets of Miletus were broad and uncrowded. There would be no real gathering in this part of the town for another hour or two, John thought wryly. Not until the storyteller, whichever twin it was today, made his appearance in the amphitheatre.

To his credit, Chaz had slackened his pace just slightly enough to allow the badger to keep up, so John and Jack had nearly caught up to them by the time the thief and the badger had entered the portal.

Jack raced through next, hardly pausing in the apparent act of running into a marble wall. John was close on his heels and cut the timing tightly enough to see the edges of the projection beginning to close in and lose their shape.

He passed through the gossamer layers and turned around for one final look at Miletus – and saw Myrddyn and Madoc dash from an alleyway and into the plaza.

In seconds the twin sons of Odysseus had spotted the unusual nature of the wall where the companions had vanished, and they moved quickly to follow, swords drawn.

But it was too late. The projection began to fade as the slide was burned dry by the incandescent bulb in the Lanterna Magica, and in a moment, the portal had closed in front of them. Ancient Greece was history.

"Curse it all," said John. "I've forgotten my watch."

CHAPTER ELEVEN
The Grail

The harsh white light of the Lanterna Magica cast deep shadows behind John, Jack, and Chaz as they stood, reeling from the chase, and realized they were once again safe in the projection room on Noble's Isle.

"The giants!" Jack exclaimed, looking around in trepidation. "Are the giants still outside?"

Reynard moved to him, making soothing gestures with his paws. "No need to fear. They retreated when they realized you were no longer here. But," he added, almost apologetic, "they may yet return. Were you successful in your mission?"

At that both Jack and Chaz looked at John, who took a deep breath. "Well, yes and no," he admitted. "I think we found the answer we were looking for – Mordred's true name – or at least, we've narrowed it down. But we still don't know how to use it against him."

Sitting to rest, the three men took turns recounting the events of the last day to Fred and Uncas, as Reynard ordered in food and drink.

Chaz hungrily tucked into the pile of cheese and bread that had been brought in by three ferrets. "Truth t' tell, I'm more sleepy

"*You know about the trials, do you not?*"

than anything," he said through a mouthful of food, "but this may be the best sandwich I've ever had."

Reynard bowed in gratitude and began to pour a cup of wine. Chaz stopped him, covering the cup with his hand. "If it's all th' same t' you," he said, looking at the others, "I'd just as soon stick t' water or ale after this trip."

"Agreed," said Jack, shuddering at the thought of how close he'd come to drinking the poisoned wine. "Thanks for the save, Fred."

The little mammal would have blushed if he could. As it was, he beamed happily and chewed a crust of bread Chaz had handed him.

"One thing's certain," John said. "We went into that completely unprepared. We can't do so a second time."

"To be fair," said Uncas, "there *were* giants at the door yesterday."

Chaz nodded grimly. "An' they could be lurkin' about even now – so we'd best get prepared and decide what t' do right."

"Is it me," Reynard whispered to John, "or didst his countenance change during your journey into the projection?"

"His appearance?"

The fox shook his head. "Countenance. His . . . appearance beneath what we see with our eyes."

"Mmm, perhaps," John mused, looking at his reluctant companion. "Maybe it has, at that."

"So," Uncas began, "how do we prepare you better for the next trip, other than giving you the hourglass this time around?"

"Yes," said John. "You saved us there, too, it seems. As to being better prepared, I don't think there is anything further that we *can* do. We simply don't have enough information to work with."

"Maybe we do," Jack said, a look of excitement on his face. "Remember? The warning! The warning in the book that was sent to Charles!"

John swore under his breath. "I'd completely forgotten about it," he admitted, "not that it would have done us any good where Verne sent us."

"What do you mean?" asked Jack. "Why not?"

"At its earliest, the representation of the Grail wouldn't have had any meaning at all until a few decades after the crucifixion of Christ. And we already know that Hugo was sent back several centuries later than that. So I don't see how his warning is relevant to Verne's mission."

"But it *is* relevant, don't you see, John?" Jack exclaimed. "Hugo gave us the answer in his message! It's the Cartographer! Mordred's twin! His own brother *would* be capable of the Binding!"

John's brow furrowed in concentration as he considered Jack's idea. It might in fact be possible – he was unclear as to the rules that regulated the power behind the Summonings and the Bindings, except that they had to be spoken by someone of royal birth. Artus was able to do it, as had Arthur, generations before him. Aven's son, Stephen, could have done it as well. And they already knew Mordred was capable of doing a Binding – so the same *might* be true of his brother.

"We know the Cartographer's existence predates Arthur's rule," John reasoned, "and we'd already suspected that Mordred did too. And remember – back on Terminus, Mordred did say that he and Artus shared the same blood. So somehow the authority to

speak Bindings and Summonings comes from somewhere beyond
even Mordred."

"Fair enough," said Jack. "That means his twin – the Cartographer – would possess the same ability. Hugo's note mentioned
the Cartographer, and Verne told us we needed to discover
Mordred's true name in order to defeat him. We can't do that
here," he said, waving his arms to indicate Albion as a whole.
"There are no other kings able to do to *him* what he can do to
us. And I don't think the authority of the Caretakers can over-
power the authority of the king."

"Mebbe that's what this 'Verne' meant f'r us t' do," said Chaz,
who was sitting against the wall, dozing, but still listening. "Mebbe
it's up t' us t' turn one of the brothers against the other."

"That's what it comes down to, doesn't it?" Jack asked. "We
have to convince whichever one is the Cartographer that his
brother will eventually turn rotten, and that the only way to prevent it is to Bind him."

"But for how long?" wondered John. "Binding can't really be
permanent, unless . . ."

Only Chaz and Reynard didn't understand John's unspoken
thought, which the others knew as part of their own history: The
only way to defeat the Winter King was to kill him. And even that
had proven to be problematic.

"Y'r still forgetting one thing," said Chaz. "He in't the Cartographer yet. And *both* of 'em were thrown out of the Archipelago,
remember? I heard 'em say it. And they were both in on th' plan t'
kill *us*, if you recall. When they was chasin' us out of Miletus, they
both had drawn swords. That says poison t' me. Both of 'em. They
be poison."

"Isn't the Cartographer your friend?" asked Uncas. "Back where we came from?"

John shook his head slowly. "I don't think the Cartographer is anyone's friend, to be honest," he said. "We went to him when we had to, and no more. And he gave us what he needed to, and no more. It wasn't so much a friendship as it was co-operation between interested parties."

"Isn't that what you're seeking now?" asked Reynard, who had been listening from the back of the room all the while. "Not his friendship, but his co-operation?"

"Yes," Jack replied, "but we have less to argue with here. Back in our world, he was a virtual prisoner, locked in the Keep of Time, behind the door that bore the mark of the king."

"Mordred's mark?" asked Chaz.

"Arthur's mark," said Jack. "Different king, but the Cartographer was just as trapped."

"What for?" asked Chaz. "What did *he* do t' piss someone off?"

John shrugged. "No one's ever said. I'm not sure if anyone really knows. None of the Histories ever mentioned it, that's for certain."

"Mayhap we should consult th' Little Whatsit," offered Uncas. "There be lots of unique knowledge there that even some scowlers may not know."

"Thank you, Uncas," John said gently, "but this is bigger than just healing blisters or making magic darts." He sat in the chair next to the badger and looked at the projector. "I wonder if we shouldn't turn it on and have a look at the next slide? That way we can equip ourselves ahead of time for wherever and whenever it lands us."

"Do we really want to do that?" asked Jack. "We can't afford to use up the hours. Once we turn it on, we have twenty-four hours maximum before the slide burns out. And we're going to need every second to convince the Cartographer to join us against his brother."

"You're probably right," said John. "We became acclimated pretty quickly in Miletus, and Chaz was useful in helping us blend in. Perhaps this really will just be a leap of faith."

John's sentiment was punctuated by a loud boom from outside and a faint tremor which shook the room.

"Oh, no," Jack groaned, slapping his forehead. "Here we go again."

"Wait," Reynard said, rushing from the room. "Let me see for certain."

Any doubt they felt as to what had made the noise was dispelled a moment later when the voice of the giant filtered through the walls of the building. *"Jaaackk,"* it said, menacing and persuasive all at once, *"Jaack . . . wee have a preeesent for youuu. . ."*

There was a crashing somewhere outside the house, and a cacophony of animal noises, then silence.

"They're being a bit more restrained than the last time," John observed. "That can't be good."

Chaz agreed. "They's up t' summat, for sure."

A moment later the fox re-entered the room.

"I have good news, and bad news, and worse news," Reynard announced. He was trembling. Whatever had just transpired outside had rattled the fox to his core.

"What's the good news?" Jack said.

"The giants will honour the king's covenant with the Children of the Earth," Reynard answered. "They will not cross our boundary and step onto Sanctuary."

"Excellent!" Jack exclaimed. "We'll be safe here, then."

"Trapped, y' mean," Chaz said glumly. He looked at the fox. "They in't going anywhere, is they?"

Reynard shook his head. "They are at the four points of the compass – one each at north, south, east, and west. They will not permit you and your fellows, or indeed, anyone else to leave Sanctuary while you are here."

"I'm guessing that's the bad news, then," said John. "Should we dare ask what the worse news is?"

Reynard leaned back and motioned for the large jackrabbit that waited in the hall to come into the projection room. The animal was carrying a small burlap sack, tied with a ribbon and bearing a card. The rabbit set the bag on one of the chairs, then hopped quickly away.

John stepped forward and looked at the card. It read simply, *To complete the set.*

He frowned and undid the tie on the bag, which dropped open.

The badgers gasped and turned away, and Jack covered his eyes with his hands. Chaz reacted even more strongly, cursing and clenching his fists in anger. As for John, he simply closed his eyes and murmured a hasty prayer before retying the bag that held his old mentor's head and setting it reverently in one corner of the room.

John turned to Reynard, wiping his eyes with the back of his hand. "There's no more time to waste," he said as boldly as he could manage. "Let's see the second slide."

◆　◆　◆

The companions prepared for the second jaunt through the Lanterna Magica's projections while trying to ignore the frequent taunts of the giants, and even more so the grisly present in the burlap bag.

John decided against including the hourglass in their supplies, making the argument that it could too easily be lost, broken, or upended. "No," he said, "I think what happened before is really our ideal. Uncas and Fred will be our timekeepers. You're both safe here on Sanctuary anyway, and you can come fetch us as the time grows short."

"They were able to do that last time because I, ah, were passin' by the portal," said Chaz. "How will they find us this time around?"

"We'll have to be aware of the time ourselves as best we can," said John, "and try to keep a bearing on the position of the portal so we'll be nearby."

"Don't worry, Scowler John," Uncas stated with a salute. "Th' Royal Animal Rescue Squad will not fail you."

"I know you won't, Uncas," John said, resisting the urge to pat the badger on the head while he was being stately. "The son of Tummeler would never let us down."

Uncas looked so proud at the compliment that John thought he might burst into tears. "Ready?" he said to Jack and Chaz.

Chaz yawned and nodded. "Enough, I guess."

"Ready," agreed Jack.

"All right," John said, signalling Reynard. "Light it up."

The fox pressed the switch that rotated the disc of slides, and the next image slid smoothly into view. John, Jack, and Chaz stepped aside to better get a view of the slide, and Uncas and Fred dutifully turned over the hourglass.

As before, the multiple layers that were projected on the wall gave everyone a slightly disoriented feeling. It took a few moments for their vision to adjust to the shifting perspectives, and then they could see what was on the slide.

In front of them, perhaps thirty feet distant, was the elaborately decorated entrance to a mosque, or perhaps a temple. The architecture was more advanced than what they had seen in the previous projection, but harder to place.

"Persian?" Jack murmured.

"No," said John. "More Egyptian, I'd say."

The wall they faced was dominated by a great arched doorway, in front of which was a broad pedestal. On it was an immense horned owl, which was clutching a piece of chalk in one clawed foot and seemed to be using it to scribble on a piece of slate.

"What do you make of that?" John asked.

"The bird?" said Jack. "I think it's an owl."

John groaned. "I know it's an owl!" he whispered back. "I mean *that*!" He pointed behind the bird.

Jack gasped, as did Chaz. Behind the pedestal, engraved into the door and embellished with golden ornaments and designs crusted with jewels, was the image of the Holy Grail, the same one that was on the cover of the book back at Magdalen College.

"So we're definitely into Anno Domini," Jack said. "Past the time of Christ."

"Or within it," said John, as a man, absorbed in whatever work he was attending to, passed by the scene in front of them. He wore sandals and a simple robe with a sash. "I can't tell from the attire. First century? Second, maybe? We'll have to suss it out for certain once we've crossed over."

"Good enough," said Jack. "Who wants to go first?"

"Don't look at me," said Chaz. "You two are the 'Scowlers.'"

"It doesn't need to be a debate," John said. "We've done it before."

"You couldn't tell from all the bickering," said a trilling voice that was airy and condescending at the same time. "If you asked me, I'd say you're all scared to death."

John and Jack stared at each other in surprise. The voice had spoken in Greek – but it had come from the *owl*.

"What?" the owl asked. "Cat got your tongues?"

The three companions all stepped through the portal and into the hallway they'd been watching. If they were going to converse with a giant bird, John figured it would be less conspicuous to do so in person than to risk anyone seeing the owl verbally upbraiding a blank wall.

"Not scared," Jack said in response to the owl's comment. "Just cautious."

"Caution, fft," the owl scoffed. "That's not really the attitude to have if you want to take over the world, now, is it?"

"Why would I want to take over the world?" asked Jack.

"Why else would you come to Alexandria?" the owl replied. "All the fashionable would-be world conquerors do."

Alexandria. So, John realized, they were in Egypt, but at the edge of the influence of the Greek world. And certainly later than the common era they'd been to in the other projection.

"It's simpler than that," Chaz said in surprisingly passable Greek. "We just need to find someone."

"Mmm," said the owl, obviously losing interest. "And what is this someone's name?"

"We're not really sure," Jack admitted.

"That would make it harder, wouldn't it?" the owl replied with no trace of sympathy.

"What's *your* name?" Chaz asked.

The owl preened. Apparently he wasn't asked his name very often. "Archimedes," he replied. "A pleasure, I'm sure."

"Archimedes? Like the mathematician?" asked John.

The owl hopped up and down in irritation. "Why does everyone ask me that? Why does no one ever think that a bird can't also be a mathematician?"

"Sorry," said John. "I didn't mean to offend."

The owl scowled. "Pythagoras should have built me as an eagle instead of an owl. No one ever questions an eagle."

"A clockwork owl?" Jack whispered. "Intriguing."

"What are you working on, Archie?" asked Chaz, looking at the slate. "Looks complicated."

Any irritation the owl might have felt at being called "Archie" was set aside by the chance to discuss the notations on the tablet.

"It's a maths problem," he said, giving John a poisonous look, "for the trials. You know about the trials, do you not?"

"We're strangers here," John began, before Archimedes cut him off with a disgusted noise.

"I *know* you're strangers here," the bird said. "I just watched you walk through a *wall*. Locals don't really do that much. And you aren't here as conquerors, or if you are, you're the most ill-prepared conquerors I've ever seen."

"We're not conquerors," Jack confirmed.

"You're the funny one in the group, aren't you?" asked the bird.

"It depends on the day," said Jack.

"People come here for only two reasons," Archimedes continued, "to start an insurrection to try to unite the world, or to prepare for the trials."

"Trials for what?" asked John.

"To become Caretakers, of course."

"Caretakers? Of the *Imaginarium Geographica*?"

"The what? No," the bird replied, exasperated. "Of the Sangreal."

"The Holy Grail?"

The bird glared at him. "Why do you repeat everything I say? You must be the stupid one of the group. Which isn't saying much, is it?

"Yes," Archimedes said as he went back to his equations. "The trials are to test those who would become Caretakers – of the Holy Grail."

Every surface was covered with maps . . .

CHAPTER TWELVE
Imaginary Geographies

The three companions retreated a few feet away to confer privately, while the owl went back to its figures and calculations.

"That seals it," whispered Jack. "It's no coincidence we came here now. The Grail has to figure into our mission to find Myrddyn and Madoc."

"I can't see how," said John, "unless they've become somehow entwined with the Grail lore this far back. Remember, we're still centuries from where Hugo ended up."

"Perhaps he discovered that somehow," suggested Jack, "and that's why he included it in the message to us."

John rubbed his forehead and chewed on his lip. "No," he said finally, "I can think of another reason they'd be here now. They've come for the trials. Remember what they claimed they wanted to do, back in Miletus?"

Chaz nodded. "They wanted t' find a way t' get back to th' Archipelago."

"Right," said John, "and to do that, they needed a route, and directions, and something else – an object touched by divinity that would allow them passage through the Frontier. And at this point in history, can you think of any other object that fits the description better than the cup of Christ?"

The companions turned and went back to the owl, who sighed dramatically. "Now what? I have work to do, you know. The trials won't write themselves, and I only have until tomorrow."

"The Grail trials are math problems?" asked John.

"Yes, oh master of the obvious," retorted the owl. "Or a part of them, anyway. The trials judge one's worth, through tests spiritual, physical, and intellectual. I'm in charge of the intellectual part."

"We'll leave you alone to work, we promise," John said. "We'd just like to ask some directions."

"Oh?" said Archimedes. "To find your nameless friend?"

"We're looking for someone who likes t' make maps," said Chaz. "Y' know anyone like that?"

"I do, actually," Archimedes replied, still distracted by his equations. "Go north three hundred paces, then open the second door. That should be the man you seek."

"Thanks, Archie," said Chaz, turning to the others. "Time's a-wastin'. Shall we go?"

"Wait," John said, still flabbergasted at having somehow become the third wheel of the trio. "He's here? In this very building?"

"Well, where else would someone who's anyone be?" Archimedes asked without looking up. "If you aren't working at the library, you aren't worth paying attention to, anyway."

John and Jack exchanged knowing glances. Of course. The seat of learning, the crossroads of culture for the entire civilized world, wouldn't just be the city. It would be the Library of Alexandria itself.

Heartened by the progress they seemed to be making, the

three companions followed the owl's directions down the passageway and opened the door.

They were looking into a broad, high-ceilinged room that was essentially one great, global map. The walls and ceilings were festooned with drawings, and all across them were lines that even connected across the floor, which was also covered with illustrations. The effect was not unlike stepping inside an immense transparent globe.

"Impressive, I know," a voice said from somewhere across the expanse of parchment that lined the tables and shelves scattered about the room. "I call the lines drawn across the maps 'latitude' and 'longitude.' Forgive me if I've forgotten a meeting. I'm not expected to present my discoveries in the rotunda until next week, but they're taking all my attention at present."

A short, pleasantly anxious man stepped around a tall papier-mâché globe he was constructing and offered them a hand in greeting.

He was olive-skinned, and he spoke with an accent that demonstrated both travel abroad and great education, but his mannerisms were those of a tailor who can't decide between creating a more finely cut suit, or a more satisfied customer. He wore a round cap and breeches that seemed to be Persian, or perhaps Egyptian. And shoes, rather than the sandals they'd seen the others wearing through the projection. They'd expected to go straight from Archimedes to one or both of the twins, and so they had not procured any appropriate clothing. However, their unusual dress seemed not to matter at all to the man, who was dressed even more oddly than they were.

John took the man's hand, which was sticky with paste, and shook it firmly.

"Oh! I'm very sorry," the man said, just realizing what he'd done. "Can you forgive?"

"Don't worry about it," said John, wiping his hand on the back of his trousers and smiling. "I'm John."

"Claudius Ptolemaeus. Call me Ptolemy," the man replied. "Did we have a meeting today?"

"We're just here for the trials," Jack answered. "To become Caretakers of the, uh, Grail."

Ptolemy squinted, as if he was having trouble with Jack's accent. "Oh!" he said finally. "Of course! The trials. Yes, a sorry business it is."

"The trials?"

"No," said Ptolemy. "The need for a new Caretaker. One of them – one of the best we've had, in fact – tried to . . ."

He paused and cupped his hands around his mouth, as if he didn't want to be heard speaking the words. "He tried to take the Grail. For himself. And he was caught and shall be executed soon. That's the reason I'm behind schedule," Ptolemy explained, gesturing at the room full of maps. "The betrayer was my own understudy, and perhaps the most talented map-maker I've ever known."

John, Jack, and Chaz all stiffened at this, but it was a testament to the swift self-control of all three men that Ptolemy never noticed their reactions.

"I was mocked in other places, other libraries," Ptolemy continued, using a small stepladder and a pointer to tap out some locations high on the southern wall. "Here, and here, and, uh" – he turned, pointing east – "and over there. I always believed that imagination plays as crucial a part in the making of maps as education. After all, how else is one to test the spatial boundaries of the world, if one cannot first imagine them?"

John pursed his lips. "That's a great argument, Ptolemy. Is it a viewpoint your understudy shares?"

The mapmaker nodded and climbed down the ladder. "Yes," he said morosely, folding his hands behind his back. "It is. That man has such a mind, such a mind, it's a wonder. And such talent! Just look at these works!"

"These are his?" Jack asked, leafing through some sheets of parchment. "Not yours?"

"Some are mine, some his," Ptolemy admitted. "Our studies we work on together. But our principal works we have done separately – the better to test their merits against each other's work."

Ptolemy pushed his way through two shelves laden with tools and buckets and retrieved a large folio. It was bound in leather and contained sheets of parchment.

"Normally," he said, placing the book in front of them, "I'd just be drawing the maps on scrolls, as scholars always have done. But keeping the latitudes straight in particular necessitated that they be cut into squares and bound thusly."

"These are maps of the entire world?" John asked as Ptolemy began to display his work to them.

"Much of it, yes," he answered. "From the Blessed Isles, here, to Thule, here, and Meroë and Serica, here." He tapped the map proudly. "Pretty good, yes?"

"It's remarkable," John agreed.

"Breathtaking," said Jack.

"The parchments are very clean," observed Chaz.

"I'd worked out most of 'latitude' myself," said Ptolemy,

indicating the horizontal lines drawn across the maps. "But 'longitude,'" he added, noting the vertical lines, "didn't really come together until my understudy arrived. He showed me ways to use some underlying cartological principles that haven't been used since the philosopher Anaximander's time to clarify my own measurements. You'd be surprised at how clearly he could articulate them."

"I'll bet," John said dryly.

"I just wish he'd been cleverer," said Ptolemy. "If not too clever to steal, at least too clever to be caught."

"Why is that?" asked Jack.

Ptolemy closed the book and dusted off the cover. "We finished my *Geographica*," he said sadly, "but we'll never have the chance to finish his." He put his book on a wide shelf and removed a second one, which was similar in size and shape but vastly more familiar to John and Jack – even in its much earlier state.

"He calls it his *Imaginary Geography*," Ptolemy said. "It contains maps to places that no one has seen, and now," he added with a sigh, "perhaps no one ever will."

The *Imaginarium Geographica*, the earliest version of it at least, was right there in front of them. It was all John could do not to grab the book and start hugging it.

"I'm happy to see it too," Jack whispered, having noted the flare of joy in his friend's eyes, "but remember – this is not our *Geographica*. Not yet."

Jack was right. As Ptolemy paged through the scant few completed maps, some were familiar, others not so much. Some of the islands of the Underneath were there: Aiaia, and Lixus, and the

Island of Wandering Rocks. A few were unmarked, but several others bore annotations.

"An addition of my own," Ptolemy said proudly. "I felt it was essential to know something more about the lands in a *Geographica* than just how to get there."

"We appreciate that a lot," said John. "More than you can know."

Chaz scratched his head. "How d'you annotate a map t' an imaginary place?"

"Just the idea was mine, not the writing itself," Ptolemy said. "But even so, how could you go wrong writing a description of an imaginary land? All that would matter is whether or not you believed in it yourself."

"Ptolemy," John said, "we need to see your understudy. Can you take us to see him?"

"Oh, I'm sorry," the mapmaker said. "He's already condemned and in his cell, awaiting execution. I couldn't—"

"Please," John implored. "It's important."

"Well, if I were to help . . . ," Ptolemy began, tapping at his chin. "How might I benefit by it?"

Jack answered, turning to Ptolemy with a determined look on his face. "If we give you something of great value, will you help us?"

Ptolemy folded his arms. "What are you offering?"

"What if I can show you a land, a new land that really exists, but that no one knows about yet?"

Ptolemy's arms dropped to his sides. "A new land? A real one?"

In reply, Jack took a stylus from a table, then grabbed a fresh sheet of parchment from a nearby stack and began to sketch. A couple of times he stood back, appraising, then kept working. Once John realized what Jack was doing, he picked up another stylus and began to add topographical details, and even a fish or three swimming in the water. When they had finished, Jack handed the sheet to Ptolemy. "There. What do you think of that?"

"Amazing!" Ptolemy exclaimed. "Where is it?"

Jack pointed to John's notations. "Here – it lies far south of Chi – uh, Sinae.

"We call it 'Australia.'"

"You'll have to wait until dark," Ptolemy explained as he traced out the route the companions needed to follow. "There will be guards attending to him through the evening, but you should be able to sneak past if you use the corridors I've marked. You don't plan to kill anyone, do you?"

John was aghast. "Of course not!"

Ptolemy took this with aplomb. "Oh, I wouldn't take issue if you really needed to. I just want to know if I have to plan ahead for anyone's replacement."

"Why would that be your worry?" asked Chaz. "Are you some sort of supervisor here at the library?"

"Actually," Ptolemy whispered, again with the hand cupped to his mouth, "I'm the king. Of Alexandria."

Chaz started to ask the obvious question: Why did they have to resort to sneaking and subterfuge to see the prisoner, if Ptolemy was in a position to simply order it?

John quickly looked at the others with a slight head shake. If Ptolemy was speaking the truth, he could be helpful; but if he was just a crazy geographer, engaging him more fully in their quest could just complicate things.

Jack rolled his eyes. "Okay," he said to Ptolemy. "We appreciate your help."

The three companions shook hands with the geographer king and started tracing the labyrinthine path he'd marked for them, which wound through the warren of rooms. They moved from corridor to corridor, each one taking them to progressively larger rooms, most of which were filled with racks and shelves laden with scrolls. It was more than tempting for John and Jack to reach out every so often to touch one of the scrolls.

"Why so delicate?" Chaz asked. "Paper don't break."

"You wouldn't understand," John replied, still eyeing a set of scrolls that bore Egyptian seals as they passed to the next room. "This library, and everything in it, represents a collection of knowledge more complete than the world will ever see again. It's tempting to just stay and read. To men like us, this is holy ground."

"Right," said Chaz, who was clearly unimpressed. "If it was so great, what happened to it?"

"The usual," said Jack. "Catastrophe, followed by a couple thousand years of regret."

In the adjacent structure they found the cluster of rooms where Ptolemy said his understudy was being held.

The hall was lined with identical doors set into stone. "Which one?" Jack asked. "They're all the same. It'll take all night."

"That one," Chaz said, pointing. "It's the only one with a guard." Without further discussion, he slipped around to the next corridor and disappeared. A moment later a second guard stopped in front of the cell door and spoke briefly to the first, who got up and began to walk directly to John and Jack's place of concealment. The other went back the way he had come.

The first guard didn't even have time to call out before John clocked him hard on the chin. The guard fell and slumped against the wall, and Jack grabbed him under the arms and dragged him to a less conspicuous spot. Just then, Chaz appeared at the other end of the corridor and trotted to them.

"What happened to the other guard?" John whispered. "I thought there were two."

"There were," Chaz whispered back, "but he couldn't handle his wine."

"You got him drunk? That fast?"

"Nah," said Chaz, pointing to his forehead. "Hit him with th' bottle."

Jack came back just in time to overhear them. "You know, Chaz," he said, only half joking, "for a thief and a traitor, you've turned out to be really useful."

"I resemble that remark," said Chaz.

"Fair enough," Jack declared. "I got the keys from the guard. Let's go and see who we find."

Jack fumbled a bit with the keys, so Chaz offered to try. The third key he put into the lock worked, and the door swung open with a gentle push.

The cell beyond was rectangular and made entirely of stone. There was a small window on the far wall, but it was blocked by wooden beams just outside. John saw at once that this room had never been intended for use as a cell at all; it had to have been a storeroom of some kind, only recently converted to hold a prisoner.

Even so, it was a cell in name only, and distinguishable from other rooms at the library solely because of the lock on the door and the guards in front of it.

There was a solitary desk and a chair, but the only light came from a small oil lamp that hung near the door, and a second positioned over the desk. In many ways, the room bore a strong resemblance to Ptolemy's workshop. Every surface was covered with maps, and there were globes and statuary scattered throughout. As they stepped over the threshold, the lamp at the door seemed to brighten, and it cast their shadows deep into the room.

"Hello?" John said cautiously. "Is someone there?"

At the desk, a man raised his tousled head up from the work he was concentrating on, and eyes that were more distracted than curious peered at them.

"Is it time already? I still have work to do, and I was hoping for a little more sleep before morning so my eyes wouldn't be puffy when you lop off my head."

"We're not here to execute you," said Jack. "We're here to, uh . . ." He looked at John, who shrugged. What were they here to do? Rescue him?

"We've got a couple of questions," said Chaz. "If you please."

The man at the desk perked up. "Three visitors, and three voices I haven't heard in oh so long," he said, standing and straightening his clothes. "You've picked a good time to visit. Another day and I'd have been unable to answer."

"So we heard," said Jack. "My sympathy would be greater if you hadn't tried to poison us, then chase us with a sword the last time we met."

"Last time, or first?" came the reply. "Not that I really care, mind you. For what it's worth, I do regret trying to poison you. It was a different time then, and I was a different man. What are your questions?"

As he said this, he stepped farther into the lamplight. He hadn't aged much but was perhaps shorter, as if gravity had noticed him more than before. Still, they couldn't quite tell if he was Myrddyn or Madoc.

John suddenly realized that the answer to one question was literally right in front of them. This was Ptolemy's understudy. Whichever of the twins this was would be the Cartographer.

"What's your name?" asked Chaz.

The man's smile was warm, but slightly weary also. "I've had many names, but at present I am called Meridian."

John's mouth twitched imperceptibly, as he tried not to sigh in relief. Meridian was the name of a line of longitude. This was the Cartographer.

"What brought you here?" asked Jack.

"I first travelled here when it was still called Rhakotis, before Alexander transfigured everything in his own image," Meridian said, pacing back and forth in front of them, so that he constantly passed between light and shadow. "That Alexander should later come here to establish a great centre of learning in the same place can be called an accident of family, I suppose."

"You're related to Alexander?" John said in surprise.

"A cousin," replied Meridian. "We descendants of the Argonauts are an ambitious lot, it seems. World conquest is in our blood. At least," he added quickly, "for some of us."

"You're not interested in conquering the world, Myrddyn?" John asked, remembering more about the twin they were facing as they conversed.

The mapmaker raised a hand. "Please. I have not gone by that name in almost two hundred years. Meridian suits me better, I think."

"And your brother?" John asked, noting that Meridian hadn't actually answered his question. "Has he changed as well?"

"Madoc is still Madoc, in name and temperament," said Meridian. "He has chosen his path, and it differs from mine. Why do you ask?"

John looked first at Jack, who nodded his assent, then at Chaz, who chewed his lip for a few seconds, looking hard at Meridian, before he also agreed.

"We have some things we need to tell you," he began slowly, "things that may seem impossible to believe. But believe them you must. And when we have finished, we're hoping that you can help us find a way to solve our problem . . .

". . . without killing your brother."

PART FOUR

The Iron Crown

"Please!" Madoc cried to her, imploring. "I'm sorry!..."

CHAPTER THIRTEEN

Betrayal

By early afternoon, Hugo Dyson and King Pellinor had arrived at the place Pellinor called "Camelot". Whatever Hugo had initially envisioned on hearing the name vanished as the cart crested the hill overlooking the shallow valley that was their destination.

Camelot was not a city, or even the castle Hugo had been half hoping to see. Instead they looked out over a broad valley ringed about with low hills and a scattering of scrubby trees. In the centre stood a number of upraised stones and a granite stairway that wound its way up a grassy mound, ending at a great stone table.

Throughout the valley were camped the various travellers Hugo had observed from a distance as they rode south. There were mud-and-wattle huts and silken tents, along with a more common scattering of simpler tents and enclosures. But in front of each encampment was a banner representing the champion who had come to compete in the tournament.

To the right, Hugo saw a flag emblazoned with a scarlet roc; and beside that, one bearing a golden griffin. To their left, he saw an immense banner crested with ships and an embroidered fish. In the distance, he could even make out one that seemed simpler, as if it had been sewn for a blanket rather than a war banner; it bore the image of a white pig.

"So," Hugo said jovially, "uh, have we got a banner to fly?"

Pellinor raised an eyebrow at him, then lifted his foot and booted Hugo out of the cart.

The scholar rolled clumsily for a moment before righting himself, spitting and brushing dirt off his clothes. "I say," Hugo said indignantly. "What's that all about?"

Pellinor shrugged and tossed the crumpled photograph at him. "I was asked to pick you up and then deliver you here. I've done that, done. And now I've my own business to attend to."

Without another word, Pellinor clicked his tongue at the old horse and wheeled it around. In minutes he'd disappeared amongst the other carts and horses and tents filling the small valley.

Hugo blinked a few times, then began to assess his situation through clear eyes for the first time. This was no joke, no illusion. And he was far out of his depth in whatever it was that was happening around him.

As if to compound his concern, a knight dressed in armour and a green-gold tunic noticed him sitting on the hillside and began walking directly towards him.

The knight stopped, towering over the scholar, who was growing more anxiety-ridden by the second. "You look as out of place as I feel," he whispered to Hugo in perfect, unaccented American English. "And that's saying a lot."

"Wh-wh-what?" Hugo stammered. This was unexpected, even after the ride with Pellinor.

"Hank Morgan," the knight said, removing his helmet. "Pleased to meet you."

"Are — are you here to fight in the tournament?" asked Hugo, eyeing the dress and armour. "Whatever this tournament is supposed to be?"

"I'm here as a watcher only," Hank replied. "I'm to observe and record, but never interfere."

"And who are you watching for?" Hugo asked.

Hank blinked in surprise. "Weren't you sent here to watch too?" he asked. "By the Caretakers?"

Hugo brightened, slightly relieved. This might be a friend. "No, I wasn't," he said, proffering his hand. "Hugo Dyson, newly itinerant friend of the Caretakers. I'm here by accident, I'm afraid."

Hank's eyes narrowed at this. "By accident?" he said, repeating Hugo's words as they shook hands. "By *accident*? How is that possible? I thought I was the only one that had happened to. Usually these jaunts into zero points are too well-planned for someone to come 'by accident.'"

Hank turned away from Hugo, muttering and grumbling under his breath. He removed the heavy gauntlets he'd been wearing and pulled a small, leather-bound notebook out of his tunic. He flipped through the pages, occasionally making a notation with a stub of a pencil, and less occasionally, glancing back at Hugo with a halfhearted smile.

Finally Hank finished checking whatever he'd needed to find in the notebook and pulled a silver pocket watch out of a pocket sewn into his sleeve.

"If you'll excuse me," he said to Hugo, "I need to let someone know about you, posthaste. You see, I don't think you're supposed to be here at all."

Hugo swallowed hard. "I keep getting the same feeling, Mr Morgan, the same feeling exactly. The problem is, I can't decide if I'm in someplace strange, or if this is a joke of some sort, or if I'm only in a dream."

Hank laughed and clapped him on the back. "I know just how you feel. The first time I 'went out', I'd been conked in the noggin by a fellow called Hercules in a factory back in Hartford. When I woke up, I was here. Well," he added, scratching his head and examining the watch, "not 'here' here, exactly. More like thirty years from now, give or take. But one thing I came to realize was that it wasn't a dream. And you'd best realize that too, if you want to keep your head on your shoulders."

Hugo gulped hard again and fingered his collar.

Hank smiled drolly. "I'm only half-joking," he said, "but I'll do my best to see you're taken care of until we're done here, and then we'll see about getting you back when you belong."

"*Where* I belong, you mean?" said Hugo.

Hank frowned. "You really don't know what's going on, do you?" he asked rhetorically. "When do you think you are?"

"It's the twentieth of September, 1931," Hugo replied.

Hank didn't reply to this but squinted at the silver watch and turned two of the dials set in its side. The watch began to chime, then buzzed harshly. He tapped it on his armour, then shook it. "Dratted machine," he complained. "Something's off. I don't think I can get a message to anyone much earlier than about a decade and a half before your prime time, but that ought to give them sufficient notice to set things aright before you leave."

He said all this as if it would mean something to Hugo, then realized that the scholar hadn't comprehended a word of it.

"Never mind," Hank said with a wave. "Just wait here and try to stay out of everyone's way. I'll send the message for you and see if the Frenchman can't help somehow, and then I have to finish my report for Sam. And I can't do either out in the open."

With that, he began to stride off, leaving the hapless Hugo sitting in the grass, holding his helmet and gauntlets. "But wait!" Hugo called. "Who's Sam?"

"The man who sent me here to begin with," Hank answered over his shoulder without turning around. "Samuel Clemens, the Caretaker Principia of the *Imaginarium Geographica*."

John and Jack took turns telling Meridian why they had come to Alexandria, with occasional contributions from Chaz. He seemed to have thoroughly mastered Greek far more quickly than they had thought possible, but however he'd done it, they were grateful. He had a keener sense than they did of which topics should be avoided and when, cutting in if he suspected they were saying too much.

The two Caretakers might have set aside the poisoning attempt in Miletus, but Chaz had not. And they didn't have Fred around to sniff out a second try.

When they had finished, Meridian sat at the table, thinking. A minute passed. Then another. Then five more.

"If all you have said is true," Meridian finally said, measuring out his words carefully, "then I have been working in error for my entire life."

"What error?" asked John. "Trying to steal the Grail?"

"That would only be the least, and most recent, of my mistakes," Meridian replied, "if it had in fact been I who deigned to take it."

"You didn't try to steal the Grail?" Jack asked.

"Of course it wasn't me!" Meridian exclaimed angrily, stopping so his face was half in shadow. "I have my work laid out to do. I'm not interested in some relic that may or may not have belonged to a false god over a century ago! Why would I risk so much, especially with my position here at the library, to gain so little?"

"Historically speaking, it's worth a great deal to many, many people," John said in answer. "Even now, you can see how it's regarded. This entire institution has been retooled to its service. And we in fact do believe it has value to you – because we know you still want to return to the Archipelago."

"What does that have to do with the Grail?"

Jack gave John a look of caution; this was a crucial piece of information to be sharing with a still uncertain ally. John shared the concern, but he was running out of options – and arguments.

"To cross the Frontier," he said, "you need to carry with you an object that has been touched by divinity. For this reason alone, I think you would desire the Grail."

Meridian narrowed his eyes, then snorted disdainfully. "Divinity? Hardly. I was a thousand years old before he was even born, and his mother was never touched by any of the gods I know. The fact that his story has become a myth believed by many people doesn't make anything he touched divine."

"It might if it's a true myth," John countered. "Ordo Maas crossed the Frontier because he carried the Flame of Prometheus – but most scholars would agree that Prometheus was only a myth."

Meridian's eyes flared at the mention of Prometheus, or so it seemed. He smiled patiently, as if he were explaining a lesson to a slow student. "Most scholars aren't descended from him," he retorted, "and if you want to believe in a new, modern god, that's your business, not mine."

"I don't, really," said Jack. "I believe in a God, but not necessarily in the Christ myth any more than I believe in Prometheus."

"And yet," Meridian continued, "you have crossed the Frontier yourselves, have you not? So you must believe in *something*."

That was an issue Jack wasn't prepared to tackle. And neither was John. Chaz broke the moment with another question.

"Mebbe *you* don't believe," he said pointedly, "but what if your brother does?"

"Yes," Meridian replied. "That would seem like a reason for his actions, to ones such as yourselves. But it would not have been mine, even if it was Madoc's. But he could not have meant to use the Grail in the way that you suggest, to cross back to the Archipelago."

"Why not?"

"Simple," Meridian replied. "We never knew that's how it was done."

John and Jack both groaned inwardly. This might be the Cartographer, but it was a gamble telling him as much as they had. The problem was, the stakes were still unknown.

Meridian smiled. "Don't worry. I reconciled myself to being here in Odysseus's world a long time ago. If – no, when – I do return to the Archipelago, it shall be in the proper time, after the proper order of things."

"One more question," said Chaz, who had clearly taken the lead in the discussion. "Why were you and Madoc exiled from the Archipelago?"

Meridian started, and actually put out a hand to steady himself against the desk. This was not a question he had anticipated, and it seemed to rattle him deeply.

"We made a mistake," he finally said, clearing his throat. "We tried to become more than we were, to become great, but we wanted to take a shortcut. We tried to open a door that was not meant to be opened, and we were caught, and punished. And that's all I can say. I shall not speak of it again."

Chaz looked at the others. All three were making their choice – whether to trust this man before them, or not. There was no way to be sure that they could. The only thing they could be certain of was that they needed to stop his twin. That was their first priority, above all.

"We wanted to know for sure it was you we were dealing with before we liberated you," John said. "No offence intended. But we had to know you were the man we could trust."

"And how do you know I am?" argued Meridian. "We've met twice now, skipping over centuries, and for less than a day each time. And, as you pointed out, I tried to have Anaximander poison you in Miletus. So why trust me now?"

His face was an open book. This was no subversion, John realized. Meridian really wanted to know.

"We trust you," John said, "because we know the man that you will one day become. Not as friends, really, but not as adversaries. And one of the reasons we're here now, the main reason, really, is that we were told by someone we do believe in that the future's sake depends on the Cartographer. So we will trust in that. And in you."

Meridian stepped between John and Jack, past Chaz, and into the empty corridor. "The Cartographer, you say? I've been called worse, but few have called me better."

"So you'll help us?" Chaz said plaintively. "You'll help us stop your brother?"

"You all have my gratitude," Meridian replied, smiling broadly and nodding. "That should mean something."

Jack quietly closed the door behind them, and it locked with a soft click. Meridian shuddered.

"I think if I'd had to spend one more day confined inside that wretched stone room," he said, with a somewhat restrained tone, "I'd have gone mad. I was grateful that Ptolemy permitted me the materials to continue my work, but I was actually starting to look forward to my own execution, just to escape.

"Now," he finished, rubbing his hands together, "let's deal with Madoc."

With Meridian leading the way, they wound back through the rooms and corridors with greater speed than before. John paced alongside him, asking questions about the rooms they passed, while Jack kept a watchful eye out for other guards, but they moved through undisturbed.

Jack noticed Chaz hanging back, moving more slowly. He seemed to be worrying over something.

"Chaz, what's up?" Jack asked him quietly. "Did you see something that's amiss?"

Chaz glanced ahead at John and Meridian, then gestured for Jack to slow down with him. "It's a couple o' things, really," he said. "F'r one thing, that seemed too easy. Too quick-like."

"I get where you're coming from," Jack retorted, "but I'm not going to complain about something going our way for a change."

"I'm not tryin' t' quiet y'r kettle, Jack, but did that look like a cell to you? Or he, like a man about t' be killed?"

"It was an unusual setting, sure," said Jack, "but Ptolemy wasn't operating on all cylinders either."

"There's summat else, though," Chaz continued. "If he – Meridian – if he does this now, won't it change history even worse?"

"How do you mean worse?"

"If we Bind Madoc now," Chaz said bluntly, "then he might not become the Winter King at all. Ever."

"And that would be a bad thing?"

"Maybe, maybe not," Chaz admitted, "but a lot of good things that happened because of him might never happen either."

Jack realized what Chaz meant. If it hadn't been for the Winter King, John, Jack, and Charles – *their* Charles – might never have met. And if it hadn't been for the events that created Albion, Chaz himself might never have come to be.

"I don't know," Jack said slowly. "It's a risk, certainly. But Jules Verne and Bert both gave their lives so that we could try to do . . . something to stop him. And we're running out of options."

Chaz stared at him for a moment, then nodded grimly and quickened his step to catch up to the others.

Meridian altered the course they took so as not to pass by Ptolemy's workshop. A confrontation with the geographer would only delay them, and might warn Madoc.

"He's here?" John said, startled. "At the library?"

Meridian nodded, his features inscrutable. "He's the other Caretaker of the Sangreal. The only one these past weeks since I was arrested for trying to steal it. It's a fine irony. The one entrusted to the care of the Grail is the very one who tried to take it."

"Madoc tried to steal the Grail?" said Jack. "Then why were you arrested?"

"The three of you are well-educated and seem to know much about my brother and me," Meridian said wryly, "and even you have trouble telling us apart. How much harder is it for that fool Ptolemy?"

"Fool?" John said, furrowing his brow. "I thought he was helping you with your work."

"He's a genius geographer," Meridian replied quickly, "and as an astronomer, he's had some astonishingly astute insights. But as a king, he's a half-full pitcher of stale water."

"So Madoc blamed you for the crime?"

Meridian nodded.

Chaz shook his head in disbelief. "And you were going to just let yourself be executed? For what he did?"

"Hardly," Meridian said with a droll chuckle. "It served my purposes not to disrupt the library more than necessary, and losing him would have done that. And as for myself, I was never in danger."

Jack and John traded sceptical glances, and Meridian laughed and looked at them with a trace of smugness.

"I'm a millennium old," he said. "Don't you suppose that room would only have held me for as long as I wished to be held?"

"Right," Chaz muttered under his breath. He knew bravado when he saw it. And he knew when a truth was whole, and when it was in pieces.

"We're here," Meridian declared. "Hello, Archimedes."

The owl squawked and looked up from his calculations. "Aren't you dead yet, Meridian?"

"I'm not Meridian, I'm Madoc."

"Then who's in there with the Sangreal?" Archimedes asked. "You're not supposed to leave your post."

"That's why my friends and I need to get in," Meridian said. "To do my job."

The bird peered at him with one eye. "How do I know you're not lying?" he asked.

"I always lie," answered Meridian, "except when I tell the truth."

The great bird considered this for a moment, then nodded and walked over to a small opening set in the side wall. He inserted one clawed foot, and the companions heard a lever inside release with a clicking sound. To the bird's right, the door that bore the image of the Grail swung open on mechanized hinges and the companions stepped inside.

"Have a nice day, Madoc," Archimedes said as he returned to his figures.

"See what I mean?" Meridian said. "We used to do that to Anaximander all the time."

"That's an impressive door," John said as it swung closed. "Those mechanisms are remarkable."

"It's a design built by the owl's creator," Meridian said as he pushed open an inner door and ushered them through. "Both were based on a curious device that I sold to him a few centuries ago. That's why it may look familiar to you. I think you called it a 'watch'."

Grinning, Meridian and John stepped into the inner chamber and stopped. Jack and Chaz were already inside, and at a loss as to what they should do next.

It was a large dome, with a massive fireplace opposite the doors, which provided both heat and light. Pillars placed through the room supported high arches, and there were two sets of stairs that presumably led to other rooms. All along the walls were pictographs showing points of recent history, a story in pictures of the Christian myth, and below them, various objects that were likely other talismans related to the Grail.

As to the Grail itself, there were several cups and saucers on the low wall that ringed the room. It wasn't readily apparent which, if any, was the true Grail. But none of the companions were focused on any of that. Instead they were transfixed by the sight of the couple sleeping on the blankets and mats that lay in the middle of the floor, as if the Grail room was nothing more than an elaborate bedchamber.

"Brother," Meridian said softly. "What . . . have . . . you . . . *done?*"

At once Madoc was awake. He was startled to see his brother – and the entourage he'd brought with him.

"Meridian!" he exclaimed. "What are you—"

His sentence remained unfinished as the girl, perhaps twenty years old, if that, suddenly awoke and pulled the cloak they'd used as a blanket over herself in fear. She had dark hair, skin that glistened, and eyes that were clear and focused.

"I can explain," Madoc began, rising.

"No need," Meridian said, taking a spear from the wall closest to him. "I now know all that I need to."

"Jack!" John exclaimed, realizing the Cartographer's intentions. "We can't let him kill Madoc!"

Before any of them could move, Meridian lunged at his brother with the spear. He missed, but only just.

The girl leaped to her feet, crying out in fear, and Madoc placed himself between her and Meridian. "Don't do this!" he implored. "You don't realize what you're doing!"

"Wrong," Meridian answered. "I know exactly what I must do."

Jack and John grabbed him, and they were surprised to realize that they could barely hold him. His strength was astonishing. "Meridian!" John shouted. "We can't risk killing him! Bind him! Then we can decide what to do!"

The Cartographer nodded and cast aside the spear.

Madoc turned to the girl, who was pulling away from him, screaming in terror now. He clutched at her robe, which tore in his hands as she ran from him, tears streaming.

"Please!" Madoc cried to her, imploring. "I'm sorry! Forgive me! Please!"

But no answer was forthcoming, and she disappeared through a second doorway at the other end of the chamber. Voices and footsteps could be heard coming from the other rooms. Her screams had alerted the library that something was amiss.

"We're about to have company," Chaz said grimly. "We got t' hurry."

Meridian leaped forward and knocked his twin to the floor, then spun him about. He held Madoc down, pinning his brother's shoulders with his knees. Meridian bit down hard on his thumb, then marked Madoc's forehead with his blood. And then he began to speak the words:

Madoc, son of Odysseus
By right and rule
For need of might

I thus bind thee
I thus bind thee

By blood bound
By honour given
I thus bind thee
I thus bind thee

For strength and speed and heaven's power
By ancient claim in this dark hour
I thus bind thee
I thus bind thee.

As Meridian finished speaking, both brothers screamed and convulsed, spines arching, as if they'd received a tremendous shock. Panting, Meridian rolled away from his brother and staggered to his feet.

"You are thus Bound, Madoc," he rasped. "By blood, and by the Old Magic, I have Bound you. And I command you . . ." He stopped and looked hesitatingly at John. It was the question none of them had any answer to. How, even Bound, could Madoc be stopped without simply killing him?

Suddenly Meridian's eyes glittered, and he turned back to his brother, who was still struggling to rise to his feet.

"Madoc, duly Bound," said Meridian, "I command you to go to the very ends of the known world, there to stay until you are summoned again, by blood."

Madoc looked stricken. For a brief instant, John actually felt compassion for him. This man still had no realization of what was happening to him, of what had been done to him – and of what fate his own twin brother had just sentenced him to.

Madoc stood shakily and reached a hand out to his brother. "I'm to be exiled?" he said pleadingly. "Again? But I don't . . . I don't . . . When?" he asked. "When will you summon me back?"

But Meridian didn't answer. He turned his back on Madoc and gave a grim smile and a brief nod to the companions. Then, without another word, he ran from the room and disappeared.

Chapter Fourteen
The Sword of Aeneas

Madoc simply stood there, looking at John, Jack, and Chaz with a stricken expression.

"I know you," he said in wonderment. "We have met before."

"Yes," John said, feeling a strong twinge of compassion that he had to fight to keep down. "And for what it's worth . . . we're . . . I – I'm sorry, Madoc."

Jack's mouth dropped open, and Chaz just looked at the others as if they were all insane. But Madoc stared back at John with that same plaintive expression. He really didn't understand what had happened.

"Why?" he asked.

"Because of who you will become," Jack said bluntly. "You needed to be Bound."

"That's not what I was asking," Madoc replied, looking over his shoulder. "Why did Meridian do that? Why did he use Old Magic on me?"

"To protect the Grail," Jack said, "and the rest of the world."

Madoc's demeanour was so confusing to them that Jack, and even Chaz, were beginning to soften.

"Protect the Grail?" Madoc said, clearly perplexed. "That doesn't make any sense."

There ... was a black sword in a scabbard, covered in the dust ...

Before they could press the matter further, a group of librarians, armed with swords and daggers, swarmed down one of the stairways. There were obviously other entrances than the one the companions had come through.

The foremost of them scanned the room, barely noticing the companions, then fixed his glare on Madoc. "The Grail is taken!" he shouted. "Hold them! Hold them all!"

With no warning, a flame exploded in the centre of the room, dividing it neatly between the companions and Madoc on one side, and the librarians on the other.

Madoc took one step, then spun about as if he were on a tether. The Binding was good, and he'd be compelled to do as he was commanded. He bent and scooped up the spear, then ran from the room. As he went, his eyes locked with John's, and the Caretaker was stunned to see there was no anger in his expression – only hurt and sorrow.

The fire had caught several floor coverings alight and was threatening the pillars as well.

"This way!" Jack shouted to the others. He led them up another stairway and out of the Grail chamber. The passageway curved around and brought them back to the entrance, where Archimedes was already sounding an alarm.

Jack didn't even pause as he exited, but rounded the corner at full speed and headed back to the main chambers of the library.

"That was lucky for us," John panted as they ran. "Talk about an opportune moment for spontaneous combustion!"

"It weren't luck," Chaz said, opening his jacket to reveal a small cache of cylinders. "I brought my flash-bangs with me in case they were needed, and it seems they were!"

John stopped, aghast, as did Jack still ahead of them.

"You did that on *purpose?*" Jack said, spluttering in anger and confusion. "Why, Chaz?"

"A distraction," Chaz said, completely baffled as to why they weren't delighted that he'd sidetracked their pursuers. "I thought you'd be happy!"

"Happy!" exclaimed Jack. "You fool – you've just set fire to the Library of Alexandria!"

Chaz scowled, still uncertain why escaping with their lives was a bad thing. John swore silently, and they all started to run again.

"Never mind," John said to Chaz. "We did what we needed to. That's what matters most."

"You know," Jack remarked, considering, "Charles is going to be mortified."

Chaz reared back. "Charles? Why would he be mortified? This is my fault."

"I know," Jack replied. "But all he's going to care about is that he seems to keep setting fire to places, whichever timeline he's in."

As they turned a corner in the main corridor, the companions passed Ptolemy, who was dashing in the other direction. He paused slightly, looking at them through narrowed eyes, as if he suspected that they'd been the instigators of the inferno, but then he turned away and kept running. John, to his great relief, had noted that the geographer had been carrying both *Geographicas* – his own as well as Meridian's.

Another one of the librarians, who had been first in the Grail chamber, stopped the king.

"It's too late!" he exclaimed, mouth agape with fear and astonishment. "The Sangreal is lost!"

"What are you talking about, Pelles?" Ptolemy answered. "Lost how?"

"A great winged beast!" Pelles cried. "It took the Sangreal into the air and away from the library!"

"No time for stories," Ptolemy said, "just because you've failed in your duties! Send word to the son of Arimathea, and take what you can to Glastonbury.

"The library," the geographer went on, "is finished."

Reaching one of the main repositories, the two Caretakers and the hapless former thief grabbed some large wicker baskets in both hands and began to shovel scrolls of parchment into them.

"Hurry!" Jack implored the others. "We have to save as many as we can!"

"It's going up too quickly," John said, scanning the rafters of the room, which were already pouring with smoke. "We can't do enough. The Histories said that the most essential works were saved. We'll just have to trust that they will be."

Reluctantly the others agreed. They dropped the baskets and headed for the portal.

All the librarians and various scholars were running in every direction, mostly away from the flames. As the companions passed the doorway to the Grail chamber, they noticed that Archimedes was no longer at his post.

"Smart old owl," Chaz remarked drolly as they turned the corner and headed for the projection.

Chaz passed through first, with Jack close on his heels. John paused at the wall and turned to look at the Grail on the door, now cracked.

Meridian was gone, to who knew where. Madoc was Bound, and banished. It had not even occurred to John that banishment could be done. If he was truly exiled to the ends of the Earth, then perhaps that was enough. Perhaps.

He tried not to think about the fact that at the moment Meridian had spoken the Binding, he had considered just killing Madoc. And he tried not to think about how relieved he'd felt when, with the banishment, he realized he might not have to.

And all it had taken was convincing the brother they trusted that he had to betray the one they didn't.

He hoped they had done enough.

John closed his eyes to the flames as they enveloped the image of the Grail, and he turned and stepped through the portal.

After receiving much more attention than he was comfortable getting, Hugo decided to camouflage himself as best as he could by donning Hank Morgan's helmet and gauntlets. After five minutes of wearing the incredibly heavy, stiflingly hot, and impossibly ill-fitting pieces of armour, he took them off and was immediately accosted by a small band of lithe, well-armed men. Or at least, he assumed they were men – they cursed like men and were dressed like others he'd seen on the field. But when he looked closely, he noticed that their ears were pointed, and they had only four fingers. And while they knocked him about, more for sport than anything else, he thought he heard them refer to each other as "elves".

He quickly replaced the helmet and gauntlets, and the elves, laughing, moved on. Hugo sighed heavily and looked around for Hank, who had at least seemed to be genial, if not a friend. Even Pellinor would be a welcome sight.

Still, Hugo had time to think. Hank had mentioned having been sent here by a Caretaker of the *Imaginarium Geographica* . . . Samuel Clemens. It took a moment for Hugo to remember why that name was familiar, and then he recalled it. The American writer. The one who wrote of riverboats, and slavery, and Adam and Eve . . . That fellow had been a Caretaker, as John and Jack claimed to be?

But wasn't Clemens also dead?

"Sam says hello," Hank said as he dropped down to sit next to Hugo. "Aren't those hot?" he asked, indicating the helmet and gauntlets.

"Terribly so, yes," Hugo replied, removing the armour. "But it seems unless I look a bit more the part of the knight-at-arms, I'm a target for mischief and harassment."

"The elves, I'll bet," Hank guessed, looking over the helmet. "There's a compact not to engage in any fighting until the actual start of the tournament, but that only applies to the champions here to compete – mostly knights and would-be kings. The elves are notorious for skirting the rules. They think they're better than everyone else, mostly because they live impossibly long lives. I think they're a bunch of pansies, myself."

"But you said you weren't here to compete," said Hugo. "So why did you come dressed as a knight?"

"Simple," Hank answered as he put on the helmet. "So I wouldn't be kicked around by a bunch of pansy elves."

◆　　◆　　◆

Hank led Hugo around the outskirts of the field to a small campsite, where they could talk undisturbed. Like all the other arrivals to the tournament, Hank had erected a banner in front. It was a long, tapering pennant with a blue and red circular design in the centre and the words GO CUBS! on both sides.

"Interesting," said Hugo. "What does it mean?"

"It was a gift from Sam," Hank explained as they entered the tent. "He said it used to represent Triumph over Adversity, but now better represents Impossible Quests and Lost Causes."

"I think I preferred not knowing that," said Hugo.

Hank grinned. "You're a Sox fan too, hey?"

In the relative privacy of Hank's camp, they were able to talk more freely, so Hugo related everything that had happened since the walk at Magdalen, and also about the dinner, and the mysterious Grail book. And he asked a torrent of questions along the way.

"I don't know that much about it myself," Hank said in response to Hugo's inquiry about the *Imaginarium Geographica*. "I know a little, thanks to Sam. But there's a fellow here who might be helpful. All the maps in here are his, as a matter of fact." He swept his arm across the interior of the tent.

Hugo had at first assumed that the stacks were fabric of some kind, or bundles of supplies for the tournament. But looking at them more closely, he could see that they were dozens of carefully drawn maps.

"I daresay he might be able to help, at that," said Hugo. "Did he make these all himself?"

"I haven't asked," Hank replied. "Didn't feel it was my business. But they are the first thing unpacked at every stop, and he handles them as if they're gold. After what you've explained to me, I half wonder if they aren't part of the reason I was sent here to watch him."

"Is he a knight or a king?" asked Hugo.

"Both and neither," Hank said, "but you know of him by reputation alone, if nothing else."

"That is either a charitable description of me, Sir Henry," a stolid, commanding voice said, "or a condemnation. And today I cannot say which I deserve more." A gloved hand parted the opening of the tent, flooding it with light, and a man, shorter than Hank but stouter than Hugo, stepped inside.

"Hugo Dyson," Hank said, rising and bowing deferentially to the new arrival, "I'd like you to meet Merlin, Lord of Albion."

Merlin was dressed formally but practically. His breeches and tunic were elegantly made, but of leather, studded throughout with iron. Not clothes for court, but for combat. He wore a headband, and his hair draped to his shoulders, flowing over the top of a cape that was fastened at his shoulders.

It occurred to Hugo that Merlin's eyes showed a flash of recognition when he entered, but on reflection, that was probably more of a reaction to Hugo's strange clothes.

"So," Merlin said. "You know who I am?"

"I know what I've read of you, ah, sir," Hugo stammered. "You're a very great man."

Merlin didn't react to the compliment, except to frown and raise an eyebrow.

"What I mean is that you are a legend," Hugo said quickly. "Everyone knows you."

"Really," Merlin replied, still unsure what Hugo was complimenting him for. "Would you say I'm a myth, then?"

It was Hugo's turn to look confused. "I might have yesterday," he said, "but I hadn't met you then."

Merlin burst into laughter. "Well met, then, Hugo Dyson," he said, handing a parcel to Hank. "You should find the rest of the day's events very enlightening."

With that, he turned and left the tent.

"Drat," said Hugo. "I should have asked for his autograph." He looked at the tent opening, then back at Hank. "Does he know about . . . ?" He pointed delicately.

"About me?" Hank exclaimed. "Where and when I'm really from? I doubt it. I made up a story when I first got here, which I'm pretty certain he saw right through. But I've been helpful to him, and loyal. So he doesn't press the matter."

"And you're here at the behest of Sam Clemens?"

"His and that of his former apprentice, a Frenchman called Verne. Do you know him?"

Hugo shook his head. "Not personally."

"Well," Hank continued, "he's the one who worked out a lot of the underlying principles behind time travel and zero points."

"Uh, zero points?" asked Hugo.

"The points in history that allow travel, or at least communication, in the case of the lesser points. There was a good one about fourteen years before your prime time that I was able to use to send a message to Verne. I don't know what it was that happened then, but it must have seemed like the end of the world."

"One or the other," Hugo said, "from what I've been told. So," he continued earnestly, "this message you sent. Will it allow Verne to fix whatever it is that happened to me at Addison's Walk?"

Hank shrugged. "I don't know. When you showed up, I thought I'd better let someone know. Mistakes like that usually aren't mistakes at all."

"You think someone deliberately arranged for me to come here?" asked Hugo.

"I do, and what's more," Hank said, checking the silver watch, "so does Sam. You're to stay here, at least for now."

Hugo was aghast. "But why? Isn't there some sort of . . . I don't know, time machine they can use to whisk me back to Magdalen?"

Hank gave a wry chuckle and scratched his neck. "It doesn't quite work that way. I'm still a novice, a foot soldier, if you will. But even I know you aren't supposed to mess around with time by traipsing to and fro."

"But you're here," Hugo protested. "Isn't that meddling?"

"No," said Hank. "I'm here in part because one of the Caretakers' Histories said I was. So I was meant to be here. You weren't."

"But don't you see," Hugo declared, having suddenly realized something. "I was. I was meant to be here. Or else how do we explain the Grail book that I supposedly wrote in?"

Hank stared back at him, puzzled. "That *is* a good question," he said, removing the silver watch again. "I'd better—"

Before he could finish speaking, the watch emitted a high-pitched squeal and began to spark, then smoke. Hank shook it, then held it to his ear. It had stopped ticking.

"That looks bad," said Hugo.

Hank bit his lip, thinking, then replaced the watch in the secret pocket. "Come on," he said, standing. "Let's see where this goes. It's high noon – the tournament is about to begin, and Merlin will be looking for me."

Hank loaned Hugo a cloak and spare helmet, which they hoped would lend just enough camouflage to the professor's appearance that he could move about more freely. It worked for the most part – although the elves kept pointing at him to get his attention, then making rude gestures.

"I'm starting to warm to the opportunity I've been given to have this adventure," Hugo said dryly, "but if I never see another cursed elf, it'll be too soon."

The tournament was centred not at the great stone table, as Hugo assumed it would be, but around a field to the west of it. There a great tent had been erected facing a low hill, on which they could see a few crumbling walls that marked rough boundaries around a shallow depression.

The participants had assembled around the front of the tent, waiting for the announcement and a proclamation of the rules.

"Taliesin's tent," Hank murmured as they approached. "Hang back a bit, so we can watch. We don't want to get too wrapped up in events. No telling what could happen if we get involved in something by accident."

Hugo was more than willing to keep a comfortable distance. He'd realized with an alarming clarity that these knights assembled here were not the same as those he'd read about in the great medieval romances. These were warriors; battle-hardened and less likely to be chivalrous than they were to be actors in a play. What's more, he wasn't certain that all of those at the gathering were even human.

There was movement at the rear of Taliesin's tent, and Hugo

saw Merlin exit from a flap in the tent, and then walk around to the back of the hill. A few moments later he reappeared at the crest of the hill and strode down into the assemblage.

"What a show-off," Hank whispered, scribbling in his notebook. "He was up there just so he could arrive last and appear to have come down to everyone else's level."

Merlin passed easily through the crowd, which parted to let him through. Apparently his reputation had preceded him. He took a position not far from the front of the tent and crossed his arms, waiting.

He didn't have to wait long. The front of the tent opened and Taliesin appeared. He was tall, bearded, and greying at the temples. He wore a simple tunic, leather breeches, and tall leather boots. There were feathers in his hair, which was swept back and grew long, almost to his waist in back.

Taliesin carried a black staff carved with runes, which seemed to glow faintly, even in the daylight. He walked to the base of the hill, then turned to address the gathering.

"I am Taliesin, called the Lawgiver," he began, his voice low but commanding in tone. "Hear my words, all ye who have been summoned.

"We have come here, to the place where once, long ago, the man called Camaalis earned for himself the mantle of king of Albion and ruled this land as his stewardship. Here he built his first castle, called after his name, and here he died and was forgotten.

"What was lost to history, and forgotten by men, is that he was to be the ruler of two worlds – both this land we know, and another, in the Unknown Region."

"The Archipelago?" Hugo whispered.

"I think so," Hank replied, writing. "This is very intriguing."

Taliesin went on. "Others have ruled parts of these lands since, but never the whole, and never the lands beyond. Those who had appointed Camaalis withdrew the knowledge and the means, until another, one worthy to rule, could be chosen.

"If there is no authority to rule, no chosen leader acknowledged by all, only a group of 'nobles' willing to destroy the land in order to wrest control of it, then the lands beyond will also remain forever apart.

"This is why the tournament has been called. To re-establish the lineage of the authority to rule. The lineage that began with the gods of myth and passed through their heirs – the heroes of the Trojan War.

"Aeneas, one of the great heroes of antiquity, possessed a great sword. When the walls of Troy finally fell, his grandson, Brutus, smuggled it away from those who would use it to further their own ends.

"He sailed far away, taking with him the sword and those who had managed to escape from the marauding Greek armies. He came here, to the island called Myrddyn's Precinct, where he founded a settlement called Troia Nova."

"Troia Nova," Hugo whispered. "New Troy, then . . . It eventually became Trinovantum, then Londinium, didn't it?"

Hank didn't hear the question. "Did he say Myrddyn's Precinct?" he asked instead. "That's rather ominous, don't you think?"

"There was another hero of the Trojan war," continued Taliesin, "called Odysseus, who had a bow that could not be drawn except by the true king. That promise and curse protected his homeland of Ithaka for generations. And the same promise and curse, passed down through the lineage of Aeneas, will protect those who would unite and rule the world – beginning here, in Myrddyn's Precinct, at the place where Camaalis was buried."

Taliesin moved aside, and for the first time Hugo and Hank could see what was in the depression on the hill.

It was a stone block, which bore the mark of the Greek letter *alpha*. It was, Hugo realized, the topmost stone of a crypt.

At Taliesin's signal, several burly men moved forward, grasped the sides of the great stone block, and slowly moved it aside. Underneath, set into the hillside, was a stone box. One of the knights removed the topmost stone and set it aside.

There, lying in state, was a black sword in a scabbard, covered in the dust of the first great king of the land.

"Caliburn," the Lawgiver proclaimed, pointing down at the crypt. "The sword of Aeneas.

"Whosoever is able to draw the sword from its sheath shall henceforth be the High King of all the lands that are. So say we all?"

The question was answered with a thundering shout, which only grew louder and louder as the seconds passed, until Hugo thought he would go deaf from the noise of it. Finally the whoops and hollers died down, and the Lawgiver Taliesin spoke once more.

"The Tournament of Champions is begun."

"I came from high in the mountains, where it is still winter . . ."

CHAPTER FIFTEEN

The Stripling Warrior

Uncas, Fred, and Reynard clustered around John, Jack, and Chaz as they stepped back through the projection.

"Is everything all right, Scowler John?" Uncas asked worriedly. "You've only been gone about ten hours."

"Fine, Uncas," John reassured him. "Reynard? Shut down the projection, quickly!"

The fox swiftly moved over to the Lanterna Magica and flipped the switch. Immediately the lamp went dark and the slide vanished from the wall, and with it the conflagration in the library.

"Thanks," said Jack, sitting in a chair and slumping over the back. "I don't think I could bear to watch."

"I was more worried about Sanctuary," John said, taking one of the other chairs. "If we could pass through, other things might be able to also. And it won't be too long before the wall we came through is on fire itself."

Only Chaz was still standing at the wall. He was touching his chest and arms, as if confirming his own solidity.

"Mister Chaz?" said Fred. "Are you all right?"

"Did we do it?" Chaz asked hesitantly. "Did we change the world?"

Fred looked at Uncas, who looked at Reynard, who shook his head. "There is no difference outside, if that's what you're asking," the fox said. "The king, Mordred, still rules over Albion, and the giants still come by every hour or so to throw stones in the harbour."

"I really hate those creatures," muttered Jack.

"I think the feeling is reciprocated," said Reynard. "At one point they were offering to tell the king the rest of your companions were dead if they'd just give *you* up."

Jack swallowed hard and managed a weak smile.

"Don't worry, Scowler Jack," Uncas said, patting him on the knee. "We told 'em we'd just as soon do you in ourselves."

"Thanks, Uncas."

Chaz exploded. "So what good did we do?" he exclaimed, waving his arms in frustration. "We found his true name! And we convinced the other one t' Bind him! And it didn't change anything at all!"

"We've only done half the task," John reminded him. "Our friend Hugo is still trapped somewhere in the sixth century, and that's what caused England to become Albion. When we confronted Madoc, and Meridian Bound him, it was only the second century. So obviously something still happens four hundred years later that we have to prevent."

"And how are we supposed to do that?" asked Jack.

"There are three more slides," Reynard reminded them. "I do not think the Prime Caretaker would have left them as mere redundancies. I think each one may have a purpose in and of itself."

Fred nodded enthusiastically. "I agree. Each time you've gone through a portal, you've come back with something you needed to know."

"That's true," Jack agreed. "The trip to Miletus revealed that Mordred and the Cartographer were brothers, and the second, to Alexandria, allowed us to tell Meridian how to Bind his brother."

"Curious, though," John pondered. "He already knew the words to do it. I think he just never would have done it if we hadn't provided the motivation."

"He needed t' know," said Chaz. "He needed t' know what his brother would one day become. And there was no one else t' tell him but us."

"So what now, John?" asked Jack. "I don't think we can handle another jaunt right away. I'm exhausted."

Chaz, already dozing, snored in agreement.

John looked to Reynard. "If we take a short nap and regain a bit of vigour, do you think the giants will cause trouble?"

The fox shook his head. "They can disturb and harass, and they may be able to damage your ship in the harbour by throwing stones. But I think it will be safe enough for you to remain, for a short while."

"Good," John replied, already stretching out on the floor. "I feel like I haven't slept in centuries."

After a few hours, Uncas and Fred regretfully roused the companions. "Sorry t' wake you, Scowlers," said Uncas, "but the giants have rallied."

John groaned and stretched, and Jack rose, looking around the room. His face fell when he saw the burlap bag in the corner, untouched as they had left it.

"Damn and double-damn," he breathed. "I'd really hoped that I dreamed that part."

Chaz jumped to his feet. The brief sleep seemed to have recharged him fully. "So what is the plan?"

John was examining the packs that the badgers had prepared for them. There were rations of food, and containers of fresh water, along with two other items: the Serendipity Box and the Little Whatsit.

"The latter is for any emergencies what may arise," explained Uncas, "an' the former, for when you're well an' truly up t' your necks in it. Just in case."

"I already used the Box," John said.

"I know," said Uncas, "but they haven't."

The badger was right. According to Bert, they could each use it once, and Jack and Chaz hadn't touched it yet.

Before John could ask anything else, they were interrupted by a tremendous crash from outside. There was a cacophony of howls, and what sounded like pounding surf, and worse, the laughter of giants.

Fred indicated to the others that they should remain in the projection room, and he rushed out the door.

A few seconds later he reappeared, helping Reynard, who was limping and bleeding badly from a gash in his skull that had nearly cost him an ear.

The companions hurried over to the wounded fox. "What's happened, Reynard?" John asked, concern etched on his face. "Are you all right?"

"I shall live," Reynard replied, "but you have suffered a loss, I am sorry to say."

"What loss?" asked Jack.

"Your ship," Reynard said, still in shock. "The *Red Dragon*. The giants have succeeded in destroying her. She's gone, shattered, sunk."

So that was it, John realized. The *Red Dragon* had been their only means of escape from Noble's Isle. Whatever success they were to have in defeating Mordred would now only be found inside the slides left for them by Jules Verne.

"Uncas," John instructed, "fire up the Lanterna Magica. We're running out of time."

The third slide showed a grassy hilltop, on what seemed to be a summer day. There was a single tall oak tree at the crest of the hill, and underneath, a young man, barely more than a boy, sleeping peacefully.

"Do you know who it is?" Chaz asked the others. "He's too young to be Meridian or Madoc."

John shook his head, as did Jack. "Not a clue, I'm afraid," Jack said, "but I mean to find out."

The three companions said their goodbyes to the badgers, and thanked the injured fox for his attempts to protect their ship. Then, Chaz leading this time, they stepped into the projection.

Unlike the previous slides, which had opened into cities on the sides of walls, this one opened a portal into open air. The three men moved quickly through the gossamer layers and turned around to look at the odd phenomenon.

"Strange, isn't it?" said Jack. "It's a bit like the door in the wood, John. There's no back side to it when you come around the other side."

"At least this one isn't going to close on us," John replied. "We'll have to remember it's to the east of the tree when we return."

There was nothing else in sight, save for miles of rolling hills and clusters of trees. No buildings, no structures of any kind, as far as they could see. Just the tall oak and the sleeping boy.

He was dressed heavily, with a cloak over his tunic and shirt, and his boots were fur. He'd come from some land that was colder than this, wherever they were.

"It's England, of course," said Jack. "Can't you tell by the light?"

"If you say so," John said, unconvinced. "Shall we wake him up? He's obviously the reason Verne had us come here."

The others agreed, and John reached down and shook the boy's shoulder once, then again. Finally the boy opened his eyes and gave them a half-awake smile. "It's about time," he said, sitting up. "I'd begun to think you would never get here."

His speech was a mix of Gaelic and Old English, but it was not difficult for John and Jack to understand. Chaz couldn't quite make it out, but he seemed to get the gist of it. The boy had been waiting for them.

"You were expecting us?" John said in surprise, offering the boy a hand up.

The boy rose to his feet and dusted himself off. "I was expecting . . . someone," he replied. "I blew the horn almost an hour ago."

He showed them a curved, golden horn that had Greek letters etched into the sides. "My mother gave it to me," he explained, "and said to use it only in a time of great peril."

Jack looked around at the countryside, which seemed empty

of life, save for a few mice on the hill and a distant bird, circling in the sky. "Peril?" he asked. "Did we miss it?"

The boy reddened. "I know. I must seem a fool for using it so lightly. But I lost my way, and I'm out of food and have little water, and I didn't think I could hold out much longer just wandering around."

"How long have you been travelling?"

"A month," the boy answered. "I came from high in the mountains, where it is still winter, riding hard. I had to abandon my horse when I crossed the water, and I've been walking for several days now. Then today I decided to use the horn. I'm already late, and if I arrive too weak from hunger and thirst, then I'll have no chance at all in the tournament."

"What tournament?" asked Jack. "Where are you going?"

"The tournament at Camelot," the boy said, "to choose the High King of this world and of the Unknown Region."

The companions looked at each other in astonishment.

"What's your name, lad?" asked John.

"I'm called Thorn," the boy said. "Have you got anything to eat?"

They opened up the packs prepared for them by the badgers and held off asking anything further while Thorn tucked into the food and drink. John stood a few feet away, watching, while Chaz busied himself reading the Little Whatsit to see if there were any language translation aids to be found there.

Jack walked around the other side of the tree, watching Chaz with an odd expression. "Do you get the impression," he said to John, "that the Chaz we've ended up with isn't the one we started with?"

"I know what you mean," John replied, looking over his shoulder at the former thief and self-confessed traitor, who had become completely absorbed in reading the badgers' handbook. "At first I thought it was just that he had a knack for languages. He is a chosen Caretaker, after all. He had the aptitude, even if he's from a timeline where he never became the educated man we know. But it's more than just remembering Greek, or being able to translate it, then speak it, after only *days* among the native speakers. He isn't struggling – he's *fluent*. He's . . . he's . . . *changing*, isn't he? Almost like . . ."

"Almost like he's becoming a lot like another scowler we know and respect?" said Jack.

"Something like that."

"How can that be?" asked Jack. "Isn't it a different world altogether? He can't be our Charles."

"It wasn't a different world for Bert," John replied. "He was, in many ways, 'our' Bert – at least he claimed to be. Maybe, in some small way, this is still 'our' Charles."

"Hey," Chaz called out, marking a page in the Little Whatsit. "I think I finally found a place that sounds worse than Albion. According to th' book, it's called 'Cambridge.'"

It was a full minute before John and Jack could stop laughing.

"I don't get it," said Chaz.

"Uncas will explain it to you later," John told him.

"Well," Jack said, looking at their empty satchels and drained flagon, "so much for our provisions."

"We haven't even been here an hour," John replied, "and we aren't even sure what we're supposed to do. Why don't you just go back into Sanctuary and restock? That way we'll be prepared for anything and won't go hungry later."

"Good idea," Jack answered, gathering up the bags and heading around the hill. "I'll be right back."

"Is Sanctuary where I summoned you from?" asked Thorn. "When I blew Bran Galed's horn?"

"We weren't summoned," John said. "It was just a coincidence that we came when we did."

"Really?" said Thorn. "What did you come here for?"

Before John could explain, Jack came running up to the tree, a panicked expression on his face.

John took his arm. "What is it? Are the badgers all right?"

"I don't know!" Jack exclaimed. "I didn't have the chance to look!"

"Why not?"

"The portal!" Jack said with rising terror in his voice. "It's gone! We can't get back!"

The tournament had gone forward in a spectacular fashion, overseen by the Lawgiver. There had been contests of not only physical prowess, but of intellect.

"Merlin nicknamed it 'Heart, Hand, and Head,'" Hank told Hugo. "Apparently, the contests are based on a series of trials once used in competitions at Alexandria."

"Like the Gordian knot?" asked Hugo.

"Something like that," Hank answered.

The contests went on throughout the day, and more than half of the hundred or so who had come to compete were eliminated. There were very few life-threatening injuries, and no deaths whatsoever.

"It was the one condition Taliesin insisted on," said Hank. "First blood only. No deaths."

"That's rather civilized," said Hugo.

"You can say that because you're not being stabbed," Hank chortled. "As Sam used to say, 'It's all fun and games until someone loses an eye.'"

By late afternoon there were only seven left standing who had not been defeated in any of the trials. Taliesin motioned for them to take up positions around the crypt that bore the sword.

"Of all those who have come," the Lawgiver announced, "you seven, kings all, have proven your worth to compete for the honour of serving the peoples of two worlds."

"Eight!" a voice bellowed. Pellinor pushed his way to the front of the gathering, eyes watery and face flushed.

"Cheated! Cheated, I was! I was told the Questing Beast would be here, *here*, when I finished the job I was given! And I was cheated! So I demand my right to draw the black sword and become the High King! It is only fair. There are *eight* great kings here!"

The Lawgiver raised an eyebrow and appraised Pellinor for a long moment, then gestured at the sword. "Fine," he said. "*Eight* great kings. If you believe yourself worthy, try to draw the sword from its scabbard."

Pellinor harrumphed and adjusted his belt as he stepped down into the shallow hole. He looked down at the sword, which was shorter and more stout than he'd imagined it to be. It also wasn't very decorative. The hilt was plain, mostly tarnished silver and steel wrapped in blackened leather, and the scabbard was a match in style and plainness. It was not in appearance the weapon of a king – but that, he figured, could be fixed with some jewels and gold flecking, and probably a new scabbard altogether.

"This should be good," Hank whispered to Hugo.

"Why?" Hugo wondered.

"Because he's doing what everyone told him not to," Hank whispered back. "I've seen this sort of thing in power plants, where some hoity-toity fellow with a degree from a fancy school starts directing the engineers on how to change everything. It usually ends when he insists on touching a cable no one else will go near."

"What happens then?" asked Hugo.

Pellinor bent down and lifted up the sword and scabbard in one swift motion. He held it, smiling triumphantly, then grasped the hilt and attempted to remove the sword – which stayed exactly where it was.

Pellinor's smile faltered, and he redoubled his effort, putting the sword between his legs for leverage and using both hands. Finally, incredibly, the sword shifted one-quarter of an inch within the scabbard.

"Aha!" Pellinor exclaimed. "That's—"

A tremendous bolt of lightning erupted from the sword itself, shooting skyward and filling the valley with thunder. It threw Pellinor out of the hole and about twenty feet into the dust, scorched and smoking.

"*That's* what happens," said Hank, shaking his head.

"Is he alive?" the Lawgiver asked.

One of the knights, who had ducked as Pellinor flew overhead, went over to where he lay and put a blade of grass in front of the old king's nose.

"He's breathing," reported the knight. "For now."

"Well and good," said the Lawgiver. "As I was saying, you seven great kings have proven your worth to compete—"

"To be the High King?" one of the seven bellowed. "To be Pendragon?"

Taliesin nodded and raised his staff.

A cheer went up from the assemblage, and the seven kings all looked at one another, each taking the measure of the others, trying to judge who among them might prevail.

"Tomorrow morning," Taliesin said, "we shall have the final contests. The seven shall draw lots, and then may choose whom to fight in single combat. The last to stand shall then be offered the chance to draw the blade from the scabbard. And if that one succeeds—"

"He shall have one more battle to fight," a harsh voice called out, "unless you are willing to admit me now as one who has the right to vie for the office."

From the eastern side of the hill a black horse sauntered in, and its rider, dressed in equally ebony clothes, dismounted. There were murmurs and growls throughout the crowd, but from two, Taliesin and Merlin, gasps of recognition.

He removed a tall, bull-horned helmet and placed it on the ground, possessively near the crypt. His skin was dark, more from weathering than pigmentation, and his features were lean. He moved with grace and the coiled energy of a serpent, which, Hugo realized, was exactly what he was. A serpent had come into Taliesin's well-ordered garden.

His clothes were unusual but seemed tailored for combat, wrapped tightly around his limbs and loosely around his torso. And as for weapons, he carried only a spear, which in contrast to his dress and manner appeared to be of Roman make.

"I declare my intention to compete. Are there any who would oppose me?" the man asked, looking directly at Merlin.

Taliesin's eyes narrowed, and he looked from the new arrival to Merlin and back again. There seemed to be an unseen struggle taking place in the very air. Finally Merlin nodded to the Lawgiver, almost imperceptibly, and Taliesin turned to the stranger. "What is your name, and by what right have you come here to disrupt this tournament?"

The man smiled coldly, as if he had been waiting for, and hating, that very question.

"I come by right of blood," he said quietly but firmly, in a tone that said he would brook no opposition, "honour-bound, after long exile. And I come because it is I, and I alone, who is worthy to draw Caliburn and become the Arthur – the High King."

"What is your name?" the Lawgiver asked again.

"I've been called many names during a long life," the man replied, "and none have served me well enough to keep. But the people who took me in, whom I have called my own for so many years, called me Mordraut. And that should suffice for this gathering."

"What?" Hank said to Hugo, straining to hear. "What did he say?"

"Mordred," Hugo said, shuddering. "He said his name is Mordred."

For almost an hour, John, Jack, Chaz, and a slightly confused Thorn circled the hill around the oak tree looking for a window in the air that was no longer anywhere to be found. Jack was distraught, and John was concerned. Of the three of them, only Chaz seemed unworried.

"Don't take this the wrong way," he said, tucking the Little

Whatsit under one arm, "but I'm not exac'ly all broken up at the thought of being stuck here. It in't perfect, but it's better than where I was at."

"Nothing's perfect," said Thorn. "I don't think anything is expected to be."

"Then what is expected?" asked Chaz.

"To become better than you are, one day at a time," replied Thorn. "Progression, not perfection, should be the goal."

"That's a very enlightened attitude," John said, clearly impressed. "How did you come by it?"

"From my teacher," said Thorn. "He ought to be coming back anytime now."

"I thought you were here alone," asked John

"I didn't think to mention him," Thorn explained, using his hand to shade his eyes from the sun. "He went off exploring after I used the horn."

"Why am you looking up?" asked Chaz, his Gaelic still rough. "Are. Why *are* you looking up?"

As if in answer to the question, a bird – the one Jack had seen at a distance, he now realized – began to spiral downward towards the oak. Moments later the great bird, an owl, had lit on Thorn's shoulder.

"You three," the owl said scornfully in flawless Old English. "You can listen to the smart one, there," he told Thorn, pointing a claw at Chaz, "but these other two are a bit slow."

"Archimedes," John greeted the owl he'd last seen in Alexandria.

"Of course," the bird replied. "How many other talking owls have you met?"

"Just you, actually," John admitted.

"See what I mean?" the owl said. "Slow."

The bird reacquainted itself with the companions as they told it of recent events, then agreed to assist them in looking for the lost window. But the addition of an extra pair of eyes, even those as sharp as Archimedes', did not help them locate the portal to Sanctuary. Jack was right – it was gone.

"Could it have been the giants?" John asked. "Do you suppose they actually went onto the island?"

"I doubt it," Jack replied. "If they were going to do that, they'd have done it much earlier."

"You came through a door with only one side?" asked Archimedes. "That's very interesting."

"I'd love to show it to you, Archimedes," said John, "but I think we've run our luck dry."

"Not luck," said Thorn. "The will of God."

"What do you mean?" Jack asked. "Which God?"

Thorn looked at him, surprised. "There's only one God, Sir Jack," he said plainly. "I don't know much about him, but I know that he sees all, knows all, and has a reason for everything he does."

"Stranding us in . . . what year is it, anyway?" said Jack.

"It's been approximately four centuries since we first met, at the library," said Archimedes. "If I had a chalk and slate, I could work it out more precisely."

"Great," said Jack. "We're in the sixth century. Do you want me to believe that it's God's will that we're trapped here?"

"You came when I summoned you with the horn," Thorn replied. "How can I think otherwise?"

"We didn't come because of the horn," Jack retorted. "We came to . . . to . . ." He stopped and turned to his fellow scholar. "I don't even know, John. What *are* we here to do?"

"I think," John said, carefully considering his words, "that we were meant to be here, now, to help Thorn get to where he's going."

"It seems we have little choice," said Jack in resignation, casting a look around the hill. "We can't go back. We might as well go forward."

"That's very astute," said Archimedes. "One might think you were an educated man."

"I've got an entire section here on Camelot," Chaz said, pointing to the Little Whatsit. "There are a few passages on tournaments and the like, but along with those are some general directions. We should be able to get Thorn where he needs t' be without much trouble."

"It doesn't help us to know where we're going, if we don't know where we're starting from," John said in a slightly officious voice. "It's one of the first things I learned watching over the *Geographica*."

Chaz blinked. "And . . . ?"

"And Thorn was already lost, and we have no way of telling where we are."

"Sure we do," Chaz insisted, pointing at the book. "We're at Grandfather Oak. See? There's a picture."

Sure enough, there was an engraving of the tree that stood next to them.

"That's insane," Jack stated. "Why would that book have a picture of this tree, of all things?"

"It seems to be an important place," said Chaz. "According to the Whatsit, it's where someone called Arthur first met the knights of the Crusade, on the day before he became the High King."

It took a few moments for the full meaning of the words Chaz read to sink in. When they finally did, John and Jack turned to look at Thorn. "Is that true?" John asked slowly. "Are you Arthur?"

"Not yet," Thorn answered, "but I hope to be, soon."

One by one . . . six opponents fell before Mordred . . .

Chapter Sixteen
The Crucible

Chaz led the way, with a conversational Archimedes circling low above his head. John, Jack, and Thorn followed closely behind, talking.

Thorn explained that Arthur was not a name in and of itself but a title of rule, and that it essentially meant "High King."

"High King of Britain?" asked Jack.

"You mean this land here?" Thorn replied. "I've not heard it called that before. It is called Albion by some, but most call it Myrddyn's Precinct. But," he added in a conspiratorial whisper, "I'm not allowed to know that."

"Why?" asked John.

"My mother would behead Archimedes if she knew he'd told me," Thorn replied, seemingly unwilling to elaborate.

John already knew the land had once been called Myrddyn's Precinct. But that was before he'd discovered who Myrddyn was. Apparently, in the four centuries since Alexandria, the Cartographer had been busy.

"Archimedes found out about the tournament," Thorn was saying, "and he convinced me that I needed to come and participate. I was against it at first."

"Against the chance to be king?" asked Jack.

"Against the need to fight for it," said Thorn. "As I understand it, the office of Arthur is to go to someone who is worthy to serve the people of the lands. I didn't understand why there needed to be a competition to find such a person."

"You don't worry that someone less worthy might take the title?" John wondered.

"Why would they?" Thorn replied. "What's the point of being in charge of the world if you don't want to help people? Hey!" he exclaimed, running ahead. "Chaz! Race you to the stone!"

"He's a good man," John said as they watched him race with their companion to a large stone up ahead. "Isn't he?"

"Yes," Jack agreed. "He's going to get slaughtered tomorrow."

As night began to fall, the companions built a small fire in the lee of the stone and set up a makeshift campsite around it. Archimedes turned out to be an excellent night watchman, and an even better cook. Using recipes Chaz found in the Little Whatsit, they gathered roots and herbs from the shrubbery and used the last flagon of water and one of Reynard's bottles to make a soup. It was thin, but tasty and warming.

With Archimedes standing guard, Thorn and Chaz soon fell asleep, but John and Jack stayed awake, talking.

"When the owl told us we were in the sixth century," John began, "I thought maybe . . ."

"Hugo would be somewhere nearby?" Jack finished. "So did I. But even if he is here, how are we going to get him back? The portal is gone."

"I know," said John, "but I'm hoping there will be another way back. We never did find out what happened to the door from the Keep."

"True, that," Jack agreed. "This Thorn is an interesting boy."

John nodded, a shadow against the stone. "He might really be Arthur – and I rather like the idea that we're to be remembered as knights of the Crusades."

"We will be," said Jack, "as long as we've got here soon enough to prevent whatever it is that Hugo did to create Albion."

"Don't worry about that now," John told him, settling down to try to sleep. "Plenty of time for that tomorrow."

It was a clear statement of intent that Mordred set up his camp not around the basin of the valley, as everyone else had, but on top of the hill, adjacent to the stone table and facing the crypt of Caliburn.

There had been some fighting among the knights and nobles, particularly those who had been eliminated earliest, but it never amounted to a formal protest, much less an outright rebellion.

The assent of the Lawgiver was enough to persuade most of them that there was in fact something substantial to the claims of the mysterious new arrival.

The look on Mordred's face was enough to convince the rest.

The fires were lit, and venison was roasted as the dinner celebrations began. It was more civilized than Hugo expected, but still more raw and primal than he was prepared for, so he and Hank retreated to their own camp to sup and discuss the day's events.

"Mordred," Hugo repeated for perhaps the hundredth time.

"That's amazing to me. Did you see how he silenced the crowd with little more than bravado?"

"More charisma than bravado, I'd say," Hank replied as he crouched over the small fire, stirring the stew he'd prepared for dinner. "He certainly has some kind of history with Merlin."

"I saw the look," said Hugo. "That's the other thing: the idea that 'Arthur' is a title. I wonder if it's possible that one or the other is actually meant to become King Arthur? That maybe he wasn't a separate man after all?"

Hank chuckled. "No, the Arthur is someone else," he said mysteriously. "More than that, I'm not allowed to say. But it's going to be very interesting to see how this all plays out."

Hugo handed Hank their bowls. "Is your watch device working any better yet?"

"Not at all, I'm afraid," he said, filling a bowl and handing it back. "I think . . ." He paused. "I think somehow time itself has been broken."

Hugo stopped, his hand halfway to his mouth with a ladle of stew. "Do – do you think that's my fault?"

"You're an anomaly, that's for sure," Hank said, blowing on his stew. "Careful, it's hot. No, I think something else has happened. But fixing it is out of our hands. It's on someone else now to try to sort out what's gone on. Not only for our sakes . . .

". . . but for the sake of the future itself."

After they ate dinner and cleared away the bowls and kettle, Hank went to sleep immediately, citing the heavy armour he'd worn all day as the reason he was so weary. For his part, Hugo could not close his eyes for a second. He was too intrigued by the turn of events at the tournament and the new arrival.

Leaving the engineer sleeping soundly in the tent, Hugo crept out and began to make his way back to the centre of the happenings. He thought he'd take a closer look at Mordred if he could, his curiosity overcoming his fear, but he was sidetracked by a light he saw emanating from the tent of the Lawgiver.

He made his way around to the rear, where he'd seen Merlin exiting earlier, and peered through the flap.

Inside, Taliesin was standing to one side, while Merlin paced in front of him, obviously agitated.

"I did not know he would come at your summoning, Taliesin," Merlin said brusquely. "I was unprepared."

"You were forgetful," the Lawgiver shot back. "Your Binding exiled him, until he was summoned again – by *blood*."

"That *was* a slip of the tongue, wasn't it?" Merlin admitted. "It never occurred to me, cousin, that another of our family might ever call out into the world for a Gathering."

"We're not family, Myrddyn," Taliesin said with undisguised rancor. "We shared a father in Odysseus, but our mothers were different, and we've never been family."

"If we were not, my dear cousin," Merlin said with deliberate emphasis as he touched the older man on the forehead, "then my Binding on you would never have worked, and we would not be here today."

"Do you believe this will be the way you will get back, Merlin? Back to the Archipelago? By deceiving your way to possession of Caliburn?"

"I believe it's the way I will conquer the Archipelago. And everything else."

"It won't work. You saw the lineage in the book yourself. Only a follower of the Grail—"

"I was a Caretaker of the Grail!" Merlin said, clenching his fists.

"Only a follower of the true Grail," Taliesin continued, "will be able to use the sword. Madoc and his own bloodline—"

"When he betrayed the trust of the Grail, Madoc lost the Mandate of Heaven," Merlin interrupted. "It doesn't matter what his bloodline spawned."

"To betray the Grail is to betray Holy Blood," said Taliesin. "How have you done differently?"

"I've betrayed nothing," said Merlin. "Madoc chose his own path, as did you."

"And my sister?" Taliesin said softly. "Did Nimue deserve *her* fate?"

"She could have ruled with me. She chose otherwise."

"Do you think her blood on your hands will let you touch the sword?"

"Our blood is different!" Merlin shouted. "We *know* our lineage, Taliesin. We know we're descended of gods. The children of the Grail are not."

"Not of our gods, no," Taliesin replied calmly, "but this is a time of new gods, Merlin. I've accepted that, and so should you. You know how his divinity was proven – and you know how this tournament will be won."

Merlin whirled away from Taliesin and was quiet for a long while. "By willing choice and sacrifice," he said at length. "That's Old Magic. It has nothing to do with new gods, Taliesin."

"We will see, Merlin."

"Yes, we shall."

Hugo would have listened longer, but a group of knights were sauntering by, and he worried about being caught and accused of spying. He worried even more that he might have to reveal what he'd heard.

He was about to leave, but his eyes widened in surprise as he noticed something just below him in Taliesin's tent. He snaked a hand inside the flap and snatched it. Then, running as quickly as he could, Hugo hurried back to the campsite to wake Hank Morgan.

"That old snake," Hank said, pounding a fist into his other hand. "That explains an awful lot."

"Can you use your device?" asked Hugo. "The silver dragon watch? Can you use it to send a message, as you did before?"

Hank shook his head. "I've tried. It still isn't working. That's never happened before – not for this long."

"What does that mean?"

"It means," Hank said with a desperate edge to his voice, "that we are completely on our own."

"Perhaps not." Hugo sat upright with a strange expression on his face. "I might be going balmy, but I think I have an idea worthy of a caretaker."

"What's that?"

"We've been too caught up in instantaneous communication," Hugo explained, "worrying too much about how soon we can contact someone via your watch device, when we really, literally, have all the time in the world."

"You've figured out another way to contact help?"

"Better than that," Hugo said, beaming. "We already *have*."

He held up the squarish book he'd taken from Taliesin's tent. The first page was blank, but the rest of the book was filled with writing – and on the cover, embossed deeply in the leather, was the image of the Grail.

"Do you have any ink and a quill?" asked Hugo.

"I have a quill," Hank replied, "but Merlin makes his own ink. I could probably put something together for you, but it would have to be done in daylight."

"No time for that." Hugo rolled up his sleeve and held out his hand for Hank's dagger. "John's going to be pleased that he called this one on the nose."

After more bloodlettings than Hugo expected, he finally had enough to work with to inscribe his message in the book. It was approaching morning before he finally began writing in earnest.

"Not to be critical," said Hank, "but wouldn't 'Help us! Help us! We're trapped in the sixth century!' suffice?"

"Now, now," Hugo admonished. "This has to be done properly. This is a work for the ages – I can't just slop it together."

"It's a plea for help, not a sonnet," Hank argued, holding open the tent flap to look outside. "Just write it out so we can be done before Merlin returns."

"I'm a professor of English!" Hugo retorted. "I don't want to be embarrassed in front of my peers when they come to rescue us, just because I slacked off in my composition efforts."

"Technically, you already read what you're writing," said Hank. "Can't you just write it out from memory?"

"I can't recall it all," Hugo said, leaning over the book. "There was a lot going on that evening, and my head was all a-muddle. I even thought it was all a joke of some kind until I actually got here with Pellinor."

"You're lucky you did," Hank said with no trace of sarcasm. "He's batty. The story goes that his ancestor, Pelles, was a guardian of the Holy Grail, who lost it when it was stolen by a dragon he called the Questing Beast. They've all been on the crazy side ever since."

"I've never seen a dragon, either," Hugo said as he began to write, "but after the past few days, I'd be willing to extend him the benefit of the doubt."

In short order, Hugo finished writing the warning to his satisfaction, and together he and Hank hid it where Merlin would not stumble across it.

"That's that," Hugo said, dusting his vest off with one hand and flexing the other, which was sore from the dagger pokes. "According to the rules of time travel, now that I've actually created the message for us to get later, they should be coming to pick us up any time now."

"The 'rules of time travel'?" Hank said with a smirk. "Do you think they're just going to be able to do some mumbo-jumbo and suddenly appear?"

"Am I really being criticized by a man who travels through time with a silver pocket watch?"

"Sorry," said Hank. "I'm not trying to be discouraging. I just didn't want you to think that even for the Caretakers, it would be as easy as just flipping a switch."

"Ah, but if I know John and Jack," Hugo said with more pride than confidence, "it is."

The final contests began at sunrise, and everyone who was camped in the valley was there to watch. No one wanted to miss the drama being played out on the hill.

Merlin came to Hank's tent to retrieve another pair of gauntlets, a helmet, and a short Roman sword. He strapped it around a Grecian leather skirt that was studded with iron, and he also took a small round shield.

He never so much as glanced at Hugo, except for a curt glance and tight smile as he left.

"Do you think he knows I overheard him last night?" Hugo asked Hank.

"If he had, he wouldn't have left you alive," the engineer replied. "Let's go see this."

The Lawgiver stood at his usual place and extended his hand to show that he held eight small stones. Seven black, one white. Whichever among the champions chose the white stone from a bronze bowl would be allowed to choose the first opponent.

One by one, they turned their heads and drew a stone, Mordred last. He turned back and opened his hand. "Of course," he murmured, looking at the round white stone. "That's just as it should be."

Merlin suppressed a grin and tipped his chin at Taliesin. The Lawgiver raised both hands. "Mordred shall be first to choose. Against which man will you raise your hand?"

Mordred looked over his opponents, considering, then extended his arm and pointed at the burly warrior to Merlin's left. "You. I raise my hand against you."

Taliesin withered slightly, as if he'd hoped for a different response. "Gwydion, son of Don, will you raise your hand against Mordred?"

The king called Gwydion nodded.

Taliesin dropped his hands. "Then it is begun."

* * *

The first contest was epic, nearly ending in a draw, so evenly matched were its contestants. But then Mordred got a swing under Gwydion's defences and slashed his right shoulder to the bone.

"First blood," Taliesin called out as the knights helped Gwydion away, and Mordred pointed at another warrior, this time to Merlin's right.

It became obvious to all that Mordred intended for Merlin to be the last, should he defeat the other kings. And with each new contest, that's what Mordred did.

One by one, some more easily than others, six opponents fell before Mordred until finally, only Merlin was left.

"My God," Hank whispered. "This has really gone the distance. I don't believe Mordred defeated them all." He kept glancing around, as if he expected something else to take place. "This is bad."

"Why?" said Hugo.

"Merlin's good, but not this good," Hank said worriedly. "He can't beat Mordred."

"We can't let that happen!" exclaimed Hugo. "We have to stop it!"

Hank shook his head. "It's not our fight, Hugo."

"Mordred," the Lawgiver said again, "against which man shall you raise your hand?"

Mordred pointed at Merlin. "Against him, I shall raise my hand."

"Merlin," Taliesin said, the sorrow in his voice almost palpable, "will you raise your hand against this man?"

Before he could answer, there was a hissing sound, and a gasp of surprise from the crowd – and from Mordred.

A dagger, clumsily thrown, was sticking out of Mordred's side at an odd angle.

Mordred couldn't decide whether to be furious that he'd been stabbed or incredulous that anyone had dared. "Who does this?" he growled, pulling the dagger from his ribs. "What treachery is this, Merlin?"

Merlin's eyes narrowed. "Don't accuse an innocent . . . Mordred," he said harshly.

"He does not," declared Taliesin, pointing. "Your own squire has thrown the dagger."

The Lawgiver was pointing at Hugo, who, in his state of shock and awe at what he'd done, still had his arm extended from the throw.

Immediately two of the knights seized him, holding him fast. Hank, pushed to the side, was too stunned to speak.

"First blood, Mordred," Taliesin said, still uncertain himself what had happened. "You've lost."

"No!" Mordred screamed. "Unfair! A cheat!"

Taliesin shook his head, and a confused smile began to spread over Merlin's face. "Those are the rules, Mordred. He wears Merlin's colours. He drew first blood. You have lost. Withdraw, gracefully."

Mordred stood, glaring mutely at Taliesin, the anger rising off him like waves of heat. Then he turned slowly towards the knights holding Hugo and extended his arm, pointing a finger directly at the terrified professor.

The meaning was clear. If it ever was in his power to make it happen, Mordred would kill Hugo Dyson.

"Hugo!" Hank cried, his head still whirling from the speed of events. "Why did you do that?"

"I had no choice," Hugo gasped. "I had to, don't you understand? I had to stop him! He would have won! Mordred would have become the Arthur! And then who would have been left to stand against him?"

Before anyone could respond, a great bird swooped over the field, screeching shrilly.

Merlin's eyes darkened, and the smile dropped away.

To the south of the hill, the crowd parted and four men strode forward to the crypt.

"Lawgiver," the youngest of them said, "I am Thorn, son of Nimue, and by right of blood and right of honour, I have come to compete."

There was an immediate reaction to Thorn's announcement, and it was harsh. The gathered throng of warriors had allowed one apparent breach of the rules when Mordred came in so near the end of the tournament, but it would not be so easy for this bold boy to breach them again by taking part so late.

He didn't have the fearsome countenance of Mordred, or the reputation of Merlin or Gwydion or any of the others. And no one cared who his mother was.

No one save for the Lawgiver, whose eyes blazed.

"Silence!" Taliesin commanded, raising his arms high. "I am the Lawgiver, and I will decide what is to be allowed!"

The angry cries settled down to a disgruntled muttering as Taliesin motioned for Thorn to come forward.

The other three men stayed at the fringes of the crowd, but Hugo nearly shouted with joy when he recognized two of them as his friends John and Jack.

Hank motioned for him to be quiet. "You're in enough trouble as it is," he said under his breath. "Let's see if the Lawgiver can sort out your mess."

"I wish to speak!" Mordred declared, stepping in front of Thorn. "I have not been given my chance to fight!"

"I have already said that you lost, Mordred," Taliesin said. "First blood."

Mordred clenched his teeth and looked down at the boy, Thorn, with undisguised loathing. Then his expression changed, and he seemed to be puzzled. The boy returned his gaze bravely and unafraid.

Mordred looked at Merlin, then turned back to the boy again. "I think I see it clearly now, Lawgiver," he said, smiling coldly. "It is an old, old story, and one I know all too well."

Without another word, Mordred went to his tent and mounted his horse, taking only his spear with him. He left his tent and everything else behind and rode away without looking back.

"Well," said Merlin, "I think that ends our tournament."

Taliesin raised a hand. "Not quite, Merlin. You, too, are out of the competition. For cheating."

"What!" Merlin exclaimed, suddenly enraged. "I never cheated anyone!"

Taliesin pointed his black staff at Hugo. "He wears your colours. He is your squire. It is you who bears the loss."

Merlin shot a poisonous look at Hugo, then another at Hank. "We'll talk later," he hissed. "This isn't over."

"Did the tall one with the staff call the other one Merlin?" John whispered.

"Yes," said Jack, who was just as surprised. "Meridian is *Merlin*."

"I don't know who that is," whispered Chaz, "but Meridian looks like he wants t' kill that scrawny fellow the knights are holding."

Merlin turned back to the Lawgiver. "The tournament itself cannot continue. None among the champions is fit to fight – even if their challenger is just a boy."

"I am a man, my Lord," Thorn said, "and I will fight my own battles, thank you." He turned to the Lawgiver himself. "May I compete?"

To Merlin's increased rage, Taliesin nodded. "I know your lineage, and you have the right. The only opponent left has been disqualified, unless you choose otherwise."

Thorn looked at Merlin. "I'm not afraid," he said. "What must I do?"

"Will you raise your hand against this man?" said Taliesin.

Thorn looked confused. "What about the other tests? The trials and contests of physical prowess?"

Taliesin shook his head. "None of those matter now. Will you raise your hand against this man?" he repeated.

Thorn considered Merlin, then smiled wryly. "If you're giving me the choice, then no, I won't."

Merlin looked confused. Taliesin turned to him, grinning like a Cheshire cat. "And you? Will you raise your hand against he who will not raise his against you?"

Merlin's face was a mix of emotions. He locked eyes with the youth, and they looked at each other in some test of wills that none around them were privy to.

After an eternal pause, Merlin broke the stare and looked around him at the assemblage. His eyes looked wild, as if he were considering option after option and finding them all leading down dark pathways and ending at stone walls. He shook his head and rubbed his temples.

"Speak it," Taliesin demanded. "Speak the words."

"I . . . I cannot," Merlin finally said, his voice barely a whisper.

It took a few seconds for Taliesin to understand that Merlin had indeed declined to fight. In relief and with renewed vigour, the Lawgiver gestured to Thorn.

"Then," Taliesin said, placing his hands on Thorn's shoulders, "only one test remains."

He pointed the staff at the black sword, which still lay in the shallow grave. Thorn turned and stepped down into the crypt, picking up the sword as he did.

"If you can draw the sword from the scabbard . . . ," Taliesin began. But Thorn didn't give him time to finish. In one swift motion, he drew the sword from the scabbard and raised it high above his head.

There was a moment of absolute stillness as a hush overtook the crowd. Then, in a fluid motion, they all fell to one knee and began to cheer.

In the noise, no one realized that six men had remained standing: Taliesin, Hank, Hugo, John, Jack, and Charles. Merlin had disappeared into the Lawgiver's tent, and the owl Archimedes was flying in tight circles overhead and singing.

Taliesin stepped forward and tapped Thorn on each shoulder with the black staff, then kissed him on the forehead. "Well done, young Thorn. You are victorious. From this day henceforth, you are Arthur."

PART FIVE

The Isle of Glass

The bird flew off, and . . . returned with the projector . . .

Chapter Seventeen
Animal Logic

The parish church was cold, Geoffrey decided. It had always been chill, but for some reason, he'd never thought of it as actually being *cold*. But that morning he'd realized that it was in fact cold, when he noticed that his own breath was obscuring the writing on the parchment in front of him.

Sighing in resignation, he laid the quill inside his leather writing pouch and replaced the wax plug in the bottle of ink, then set about finding some tinder to put in the hearth. He carefully made his way down the steps and then opened the stout wooden door. The weather at Caerleon was always a bit ratty. He could understand why St. Cadoc had never wanted to fight any battles. It would have been too cold to lift his sword.

Still, it was a good enough place to build a church here and name it after him, Geoffrey decided, and if St. Cadoc could bear the weather, then so could he.

As he bent to pick up some sticks of wood at the tree line, a gust of wind caught his attention, and he looked seaward.

He had seen some mysterious storms out over the water of late, and more south of the parish. He didn't know what they meant, but he understood well enough to keep to his work, rather than look too closely.

But tonight the storm seemed different. The clouds were taking shape...

He dropped the sticks and crossed himself as three giants came striding out of the surf, directly towards the town. They were massive creatures that towered over the tallest trees in Caerleon. Behemoths such as these might have cowed even Arthur, Geoffrey thought. Yes, even he.

Then, as quickly as the apparitions had appeared, the giants paled, then faded, then disappeared completely, leaving behind less than smoke in the air.

Geoffrey lifted his robe and hurried back to the church. If nothing else, he intended to get his transcriptions done and turn in early. He could tell a sign when he was given it. No need to burn any bushes for him.

Although, he thought as he trudged back up the stairs, that *would* have made him warmer.

He reached for his door, and oddly, found it jammed from within. He rattled the latch, and from inside he heard a soft cursing, followed by the sound of tearing paper.

He pressed harder, and suddenly the door flew open.

The room was empty save for his small fireplace, his table, his chair, and the parchments he'd been working on. The window was locked. And there, on the floor, lay the ancient book he'd been transcribing.

Somehow the first few pages had been torn out diagonally, from the upper left to the lower right side. Only the left-hand pieces remained. There was no sign of the torn pages themselves.

Shaking his head, Geoffrey crossed himself again and closed the door. Something beyond his ken was happening here, and he hadn't the presence of mind to deal with it. Not while it was so cold. The history of the kings of England would have to wait until later.

Still mulling over what the vision might have meant, and trying not to consider the possible ways someone could have entered his study invisibly, Geoffrey of Monmouth fell into a fitful slumber. As he did, all around him, time itself shook and trembled like a tree in a thunderstorm. . .

Being declared the High King of the lands both known and unknown has its benefits, and when John and Jack made it clear that Hugo was their friend, Arthur immediately pardoned him and ordered him released.

The Lawgiver took Arthur aside to discuss matters of his new office, and the rest of the knights immediately began to start a celebration – which, Hugo decided, was practically identical to the tournament, with less of a point.

Of the companions, only Chaz had noted that not all the cheers were heartfelt, and not all the new subjects seemed to be pleased with the King, or the process by which he'd been chosen.

Hugo was mostly just relieved to see his old friends from Oxford. "I knew it!" he exclaimed happily. "I knew you'd be here to fetch me!"

"And just in time, it seems," John noted. "It looked like you were about to be drawn and quartered."

"All under control, I assure you," Hugo said with a wave. "But I'm not going to complain about your timing." He turned to Chaz and took his hand, which he began pumping frenetically. "And you, dear boy! So happy to see you, too! What happened to your face?"

Chaz pulled his arm free and tightened his collar. "Ah, I'm happy to see you well, Hugo."

John gave Chaz a quizzical look, and Chaz took him aside, out of earshot of the others. "I didn't want t' give him anything t' regret," he said flatly. "He doesn't know I'm not Charles, and he doesn't need to know where I came from or," he added with a quick glance back, "what else transpired there."

John nodded. "I understand. You're a good fellow, Chaz."

"Don't rub it in."

They rejoined the others, who were now conversing with Hank Morgan. He showed them his watch and seemed as pleased as Hugo that they'd come.

"It still isn't working," he said, shaking the watch. "When you return, can you get a message to Verne?"

"I'm sure we can," said Jack, "one way or another. What year is it, exactly?"

"It's the year 498 AD," said Hank, "give or take a few weeks."

"Not quite the sixth century," said John.

"Close enough," said Hugo. "So," he added, rubbing his hands in anticipation, "when do we go home?"

"That," John said, putting his arm around his friend's shoulders, "is something we need to discuss."

Back at his tent, Hank prepared another stew for his hungry new guests as John, Jack, and Chaz offered an abridged version of what had happened to them.

Hugo had barely begun his reciprocal tale, starting with his trip with Pellinor, when the High King poked his head inside the tent.

"Sorry to interrupt," Arthur said, "but Archimedes has just captured something for our dinner."

"He's an industrious bird," said Chaz. "Tell him to bring it here, and we'll add it to the stew."

"That's the problem," said Arthur. "It's talking – and insisting it's here to rescue something called scowlers."

John and Jack beamed and simultaneously sighed in relief. John dashed out of the tent, and Jack clapped Hugo on the back. "Hang on, old sport," he said, smiling broadly. "The cavalry's here, and they're short and furry."

John followed Arthur to the crest of the hill, where Archimedes was grappling with an extremely agitated Uncas.

"Stupid bird!" Uncas exclaimed. "What are you, a cannibobble?"

"I'm a mathematician, if you must know," the owl replied, still keeping a grip on the badger with one claw.

"Let him go, Archie," Chaz said as he and the others caught up to John.

The bird immediately loosed the badger, who snorted at it, then patted down his fur. "I come on a rescue mission, and nearly get et by a cannibobble," Uncas muttered. "No respect."

"We respect you, Uncas," Jack said, sweeping up the badger in a tight hug. "I'm thrilled to see you."

"Scowler Jack! Scowler John! Mister Chaz!" Uncas shouted. "I finally found you! I knew I would!"

The little fellow was so happy, and they were so relieved, that none of them noted that it was actually the owl who'd brought him to them. "What happened?" asked John. "We went back to the proper spot, but the portal was gone. It had only been a few minutes."

"That'd be my fault, Scowler John," Uncas said, looking as embarrassed and forlorn as they'd ever seen him. "Mine, an' mine only."

Jack knelt down and took the little fellow by the shoulder. "It's all right, Uncas. Mistakes happen. What did you do?"

"I, uh, I tripped over the cord, and accidentally unplugged the projector."

"Okay," said Jack, suppressing a grin. "Then why didn't you just plug it back in?"

"I tried!" Uncas wailed. "But I got all tangled up in it, and then I pulled over the whole thing, and it breaked! I mean, broked. . . Um, I cracked it, is what I mean t' say!"

"So how did you get here?" asked John.

"We fixed it up – Reynard is a work an' a wonder with lenses – and plugged it back in. But by then you were gone."

"How long did it take you to repair it, Uncas?" asked Jack.

Uncas closed one eye and estimated. "About an hour."

Jack's shoulders slumped. "Then we're still in trouble," he said, shading his eyes and looking at the afternoon sun. "It's been twenty-four hours already, plus the hour it was down. The slide will have burned out by now."

"We thought of that!" Uncas said, preening. "Fred and I looked all over for you around that old oak, until just an hour ago. Then we stopped it before we ran out of time."

"Is Reynard simply going to turn it back on so we can return?" asked Jack.

Uncas looked crestfallen. "That would have been a good idea," he admitted.

"But he would have no way of knowing Uncas found us," Chaz said, "and the slide would still burn out."

"He's right, Uncas," John said, still confused, "how do we get *back?*"

"Easy," Uncas said, bursting with the ingenuity of his plan. "We brung it with us – the entire Lanterna Magica."

They had Arthur ask Archimedes to return to Grandfather Oak, to look for a second badger and a small machine, and to return, as carefully as possible, with them both.

The bird flew off, and inside of an hour returned with the projector in his claws and Fred riding on his back.

"Please don't drop the time machine," said Jack.

"Or the badger," added John.

"I meant to say that," said Jack.

Archimedes spiralled slowly down and lowered the Lanterna Magica to the grass, and Fred leaped off his back and hugged Uncas.

"Did you see, Father?" Fred exclaimed. "I flew! In the air!"

Uncas hugged his son back and glared at the bird. "I had the same trip, under less pleasant circumstances."

John and Jack stared at the projector. The badgers had indeed managed to bring it through.

"It was Reynard who figured it out," Fred explained. "He used an extra lens to keep the projection large as we pulled the machine closer to the screens. Then, when it was almost inside, we pulled it through, and the portal closed behind it."

"It almost didn't work at all," said Uncas. "The cord in the back was barely long enough to let us pull the projector through before it came out of the socket."

"That's actually my next question," Jack said, already knowing –

and dreading – the answer. "We're at the end of the fifth century. Where are we going to plug it in?"

The mournful howling of the two badgers was so pitiful that the companions had to move them down the back side of the hill, away from the celebration and into the woods.

It took several minutes and the combined efforts of John, Jack, and Chaz to settle them down. Then the companions began to discuss any ideas they might have to get back to Sanctuary.

"The Lanterna Magica used to be powered by a candle," John suggested. "Maybe we don't need the electricity."

Jack shook his head. "I was looking it over with Reynard. We'd have to take it apart to do something like that, and we don't understand enough of how it works. What if we broke the mechanism that makes it function?"

"I wish you'd thought to bring a generator, too," John said to Uncas. "Not," he added quickly as the badger started to tear up again, "that I'd have thought of it either."

"The Serendipity Box?" asked Chaz. "Could it give us a generator?"

"Not likely," John said, eyeing the box. "It's too small, and too big a risk to wish for something it can't give us."

"We might just as well wish for a generator," said Jack. "It could fall into our laps this very minute."

"Not quite that fast," someone said, "but give me a few days, and I might be able to arrange it."

It was Hank Morgan who had spoken. "I'm only an amateur time traveller," he said with some degree of modesty, "but in my day job, I'm an electrical engineer. I'm certain we could construct an electrical generator in a few days, give or take. And then we can power that thing up and get you on your way."

"Perhaps we could fix your watch," John suggested. "Could you take us back with you?"

"I wish I could," Hank replied, "but I'm afraid the device doesn't work that way. Not yet, anyway. It's a one-person contraption. I've tried to take a passenger, but it just left them standing and clutching empty air. But perhaps in the future something can be done to change that. It's busted, anyway. But if I ever get another one, I'll give it to you. You really ought to have a watch if you're going to be travelling in time."

"I'd appreciate it," said John. "I'm going to catch hell for the last one I lost."

The group returned to Hank's tent, where he kept a large bag filled with various handmade tools and implements, and a second one filled with raw materials.

"Ever the Boy Scout, eh?" said John.

"The what?" said Hank. "No, I just like to always be prepared."

"Couldn't you have just used that watch of yours to pop back and forth in time, and simply bring back the tools you need?" asked Jack. "That would be a lot easier than fashioning everything by hand."

"Would if I could, brother," Hank replied. "It just doesn't work that way. The only thing I can actually take back and forth is the watch. Everything else has to be created or acquired."

"Does that include . . . ?" Jack asked, indicating Hank's clothes.

"Yep," Hank admitted with a slight blush. "First trip out, I found myself absolutely starkers. Should have seen the first knight who stumbled over me. He thought I was some kind of crazy man."

"It didn't say that you were naked in the book," said John. "Not that I recall, anyway."

"A favour from Sam," Hank explained. "I have to preserve my dignity where I can, you know."

"But I've seen you take notes," said Hugo. "Should I even ask how you get them back?"

"Better for us both if you don't," said Hank.

As Hank worked, the companions remained apart from the celebrations and revelry, so as not to risk disturbing the timestream worse than they had. Now that they had Hugo, all John and Jack wanted to do was get home.

Fred, Archie, and Chaz turned into an unexpected trio of friends, who passed the time playing logic games. Uncas mostly stayed at Hank's side, feeling as he did responsible for the entire mess. If he could help, he would.

As it turned out, the Little Whatsit was a great benefit to Hank's efforts, providing him with instructions and diagrams that he otherwise would have had to work out himself.

"With that book," Hank said, wiping his brow, "we should be done tomorrow."

"That quickly?" asked John. "Excellent. Good show, Hank."

Jack seemed a bit put out that Arthur was not spending more time with them. "We are the ones who brought him here, after all," he complained. "If not for us, he'd still be asleep under the tree."

"Now, Jack," Hugo said consolingly, "he is the High King, after all. He's got a lot to do, I'm sure."

Of Merlin there was no sign. And Mordred never rode back to the camp. In his stead, Arthur had moved in to occupy the tent he left behind.

"There's a metaphor in there somewhere," John remarked, "but I'll be damned if I know what it is."

By late the next morning, the generator was assembled and running.

"Should we say goodbye to Arthur?" asked Jack.

"Best not," John replied. "We'd have to explain too much about where we're going and why. And I'd prefer to let history take its course without any further help from us. And you, Hank?" he said to the engineer. "Will you be all right?"

"My device is still not working," Hank said, holding the silver watch to his ear, "but no matter. If I have to stay awhile, so be it. Sam and Verne will straighten it out. Besides, it's good weather – I'm thinking about organizing a few baseball teams and having a tournament of my own."

"Ah . . . Go Sox!" said Hugo.

"Attaboy!" said Hank. "Good luck to you, gentlemen . . . and badgers."

They plugged in the Lanterna Magica and crossed their fingers. "Ready?" Hank asked. Everyone nodded, and he gave a signal to Uncas, who threw the switch.

Against the wall of Hank's tent, the brilliant projection sprang to life. But instead of the room at Sanctuary they were expecting to see, they saw a tree on a hillside, with a young man sleeping underneath.

Jack realized it first and slapped his forehead. "Of course," he moaned. "This isn't like the doors, where it's two-way. The Lanterna Magica only projects a portal into whatever's on the slide."

"In this case, a couple of days ago, when we got here," said John.

"Can we go through there," asked Chaz, "before we got shut out?"

John shook his head. "We'd still have no way to get to Sanctuary, and," he noted bitterly as the edges of the slide began to thicken and fade, "this slide is nearly finished, anyway."

"Can we go through one of the other slides instead?" asked Fred.

"Too risky," said John. "They would just take us to another spot in our past, and presumably, another encounter with Mordred. And now that Arthur's taken control, I don't want to chance another change."

"I'm sorry," Hank said as the slide burned away and the projection turned clear. "I got her going for you, but after that, I'm fresh out of miracles."

"You might be, but we aren't!" Jack said, snapping his fingers. "The Serendipity Box!"

John pulled it out of his bag and handed it to Jack as Chaz explained the workings of it to Hugo and Hank.

"All I want," said Jack, closing his eyes, "is a ticket home." He opened his eyes and the box at the same time, and everyone leaned in close to see what it had given him.

Inside the box was a miniature ship inside a bottle. Jack took it out and looked closely at it.

"A ship?" said John. "I have no idea what that's supposed to do for us."

"Neither do I," admitted Jack, deflated. He'd hoped for something more clearly useful, but this ship in a bottle was, according to the box, the thing he needed most.

"There's no time limit, remember," John pointed out. "It doesn't seem to be constrained by the urgency of the moment. Bert's scarab brooch wasn't needed for years."

"Grand," Jack said, pocketing the bottle and closing the box. "Now what do we do?"

"Let me try," Chaz suggested. "It is more my world we left from, after all. Maybe it'll be my need the box responds to."

Jack shrugged and handed it over. "I don't see that we'll lose anything if you try."

Chaz rubbed Uncas's head for luck. "If it's not a magic carpet t' home," he said cheerfully, "let's hope for some oyster crackers, eh?"

Chaz opened the box.

"Oh, drat again," said Uncas. "And after you got my hopes up an' all."

Chaz reached inside and removed a small photographic slide. In it they could see the projection room back at Sanctuary, and even a miniature depiction of Reynard, still watching for them.

Jack removed the disk from the projector. "It has a sixth slot," he said with a trace of surprise, "almost as if it had been left open for a reason."

Hank and Uncas fitted the slide into the slot, then replaced the disk. "Here goes nothing," Hank said, firing up the generator again.

In a moment, the image of the projection room sprang up on the tent wall. The image was coarser than the others they'd gone through, but this one seemed no less viable.

"Only one way to find out," said Jack, and he stepped from the tent into the house on Sanctuary.

"Come on!" he implored, waving them over. "It's a bit more like moving through soup than air, but I'm here just fine."

"I think I can duplicate that trick with the lenses," Hank said to John, "so you can take it back through with you."

"Are you sure you don't want to come with us?"

The engineer shook his head. "Not my place or time," he said. "Thanks for the offer, though. Just get a message to Verne."

"I will," John said, and he stepped through the portal, with Uncas and Fred close behind. Hugo gave Hank a warm, two-handed handshake and, swallowing hard, threw himself through the portal, landing in a sprawl in the room, much to the delight of everyone there.

Only Chaz remained in the tent. He made no move to go through.

"Chaz?" called John. "Are you all right?"

"I don't . . . I don't want t' go back," he said.

"But why not?" exclaimed Jack. "We've got Hugo back and assured that Arthur has the throne he's supposed to have. When we get back to Noble's Isle, everything will have changed back to the way it's supposed to be!"

"You mean," Chaz replied softly, "everything will have changed back t' th' way it's supposed t' be . . . for *you*. If everything else changes," he continued, "will I just become 'your' Charles? Will I even remember who I was before?"

"I honestly don't know," offered John. "I hadn't thought much about it — no offence," he added quickly. "It's just that you've become so much like . . ."

"So much like him that you hadn't noticed I wasn't him?" Chaz said with a trace of bitterness. "Well, I'd noticed," he said, jabbing his thumb at his chest, "and I don't want to go anywhere if it means I'm not going t' be me when I get there."

"I don't think it'll work like that," said Jack. "I think you'll stay 'you' no matter what. You're one of those implementing the changes in the timelines. So I think you'll remain unaffected – stay Chaz-like, as it were."

"I agree," John said. "Bert mentioned that he and Verne travelled outside the timelines somehow, and despite going to times and places they'd already been, they always kept a memory of events. I think it'll be the same with you."

"There is another thing to consider," Hugo put in. "If you stay, you will probably affect the timeline for us. After all, isn't that why you all came back? To bring me home, so I don't mess up whatever I, ah, botched in history? What if you stay there, and the same thing happens?"

Chaz looked at each of them through the projection, considering, then stopped at Hugo. "That's really th' best reason, isn't it?" he said. "Whatever else goes wrong, I don't want t' be th' cause of Mordred taking over th' world. So let's just pull me over and be done, hey? Before I change my mind?"

"Mordred taking over the world?" Hugo said to Jack. "What's happened while I've been gone?"

"We'll explain later," Jack told him, "hopefully back in my rooms at Magdalen."

Chaz put his hands through the projection, and John and Jack pulled him through. Then, with some coaching from Reynard, Hank adjusted the lenses on the Lanterna Magica and moved it closer, until the men in Sanctuary could touch it, grasp it, and pull it through its own projection. Hank waved a last farewell as he pulled the cord and tossed it through. An instant later the wall went blank. They were back in the room on Sanctuary.

Jack started to cheer, but John held up his hands. "Wait," he said. He didn't know if Reynard, or the room, or the entire island would have been affected by the change they made in the past by returning with Hugo.

He looked at Chaz, who patted himself down and then shrugged. Chaz was still Chaz.

"Reynard," John said cautiously, "has anything changed in our absence?"

"Changed?" asked the fox. "In what way?"

As Reynard spoke, John realized he was bandaged – he still bore the fresh wounds he'd got trying to protect the *Red Dragon* from being destroyed.

"John," Jack said tonelessly, pointing at the corner of the room. "The burlap bag. It's still where we left it."

John sat down heavily in a chair and began to shake. There was too much that had been overcome, at too great a cost. Even when the impossible had been needed, they had still managed, somehow, to prevail. And none of it had done them any good at all.

"It's still Albion. Still the Winterland," John said bitterly.

"We haven't changed anything."

CHAPTER EIGHTEEN
The Sacrifice

There was no choice then but to explain to Hugo the complete story of exactly what had taken place after he stepped through the door in the wood. When the companions had finished, Hugo was shaken, but reciprocated with his own tale, looking askance at Chaz as he spoke.

After the Caretakers had explained who he really was, Hugo had accepted it with aplomb, but a feather's uncertainty remained. If it were not for the scarring on his face, and the occasional lapse into vulgar language, Hugo might have thought it was another joke being played on him.

"The book was sent to Charles, and Pellinor had been instructed by someone to retrieve the man in the photo – you, Hugo," Jack summarized. "Then, a time traveller who was working with Samuel Clemens, another Caretaker of the *Imaginarium Geographica*, appears at a tournament in fifth-century Britain. This is all being orchestrated by someone, somewhere."

"I still think Mordred has everything to do with this," suggested Chaz. "I know him – at least, the Mordred of the Winterland – better than any of you. And this is exactly his kind of scheme."

In answer, Arthur began to raise the black sword, Caliburn . . .

"It wasn't Mordred I heard scheming," said Hugo. "It was Merlin – the Cartographer. He's the one I wrote the message to warn you about."

"I understand what you think you overheard, Hugo," John offered, "but remember, we know what the Cartographer became. We've had several encounters with him through the slides in the Lanterna Magica, and we know his predilections. But we know where he ended up, too. And he's an ally, not a threat."

"Fair enough," Hugo said, a bit nonplussed at the easy dismissal of his story. "After all, I share your concerns about Mordred. As a scholar of Arthurian lore, I knew I couldn't allow him to defeat Merlin and become the Arthur. That's why I did what I did. I'm just lucky you came along with the real Arthur."

"Yes, lucky," Jack said, rubbing his chin in thought. "But I'm not certain it was luck.

"Consider this," he continued. "Verne and Bert did what they did in response to Hugo going through the door and altering time. They had no way of knowing what specifically had happened – just that something had. And so they responded, and then left us the means to resolve what had gone awry."

"What are you getting at, Jack?" asked John. "Everything changed after Hugo went through the door and the badgers closed it. Of course the thing to do was to find him and bring him back."

"That wasn't what Verne directed us to do," Jack insisted. "He gave us the mission of defeating our adversary. He never mentioned bringing Hugo back as a means for doing that."

"So all this death, and destruction, and whatnot that happened," Hugo said carefully, "it might not, in fact, be my fault?"

"Not all of it, anyway," said Jack, "no."

"Oh, I'm so relieved," Hugo said.

"I know *exac'ly* how you feel," said Uncas, patting Hugo's knee. "Exac'ly."

Reynard and the jackrabbit entered the room carrying trays of potato sandwiches and a hot drink that resembled tea and smelled of chile and cinnamon. "To revitalize you," Reynard said as he passed out the cups. "It's an old recipe, given to us long ago by the wife of the shipbuilder."

The companions drank the tea, and ate the sandwiches hungrily. Despite the camaraderie of Hank Morgan and the interest they had in young Arthur, they were relieved to be able to rest, even temporarily, in a place where they felt civilized.

"The other slides," John said suddenly. "We still have two slides."

"Like the one Charles got out of the box?" asked Hugo, rising and walking over to John's pack. "I didn't realize there were others in here."

"Hugo, wait!" Jack shouted, leaping to his feet and scattering cups and saucers as he did so. But he was a fraction of an instant too late. Hugo flipped open the lid of the Serendipity Box and peered inside.

"Huh," Hugo exclaimed, holding aloft a flower. "It's a purple rose. Was this in here before?"

"It's not purple. It's indigo," said Jack, sitting back down in one of the chairs. "And no, it wasn't. It was there just for you, because it's apparently what you needed the most."

"Strange little whatchamacallit," Hugo remarked as he handed the box to John, then inserted the rose in one of his jacket pockets. "It's pretty, but I'm not really in need of a flower."

"You may be," said John. "It doesn't give you instructions. And each person can open it only once. We'd expected to save your turn until we were in trouble."

"You just finished explaining to me how the entire world is under Mordred's thrall, our only transportation was a ship, now destroyed, and there are giants waiting to kill us if we go outside. How is this not the appropriate time to open the box?"

John looked to Jack and Chaz, who both shrugged. "He has a point," said Chaz.

"It seems to me," Hugo said, sniffing the rose, "that we should follow the mandate of Jules Verne. He gave you five slides. Two remain. We should use those to see if what's been broken can, in fact, be mended."

All the others considered this, then nodded in agreement and got to their feet to start preparing for another trip through time.

Fred and Uncas assured the companions that there would be no mishaps with the cord, and they promised that it would stay put where it belonged on Sanctuary. As before, the companions took supplies to sustain them throughout the day, but they briefly debated whether or not to leave the Serendipity Box behind.

"The 'imp' may not appear for any of us again," Jack said as he and Reynard placed the box in a bag, "but I'd rather keep a hand on the 'bottle,' if you follow my meaning."

"Fair enough," John declared. He turned to the badgers. "Okay, Uncas. Let's see when we're going next."

The badger turned on the projector, and for a moment it seemed as if the image was unable to focus. It shifted and blurred, and finally clarified to a clear but dark scene in a very familiar setting.

The projection on the wall was almost identical to the one they had gone through last: an image of Grandfather Oak, in the centre of the hill not far from Camelot.

"Did we use the same slide again?" Jack asked Uncas. "Is this the burned one?"

Uncas shook his head. "The other one's all used up, Scowler Jack," he said. "This is slide four, as y' requested."

"It isn't the same," Chaz said suddenly. "Look – the tree. It's taller, older. And the trunk is split."

Looking more closely, they realized Chaz was correct. The tree was the same shape, but taller and stouter, and there was a nasty gash along one side, as if it had been struck by lightning. It was a bad enough split that ultimately the tree would not survive.

Chaz flipped through the pages of the Little Whatsit to the entry on Grandfather Oak. "It says here that the tree is still standing," he said, indicating a passage in the book. "What does that mean?"

"It means," John reasoned, "that whatever caused the changes to the world that resulted in the Winterland already happened. Maybe when we were there, in the fifth century. Maybe after. But whatever happened to the tree might be happening everywhere."

"Is this what Verne meant for us to do?" asked Jack. "Are we supposed to find the exact cause of the change and fix it? Can we do that, if it's already happened?"

"I don't know," said John, "but I'm going to go with Hugo's assessment. These slides aren't redundant. They've all been left for a reason. We've got Hugo back now, thanks to the last one. Perhaps this one will bring us closer to the finish."

"I hope so," Jack said as he stepped through the projection. "I need something to believe in."

◆ ◆ ◆

The tree, Grandfather Oak, was indeed dying, and the rest of the countryside looked no better. It was bleak, stricken, as if it was diseased. A thick odour hung in the air, an odour of death and decay.

"What's happened?" Hugo exclaimed. "How long have we been away?"

"Years, certainly," said John. "Decades, perhaps, judging from the size of the tree," he added, stroking the bark. "A shame we won't see it again after this."

"This must be a different timeline," Chaz said. "Different from yours, I mean. This looks more than familiar t' me."

They started walking the same route they had taken before, but other than the topography of the land, nothing was familiar.

There were scattered houses and a number of crumbling and broken walls. There were fires in some of the structures, and a few carcasses of horses and cattle that looked as if the animals had died of consumption rather than in a conflict.

Far off in the distance, they could just make out through the smoke and haze the crenellated towers of a castle.

"Camelot," John said dully. "Or what's left of it."

"Let's make haste," Hugo urged, beckoning them on. "We need to get to the bottom of things as quickly as we can. It's early in the day, from the position of the sun, so we can be there in a few hours if we hurry."

The companions ran as long as they could, finally slowing to a walk to conserve their strength for any unexpected surprises. The closer they got to the place they had known as Camelot, the more barren the landscape had become. It had been stripped bare of trees, stones, and anything else that could have been useful in a siege. And a siege was exactly what was taking place.

From the hilltop where they were, the companions could see the fields in the shallow valley where the tournament had taken place. Massed along the valley floor were thousands of warriors, many bearing banners they'd seen at the competition. There were battering rams, and trebuchets, and various machines of war that were completely unfamiliar in design, but evident in their use. Destruction was their purpose, and they were being used by warriors willing to smash everything in their path.

The armies were circled around the castle that had been built on the hill where the stone table stood. It was a motte-and-bailey castle of raised earth and wood that had been fortified with stone. The traditional courtyard that enclosed the town below had been obliterated by the invaders, who were now pressing their attack with fire and steel up against the walls of the castle itself.

The castle and its defenders would not last the night.

"This is it, isn't it?" Jack whispered, awestruck by the spectacle in front of them. "This is the beginning of the Winterland."

"No," John replied. "This is just the result. Whatever set things on this path has already happened."

"But how can we fix this?" Hugo asked, sitting on the ground and clutching his knees. "This is war!"

Hugo had lived through the Great War – but unlike John and Jack, he had never witnessed the kind of savagery that permeated every aspect of a battle that turned on blood and steel. Hand-to-hand combat with spears and swords was a different kind of warfare, and it was frightening Hugo into a stupor.

"Hey, Hugo," said Chaz, pointing at the Little Whatsit, "give me a hand here, will you? I can't make sense of some of this."

John started to remark that Chaz hadn't had a problem with reading it before, when he glanced at Chaz and Hugo and realized that Chaz still needed no help. He'd asked Hugo to assist him to break the professor's coma of fear. And it worked. With his attention drawn away from the battlefield before them and focused instead on the unusual academia of the Whatsit, Hugo was getting his colour back.

Chaz looked up at John and gave him a half smile and a nod, then went back to examining the book.

It occurred to John that it had only been through necessity that they'd brought Chaz with them. But just that degree of contact had changed him, perhaps permanently. He would never be the same Chaz they had first met. Perhaps never Charles – not their Charles, at any rate. But not the same as he'd been.

Jack interrupted John's reverie with a squeeze of his arm. "Someone's coming," he said. "But I think he's a friend."

"Why do you say that?" asked John, already stiffened in expectation of a row.

"Because," Jack replied, "he's carrying a sword, a shield, and a baseball bat."

The figure of the knight trudging towards them finally realized that the men in front of him were not fleeing, but merely watching. He took a defensive stance, and then looked more closely at their clothing.

"Who goes there?" the knight called out. "Identify yourselves, and state your allegiances."

"Hank?" Hugo exclaimed. "Is that you?"

The knight straightened up and lowered the sword, then after a long moment, removed his helmet, which was streaked with blood. His gauntlets and breastplate were similarly stained, but his face was welcomingly familiar.

It was Hank Morgan.

Hugo strode down the slope, arms outstretched. "Hank! Well met, old sock! Well met!"

Hank held out a cautious hand. "I'm sorry, but I don't know you. How is it you're here now?"

Hugo stopped and lowered his arms, confused. "You may not know us, but we know you, Hank."

"You know me?" Hank exclaimed through gritted teeth. "That's impossible."

"No, it isn't!" said Hugo. "We're time travellers as well! We actually met you here, some years ago!"

The bloodied engineer shook his head. "I don't know what you're talking about," he said brusquely. "I've never travelled in time before. I don't know how it happened. I was having an argument at my factory in Hartford, and a crusher named Hercules cracked me in the skull with a crowbar. I woke up underneath a great oak tree not too many miles from here."

"We know the place," said Hugo. "How long have you been here?"

"About six months, give or take," Hank replied. "Just long enough to see the whole place going straight to hell in a handbasket." He dropped the bat and shield and moved up to shake hands with Hugo. "Sorry about the reaction," he said. "It's been a long time since I saw a friendly face."

"What's happened here, Hank?" asked John, pointing at the castle. "Who's attacking them?"

"Who isn't is a better question," Hank replied. "All the tribes and fiefdoms have united against King Arthur."

"*Against* Arthur?" John deadpanned. "Arthur united the tribes and kingdoms. Who would dare raise a hand against him?"

"From what I've learned, the nobles have always resented him," Hank replied. "There's a deep-seated belief that he came by his crown though deceptive means, that he never truly earned the right to become the High King thirty years past. And it all came to a head a few months ago when his own adviser, that bastard Merlin, united the nobles and besieged Camelot.

"Actually, the place would have fallen weeks ago," Hank continued, "if Arthur's uncle, Mordred, hadn't shown up to help defend the castle."

The companions were horrified.

"His *uncle?*" Jack exclaimed, eyes narrowing. "When did *that* happen?"

"It isn't in the histories," said John. "None of the ones I've read, anyway."

"I don't care if Mordred's his nursemaid," said Chaz. "Why is *Merlin* attacking Arthur? I'nt he s'pposed t' be the *good* one?"

Hugo was overcome with a different emotion: guilt. "This is all my fault," he began.

"It's not over yet," John said, cutting him off. He turned to Hank. "We have to get to Arthur. Is there any way we can get close to the castle? Any way at all?"

"There just might be," Hank answered. "Follow me."

About half a mile to the north of the castle, where an assault was impossible because of the thickness of the rocks and trees that bordered the river just beyond, Hank led them to a massive stone.

On the stone, almost completely faded with age, were markings in ancient Greek.

"Arthur showed this to me when I first got here," Hank explained. "A man called Brutus created the passageway centuries ago, modelled after one he'd used to escape the siege of Troy. There are several more scattered around Albion."

The companions all shuddered involuntarily on hearing the name. "Britain, if you please," Jack said, looking around the stone. "Where is the passageway?"

Hank gave the massive boulder a shove, and they heard a mechanism underneath grind into action. The stone levered over on its side, revealing a long-unused set of stone steps that spiralled down into darkness.

"I think it leads to a spot right in the centre of the castle, and there are oil lamps throughout," said Hank. "Anyone got a match?"

Lamps blazing, the companions moved quickly through the narrow underground passage. Hugo led the way, having renewed his courage since seeing a familiar face – even if the engineer didn't recognize him in turn. Hank followed behind him, then Chaz, with John and Jack in the rear, making sure they were not being followed.

Suddenly Hugo stopped. There was something partially blocking the narrow passageway. It was a bird, an immense owl, which lay unmoving on the flat stones.

"Archimedes," Chaz breathed, pushing past the others. He

knelt down and pressed his ear to the bird's chest. "He's functioning, but barely. I think there might be something in the Little Whatsit I can use to fix him up."

"We don't have time for a stupid bird," Hank hissed. "What are you doing?"

"I'm not leaving him behind," said Chaz, dumping a few other items out of his pack. "I'm taking him with me."

"Your business, not mine," Hank retorted, turning around. "Come on. We're almost there."

"Do you believe," John whispered to Jack as they watched Chaz gently wrap the damaged owl and put it into his bag, "that this is the same fellow who wanted us to give him Uncas to eat?"

"Miracles never cease," said Jack. "Look – the passageway is sloping upward to more steps."

The passageway levelled out, then pitched steeply upward, ending at a stone ceiling. "Stand aside," Hank instructed the others, taking up the bat. He got a solid grip on it, then swung it up into the stones.

They shivered, and a light rain of dust fell. Hank adjusted his grip and swung again, then again, and with a sharp crack, the stones broke apart and crumbled down onto the steps. Above them, they could see a stone covering that was slightly ajar, so light could come down into the tunnel. And they could hear voices; harsh, almost shouting.

"You think I don't know?" one was saying. "Don't you think I knew all along what I had lost?"

"I can't let you do it," another voice pleaded. "I can't let you kill him."

"You must."

"I can't!"

"That's Mordred," said John urgently. "And Arthur! We have to get up there, now!"

Pushing together, Hank, John, and Jack hefted the large stone off the entrance and shoved it aside. They climbed out to an astonishing realization: The stone had been covering the crypt of the old king, Camaalis. The tunnel led to the very spot where Caliburn had lain for centuries until Arthur claimed it.

A short distance away, in the centre of the castle walls, Arthur and Mordred were facing each other across the ancient stone table. They had ignored the clamour of the falling stones in the passageway, but ceased arguing when they realized that they had an audience.

Arthur was bewildered at first – he hadn't seen the companions long enough to immediately recall them after three decades. But Mordred recognized them instantly.

"I don't know why you're here," he said, his voice low and dangerous, "but you have followed my brother and me across the centuries, always appearing at these pivotal points in our histories. It's only right that you are here to witness this now."

Arthur, older and bearded but still bearing the youth and noble countenance of the boy they remembered, spun back to his uncle. "I can't allow it, Mordred."

Mordred raised his spear – the one he had taken from the chamber of the Grail in Alexandria. "You cannot stop me, boy. Not in this."

In answer, Arthur began to raise the black sword, Caliburn, as he stepped forward.

"Arthur, please!" Mordred cried out as he stepped up onto the table to meet the younger man's approach. "Please, don't—"

The corner of the table, worn and pockmarked with age, gave way under Mordred's foot, and he fell, twisting, against Arthur, who caught him against his chest.

There was a terrible cracking sound, and thunder shook the castle walls, raining stones down all around them.

The sword Caliburn fell to the ground. The blade broke off just above the hilt.

Mordred looked down at it, disbelieving, and stepped back from his nephew, letting go of the spear.

Arthur looked down at the shattered sword, then at his chest, where the spear, the Lance of Longinus, had pierced his heart. He pulled it free, then fell to his knees on the stone table. He whispered something to Mordred, then fell.

The companions raced over to the table just in time for John to catch the king. He looked up, stricken. "We've arrived too late," he said mutely. "The one, the Arthur . . .

". . . is *dead*."

Circe held up the golden bowl. "Choose," she said.

CHAPTER NINETEEN
The Enchantresses

The girl walked along the island's shoreline, idly dragging one foot through the surf. The old fisherman watched her, knowing, as she only suspected, that this was the last day they would spend together.

"You know," he said jovially, "you're going to scare all the fish."

"Sorry, Grandfather," she told him. "I was just thinking."

"I could tell. But you're not afraid?"

She considered her answer. "No," she said finally. "Not afraid. But I know that my childhood is nearly over. And it makes me sad. Leaving you makes me sad."

He nodded. "I understand. It was the same with your uncle Telemachus. But nothing is forever. We'll meet again someday."

"Will we? Does that mean I'll live to see tomorrow?"

"None of us knows that for sure," he replied, "but I'd say the odds are in your favour."

She didn't answer, but simply stared out across the water, towards the line of storms that never seemed to change, and wondered if she would ever see what lay beyond them. She hoped she would.

♦ ♦ ♦

Mordred hadn't moved. He just stood there, confused, looking from the bloodied spear that lay on the ground to Arthur and back again.

"What did he mean?" Mordred whispered to no one in particular.

The companions approached cautiously, uncertain of what was happening. John cradled the lifeless form of Arthur in his arms and looked up as Mordred repeated the words. "What did he mean?"

"What did he say to you, Mordred?" Jack said, stepping closer. Once, years before, in his own timeline, he'd shared a connection with Mordred that had been forged more because of his youth than poor judgment, and nearly lost his shadow – and soul – because of it. But he knew a personal struggle when he saw it.

Mordred looked at him, his face a mixture of emotions. "He said, 'You are strong enough to bear this.' What did he mean by that?"

John's mind raced. The crucial moment had passed, and they'd missed their chance to undo whatever had been done. Whichever brother had been their true adversary no longer mattered. Arthur was dead. Now the only hope they had was to prevent the ascent of Mordred to the throne. To keep him from becoming king and turning the world and the Archipelago into the Winterland.

"Mordred," John said cautiously, "what were you and Arthur arguing about?"

The question seemed to snap Mordred out of his trance. "Arguing?" he repeated. "We were arguing about what I am compelled to do. Arthur disagreed. But now," he added ruefully, as he looked at his nephew's body and the realization of what had happened hit him fully, "the path is clear. And there will be none who can oppose me."

"This is what Arthur meant, Mordred!" Jack exclaimed. "You are strong enough to bear this! We saw what happened. We know you didn't mean to kill him. Don't let his death force you into a path—"

"Force me?" Mordred said with a barking laugh. "As with a Binding? Don't you think I worked out long ago who had suggested to my brother that I be Bound? Who it was that was responsible for my exile?"

John and Jack looked grimly at each other. There was nothing they could say.

"If I had not been summoned to the tournament by Taliesin," Mordred continued, "I would have remained in exile. And your treachery" – he pointed at Hugo – "is what cost me the throne that was rightfully mine."

He stepped over the spear, and all the companions reared back in trepidation. "I have a promise to keep," Mordred said as he moved around the table, "and order to restore to the land that has been decimated. But when that is done, we shall have a reckoning of our own."

With that, Mordred glanced upward at the sky, then turned and ran towards one of the great castle doors, where he disappeared.

As one, the companions looked up too. High above, the sun had reached its zenith – but instead of shining brightly, it was obscured by shadow and soon would be in full eclipse.

◆ ◆ ◆

"Why didn't he kill us?" Hugo asked. "Not that I'm complaining, but I'm certain he really, really wanted to."

"I don't think he can," John answered. "Not here, in this place. And not after killing Arthur." He looked up at the vanishing sun. "I think that's what's happening now. Mordred's broken some law of the Old Magic."

Outside, in the direction Mordred had gone, the din of battle rose. It meant the escalation of the war. Worse – if that was possible to imagine – it meant that the creation of the Winterland was closer than ever.

"We have to find a way to stop this!" Jack exclaimed.

"We will," John said. "But first we're going to take care of Arthur's body. I'm not just leaving it here, uncovered."

As John and Jack wrapped the body of Arthur and laid it in state on the stone table, Hank moved around to the doors, barricading them. "There," he said, breathing hard from the effort. "No one's going to be coming through. Not for a while, at least," he added with a fearful glance at the ramparts, which were being sparsely defended by the king's followers.

Hugo and Chaz sat in the grass, still numb from the events they'd just witnessed. "You know more about this Arthur fellow than I do," Chaz said. "Can I ask you a question?"

"Certainly," said Hugo.

"Is this the first time or the last time that Arthur was killed?"

Hugo's brow furrowed. "I don't understand what you mean by 'first time' and 'last time.'"

Chaz showed him some pages he'd dog-eared in the Little Whatsit. Hugo scanned the passages Chaz indicated, then frowned. Suddenly he sat upright, and his eyes widened in shock and realization.

"John! Jack!" Hugo shouted. "Come here!"

As the Caretakers approached, Hugo gestured to the book. "Here, Chaz!" he said excitedly. "Read them what you've found!"

"I've been trying t' catch up," Chaz explained. "The rest of you knew so much already about Arthur and Mordred and Merlin, that I've been reading up on them. Do you know if this is the first time, or the last time that Arthur was killed?"

"What's the difference?" asked Jack, his tone sceptical. "He's just dead."

"Well, it says here that he might not have t' be," Chaz replied. "The Little Whatsit says that Arthur ruled on the Silver Throne for a hundred years before he died, but that he'd been killed once before – then restored to life."

That got the Caretakers' attention. "Does it say how he was restored?" John asked, trying not to get his hopes up.

Chaz nodded and quoted from the book. "It says that he was 'saved to bring light back into a world of eternal darkness, by blood, by faith, and by the power of the Sangreal.'"

"The Holy Grail," Hugo said breathlessly. "Arthur can be brought back by the Grail."

"Is it true, John?" Hugo asked. "Does the Grail really exist?"

"I never saw it for myself," John answered. "It disappeared from Alexandria while we were there. Merlin was supposed to have tried to steal it, but he claimed Mordred was the real thief. Then we found Mordred in the chamber, sleeping with one of the priestesses who tended the Grail itself, and that's when Merlin Bound him. And the Grail vanished."

Hugo groaned. "So Mordred may have the only thing that can bring back Arthur? How do we convince him to use it?"

"I don't know that he does," said John. "We don't even know that it's an object, really. It's a translation conundrum that no one, not even the Caretakers, have been able to sort out.

"One way of reading *san greal* means 'Holy Grail,' or the cup of Christ," he explained, "but the other way, *sang real*, means 'royal blood.' What we need might be a person. An actual descendant of Jesus Christ himself."

"The legend of Joseph of Aramathea," said Jack. "He was Christ's uncle, and supposedly took his nephew's *children* away from Jerusalem to Glastonbury, in England."

Hugo started. "That night in the tent," he began, excited that he could add a piece of the puzzle, "Merlin and the Lawgiver were arguing about how betraying the Grail meant betraying Holy Blood. And Merlin said something about the children of the Grail."

"So is it the cup, or is it the bloodline?" Jack asked rhetorically. "Not that it will help to know, since I haven't the faintest idea where it can be found."

"But I do," a voice said behind them, "and if you are worthy, you may yet find out the truth for yourselves."

The companions turned as Taliesin the Lawgiver stepped up out of the stone passageway.

"Taliesin," Hugo said in greeting. "How has this happened?"

The Lawgiver's eyes were filled with tears, and he deliberately avoided looking at Arthur's body. "A journey of a thousand regrets," he said simply, "begins with a single step. Follow the path of your adversary to the beginning, and perhaps you will find the means to alter his course."

"If you are who I think you are, then you had as much right to claim Caliburn as Merlin and Mordred," said John. "Why didn't you stop this three decades ago?"

The Lawgiver briefly raised his hand to his forehead, touching it. "I was Bound, and was kept from doing all I might have had I been released. And now the future is certain unless you find the Grail and restore the true king."

"Where?" Jack wondered. "Where can we find it?"

"At your adversary's beginning," said Taliesin, "and my own."

"In the Archipelago?" asked John, his heart sinking as he anticipated the possibility of a long, arduous journey ahead. "Do we need to find Odysseus? Was that the beginning you mean?"

Taliesin shook his head. "Our father is long gone," he said flatly, "but our mothers remain. The Grail may be found with them."

"Calypso and Circe," said John. "They're still alive?"

"They, or an aspect of them," answered Taliesin. "On an island of glass, that is both here and not here. In this time, they are often called the Pandora, after our ancestor."

"The Morgaine," Jack declared, shaking his fist triumphantly. "The Morgaine! Of course! That means the Grail is on Avalon!"

"And of course," Hugo said, "you just happen to know how to get to Avalon."

"Of course," John told him. "Why wouldn't we?"

"Just asking," said Hugo.

"There's a river near the great stone," Jack said to Hank. "Are there any boats nearby? Anything we might use?"

"They've all been destroyed," Hank said. "Used for raw

materials in the siege. I don't think there's even a toy boat to be had for a thousand miles."

Jack scratched his ear. "Huh," he murmured. "What do you know."

"What?" said Hank.

Jack stuck his hand in his pocket. "We do have that much at least, right here," he replied, removing the miniature ship in a bottle he'd been given by the Serendipity Box. "Take us to the river."

Taliesin offered to stay with the body, to protect it, and the companions bade him farewell and re-entered the stone tunnel. Jack followed last, pausing only to retrieve Mordred's spear. "I don't intend to use it," Jack told the others, "but I'd rather that Mordred didn't have the chance to use it again either."

At the other end of the passageway, as before, the forest was empty. "Thank God for small favours," said Hank. "They're all massed at the gates."

It was not far to a sloping path that led the companions to the flowing water of the river. It was thickly clotted with debris along the shore's edge, but ran clear in the middle, and not too many miles distant, opened up into the sea.

"What do you think, fellows?" Jack asked, cradling the small bottle in his hands. "How do we get it out?"

"Bert simply threw the scarab brooch," said John. "Maybe you should toss it into the water."

"And what if it just sinks?" Jack retorted. "Then where will we be?"

Hank grabbed the bottle out of Jack's hands, and before the others could stop him, he had dashed it against the stones in the shallows. But they realized at once that Hank had done exactly the right thing. The tiny boat, immersed in the water, was beginning to grow.

It took less than a minute for the toy boat to grow into a full-size, functional vessel. It resembled a small Portuguese caravel, with room enough for the companions and their bags, and at the front was the carved representation of a scarlet dragon.

John and Jack nearly cheered at the sight of it. A Dragonship had considerably more meaning for them than it did the others, who were nevertheless still very impressed by the appearance of the instant boat.

"It gave you just what you needed most," Chaz said to Jack. "We just didn't know it at the time."

"Thank God," Jack replied, casting his eyes skyward. "And I mean that literally."

Chaz got in first, still carrying the bag that held the unconscious Archimedes, followed by Jack, then John. Hugo got in next and extended his hand to Hank.

"I'm sorry, fellows," Hank told the others, "but this is as far as I go."

"It's an adventure!" Hugo said brightly. "We're searching for the Holy Grail, don't you see? This is the first Crusade!"

Hank smiled blackly and folded his arms. "I understand your excitement and enthusiasm, Hugo," he said. "I felt the same way when I first got here. But I've been here for too many months, and seen more than I wanted. And I think I've had my fill of adventuring."

"There's a chance this will all change, you know," Jack pointed out. "That's what we're trying to do, anyway."

Hank glanced over his shoulder at the rising clouds of smoke that were darkening an already blackened sky, then up at the haloed sun that was nearly in full eclipse. "I always remain hopeful, but in this case, I think the game's already been called," he said bleakly. "If this isn't the end of the world, it's a damn good imitation. And at this point, I think all I can do is try to stay at the edges of the chaos, and record what I can, before . . ." He let the words trail off.

"Can't you go back?" Hugo implored. "With the watch?"

"The what?" asked Hank. "I don't even know how I got here, much less how I'm going to get home."

"The watch," Hugo repeated. "The one that Sam Clemens gave you, that allows you to travel in time."

Hank looked at the professor as if he were crazy, then chuckled wryly. "I'd say you were losing your marbles, if we weren't where we are. If, by some miracle, you ever come across one of those watches, let me know, will you?"

Hugo turned and looked pointedly at John, who opened up the bag he was carrying. "Maybe you can find it yourself," John said, removing the Serendipity Box and handing it to Hugo, who handed it to Hank. "Open that and tell us what you see."

Obediently Hank lifted the lid and smiled in confused surprise. "You've been having me on the whole time, haven't you?" he asked as he took out the small silver pocket watch that was inside the box. "What does the dragon represent?"

"Hope," said John. "It represents hope."

"How does it work?"

John shook his head. "I don't know. But we were told – by you, actually – that it will let you travel in time."

"There's a note underneath," Hank said. "It reads, 'Midnight takes you back.'"

"The rest is up to you, it seems," said Hugo, clapping Hank on the shoulder. "Remember us to Sam, won't you?"

"Verne," Jack said suddenly. "That's what we need to ask of you, Hank. Remember us to Jules Verne."

"Okay," Hank agreed, still uncertain of what he was being asked or expected to do. "How do I contact him?"

"I think you'll see him when you leave this place," Jack told him, "in another time. Just remember to tell him when and where you got the watch, and from whom."

"I will," said Hank, tapping the dials. "What happens when I turn it to mid—"

Hank vanished.

"That's that, boys," Hugo said, dusting off his hands. "I think he's going where he needs to go, and now, so must we."

He sat in the bow of the boat, which then pulled away from the cluttered shallows and into the swiftly flowing water at the middle of the river.

"So we're on an actual Crusade, then?" Chaz said. "Your Charles would have loved this, wouldn't he?"

"He would, absolutely," said John.

The small boat, which John had dubbed the *Scarlet Dragon*, operated in exactly the way they had hoped. In only a few minutes, the smoke in the air had turned to fog, and it clouded thickly around the craft and its passengers.

Moments passed, and the fog began to thin, then clear completely, and they were sailing in open waters, far from any shore.

"Extraordinary," Hugo breathed, looking around at the horizon. "It's like we've come into another world entirely."

"Not entirely," Jack said, pointing at the sky. The sun above was still eclipsed and hadn't changed. "Avalon lies on the transition line between our world and the Archipelago, so we won't have to completely cross the frontier. But," he added tensely, "if this doesn't work, that may not matter."

Within a few hours, the familiar outlines of the island of Avalon appeared on the western horizon. The sky was already dark enough that they could barely make out the thunderheads beyond that marked the true line of the Frontier – the boundary that protected the Archipelago of Dreams.

As the *Scarlet Dragon* approached, it became evident that this was not entirely the island John and Jack knew. Their Avalon was almost abandoned. Only the three who were one, the witches known as the Morgaine, lived there, with an occasional guest, and were guarded by a succession of old knights. While this Avalon appeared similarly empty, the buildings were not in ruins, as they were in the Caretakers' time. The temples, all Greek, were whole and untouched by time or man.

The shore was clean and afforded an easy landing on the beach in front of them. They pulled the *Scarlet Dragon* up onto the sand, then turned to decide where to go.

"We should be wary," John cautioned. "The Green Knight of this time would not know us, and he won't be as feeble as Darnay, nor as stupid as Magwich."

They approached the centremost temple, but no one greeted them, no knight, no squire. "Well," Jack declared, "I don't think anyone's home."

In defiance of Jack's statement, the torches along the walls suddenly blazed into life, and a chill wind swept through the courtyard.

The companions instinctively backed towards a group of the white marble columns for cover and scanned the buildings to see if they were still alone.

They were not.

From the north a regal woman appeared, hair bound up in the classical Greek manner, underneath a silver circlet. She was dressed in a flowing gown of gossamer silk, with a golden belt that matched her sandals, and walked with the assurance of someone who wielded great power. She strode to the centre of the courtyard and stepped up to a dais, where she sat on an elegantly sculpted bench.

From the south another woman had appeared, just as beautiful as the first, but whose countenance shone with a terrible power. Her long, beautiful hair reached nearly to the floor, and she carried a broad golden bowl. Barefoot, she walked to the dais, where she stood next to the other woman. Both faced the companions.

"I am Circe," the standing woman said, "and we have allowed you here on Avallo because you have come bearing the sign of the Pendragon."

"The boat," Jack whispered. "She means the Dragonship."

"Where's the other one?" John whispered back. "There should be three."

"Speak," Circe commanded. "Tell us why you have come here and what it is that you wish."

The companions turned to John, deferring to his authority as the Caveo Principia. He gulped and stepped forward. The Morgaine were unpredictable and usually played games. There was no reason to expect things to be different now, in the past. But what question to ask?

"We've come seeking the beginning of the men called Myrddyn and Madoc," said John.

Circe smiled, but it seemed to John – incredibly – that the other, who must be Calypso, actually winced, then blushed.

"Their beginning," Circe said, "is known to us. They began as all men did, and with the same potential. But they forgot how to choose."

"Forgot how to choose what?" asked John.

"How to choose," Circe answered sternly, as if John were a bit stupid. "They forgot that choosing is always an option. There is always a choice to be made."

"Why are you here?" John said. "On Avalon? I know that your island is called Aiaia."

Circe bowed her head. "It is. And hers was Ogygia, before she came here," she said, indicating Calypso. "We came here to the temple of Diana, which was erected by Brutus, to await our children's return."

"This is the island," Jack interjected. "This is where they wrecked the *Argo*."

Again Circe bowed her head. "Brutus built the temple with those who escaped from broken Troy, before he went to the isle of giants, called Albion, to build a kingdom of his own. No man, save for one, an old fisherman, ever returned to this island until Myrddyn and Madoc were exiled here."

"The fisherman was the one who helped Anaximander rescue them," said John.

"He was," said Circe. "Odysseus was a vain and fickle man, but unlike Iason, he always returned to watch over his children."

"I wanted to ask about the *Red Dragon* . . . ," Jack began.

"Too many questions!" Circe exclaimed. "Enough!"

"I'm getting a good idea which of them turns into Cul," Jack whispered.

"What is it you wish of the Pandora?" Circe demanded again. "Speak."

"We come seeking the Grail," Hugo said. "The Holy Grail."

John swore silently and threw a helpless glance at Jack. Hugo was not accustomed to dealing with the witches; he didn't understand how they responded to direct statements like that.

"At last," Calypso said. "A plainspoken man."

Circe held up the golden bowl. "Choose," she said. "The Cup of Albion, or the bloodline of Aramathea."

"The cup?" John whispered. "That's not a bowl. It's the cup of the giant Brutus slew."

"The bloodline of Aramathea," Jack mused. "That's what we thought of as well. Both have ties to Britain, and to the heritage of Arthur. But I don't know what to choose."

"Don't look at me," Chaz said, paging furiously through the Little Whatsit. "I can't even take a guess."

"Let me," Hugo offered, stepping forward. "I choose the bloodline," he said with no hesitation.

Circe and Calypso nodded at each other, and a third woman, plainer than the others but still lovely, came up the steps behind them to take her place on the dais.

"Are . . . are you . . . ?" Hugo said hesitantly. "Are you the Grail?"

"Gwynhfar," the woman replied, bowing her head. "I am called Gwynhfar."

. . . the knight . . . stood at the entrance of the temple . . .

Chapter Twenty
The Good Knight

"*I have seen you* before, haven't I?" John said gently.

"Yes," said Gwynhfar, glancing at him. "Once, long ago, in a faraway place."

"Alexandria," Jack said, realizing who she was. "You were the girl with Madoc, in the Grail chamber."

"Are you really a descendant of . . . ," Hugo began. "Are you truly of the Holy Blood?"

"Five generations ago, my ancestor was put to death," Gwynhfar said. "He died at the hands of the Romans, who could not bear to see their own beliefs supplanted by those he left in his wake as he travelled, teaching. And so when he returned home, they killed him. And soon after, many who followed him. So my great-great-great-granduncle Joseph gathered the family together and fled the land of our birth for a new world.

"But," she continued, "the beliefs and practices of the old world still held sway there, and it was not safe for us to remain. All who were descended from the great Teacher were eventually killed, save for myself and Uncle Joseph. So he arranged for me to be taken to the one place where I would be guarded, where all the great scholars of the world had come together. A place where new beliefs might be forged and fought for."

"And even there, in the library itself, you were not protected," Jack murmured.

Gwynhfar nodded. "There were those who would use me, and what I represented, to further their own aims."

"So when Madoc forced himself on you . . . ," Jack began.

Gwynhfar looked at him in confusion. This meant nothing to her. "Forced?"

"What I mean to say," Jack tried again, "is that when you were, uh, attacked in Alexandria by Madoc, and he violated you—"

"You misunderstand," Gwynhfar interrupted. "I was not attacked. I was not . . . violated. Not by Madoc. How can you say that I was?"

Jack looked at the others, now clearly confused himself. "But we thought . . . When Meridian spoke of his brother betraying the Grail . . ."

"You are mistaken," Gwynhfar said coldly.

"But we were there," Jack said cautiously, with a quick glance at John. "We saw you with Madoc and heard you scream as you fled the library." He extended his hands, trying to understand. "Meridian defended your honour!"

Gwynhfar snorted derisively. "You assume, and conjecture, and misread everything," she said. "You would have been completely inadequate as my Caretakers."

"We do have our moments," John said, not sure if his own words were a defence or an admission. "Please, tell us what really happened."

Gwynhfar stepped down from the dais to get closer to them. She was shorter than all of them save Hugo, and surprisingly delicate.

"Meridian and Madoc were there as two of my Caretakers," she began, "but once Meridian discovered who I was, and why I was valued, he lost interest . . . mostly," she added. "His interest in the library had more to do with the objects gathered there, such as the Cup of Albion and the Horn of Bran Galed."

"Old Magic artifacts," said Jack. "But not the New World treasures, like the Lance of Longinus or . . ."

"The Sangreal," Gwynhfar finished. "Except for uses more common."

Her meaning dawned over the companions. "So when Ptolemy said Meridian had tried to take the Grail . . . ," John began.

"He tried to take from me, against my will," Gwynhfar explained, "that which I freely shared with Madoc, whom I loved, and who loved me in return."

"And we believed he was evil," Jack said dully. "We sided with Meridian and helped to Bind his brother. And Madoc was the good one all along."

"Y' mean he might have been," said Chaz, "if we hadn't come along an' mucked him up."

"Both of my sons have made poor choices," Calypso clarified. "Both were exiled from the Archipelago. But of the two, Madoc was the one with a spirit."

"Soul," John said quietly. "She means soul."

"What is the difference?" Calypso asked, hearing the word John spoke. "It is the breath of the gods in him. It is his life. It is himself."

"Spirit, breath, wind," Jack intoned. "My God, John, what have we done?"

"We need to do our duty now," replied John. "We are the

Caretakers of the Archipelago." He turned to Gwynhfar. "We need you to come with us. Something terrible has happened, and only you can help us."

She shook her head. "I am of the Archipelago now. The island of Avallo is as far as I will go towards the world that was."

"We should have brought him with us," said Chaz. "Is there time t' go back?"

John shook his head. "It's been too long already," he said, noting the eclipsed sun. "Every moment takes us farther into the Winterland. And we may never be able to reverse it if we don't do it now."

"I must stay," said Gwynhfar, "but the Holy Blood might be taken back with you, to do what must be done."

"You want us to take your blood?" asked Hugo.

"No," she said with a faint smile, "I want you to take my child."

Gwynhfar turned and walked between Circe and Calypso, gesturing for the companions to follow.

They walked out of the temple and down a long procession of steps that ended up splitting into two separate paths. The one to the left followed the ridge of sharp cliffs that rose above the western side of the island. Jack and John looked at each other and grinned in recognition. That path led to the cave where they were most familiar with seeing the Morgaine, and where they would one day meet the distant heir to Arthur's throne. If Arthur might still have heirs, that was.

The path to the right dropped sharply down to a pebbled beach, where a number of rusted weapons and tools were scattered in the sand.

There ahead of them, watching through an old iron grate half-buried in the sand, was a young girl. She was auburn-haired, with wide green eyes and a face that bespoke innocence. She was playing with an assemblage of gears that resembled the insides of a watch.

Gwynhfar walked to the girl, who stood and kissed her mother on the cheek. "I've brought you some visitors," said Gwynhfar. She introduced the companions one by one, and the girl nodded and smiled at each of them in turn.

"And what is your name, my dear young lady?" asked John. "How are you called?"

Gwynhfar answered instead, shaking her head. "She has never been named. Her father has never seen her or spoken her name. So she has waited to choose her own name."

On impulse more than anything else, Hugo reached inside his jacket and removed the indigo rose he'd been given by the Serendipity Box. He looked to Gwynhfar, who gave him a curious look in return, then nodded, and he turned and gave the flower to the girl.

"It's called a rose," he said mildly. "I . . . I think I brought it for you. Will you come with us? Will you come, and help us?"

The girl nodded. "May I give you a thimble?" she asked, and kissed him on the cheek before he could reply. "Thank you for my name. I've been waiting for you a long time."

"It's a flower, not a name," Hugo stammered, still blushing from the kiss.

"A thimble might be a kiss, a flower might be a name, and a dragon might be a ship," said Gwynhfar. "Sometimes things are simply what we need them to be. And sometimes things are not what we expect."

She turned and walked up the steps, expecting the others to follow. Her daughter and Hugo went behind her, then Jack and Chaz.

John was about to follow, when he caught sight of a movement farther down the beach. He stopped and looked more closely, then realized it was an old fisherman, bent over his nets.

The fisherman saw John and lifted an arm to wave. John waved back, then trotted up the steps to catch up to the others. "He always returned to watch over his children," he murmured. "That's the way to do it, old-timer."

Back in the temple of Diana, the companions stood with the enchantresses, Gwynhfar, and the girl.

"Thank you," John began. "We cannot express what this will mean to the world that you are helping us."

"Your gratitude is not necessary," Circe said. "It is a fair exchange, in the manner of the old ways."

Exchange? John thought wildly. *What exchange?* He'd forgotten that the Morgaine rarely gave anything freely; they usually expected something in return. But they had brought nothing with them except . . .

"You don't mean to take our boat, do you?" John said. "We need it to—"

"Not the Dragonship," said Circe. "It has not the value."

"Then what?" asked Jack. "What is it you want?"

"Blood for blood, a life for a life," Circe said simply. "It is the Old Magic, and it is the Law. If the child is to leave Avalon, then one of you must stay."

"You're going to sacrifice one of us?" Hugo gulped.

"No one will be sacrificed." Calypso sighed. "But he who stays will be expected to serve, as our daughter will serve in the Summer Country."

"The Green Knight," Jack said suddenly. "They mean for one of us to become the Green Knight."

John understood. That was why they hadn't seen one of the familiar guardians of the island. There had been no guardian, not until this point in time. And one of them would have to stay behind and take up the mantle, if they were going to have the chance to save Arthur.

Chaz stepped forward. "I can do this. I want to do this."

Jack shook his head. "No," he said flatly. "You don't realize what you're offering, Chaz."

"I know one of us has t' stay," reasoned Chaz. "What else do I need t' know? You two are real Caretakers. You have t' go back. And rescuing Hugo was part of the reason you've done all this t' begin with. I'm the only one who *can* stay."

"We'll find another way," John began. "There must be another way, Chaz!"

"Blood for blood, a life for a life," Circe repeated. "There is no other way."

"I've been wondering all along," Chaz said slowly, eyes downcast, "if maybe things back in Albion might have been different, if I had only been more like Charles instead of Chaz, then. We're not that different now, he and I, I think."

"Chaz," said Jack, "you can't hold yourself responsible. The Winter King was centuries old before you were even born. He had thousands and thousands of minions at his command. Against all that, what can one—"

"What can one man do?" Chaz asked, looking up at Jack with a grin. "Is that what you were going to say, Jack? I've been wondering that myself. Especially with things I've been reading in the Little Whatsit. And it seems that one man, in the right place, an' at th' right time, can do an awful lot. And I could have, and didn't. Not when it meant the most."

He was talking about Bert, John realized. Since the last passage from Sanctuary, they hadn't mentioned the death of the old traveller, but now he understood that it had weighed as heavily on Chaz as it had on him or Jack, and perhaps more so.

"Besides," Chaz went on, "in't all of what we're doing based on one man, anyway? This 'Christ' everyone's been going on about? He was just one man, wasn't he?"

"That's different," Jack replied. "That was . . . well, a mythology. A real mythology, based on a real person, but you can't use that story as a reason for choosing to sacrifice yourself in this way."

"And why not?" Chaz shot back, annoyed. "Isn't that why we come all this way, to this island? T' find the Holy Blood who are his children?

"You say it's just a mythology, a story," Chaz continued, "but here we are anyway, centuries later, pinning all our hopes for the future of the entire world on whether or not this girl is his kin, and carries his blood. And maybe she is, and maybe she isn't – but what else are stories for, 'cept t' learn from, and improve yourself? T' learn t' do th' right thing?"

"Because the story is *mythical*," Jack retorted. "There probably *was* a man called Jesus Christ, and he probably *was* crucified. But all the value of that sacrifice came from the mythology that sprang up around it, and maybe the whole reason that there is power in his bloodline is because people have chosen to believe in it – not because of the value of the literal event itself."

"What's the difference?"

Jack started to reply – then realized he couldn't. Not that he didn't want to, but because he really had no way to answer the question.

Chaz stepped over to Jack and put his hands on his shoulders. "If I do this," Chaz went on, his voice low, "it will be literal, not mythical. Only you, those here with me, will ever know the literal truth of the choice I'm making. But maybe, in time, my friends will make a story out of it, and it might even become a myth. And others can learn from my example, the way I've learned from the ones I've read about, and seen, and become friends with."

Jack met Chaz's eyes and realized that his unlikely ally had indeed become a friend. "You realize," he said, struggling to voice the words, "what we're trying probably won't work, right, Chaz? We're taking this child to a battlefield to resurrect a dead man who may or may not have been the rightful king. And there's no way of knowing if it will work."

"That's where – what did you call it, John? Faith? That's where faith comes in, doesn't it?" Chaz said. "You have t' admit, it sounds familiar . . . sacrifices, and bringing someone back t' life . . . Even if it doesn't work, it'll be a great story. Just don't forget me, hey?"

"Never, Chaz," Jack said, embracing his friend in a tight hug. "I'll never forget."

John also gave Chaz a hug and a solid clap on the back, and even Hugo gave him a warm two-handed shake.

Chaz turned to the enchantresses and spread his arms. "Okay," he said with as much bravado as he could muster. "Y' got me."

Circe looked at Calypso, who nodded and looked at Gwynhfar, who also nodded. Then the three of them beckoned to Chaz to come forward.

He took a few slightly unsteady steps, then strode forward to the top of the dais. Circe moved behind a pillar and re-emerged carrying a silver tray. On it was a small cake and a crystal bottle with a stopper.

"Choose," said Calypso. "Choose your form, Chaz, and thus become the Guardian of Avalon."

"I've avoided drinking things lately," Chaz said decisively. "Nothing personal, but everyone in history seems obsessed with poisoning everyone else. So if it's all the same t' you, I'll have the cake."

"As you wish, Chaz," said Circe.

"Don't mind if I do," he replied, taking the small cake from the tray and popping it, whole, into his mouth. "And please, from here on – call me *Charles*."

The cake took effect almost immediately, and Chaz – Charles – bent over in pain. Jack began to rush forward to the dais, but John held him back. "Wait. Just wait, and watch."

The two enchantresses and Gwynhfar stepped around the agonized man, forming a loose circle. All three were murmuring words – words of comfort, or spells? John couldn't tell. His friend twisted about, seemingly in agony. But even through the tears, they could see he was smiling.

Suddenly leaves shot out from his joints, and around his neck and waist, shredding his clothes. His skin began to darken, as if it had been aged and stained to a fine, rich sheen. As one, the three women moved away and removed pieces of armour from the alcoves around the dais. They returned just as the transfigured man was getting to his feet, and they dressed him, reverently, almost gratefully.

Next, Gwynhfar signalled to her daughter, who dashed off to one of the rooms and returned with a great rectangular shield, which she handed to him.

"And now," Calypso stated, "we must choose a weapon for you."

"I think I have just the one," Jack said, and dashed down the steps to the *Scarlet Dragon*. He returned to the temple carrying the Lance of Longinus.

"This was Mordred – Madoc's," he explained, "and it has a history with your ancestor as well, Gwynhfar. I think it being wielded by the Guardian of Avalon would be an appropriate use for it."

"Well spoken," said Circe.

Jack handed the spear to Gwynhfar, who presented it, reverently, to the Green Knight.

"It is done," said Circe. "The Old Magic is satisfied."

The girl kissed each of the enchantresses farewell, then embraced her mother. The companions said their goodbyes to the knight, who then stood at the entrance of the temple, ready to assume his duties.

"Tell Fred and Uncas I will miss them," the Green Knight called out as the small boat moved away from the shore. "Tell them I said thank you, for helping me to find my destiny. And look after Archie, will you?"

"We will," Jack said, waving. "Goodbye . . . *Charles*."

The *Scarlet Dragon* passed back into the Summer Country as easily as it had left, and in a matter of hours, the companions were once again racing through the stone passageway that led to the castle.

When they emerged from the crypt, they found Taliesin still watching over Arthur's body. The Lawgiver seemed astonished to see them back.

"The battle does not go well," he said, "and you have increased Mordred's anger tenfold."

"Us?" said John. "Why?"

"He came back for the lance," said Taliesin, "and flew into a rage when I told him you had taken it."

"Hah." Jack smirked. "It's in a far, far better place, and being used for a better purpose than Mordred had managed." He looked down at Arthur's body. "I only hope we've returned in time."

"I don't even know who's supposed to win anymore," said Hugo. "Do we want Mordred to win? Or Merlin?"

"We want Arthur, the true High King, to do what he's meant to do," said John, moving aside to allow the girl to approach the table. "That's what we brought her to do, if she can."

Taliesin gasped in recognition, then bowed his head as the girl approached.

She touched Arthur's face lightly. "Hello, cousin Thorn," she said as if he could hear her. "My name is Rose. And I've come here to help you."

"The blood that took his life must be the blood that restores it," Taliesin murmured.

"He's not going to hurt her, is he?" Hugo asked, eyeing the Lawgiver.

"I don't think so," Jack said, holding him back. "Watch."

Taliesin touched Rose's hand with the black staff, and the runes flared briefly with eldritch light. She looked at her hand and saw the small cut across her palm.

Rose marked both of Arthur's cheeks with the blood from her hand, tracing the line of the bones to his chin. Then, reverently, she laid both of her hands on his head, closed her eyes, and began to speak.

By light's power driven
For need of right
I restore thee
I restore thee

By blood bound
By honour given
I restore thee
I restore thee

For life and light and protection proffered
From blood and will my life is offered
I restore thee
I restore thee.

Rose removed her hands from his head and crumpled to the ground. Hugo rushed forward and caught her, but the others had no time to react to what happened next.

There was a pause, as if the world had stopped.

No sound, no movement. Even the constant rumble of the battle outside had ceased. The stillness was everywhere, and everywhen. And then, overhead, the dark circle eclipsing the sun shifted. The light on the edge of the sun brightened, then rays burst forth, striking directly below in the centre of the castle, on the ancient table made of stone, which was carved with the runes of the Old Magic.

Suddenly, impossibly, Arthur raised his hand and reached into the light. Then he sat up, swung his legs off the table, and rose to his feet.

The High King, Arthur Pendragon, was alive.

PART SIX

The Silver Throne

The older dragons . . . almost looked as if they were grinning . . .

Chapter Twenty-one
The Fallen

A tall stack of bound manuscripts tottered, then fell, setting off a chain reaction in the small writing chamber Geoffrey kept on the topmost level of the church.

In seconds, the pages he'd been working on were swept away in a tidal wave of aged leather and the decaying writings of monks long dead.

Geoffrey sat on the floor and sighed. This was becoming a more and more frequent occurrence. He'd got into the habit of acquiring old books and manuscripts in his younger days, at the upswing of the twelfth century. But now, at its midpoint, he was beginning to grow weary at the futility of it all.

He reached for the nearest tome and smiled as he realized what it was. Nestor's *Primary Chronicle*. One of the first and greatest of the world histories. Not complete, by any means, and certainly slanted towards the Slavic, but indispensable nonetheless. After all, few chronicles ever attempted to begin as far back as the pharaohs, or even the Deluge. Even his own works were meagre contributions to his own library compared to Nestor's works, dealing as they did with the histories of the lineage of Britain's kings, and of the great enchanter and philosopher Myrddyn.

Geoffrey had only just begun to clean up the disaster when he heard a knocking at the door downstairs. He quickly made his way down the stairs, but when he opened the door, no one was there.

Instead he found a parchment rose, which had strange markings on the petals, and a roll of paper, cream-coloured and tied with a cord. It was addressed to him. Cautiously he unrolled it and read what was written inside.

He blinked at the rose and the strangeness of the message, then read it again, then a third time.

Quickly he shut the door and hurried back up to his study, where he tossed the rolled paper into the embers of his fireplace, then stoked the coals until it caught fire. He stood and watched it until it was nothing but ash.

"Is this a dream?" Arthur asked. "It must be, because Merlin's War Leader is here and seems to have been weeping over me."

"He was Bound," John said, "by Merlin."

Taliesin knelt and took Arthur's hand. "You are the true High King, the true Arthur."

"Bound?" asked Arthur. "As in Old Magic?"

"Yes," said Hugo. "He's been Bound all along, ever since the tournament."

"The tournament," Arthur said wonderingly. "That's where I met you two before, isn't it? You met Archimedes and me at Grandfather Oak and helped me find my way to Camelot."

"We did," Jack confirmed.

"I wish you'd stayed around," Arthur remarked. "You three seemed reasonable men. And there has been a shortage of reasonable men these last thirty years."

He suddenly noticed his bloodstained tunic and touched his chest, probing. "I . . . I died, didn't I?"

"You did," said John. "It was an accident. Mordred didn't mean to do it."

"Then how is it I am standing here now?"

"Because of her," Hugo said, cradling the still weak girl. "Mordred's daughter – your cousin, Rose. The heir of the Grail."

"I can't believe you have that kind of power," Jack breathed, as he and Hugo helped her to her feet. "You brought him back, Rose."

She shook her head. "Not I, and not my power."

"It was someone's power," reasoned Jack. "He was dead, and then he was not."

"That is the blessing of the Old Magic," said Taliesin, "and the power of belief."

"Oh no," Arthur cried, kneeling. "What happened to my sword?"

"It shattered when Mordred stabbed you," John said. "When his spear clashed against your sword."

"That should not have happened," said Taliesin, looking over the broken halves of Caliburn with Arthur. "Caliburn should have been stronger."

"I don't think it was Caliburn that was weak," said Arthur. "*I* was. I think I was afraid to use the strength that was needed to end this sooner."

"Now is your chance, boy," a harsh voice called out as one of the heavy inner doors splintered apart. The companions whirled about to see Merlin force his way into the castle's centre. "It's only right that I should find you here, where it began," he said angrily. "Where you took what was rightfully mine."

He seemed to notice only then that there were others present and, with no small surprise and a rising anger, realized that he knew them.

"You," he said accusingly to the companions. "You have followed me for much of my life. If you value your own, you won't interfere."

"You didn't mind when it benefited you," John pointed out.

"I did mind, when you changed my own history," Merlin spat, "and disqualified me when I was one breath away from gaining my throne."

"You would have lost, Merlin," Taliesin said. "Mordred would have beaten you."

"I lost, traitor," Merlin replied, "when I didn't learn my lesson the first time, to make my Bindings more specific."

He tightened his grip on the short Roman sword he carried and stepped towards Arthur. The companions circled protectively around the king, and then another player joined the deadly game.

"This has been a long time coming, brother," Mordred said, stepping out of the crypt passageway. He stopped in shock when he saw Arthur, and even took a step backwards when he saw Rose.

Then he seemed to steel himself. He took a firm grip on the scimitar he was carrying and walked purposefully towards Merlin.

"Mordred," Arthur began.

"Stay back, Arthur," Mordred commanded, "and this shall be ended in a trice."

Merlin acted first, leaping with a snarl at Arthur. His blow was parried not by the king, but by Mordred's scimitar. Mordred pulled back and struck out at Merlin, but found his blow deflected by a short sword, expertly wielded – by Arthur.

"What are you doing?" Mordred asked, incredulous.

"What I must," said Arthur.

"As am I," said Merlin, swinging the sword again. Arthur dodged it easily, then pressed around the table to block Mordred.

Merlin jumped atop the table, only to have his feet knocked out from under him by a vicious blow from the scimitar. Mordred pushed Arthur aside with a shove, then leaped up to deliver a killing blow to the disoriented Merlin.

"This is the end, brother," Mordred said, holding Merlin at the throat with one hand, while drawing back the scimitar with the other.

Merlin screamed.

Mordred struck.

And suddenly he realized that his scimitar was lying on the ground, still clutched in his hand.

He cried out in pain and horror and held the bleeding stump of his forearm to his chest.

"I couldn't let you do it, Mordred," said Arthur, the bloody sword in his hand dropping loosely to his side. "I couldn't let you kill him."

Mordred staggered, then fell. Kneeling in the dirt, he curled in on himself. After a moment, his shoulders began to shake.

Dear Christ, thought John. *Mordred is* laughing.

Mordred threw back his head, eyes wild, and in a moment his frenzied laughter turned into an agonized, soul-searing scream. He rose to his feet, still bleeding, and pushed past Arthur and Taliesin to the crypt, where he disappeared into the passageway below.

The companions moved back to the table, where Merlin was sitting and holding his head in his hands.

"Are you all right, Merlin?" John ventured, staying back out of reach of the short sword.

"I was going to kill you myself!" Merlin cried, looking at Arthur with a bewildered expression. "Why, Thorn? Why did you prevent Mordred from killing me?"

"Because," Arthur replied, "I didn't believe then, and don't believe now, that anyone needs to die to become the High King."

"That," said Taliesin, "is the reason you were able to draw Caliburn at the tournament."

"Then how was it that Mordred's spear shattered Caliburn?" asked Jack. "Arthur is far more noble than Mordred. In my opinion, anyway."

"It wasn't a matter of nobility, but a matter of belief," Taliesin replied. "In the moment that they met, Mordred's belief in his motivation was greater."

A tremendous crashing arose from within the walls of the castle, and the clashing of steel could be heard. The war was coming to the heart of Camelot.

"Is it Arthur's forces, or Merlin's?" asked John.

"It doesn't matter," said Arthur. "My main support had been Mordred's, and the soldiers were his as well. Everyone else, all the other tribes, had been united under Merlin before he tried to overthrow me."

Taliesin agreed, with sadness and regret radiating from his face. "Under the Binding, I had trained them all to respond to the will of Merlin, on Arthur's behalf," he said, "but none of that will matter now. If you have the means to take him away, Arthur must flee, and rule in exile."

John and Jack knew what it would mean if Arthur left now. Merlin would try to rule until he was overthrown by Mordred.

And then, despite all they had done, the Winterland would still come to pass.

"There is a way."

It was Merlin who spoke.

"When you drew Caliburn," he began, "and won the tournament, you were acknowledged as the High King. As the Arthur, Pendragon. The liaison between the Summer Country and the Archipelago of Dreams. But there was one step you didn't take . . . were not allowed to take. One I never allowed those who knew," he said, looking at Taliesin, "to tell you about.

"There are those more powerful than the armies of man," Merlin went on in a sombre voice, "and as High King, you have the right to command them."

"Where?" asked Arthur. "Who are they?"

Merlin turned to John. "You know where, and you know how," he said. "Don't you?"

"Stonehenge," John said breathlessly. "We can use Stonehenge, the Ring of Power, to summon the dragons of the Archipelago."

The small group, including Merlin, left the castle through the crypt passageway, pulling the cover stone over it as they went. It would not take long for it to be discovered, but by then they would be miles away.

Taliesin, with some assistance from Jack, secured horses for all the companions and took the lead, heading towards the standing stones John called the Ring of Power. As they left the passageway and waited for the horses, Arthur was anxiously scanning the countryside, looking, hoping, but to no avail.

Mordred was nowhere to be seen.

◆　　◆　　◆

It took several hours for the companions to reach Stonehenge, and all the while they rode, the skies behind them filled with smoke. Camelot was in flames.

Arthur glanced to his left, at the girl called Rose, who was riding behind Hugo on a black mare. There had been little time for discussion, but he was wise enough to have pieced together who she was, and what she had done to save him. He watched her, saddened, and hoped that their support of each other would extend beyond the present moment. That was, he believed, how it should be. In a family.

He patted the bag at his side, taking comfort in the feel of Caliburn, while also feeling shame. Was it possible to betray, even by weakness, a weapon? Even one as storied as Caliburn?

They dismounted and tied the horses in a nearby grove, then walked over to the ancient standing stones.

"The last legacy of the sons of Albion," said Taliesin, stroking one of the massive stones. "And the last connection they kept to the world of their birth."

"Do you know what to do?" Merlin asked Arthur.

"We can show him what he needs to do and say," Jack said, his voice firm, "and if it's all the same to you, I think you need to stand back."

"Of-of course," said Merlin, bowing his head.

He moved to a shallow field where he could watch without disturbing Arthur. The others remained apart from him, until Rose moved over to him and took his hand. Then Hugo followed, and finally Taliesin.

John and Jack took Arthur to the centre of the stones and explained to him what it was they hoped he would do. They explained the means, and the ritual, then left him alone and joined the others.

Arthur stood a long while, arms folded behind his back, head bowed, as if in prayer. Finally, he lifted his head and began to speak.

> By right and rule
> For need of might
> I call on thee
> I call on thee
>
> By blood bound
> By honour given
> I call on thee
> I call on thee
>
> For life and light your protection given
> From within this Ring by the power of Heaven
> I call on thee
> I call on thee.

He finished speaking the Summoning and looked around at the mottled sky. Then he turned and called out to the others, "Now what happens?"

"Now," John said grimly, "we wait. And hold out as long as we can."

They did not have to wait for long.

A dozen dragons, of various shapes, sizes, and colours, dropped out of the sky and landed on the hillside near the stone circle. The first among them was not the largest, but was by far the most familiar to John and Jack.

"Samaranth!" John exclaimed. He was almost giddy at seeing one of their strongest allies. Both he and Jack rushed forward – and stopped in their tracks.

The large, reddish dragon with the white mane of hair looked at them with a gaze that was clear in its meaning: Come no closer.

John looked at Jack in puzzlement. Then they both realized what was wrong. They were still in the sixth century and would not meet Samaranth, the oldest dragon, for nearly fourteen hundred more years. He would not know them, here, now. And he, as well as the other dragons, would be wondering who had known to summon them using the Ring of Power.

"Ah, what do I do now?" asked Arthur. "Offer to shake hands?"

"Not a good idea," said Jack. "John?"

John's mind was racing. He hadn't really thought it through this far. He'd simply taken a wild chance that the king would be able to summon the dragons. But he needn't have worried – someone was already in charge and knew how to proceed.

"Why have you summoned us here?" the great, smoky voice of Samaranth rumbled. He swung his head around to Arthur, who, to his credit, stood his ground and faced the dragon fearlessly. "You," Samaranth said. "You spoke the Summoning. What gives you the authority to do so? Who has given you the words that called us here?"

"I called you of my own authority," Arthur answered, emboldened by the fact that the dragon hadn't simply bitten his head off straightaway. "And the words to speak were given to me by your servants, the Caretakers of the *Imaginarium Geographica*."

Arthur made a gesture with his hands, indicating to John and Jack that they should step forward.

"Sons of Adam," Samaranth asked, "what does this mean?"

"It means that we are also Caretakers of the Archipelago of Dreams, and true and loyal servants of the High King," said John.

"And you support his rule?"

Jack and John both nodded. "We do."

"Are there any others who will stand with you, little king?" asked Samaranth.

Screaming a ferocious battle cry, King Pellinor burst through the shrubbery at the edge of the trees, charging straight at the dragons. He was dressed in rags, which were tied around what little remained of his rusted and abused armour, and was running barefoot. Seeing the dragons, the king suddenly skidded to a stop – apparently, when he saw that his legendary "Questing Beast" had finally come to Albion, he had neglected to notice that several others had come as well.

Pellinor stood there, staring mutely at the dragons while his mind reeled. This was not the end to the quest he'd envisioned, nor had his grandfather, or his grandfather's grandfather. Finally he let out a yell in frustration. "Which of you is it?" he shouted. "Which of you is the Questing Beast, appointed by destiny to be slain by the lineage of Pelles?"

The older dragons at the front almost looked as if they were grinning, John thought, if he really believed a dragon was capable of grinning. Then, in the back, a largish orange dragon with a short, stout body and a long, thick neck raised an arm and waved at Pellinor.

"Aha!" the old king exclaimed as he dropped his visor and drew his sword. "Have at thee, beast!"

Pellinor set off at a full run directly at the dragons, who moved aside to let him through to his target. Pellinor barely came up to the dragon's knees – which did not deter him from stabbing the dragon directly in the shin. In response, the Orange Dragon reached out with a great clawed foot and stomped down on the blustering Pellinor with a crunch.

When the dragon lifted his foot, Pellinor's right leg and left arm were twisted at sickeningly odd angles. Still, the old king persisted in stabbing at the dragon with his sword.

"This?" Pellinor bellowed, glancing at his ruined arm. "It's just a flesh wound! I've had worse!"

"Your leg is also broken, you old fool," the dragon noted.

"Making excuses not to fight me, eh, beast?" challenged Pellinor, and he attempted to chop at the dragon's foot. "Coward! I'll have your guts for garters!"

The Orange Dragon sighed and picked Pellinor up by the neck. He walked over to the tree line and deposited the raging king into a stout, hollow oak.

"Think you've won, eh?" shouted Pellinor with a now barkmuffled voice. "I can still see you, beast! I can still, uh . . ." There was a brief pause, as the ratty old king realized that not only was he halfcrippled, but he was also completely immobilized within the trunk.

"I can still curse you!" Pellinor yelled, looking through a knothole. "With my last breath, I shall curse at thee, from the very heart of . . . ah, well, this tree!"

The Orange Dragon shook his head and walked back to join the others.

"Any others, little king?" asked Samaranth.

"I think he was the last one who would have backed me," Arthur said, embarrassed, "and he only did that much because my uncle asked him to."

"Ah yes," Samaranth mused. "Your uncle Mordred. He was a favourite of mine. A very good student. But he has always let his belief that events and creatures are unchangeable manipulate his choices. And that, above all, is a stupid way to live."

"And his brother?" asked John. "Was he also your student, Samaranth?"

"He was mine," said a smallish, lithe dragon, who stepped to the fore of the drive. "I was his teacher, and he, too, was an excellent student."

"The Indigo Dragon speaks true," said Samaranth. "The sons of Odysseus have always had great potential. But it has been warped, and misused, and they lost their way."

There was a great, choking sob from behind the companions. Merlin, his eyes filled with tears, stepped forward, hands outstretched. The Indigo Dragon took him, pulled him close, and embraced him. "Ah, little boy-king." The creature sighed. "I had hopes for you. I did. But now it seems another will have to serve in your stead as the Indigo King."

"Was there no time I chose correctly?" Merlin asked. "No chance I had to redeem myself?"

"Almost," said the Indigo Dragon. "Had you chosen – truly chosen – to step aside for the boy, it would have been you who was worthy to wear the Indigo Crown and sit on the Silver Throne."

Merlin looked anguished, then nodded sadly and walked back to the companions.

"Thousands of years ago," declared the Indigo Dragon, "as the world of men ceased believing in magic and wonder, we, the Guardians of the Archipelago, began to draw a veil over it, to prevent passage except by those who travelled in vessels that bore the mark of divinity.

"But that mark had less to do with power than it did with belief, and intention. This was a lesson we ourselves learned, many thousands of years ago. But we also learned that once fallen, we could also rise again if we so chose. And many of us did.

"There are many who will aid you, both in this world and in the Archipelago. There are objects of both power and influence, born of magics old and new. But above all, you must believe in your cause and have the righteousness of intention to see it through, and you shall always prevail.

"This is your secret, young king. Yours, and those who are the Caretakers of the lands that lie beyond," the Indigo Dragon continued, indicating the companions with his great claw. "Guard it well and call on us in time of need. We will aid you, as long as you are worthy."

"You will come, if called by one of royal worth?" said John.

"A misunderstanding," the dragon said. "The authority does not now and never has lain with those of royal blood. Rather, it lies within those of noble worth. And having one does not necessarily guarantee the other."

"These are the duties of your office, young king," Samaranth said. "Will you accept, knowing all that you face? Knowing that the world is united against you, save for these few, and those such as ourselves?"

Arthur nodded with no hesitation. "I will."

The great old dragon looked skyward, as did all the others. Where there was dark smoke obscuring the sky and light of the sun, a thousand pinpricks of light had appeared, breaking apart the darkness.

"Then as you have Summoned us," Samaranth concluded, "the dragons of the Archipelago shall serve."

In minutes the sky was filled with a multitude of dragons, all flying towards Camelot. The dragons in the great stone circle indicated to the companions that they should climb onto them to travel more quickly, and in moments they too were airborne.

In the distance . . . the passenger . . . could make out the island . . .

CHAPTER TWENTY-TWO
Exiled

With the aid of the dragons, it was not long before order, or at least a more manageable chaos, was established in Camelot. The fires were quenched and the armies routed. And backed by the might of the great winged beasts, Taliesin was able to reassert his authority as war leader over many of the tribes. Not all of them. But enough. And as the sun began to set, it was evident to all the companions that it would be setting on Arthur's Britain, and not on Mordred's Albion.

At the stone table, the dozen dragons who had appeared at Stonehenge converged again with the companions. The Caretakers, Hugo, and Rose had stayed well away from the battles. This was not their war. And Arthur had gone to the front of the conflict, to show to the soldiers that Taliesin was indeed now taking orders from, and obeying, the true king.

Merlin, for the most part, sat at the back of the hill, neither moving nor speaking.

"Have you any further need of us, Arthur?" asked Samaranth. It was the first time any of them had addressed him by the title, and for the first time in thirty years, it felt earned.

"I believe we have it well in hand," said Arthur, "or at least, well enough for all practical purposes. But there is one question I do have." He cast a glance back at Merlin.

"His betrayal of those he trusted in the Archipelago caused him to be exiled here," said the dragon. "It is you who was betrayed here in the Summer Country, and it is you alone who shall decide his fate."

Arthur bowed his head. "Very well."

"Others have been summoned," the Indigo Dragon said. "Your education in the ways of the Archipelago and its peoples is sorely lacking. This must be remedied as soon as can be managed.

"You will have three teachers. The first of them will be waiting for you at the water's edge at sunset. The others will come in time," said the dragon. "All else is now entirely in your hands. Choose wisely. Choose well."

"I will do my best."

The dragons all extended their wings and stroked the air, rising high into the dusk.

"Rule wisely and fare thee well," the Indigo Dragon said again, "Arthur Pendragon, King of the Silver Throne."

The companions gathered together their few belongings and followed Arthur and Merlin to the water, where the river began opening itself up to the sea.

Taliesin remained behind so that a semblance of order might be maintained at the castle. Hugo and Rose took responsibility for the damaged Archimedes. Arthur agreed that the bird would need repairing, and also that he might be a good and eminently appropriate teacher for Rose.

Jack carried the Little Whatsit and the Serendipity Box, and

John, acting as Arthur's squire, carried the scabbard and broken sword Caliburn.

Arthur rode to the rear in silence, with Merlin close at his side. There was little that could be said between them, or perhaps little they felt that they were capable of saying.

At the water, they left the horses near the tree line and walked down to the sand on foot. There, standing starkly against the rays of the setting sun, was a sight that reassured John and Jack even more so than the dragons themselves had.

It was the ship, the *Red Dragon*. And at the helm stood Ordo Maas.

John started to wave at the old shipbuilder before Jack reminded him that Ordo Maas would not know them any more than Samaranth had. So it was particularly surprising when the old man, still carrying his long staff with the eternal flame, disembarked from the ship and came straight towards them.

"Which of you is John?" he asked pleasantly.

"That would be me," said John.

"Here," said Ordo Maas as he handed something to the Caretaker. "I was told you misplaced something very like this a long time past, and a friend didn't want you to go too much longer without."

It was a silver watch with a matching chain and fob, and on the back was a red engraving of Samaranth.

"Is it a time machine?" Jack asked. "Will it let us travel through time?"

"I believe it will," Ordo Maas replied. "I've found for every minute I watch it, I move a full minute farther into the future."

The shipbuilder turned to Arthur. "I am to be your first teacher,

High King. And tonight we go for the first of your many lessons."

"I understand," Arthur said. "May I attend to some business first?"

Ordo Maas bowed. "As you wish."

Arthur took the broken pieces of Caliburn from John and walked to the water's edge. "I drew this sword," he murmured, "and thought I had become a king. Then it broke, and only by going without it at my side, and in my hand, did I truly prove myself to be a king.

"I should like to give it over to the safekeeping of another, until such time as I shall need it again, or until another more worthy than I chooses to seek it out."

"Who is he talking to?" John whispered.

"I have no idea," Jack whispered back. "This is new ground for me, too."

The water near the banks of the river, just past the rushes, began to roil, and a figure rose, spectral-like, out of the water.

She was beautiful in a stern fashion; her eyes were cold for all but Arthur, and she spoke to him alone.

"Will you take it, Mother?"

Nimue reached out and took the shards of Caliburn from her son, then leaned in to kiss him on the cheek before sliding swiftly and silently back into the depths.

John noticed that during the entire encounter, Merlin had kept his back to the woman and stayed far from the water's edge.

"I have one more matter to attend to," said Arthur. "Merlin. Come to me."

The would-be king approached the younger man and dropped to one knee, but to everyone's surprise, Arthur pulled him to his feet. "You do not kneel to me," he said blithely. "Never do you kneel to me." And then, even more surprisingly, he pulled Merlin in for a tight hug, which Merlin reluctantly returned.

"You understand what I must do?" Arthur said.

Merlin nodded.

"I know you still love your maps," said the High King. "Do you still carry the tools to make them?"

Merlin nodded again. "I have a quill, and ink, and a bundle of parchments," he said, "but I have not used them in almost a century."

"You'll have time to do it again, I think," said Arthur. He rubbed his cheek where he'd been gashed earlier, then touched a blooded finger to Merlin's forehead and began to speak:

> Myrddyn, son of Odysseus
> By right and rule
> For need of might
> I thus bind thee
> I thus bind thee
>
> By blood bound
> By honour given
> I thus bind thee
> I thus bind thee
>
> For strength and speed and heaven's power
> I call on thee in this dark hour
> I thus bind thee
> I thus bind thee.

"You are thus Bound, Myrddyn," pronounced Arthur, "by the Old Magic, and by blood. And thusly Bound, I command thee to seek out Solitude and to remain there, until released by blood, or by my command."

Merlin looked at him with less sadness than resignation and nodded. "As you command, Arthur."

Arthur took off his torn and bloody cloak and handed it to Merlin. And then, almost as an afterthought, he handed him the scabbard of Caliburn. "Here," he said. "Perhaps one day you will find a use for this. Or choose to use it in the way it was meant to be used, when you are ready."

Merlin stepped into the water and stopped. "How am I to . . . ?" he began.

"My king," said Ordo Maas. "If you'll permit me?"

Arthur nodded, and Ordo Maas raised his staff. A moment later, sailing smoothly along the river, the *Scarlet Dragon* appeared.

"Our boat?" Jack exclaimed. "My boat?"

"Chin up, Jack," said John. "It's not as if we planned to use her again."

Ordo Maas stepped into the water and stroked the *Scarlet Dragon*'s head as he whispered to it. He reared back as if listening, then smiled and patted the boat on the head.

"She will take him," Ordo Maas said to Arthur, "to Solitude. You will learn of it yourself from a teacher other than myself, but for now, there is a place he can go where he can think and dedicate himself to his work."

"Thank you," said Arthur. He gestured at the boat, and Merlin stepped aboard with his few meagre belongings. Merlin stood, facing away from the others, and spoke.

"Why?" he asked. "Why wouldn't you allow him to kill me, Arthur?"

Arthur took a deep breath. "You betrayed your brother," he said evenly, "and my mother. And as a child, you even betrayed me, staying only long enough to give me a name. And when I grew older, all that you had feared in me are those things that came from you.

"You have been afraid your whole life. And I cannot bring myself to kill – or allow to be killed – someone who had made the mistakes you've made, just because you are afraid."

The *Scarlet Dragon* took that as a tacit approval to leave, and she pulled away from the shore.

"Thank you, Thorn," Merlin said without turning around.

"You're welcome," Arthur answered. "Farewell . . . Father."

The companions all watched from the shore until the *Scarlet Dragon* vanished from sight.

It took only a short while to arrive at, and cross, the Frontier. *So simple a thing,* Merlin thought to himself. *So simple, when done the right way. It was all I wanted for so long, and now, to have it given to me so easily . . .*

But no – the thoughts themselves caused the blood on his forehead to burn.

He had been marked.

He had been Bound.

And he had returned to the Archipelago.

The *Scarlet Dragon* sailed for days, perhaps longer, before finally approaching their destination.

In the distance, shrouded by mist, the passenger of the small boat could make out the island, and on it a tower that had no end.

And suddenly, with a mixture of shame and surprise, he realized where he was going.

In a short while he would be there, and he would climb the stairs until he found what he had been commanded to seek. Somewhere, there in the Keep of Time, he would at last find Solitude.

Arthur said his farewells to the companions, then stepped onto the *Red Dragon* with Ordo Maas, and the second Dragonship of the evening pulled away from the shores and set course for the Archipelago. The companions watched as the ship sailed away, and then made their way back to the stone passageway.

"One final matter remains," said Hugo. "What is to become of young Rose?"

"We're taking Rose with us," John and Jack said together. It seemed that all three of them had come to the same conclusion.

"Blood for blood, and a life for a life," Rose said, nodding her head in agreement. "Your companion stayed on Avallo, so it seems right that I return with you."

"And if no one has any objections," Hugo added, "I'd like to take Archimedes back as well. Chaz asked that we care for the bird, and Arthur has enough advisers, now."

"Good enough and done, then," said John, looking at the rising moon. "We're running close. We'll have to ride hard to make it."

With horses and best wishes given to them by Taliesin, the companions arrived at Grandfather Oak just as the projection was starting to waver.

"The badgers will be frantic," said John.

"Badgers?" asked Rose.

"You're going to love them," said Hugo. "Ready?"

Rose nodded, and together the foursome stepped through the projection and into the future.

Once more they were back in the projection room on Sanctuary. There was a brief flurry of greetings and explanations to satisfy the badgers' questions – mostly about why they had brought back a sick bird in a bag, and why Chaz seemed to have been turned into a girl.

"I'm not Chaz, I'm Rose," she said. "Pleased to meet you both."

"First things first," said Jack. "We need to know if it worked this time."

From inside the room, nothing seemed different at all.

"Well," John said. "I guess we'll just have to go outside and take a look again, and see if this time it did the trick."

"John!" Jack cried out. "Look! In the corner! The burlap bag is gone! We have changed things, after all!"

"Did you move the bag?" John asked the badgers. "Set it aside, perhaps? Or did Reynard move it?"

Uncas shook his head.

"No, we never touched it," answered Fred. "I never realized it was gone until you mentioned it just now."

"Where's Reynard?" Jack said, looking around the room. "We need to have him check outside, to see if the giants are still lurking about."

"He went out a while ago," said Fred, heading for the door. "I'll go ask after him."

The little badger opened the door and stepped outside – and disappeared with a yelp.

The companions ran over to the door, which opened not into the hallway they expected to see but into an endless black void. Fred had fallen when he stepped over the threshold, and he was desperately hanging on to the door frame by a single paw.

Jack reached down and grabbed him up, holding him tightly. "Don't worry, little badger," he soothed. "I've got you."

"Thank you, Jack," Uncas said gratefully. "I couldn't bear t' lose my boy!"

"What in Hades is out there?" John said to no one in particular.

"It's Nothing," Hugo said simply. "The door opens into Nothing."

John closed the door and stepped away from it, thinking. "We've changed something," he said, gnawing on his fist in thought. "I think we *did* change the world, after all. Because the one we came from, Chaz's world, is no longer there. At all."

"But this room still is?" asked Jack. "How is that possible?"

"Perhaps we've changed things again," John said morosely. "We left Chaz, centuries ago, in a world that didn't turn into his. And we took away someone who was already there." He gestured to Rose. "Who's to say we didn't do exactly the wrong things?"

"Do you believe that?" Hugo asked. "Do you believe either one of those choices could have been different?"

"No, I don't," John answered. "That's what confuses me. I don't see any other path to have taken other than the one we have."

"Then we should follow it the rest of the way," said Hugo. "We can't go out of this room by the door – so I think we're meant to go through a projection one more time. Why else would it still be here, waiting?"

"I think you're right, Hugo," said John.

"Should we try to take the projector with us again?" asked Jack. "It might be useful."

"To what end?" John replied. "We're out of slides. And unless another one magically appeared, we couldn't use it anyway. No," he said with finality, "I think the room was still here because the projection tied us to the other timeline. It kept it intact, for as long as there's a projection."

"So what happens when the slide burns out?" Hugo asked with a gulp. "Do we vanish into the Nothing too?"

"I don't plan to be here to find out," John said, grabbing his pack. "Take everything we can fit into our bags," he instructed. "We have two choices. We can go back through to Camelot and take our chances, or we can use the last slide Verne left for us and have faith that we're being looked after, even now."

"Do you have that much faith, John?" asked Jack.

John looked at the silver and red dragon watch given to him by Ordo Maas, then at Rose, who had come with them into an unknown future. "Yes," he answered. "I do."

With no more discussion, the companions gathered their few belongings together and prepared for a final trip in time.

"Of course you'll be coming with us," Jack said to Uncas. "We're all going together, wherever and whenever it is."

Verifying that everyone in their small party was ready to go, John gave the signal, and Uncas switched the slide from the sixth-century picture of Camelot, which was already charring at the edges, to the last slide.

It was not what they'd expected.

In front of them, on the wall, a startled monk dropped the bundle of wood he was carrying and crossed himself. That was not what they'd hoped, that the portal was opening in the presence of someone, but not unexpected. But they were unprepared for the effect the last slide had on the projection room itself.

It trembled and shook and began to come apart at the seams and fall away into Nothing.

John and Hugo pushed Rose through the portal, then began to step through themselves. "Hurry, Uncas!" John shouted over the howling winds that were sucking at the walls of the room. "Hurry!"

The door shuddered, then ripped away from the wall, spinning off into the dark. The wall itself followed seconds later. Uncas and Fred rushed forward and jumped through, rolling in the brush on the other side.

Jack tossed the bags and packs through the portal as the other side wall ripped away, and the chairs began flying around the room, then up through the shattering ceiling.

Hugo crossed over, and then Jack. John took one last look into the room and stepped away just as the floor began to disintegrate.

Standing safely amidst the shrubbery and trees that had been visible through the slide, the companions watched in chilling fascination as the rest of the room fell away into Nothing, finally taking the projector with it, and in another instant the projection blurred, then blinked out.

The room, and the Lanterna Magica, were gone.

They found themselves standing in the company of a slightly frightened and extremely bewildered monk.

"Be ye angels, or be ye demons?" he asked in clear Old English.

"We be . . . I mean, we are men," said John.

"And badgers," added Uncas.

"And you?" the monk asked Rose.

"I'm Rose," she answered simply and, to the companions' surprise, in the monk's own language.

"Of course you are," the monk replied. "Are you seeking sanctuary?"

"We've actually just come from there," said Hugo, "but if you've some handy, we wouldn't decline."

The monk looked at him and shook his head. "I'm not sure what you mean by that, but I am happy to help. You are not quite what I expected, but if you carry the sign . . ."

The companions looked at one another with puzzled expressions. The sign? What was he talking about?

Then, on impulse, John reached into his pocket and withdrew the watch that bore the image of the red dragon, Samaranth.

The monk's expression changed from one of cautious surprise to one of relief. "You do bear the sign. That means you are the . . . how did he call you? The Caretakers?"

It was the companions' turn to be surprised. "We are," John said, nodding.

"I'm Geoffrey of Monmouth," the monk replied. "I've been waiting for you."

. . . the door . . . was still standing slightly ajar.

Chapter Twenty-three

Restoration

Geoffrey led the companions up the claustrophobic stairway and into his study. "The message said that I was to wait for three scholars, called Caretakers, who carried the sign of the dragon, and that when you arrived, I was to use the, uh, flower to contact the knight."

"You have a Compass Rose?" Jack said, suddenly excited. "Which knight?"

Geoffrey shrugged. "I couldn't tell you," he said, moving aside several piles of parchments. "I'm just riding along on the skiff. I haven't any idea where the river is flowing."

"Jack," John said, looking over the monk's accumulations. "I think I've read some of these! I think these are some of the actual Histories!"

"I can do you one better," said Hugo. "There's one over here that I actually *wrote* in."

The others clustered around Hugo's discovery and realized they recognized it themselves. It was the Grail book that had been sent to Charles.

"Oh, yes, that," Geoffrey said from behind a mound of books. "A very odd Frenchman gave it to me only recently. I had just begun transcribing it, but then parts of several pages mysteriously disappeared. I can't imagine what happened to them."

"That's too bad," said Jack. "I'm sorry your work was interrupted."

"Oh, it didn't slow me down too much," Geoffrey told him. "I'm quite good at, uh, extrapolating details from limited information."

"Making things up out of whole cloth, you mean," said Jack.

"More or less, yes," Geoffrey admitted. "Sorry about the mess, by the way. I've been collecting these writings for years, and I just ran out of places to keep them all."

"I think we can fill in some of the fabric here," said Hugo, "at least where my own contribution is concerned."

On a clean sheet of parchment, Hugo recreated the entire message he'd actually written, which had been truncated by the torn page:

> The Cartographer is Merlin, who cannot be trusted.
> He who seeks the means to conquer and rule
> the islands of the Archipelago and our own world
> will follow the true Grail and the children of Holy
> Blood will be saved, by willing choice and sacrifice
> that time be restored for the future's sake.
> And in God's name, don't close the door!
> —Hugo Dyson

John breathed hard and rubbed the back of his neck. "If we'd only had this whole message," he said to Hugo, "we might have made all kinds of different choices, starting with never having trusted Merlin."

"Oh, Merlin?" said Geoffrey. "I've written a biography of him. A fascinating man."

"You don't know the half of it," Jack told him dryly.

"Someone sent the book to us," said John. "So someone, somewhere, somewhen, knows more about this than we do."

"Found it!" Geoffrey exclaimed happily. "Now, if I can just remember the working of it . . ."

"Here," Jack said, taking the Compass Rose. "Allow me."

He swiftly found the appropriate place and made the mark that would bring someone from the Archipelago.

"One thing's certain," John said as Geoffrey, accompanied by Fred and Uncas, went to fetch some bread and cheese for his guests. "We prevented Mordred from establishing the Winterland. Geoffrey of Monmouth is in the twelfth century. If Mordred had regained the upper hand, Geoffrey wouldn't be here now, in our England."

"So you've achieved what you set out to achieve, then," Rose said as she examined Archimedes. "This is good, is it not?"

"It is," John replied, clearly uncomfortable discussing Mordred in front of his own daughter. "Now our objective is to simply return home to our own time."

"You're here now," said Rose. "Doesn't that make this time your time?"

John rubbed his temples. "She's another one of those, isn't she?"

"I'm afraid so," said Jack. "And more are on the way, unless I miss my guess." He pointed at the Compass Rose, which had begun to glow. "Company's coming."

Geoffrey and the badgers had just returned with the food when there was a sharp knock at the door below.

Rather than bring someone else into an overcrowded room, they all went down to meet the new visitor.

It was the Green Knight.

Jack and John both cried out in joy at the thought of a reunion with Chaz, but an instant later their faces fell. This was indeed the Green Knight, but it was a different one.

"I am called Abelard," the knight said in a clipped French accent, bowing deeply. "Have I the honour of addressing the Caretakers?"

John and Jack stepped forward. The knight looked confused. "I was told to bring you all with me. You are not all Caretakers?"

"We all are indeed," John said hastily, "after a fashion, that is." The Green Knights were not traditionally known for their intelligence, and the last one he knew personally, Magwich, would sell his own mother, then forget to collect the money.

Geoffrey was taking both the strange appearance of the knight and the invitation with aplomb. John admired that – even if he was a bit bemused at the monk's rather disorganized personal style. Suddenly, looking up the stairs, all the elements of the happening came together for John in a burst of insight.

"Geoff," John said, tapping him on the shoulder, "how would you like to relocate your collection of books and manuscripts and receive a special education on the history of the kings of Britain, all at the same time?"

"That sounds very intriguing," Geoffrey answered, rubbing his hands together. "What must I do?"

John smiled. "Grab your hat," he said briskly, sizing up the Green Knight. "We're going visiting."

* ✦ ✦

The Green Knight had come to Caerleon in the beasts' ship, the Green Dragon. It was one of the larger of the Dragonships, and also the most wild and free-spirited. With the knight's help, and under Geoffrey's mostly efficient direction, the companions were able to load the monk's entire collection onto the ship in a matter of hours.

With the work done, they all boarded the ship one last time, and slowly it pulled away from the shore and set sail for the Archipelago.

"It was good of you to wait and help us bring all the books and manuscripts," John told the knight. "We appreciate it very much."

The knight bowed. "It was my pleasure, Caretaker."

"Are you the Abelard I would know of?" asked John. "The philosopher poet?"

The knight seemed startled by this, then regained his composure and bowed again. "I am honoured that you would remember me as a poet," he said with a lilt of pride in his voice. "It was, in truth, one of the later accomplishments in my life."

"How is it that you were chosen as a knight of Avalon?" asked Jack.

The knight sighed. "It was Bernard of Clairvaux," he said, the shimmying of the leaves on his shoulders attesting to the emotion he felt in sharing the confession.

"He had succeeded in having me accused of heresy. I became ill at the priory of St. Marcel, and it was there that I was approached by my predecessor, a knight called Gawain. He offered me the chance to serve, and I accepted, most gratefully."

"I know of your work too," Geoffrey said quietly. "In fact, I have the only complete copy of your *Historia Calamitatum*."

"I am pleased by this," said the knight, and it showed. He looked near to bursting.

"Your predecessor was Gawain," Jack mused. "Who was his predecessor?"

"The greatest of us all," the knight replied. "He served for many years as the first Guardian of Avalon and set the example by which those who came later follow."

"Are we going to Avalon, then?" Jack said, almost tearing up at the description of Chaz.

The knight shook his head. "That was not my instruction. Tonight we are going to the Chamenos Liber."

"We're going to the Keep?" asked Jack.

The knight nodded. "Someone has asked to see you."

John and Jack looked at each other and traded knowing smiles. There was only one man in residence at the islands of Chamenos Liber – only one man who could have requested them by the title of Caretaker here, in the twelfth century.

At the Keep of Time, the companions all disembarked and began to climb the stairs of the impossibly tall tower. Finally they reached the top of the steps, and the door that was second to last in the Keep.

The door was locked, and the keyhole under the mark of the High King seemed so new it might have just been installed that hour. John was about to knock when Rose reached out her hand and touched the door. The lock disengaged with a soft click.

"Come in," said a now familiar voice. "Enter freely and of your own will."

John gave the door a gentle push, and it swung open to reveal a room that was only just beginning to be filled with the clutter of maps and globes and the accumulated cultural bric-a-brac of two thousand years that they remembered from the first time they'd seen it. And sitting in the centre, working at his desk, was the Cartographer of Lost Places.

The Cartographer gave the companions a careful, lingering look of appraisal before speaking again, and when he did, it was to Rose. "Greetings and salutations, daughter of Madoc."

Unexpectedly, Rose walked to the Cartographer and kissed him on the cheek. "Hello, Uncle Merlin."

He shook his head at this and gently pushed her back.

Was that a tear on his cheek? John wondered. Or just a trick of the light?

"No," the Cartographer was saying, "I haven't needed a name in a very long time, and it's doubtful I'll need one again. It's best for all concerned, especially you, dear Rose, to simply call me the Cartographer."

"As you wish," she said, stepping back and taking Hugo's arm. She was trembling, he realized suddenly. The gesture had been more difficult for her than it had appeared.

"You hesitate," the Cartographer said to the others, noting that they had come inside the room but remained clustered by the door, as if they were comforted by the option of easy escape. "With good reason, probably. I was an excellent example of what not to do when you've been gifted with near immortality and unlimited opportunity."

"It's been a revelation, that's for sure," Jack said brusquely.

"Merlin?" asked Geoffrey, pulling at his collar. "As in, the real Merlin?"

John chuckled. The knight made of wood and leaves hadn't fazed the monk, nor had the talking badgers. A living Dragonship was similarly accepted, as was a tower made of time. But the thought of actually meeting the man whose life he'd been chronicling made Geoffrey twitch and shift about as if his bladder were full.

"Real is a matter of perspective," the Cartographer said, "and it's a matter of what is worth remembering and what is worth passing on to those who inherit the future."

"We almost lost, didn't we?" said John. "We almost brought about Mordred's victory."

The Cartographer looked at him for a breathless moment, the nodded. "We almost did. All of us, together, who were there."

"What happened?" Hugo asked. "What did I do to cause the crisis in time?"

"In the history you remember, the one you first came from," the Cartographer replied, "Mordred defeated me as you feared he would, and then was challenged by the boy. Mordred broke the rules of the tournament and attacked Arthur after he'd chosen not to fight his uncle. The boy, bless his scrappy heart, fought back and actually won.

"He drew Caliburn, became High King, and united two worlds. Because he had beaten Mordred in fair combat, the tribes united under his rule."

"So when I interfered by throwing the knife and disqualifying both Mordred and yourself . . . ," Hugo began.

"Arthur won by default when I refused to fight," the Cartographer finished. "And though he was worthy to draw the sword, he did not unite the people. And I . . ." He paused, composing himself. "I used that against him, until you came and set things right again."

"How can you remember all of that?" asked Jack. "What happened the first time? That was a different timeline than the one we changed."

"I have an acquaintance," the Cartographer explained. "One of the more recent kings of the Silver Throne, Arthur's son Eligure, chose to allow me a visitor. And that visitor has shared certain knowledge with me about pasts that were, and a future that may be."

"Verne," said John. "You mean Jules Verne."

"The same," he confirmed. "He has impressed upon me the need to keep detailed Histories of the events of the Summer Country as well as of the Archipelago. That's why I asked Abelard to fetch the monk — what was your name again?"

"G-Geoffrey," came the reply, his voice shaking with trepidation. "Of Monmouth."

"Ah, yes," the Cartographer said. "I understand you have amassed quite a library as it is, am I correct?"

"You are," said Geoffrey. "It's in the ship below."

"Excellent," said the Cartographer. He started rummaging through a stack of maps in the corner. "Eligure's brother, Artigel, has already created a great library within the city they are building on the island of Paralon," he went on, removing a large, leather-bound book from the pile. "All of your collection can go there, but this" — he handed the book to Geoffrey — "must be in your possession always."

It was the *Imaginarium Geographica*. The first *Imaginarium Geographica*, which the Cartographer had begun in Alexandria centuries earlier.

"In this atlas," he explained, "are maps to every land in the Archipelago. At least, those I have managed to remember. Abelard brings me scraps of stories of new lands, and I make new maps. But these, the finished works, should be looked after by those who also write its Histories. Will you accept?"

Geoffrey looked flustered, then bit his lip and bowed gravely. "I am your servant."

The Cartographer shook his head. "You serve the Silver Throne and the peoples of the Archipelago. I am only a map-maker."

"I have to ask," Jack said. "Did we fix it? Is the world, the timeline, proceeding the way it was meant to after the battle at Camelot?"

The Cartographer nodded. "It was not the last confrontation between Arthur and Mordred – but it was the last that you were witness to. There were other encounters between them, and much more to Arthur's own history that you have not yet learned. The building of the Dragonships. The forging of the great rings from the Cup of Albion. Your learning of these things may yet be in your future, and events must still follow the paths already taken, if you are to return to the world you know."

"We can go home?" Uncas and Fred exclaimed together. "Really?"

"Yes, little Children of the Earth."

"And you'll remain here, Bound by Arthur," said Jack. "It's just, I think. But having been Bound once myself, by Mordred, I can't say I don't have some sympathy for you."

"It must be a strong magic," said Hugo, "to keep you here so long."

"Magic, and Bindings, and Openings, and Summonings have far less to do with actual power than they do with belief," the Cartographer said. "Belief in what is possible, and belief in what is necessary."

He gestured to Jack. "You say that my brother, Madoc, once performed a Binding on you? With a ritual? And blood?"

"That's right," said John. "On all of us. It took a remedy from within the badgers' book, the Little Whatsit, to free us."

"Did it now?" came the reply. "So ask yourself this: Why did it work to begin with?"

"Because, ah . . . ," John started. He looked at Jack, who shrugged.

"Mm-hmm," said the Cartographer. "And why did the badgers' remedy work?"

John and Jack had no answer for that, either.

The Cartographer nodded, almost melancholy, and rubbed Fred on the head. "And you, little Child of the Earth. Can you tell me why the Binding worked, and why your remedy did as well?"

"Because we wanted them to," Fred answered.

"Because," the Cartographer said simply, "you had *faith* that they would."

"If it's a matter of faith," Jack retorted, "then why wouldn't the talismans you found, like the Spear of Destiny, allow you passage back to the Archipelago?"

"Oh, I found many other talismans," the Cartographer said. "A dozen. Dozens. Maybe a hundred. It doesn't matter. What matters now, as it did then, was the reason that those 'divine' objects wouldn't allow me to pass through the Frontier into another world."

"Because you didn't believe," said Jack. "Because you had no faith that they were, in fact, divine."

"Exactly, my boy," the Cartographer said. "I was searching, and acquiring, and trying to use objects that had value, worth, to other people. Not one of those things meant more to me than that. As a means to an end."

"But if they had . . . ," Jack began.

"If they had," the Cartographer finished, "I'd have crossed over easily, no bones about it. If I'd had a belief in just one of those things, I'd have passed."

"But the sword, Caliburn, was from your world, your gods," said Jack. "Why couldn't you use it?"

"For exactly the opposite reason," the Cartographer said. "I had the belief in it, but I also didn't think I was worthy. And I refused to test myself to have that fear proven for all to see.

"Well," he went on, rubbing his hands together, "I've enjoyed this, but I really must get back to work. Autunno isn't going to annotate itself."

"What are we to do now?" John asked.

The Cartographer blinked. "Abelard is taking Geoffrey to Paralon," he said, "and I expect you'll be going home."

"How do we do that?" asked John. "We used our last means of time travel to get here – and no offence, but it's far from when we want to be."

"Don't you have a talisman of your own?" the Cartographer inquired. "One that can magic up what you need most?"

"Yes," John replied, "but we've all used our turn with the Serendipity Box. It won't work again."

"I haven't," a voice said, small but firm.

It was Fred.

"I haven't opened the Serendipity Box," he repeated. "I've thought about it several times but never did. I wanted to wait until it looked as if there really were no other options."

"Animal logic again," John said gently, kneeling to look the badger in the eyes. "You may turn out to be the wisest of us all, Fred."

Jack and Uncas removed the box from the satchel they'd been carrying and handed it to Fred. The little animal didn't give a pre-amble speech or make any dramatic gestures, but simply lifted the lid and looked inside.

The box seemed empty at first, until Fred realized that in the corner was a small silver key. He took it out and closed the box.

"It's the key to your future, I'd imagine," the Cartographer said.

"Is that a metaphor?" asked John.

"The future. Upstairs – the next door," the Cartographer replied, exasperated. "That's the problem with scholars. You always think there are layers and layers to everything, when sometimes, the literal meaning is all you need. It is," he repeated pointedly, tapping two fingers into his other palm for emphasis, "the key, to, your, *future*."

Jack and John both realized it at once. The last door in the Keep. The one always out of reach, because the stairs ended at the Cartographer's door, while the tower continued to grow.

"Have you ever gone through it?" John asked. "Have you ever gone into the future?"

The Cartographer turned away from them and did not answer for a long, long while. Finally, still facing the wall, he began to reply.

"I have not gone through it myself," he said quietly, "but it wasn't for lack of desire or effort. It had opened, just the merest fraction of an inch, just enough for a single look, before it was slammed shut and placed forever out of reach."

John realized what the Cartographer had left unspoken. "You didn't get to look through the door, did you?"

"Not I," the Cartographer said, turning to look at Rose, "but my brother did, and what he saw broke his heart, and he spent the next dozen centuries trying to change what he saw. And he never succeeded, because I spent just as many years trying not to. And I will never be able to erase that shame, or ease the pain I caused him."

"That was why you were exiled from the Archipelago, wasn't it?" asked John. "For trying to go into the future."

"Almost," came the reply. "I – we – were exiled not for attempting to see the future, but because we wanted to use that knowledge to shape the world to suit our own purposes. That was not permitted then, or now."

With that, the Cartographer resumed his work, head bowed low to the paper. It was, the companions realized, the end of the conversation.

"Be well, Uncle Merlin," Rose said, as she and Hugo stepped out the door.

Jack bowed his head. "Farewell, Meridian."

"Goodbye . . . Myrddyn," said John.

"I am the Cartographer now," he replied, not looking up, "and that is enough. In truth, it always was."

At the edge of the stairs, the companions found a small keyhole, almost covered over with spiderwebs.

Fred inserted the key into the opening and turned it. There was a small click, then nothing.

Suddenly, as if they were leaves of a plant breaking through soil to sunlight, nubs of stone began to appear along the wall. They pushed outwards, groaning and creaking as they grew, until in moments there were several new steps extending from the stairway that ended at a just-appearing platform beneath the last door.

"Lead on, Fred," said John. "It's your key, after all."

Fred and Uncas stepped cautiously up the stairs to the door, which they realized was still standing slightly ajar.

"They never closed it," Jack murmured.

"We'll make sure we do, then," John stated. He pushed it open, and together they moved into the future.

It was dark until John closed the door behind them. Then, just like the door Hugo had gone through, this one disappeared.

They were in the wood, along Addison's Walk, at precisely the spot where the first door had been. And if there had been any doubts whatsoever that they had been returned to the right place, they vanished when the companions heard the whoops and hollers from the Royal Animal Rescue Squad.

The badgers swarmed off the Howling Improbable, which was exactly where John and Jack had last seen it, at the side of the path, just along the trees.

Jubilantly the badgers embraced Uncas and Fred, and even the humans, including an astonished Hugo and a delighted Rose.

Rising above the trees was the comforting, familiar sight of Magdalen Tower, and beyond that, the buildings of the college itself.

"We're back," John said, hugging Jack's shoulders. "We're home."

Jack didn't answer, but just smiled a small smile and watched the badgers dancing around the clearing.

"Never doubted it for a minute," said Hugo.

The Royal Animal Rescue Squad departed after promising to give a full report to King Artus. As the principle sped away, John also said that he had to get home right away. He looked exhausted.

"It must be nearly three in the morning," he said. "This was quite the extraordinary adventure, wasn't it? Quite the mythopoeia."

Jack responded to the comment with a half smile. "It's certainly going to make a grand story," he said as the four companions walked back to his rooms at the college, "but I don't think I'll ever view the myths again in quite the same way."

"Why is that?" John asked.

"Because," Jack replied, "I've . . . felt them now. I've tasted them. They've become more than stories to me. And I'm going to be thinking about all this a long, long while."

They crossed the quadrangle, and Jack unlocked the gate next to Magdalen Bridge. As they said their goodbyes to John, Hugo remained a bit longer as they went to Jack's rooms at the New Building and discussed what would be best to do with Rose.

"There's a boardinghouse in Reading," Hugo said. "It's near the college, and it wouldn't be any trouble to put her up there as my niece. And Archimedes can stay with me so she can see him every day."

He wrapped an affectionate arm around Rose, who yawned.

"We'd best be going," said Hugo. "I'll call you up tomorrow to let you know all's well."

Jack closed the door behind Hugo and sat at his desk. His mind was still racing with the events that must have happened in a single night – and had lasted for a lifetime, it seemed.

Sunrise was still hours away, and there would be plenty of daylight in which he could do what he was considering. But he couldn't wait. He had to know if they'd made the right choices, if they had done enough. If they had believed enough.

Jack took out a key that opened the hidden drawer where he kept items pertaining to his duties as Caretaker. It contained some documents, a few items of an unusual nature, and a flower, made of parchment.

He removed the Compass Rose, and with a stick of graphite scratched onto one of the leaves the small mark that would summon a Caretaker from the Archipelago. With John nearby in Oxford, and Charles still in Paris, there was only one other person who might respond to this specific summons.

A tapping at the door an hour later woke Jack from where he'd fallen asleep at his desk.

Bert – all of him, both arms, both legs, and a fully attached head – was standing outside the door.

Jack fell back, stumbling, as his mentor rushed into the room.

"Jack, lad, what is it?" Bert asked, his face a mask of concern. "You look as if you've seen a ghost."

"It – it's good to see you, Bert," Jack said, before his voice finally cracked and he collapsed, sobbing, into the old man's arms. Bert held his friend, not talking, until the sun rose.

"Gentle Caretakers," Burton said cheerfully . . .

CHAPTER TWENTY-FOUR
The Bird and Baby

"*Utterly unbelievable,*" Charles said.

He returned to England from Paris on Monday, and John and Jack arranged for a meeting in Jack's rooms the following Thursday, so that Charles could come up from London and hear the entire incredible story of what had happened to them.

"Unbelievable," Charles repeated, pouring himself a second glass of rum. "I can't decide if I'm more envious that I missed out, or grateful that I didn't have to go through it all myself."

"You did experience it, in a manner of speaking," said John, who was draped comfortably over the back of a chair. "At the end, Chaz had become very much like you."

"That's fascinating," Charles said. "I've been theorizing about the possibility that different worlds, different dimensions, do in fact exist. Changing the timeline is exactly the kind of method that could be used to travel to those other dimensions."

"Thanks anyway," said Jack, "but I think I like this dimension just fine."

"But don't you see?" Charles exclaimed. "You aren't in the same dimension you started from."

Jack sat upright. "What are you talking about, Charles?"

"You may have prevented the Winterland," Charles said matter-of-factly, "but you did in fact alter the past, and with that change, you affected everything that followed.

"All we knew of the original Green Knight was that he was a Crusader," Charles explained, "but in taking Chaz back, who was from a present that wasn't your own, you inserted a new element into a past that was. You also ensured Arthur's rule — but it came about thirty years later than you say it happened in our Histories."

"You can check that for yourself," said John.

"I have," replied Charles, "and the events happened as you told me they did, after your trip. But that's not how I remember reading about them before."

"You're remembering incorrectly, then."

"No," Charles said. "I just remember it *differently*."

"This is all making my head hurt," said John. "All this talk of multiple dimensions and whatnot. Are you saying you're not, in fact, 'our' Charles?"

"I'm saying," he replied patiently, "that there are an infinite number of worlds, with an infinite number of each of us in them. There are worlds where we never met. There are worlds where we never became Caretakers. And there are worlds where we might have been lesser men than we are. It may even be possible for the traits of a man in one world to be passed to his twin in another, and vice versa. That might account for Chaz's ability to learn languages so swiftly. He wasn't *learning* so much as drawing on the abilities I already have."

"Does that mean you might start assimilating Chaz's mannerisms?" asked Jack. "I don't know how I feel about that."

"I like to think," Charles replied, "I have hope, that in all of those worlds, there would remain in each of us the potential to choose to better ourselves. And isn't knowing that, believing in that, the most important thing?"

John nodded and raised his glass. "To Chaz."

Jack and Charles raised their glasses too. "To Chaz."

"I'd still like to find out," Charles said as he drained his glass, "who sent this to me and started everything."

He moved over to Jack's table, where the Grail book lay, and traced the image on the cover with his fingers. "It's a shock discovering what the true Histories are," he said wryly, "but at the same time, it's comforting to know that fictionalizing our adventures didn't just begin with Bert."

"Geoffrey was quite the tall-tale teller," said Jack. "You'd have had a wonderful time exchanging Grail lies, I'm sure."

"Yes, but Bert did it out of necessity, to protect the Archipelago," said Charles. "Geoffrey seems to have done it just for a lark."

"Speaking of Bert," John said as he checked the time on his watch, "we'd best be hurrying along if we're to be on time meeting with him and Hugo and Rose at the tavern."

"That's right." Jack got to his feet and grabbed his coat. "It's at that new place that Bert discovered, isn't it? What was the name again?" he said, scratching his head. "The Eagle and Child?"

"That's the real name," Charles said as he closed the door behind them. "But everyone who's a regular there just calls it the Bird and Baby."

The fog had settled thickly around Oxford, hanging low and dense in the air. Usually that meant there would be weather – but on this particular Thursday, the Caretakers knew it meant someone needed cover to land an airship.

"I have to say," Jack commented, "the *White Dragon* being an airship instead of a sailing vessel makes it a hell of a lot more versatile. I wonder if any of the other Dragonships would be amenable to making the conversion?"

"I think Ordo Maas went along with Bert's suggestion just to give him a countermeasure to the *Indigo Dragon*," John said, wincing at having mentioned their long-missing stolen ship as he checked his watch again.

"You really like that thing, don't you?" said Charles. "What did Pris say when you told her you'd lost the other one?"

"She started to get upset," John answered, "but I managed to distract her by telling her a story from the new book. She loves the parts with the elves."

"Oh no," a familiar voice moaned. "Not elves. Give me anything but elves!"

"Well met, Hugo," John called as the professor and his adopted niece rounded the corner in front of them. "Hello, Rose."

"Hello, Uncle John," Rose said, kissing him on the cheek. "Hello, Uncle Jack."

"Oh my stars and garters," declared Charles, stunned. "You must be Rose."

"Hello, Uncle Chaz," Rose said as she kissed him.

Charles touched his cheek and blushed. "I, ah, I'm not Chaz, you know."

"It's hard to tell," she said, looking at him appraisingly. "I only met him once, but he is the reason I could come here. In many ways, he was you, and I think, in all the best ways, you are him. I think he was the bravest knight I've ever known."

"So are you an apprentice Caretaker now, Hugo?" Charles asked, trying to change the subject before he blushed again. "Now that you know where all the bodies are buried, so to speak."

Hugo frowned, then raised his eyebrows. "I rather expect I am, at that," he said. "Do I get some sort of certificate or something?"

"Maybe we'll get you a dragon watch," John said, "as long as it's exactly like the one Verne left for me."

"What does it do?" asked Hugo.

"It tells me the time," John replied, "and nothing else."

"Oh, drat," said Hugo.

At the tavern, Hugo and Rose went inside to secure a table in a private room, where the group could talk relatively undisturbed, while the Caretakers went to the back to retrieve the last member of the party.

They waited only a few seconds before the rope ladder dropped down from the ship hidden somewhere above in the fog. "Dratted ladders," Bert grumbled as he climbed down from the very patient *White Dragon*. "We can build a ship that flies but can't manage a way to get off it that doesn't involve self-strangulation."

"We're already a bit late," said John, "but we can spare a few minutes to unwind you, I think."

"Remember," Bert noted, half upside down, "in the end, it's not the years in your life that count. It's the life in your years. Chaucer said that, I think."

The companions laughed and helped their mentor untangle himself from the ropes. Jack was rather less animated than the others and acted as if he didn't want to miss a second of conversation with the Far Traveller, wrapping an arm around his shoulders and marching him to the door of the tavern. Bert went in first, and Jack held the door for the others.

"Chaucer?" said John quizzically. "He must be mistaken. I've never read that quote."

"You know," Charles said to John, holding him back at the door, "it used to really intimidate me how frequently Bert could quote even the most obscure lines from great works of literature."

"Yes," John said with a smirk. "Jack does it too, and for the same reason – to show up his students."

"Well, I found something interesting," Charles offered, taking a small paperback book out of his jacket. "I pinched it out of his hat when he was tangled up in the *White Dragon*'s rope ladder."

"You *pinched* it?" said John. "That settles it. I'm calling you 'Chaz' for the rest of the night."

"Har har har," said Charles. "Take a look at this, John."

The book was called *Great Quotes from the American Presidents*, and it had been marked on nearly every page.

"He's quoting the American presidents?" John said, unsure whether to be shocked or impressed.

"Why not?" said Charles. "Short, pithy, and designed to rouse the troops. And it makes him look smart. But that's not the best part."

"What is?"

"This," Charles said, tapping on the copyright page. "This book won't be published until 1976. And do you remember that quote from Milton we could never find? It wasn't Milton at all – he was quoting a President who ends up getting killed on" – he checked the listing – "November 22, 1963. I wonder if we should find some way to warn him?"

"That he'll be killed, or that Bert is misattributing his quotes?" Jack said wryly, motioning for them to come inside. "After the adventure we've just had, I want as little as possible to do with time travel, and fate, and destiny. And besides, I don't think any man should know the day he's supposed to die – in any reality."

Together the three men entered the Eagle & Child and were shown to the room near the back where they would be assured of as much privacy as was possible in a local tavern.

"The Rabbit Room, hey?" said Charles as they walked in. "We'll have to tell Tummeler—" He stopped, stunned, as did John and Jack.

At the mantel, gesturing to them with a glass of beer in hand, was a man John had once described as a "wild-eyed gentleman". But that was before they'd met, which was long after the man was supposed to have died. Then again, if nothing else, Sir Richard Burton was resourceful. Maybe the most resourceful man they'd ever met.

Five years earlier, the companions had found him in the Archipelago, where he had done his best to kill them, their friends, and Peter Pan – after which they rescued his daughter, an act which he repaid by stealing their Dragonship.

"Gentle Caretakers," Burton said cheerfully, "come, let us sup together."

Bert, wearing an angry and pained expression, sat at the far side of the long table, and a bewildered Hugo sat across from him. Rose, who was calmer than anyone in the room except perhaps Burton himself, was sitting next to Hugo, eating a cracker.

John, who was behind the other Caretakers, looked around warily. Was this a trap?

Burton laughed and took a seat at the table near the fireplace. "It's no trap, John. Just a friendly meeting of peers. Or," he added a bit more precisely, "respectful adversaries."

"Burton?" Jack exclaimed as he stepped into the room. "What are you doing here, you son of a—"

"Now, Jack," Burton admonished. "Language."

"Where is my ship, Burton?" Bert demanded, barely containing the fury in his voice. "Where is the *Indigo Dragon?*"

"Where she's been all along," Burton replied. "Serving those who serve the true heirs of the Archipelago."

"Who, you?" John spat.

"The Imperial Cartological Society," Burton replied. "Have you forgotten already?"

"The door," said John. "You're responsible for putting the door in the wood along Addison's Walk, aren't you?"

Burton merely smiled and took a long swallow from his glass.

"It didn't do you any good," Jack said. "We sorted it out, as we've always done."

"Whatever you say, Jack."

"You couldn't even entrap one of *us*," John said. "You tangled up Hugo instead."

Burton hesitated. The mix-up, apparently, had been an obvious flaw in his plan. "It wasn't perfectly executed," he admitted, looking into his empty glass and reaching for a second ale on the table.

"I'll tell you straight out, we were hoping to catch – and convert – *you*, Charles."

"Convert me?" Charles exclaimed. "To what?"

"From your belief and support of the wrong heir," Burton replied. "We at the society know the Histories as well as you. After all, we were all Caretakers too . . .

". . . *almost*."

"You wanted Mordred to win!" John said incredulously. "Why, Burton?"

"You've been through the Histories," he shot back. "You know what Myrddyn became, who he really is. He's the one who set the path for all the Caretakers. Can you really tell me that is a man you would risk your lives for?"

"Yes," John said evenly. "I can."

"If you'd wanted to convince us the Cartographer was evil," said Jack, "you shouldn't have tried stealing the Grail book. It was one of your people who tore out the pages, wasn't it?"

Burton actually reddened. "Yes, well, some members of the society are being disciplined for that. When they tried to retrieve it, Monmouth surprised them, and one of them dropped it, tearing the pages. He could only bring back that part he'd torn. The fool."

"Harry," said Bert. "You must mean Harry Houdini. He always was a butterfingers. Good for locks, not for espionage."

"Was he the one who put the door in the wood?" asked John.

"He and Conan Doyle," said Burton. "We hoped you'd go through and see what was taking place at Camelot – that Mordred had become a villain only because Arthur and Merlin made him so. We didn't anticipate that you would be foolish enough to close the door. How *did* you get back, anyway?"

"That's a Caretaker secret," Jack replied, knowing the answer, believed or not, would make Burton seethe.

"If you just wanted to make Mordred's case," said John, "why did you need a door from the Keep?"

"To put you in the position to see for yourselves," explained Burton. "So you could see who Mordred and Merlin really were, and which was more noble."

"You didn't benefit," John stated flatly. "All that effort, and nothing came of it."

Burton tipped back the second ale and drained the glass in a swallow. "Oh, I wouldn't say that." He wiped his mouth on his sleeve. "We learned from our mistakes. And we may have found something that I once thought was lost. And it was in our hands the entire time."

"And you nearly caused the destruction of the world!" Hugo exclaimed. "Why, the Winterland that Mordred created—"

"Hugo, please," Jack said, squeezing his shoulders sharply. Hugo realized too late what he'd revealed – Burton had no idea what had been caused by the changes in time, because the Caretakers had managed to repair most of the damage.

Burton smiled. "I think I understand," he said, rising. "And now it's time I take my leave of you. This has been entertaining, but as usual, you Caretakers ask all the wrong questions."

"How can the questions be wrong?" asked Charles.

"You focus entirely on the past, on filling in the holes in events that have already happened," Burton answered. "You are obsessed with what was and miss entirely what is. And that is why we shall control the future."

"What questions?" Charles insisted. "What haven't we asked?"

"All right," Burton said. "Since it is just the six of us in here, all men of learning, I'll give you a lesson you haven't earned.

"You ask why the door was in the wood – but not how we got it, or if there are others like it. You ask why we might want to convert Charles to our cause, without asking what our intentions are in doing so. And you have travelled in time and made choices based on what you experienced in the past – while ignoring the most important revelation of all . . .

". . . that time moves in *two* directions."

Burton took his hat and coat from the rack and bowed. "Farewell, Caretakers," he said, smiling. "Settle my bill, will you?" And with that, he walked out of the tavern and vanished.

"I wasn't pleased to see him," said John, "but at least we know. We know why this happened."

"Was that really Richard Burton?" asked Hugo. "He's charming, but he smells."

Bert scratched his head. "There was something else," he mused. "Something very, very interesting. I don't think he was able to even see Rose. Not at all."

"What would that mean?" said Jack. "How could he not see her?"

"It could be her unique bloodlines, or perhaps the fact she might be from an alternate dimension," said Bert. "At any rate, it's worth discussing with Jules, and it's about time you met him anyway. This latest escapade proves that. We need to accelerate our plans. Soon. Very soon."

None of the companions broached the topic again to ask what Bert meant by this, and Hugo and Rose seemed to be more interested in ordering dinner than in more debates about Archipelago business.

They ordered some food, and more drinks (noting that Burton had left a sizeable tab), and ruminated on what had happened just a few days earlier. One thing was clear – their adversaries were more aware of them than they had been. And they'd been much more active. And that would have to change, John promised himself. It was no longer good enough to simply react.

"So everything Burton did was predicated on the belief Charles would be walking in the park with us Saturday night?" said Jack. "What a stroke of luck that you were detained in Paris!"

"Not luck, but Jules Verne," said Bert, "and the power of cause and effect." He turned to Charles. "Jules deliberately had you detained so that you wouldn't be at risk, then sent the Grail book to Jack."

"But Hugo's warning was incomplete," Jack stammered. "How did that help anything? Why couldn't Jules simply warn us outright?"

"Cause and effect," Bert repeated. "By the time he stopped Charles, he discovered Hugo *had* to go, and in fact, had already *gone*."

"This is very confusing," said Hugo.

Bert nodded in understanding. "It gets worse. He got the first inklings of what was going on when Hank Morgan showed up at Sam Clemens's house carrying the dragon watch. He told us where and when you were, and Jules began to prepare the room on Sanctuary with the Lanterna Magica. Jules arranged for Pellinor – who was meant to be the first Green Knight, incidentally – to be at the river where Hugo would appear, and persuaded him to take you to Camelot by promising him a chance to battle his 'Questing Beast.' You botched that up, Hugo, when you stabbed Merlin. Our concerns were realized and verified later, when Hank sent us a message that he'd indeed met Hugo Dyson."

"That was the message you got fourteen years ago, when you came back to London to find us," said Jack. "But you – the you in Albion – told us that you'd been trapped there and had to wait for us. How is it you're here now ali – unharmed and whole?"

"That was the risk we took," said Bert, "that you would change what had happened. And you did."

"I'd like to meet Verne for one reason more than any other," put in Jack.

"What's that?" said Bert.

"I want to show him his own skull," Jack said as he took a drink of ale. "It's on the desk in my study."

"It just occurred to me," John said. "Did anyone ever get Pellinor out of the tree?"

Bert pulled a copy of the Little Whatsit out of his bag and thumbed through to one of the back pages. "Ah, no," he replied with a smirk. "They didn't."

"We're going to need to spend some time at the Great Whatsit on Paralon," said Jack. "We have a lot of history that we'll have to unlearn, beginning with the chronicles of Arthur, as the Cartographer was suggesting. We need to know what's changed as a result of this little adventure, and what hasn't."

"Jules has already begun tracking the changes," said Bert. "There have been some discrepancies found here and there in the Histories. One in particular came to our attention fourteen years ago, as Jules began keeping a Chronologue of the various jaunts through time."

"Discrepancies?" said John. "With what?"

"Oh, nothing attached to you, dear boy," Bert said, turning to Jack with a Cheshire grin. "But you, lad, are another matter entirely."

"Me?" Jack exclaimed. "I'm sure I don't know what you mean."

"Then how do you explain the apparently nonfictional, absolutely true, two-thousand-year-old tale that begat the story of Jack the Giant Killer?"

"Oh, for heaven's sake," said Jack. "Not all stories are true, are they? Not all of them really happened." He paused. "Or did they?"

"Time will tell, my boy," said Bert. "Time will tell."

Epilogue

Chancellor Murdoch entered the small room where the leaders of the world had gathered together to plan and play their little wars.

The meeting proceeded as he had expected it to; each proposal was met with open enthusiasm and fully proffered support. It would be, he realized, the easiest conquest he'd ever planned, and the most successful, because it would be his last. When this was done, there would be no players on the board but himself.

The rallying offensives of the past year had made his allies arrogant, especially the American president. He was the weakest of them physically, but he commanded the same sort of loyalty as others he had known in the distant past. And he was heading for the same great fall.

If they had not been so concerned with the plans for the war itself, and so enthralled by any credible promise of an added advantage over their enemies, they might have noticed the gentle whirring sounds that the chancellor emitted as he spoke, or the slightly mechanical nature of his movements. But they had not, and so when they left the room, no one looked back at their strange new ally, for if they had, they might have noticed that his shadow had a will of its own and moved of its own accord.

Of course, none among them would have known that it was the shadow that provided the motive power to the Clockwork Man that had been created by talking animals and a man called Nemo, and in another world had been known as the Red King. And if any of them had suspected, they did not care. All that mattered was that he had brought them the weapon that would see them to victory, when the time was right.

It was ironic, he thought. To have sought the weapon once called the Lance of Longinus for so many years, only to discover that it had been in the possession of the Green Knight. Most if not all of their long line, especially the first, would not have entertained the thought of giving it up to one such as he, even if they had been unaware of his plans for it. But the last, Magwich, had been his own servant, and he gave it up for the asking. It had taken time, but the world was once again in flux, and he would have the chance to prove his worth.

And time, the chancellor thought to himself as he cradled the Spear of Destiny in his hands once more, was what it was all about. Time, and how to use it. Because once that question was answered . . .

. . . he would rule the world.

In many ways, the chance to tell the story I created in *The Indigo King* is the reason the Chronicles of the Imaginarium Geographica exist. The heart of it is a very real event that took place on an evening in September 1931, when J. R. R. Tolkien, C. S. Lewis, and Hugo Dyson took a stroll on the grounds around Magdalen College, and discussed the story behind Christianity in the context of its meaning as a mythology rather than a religion.

Lewis had been if not a complete atheist, then something very close to it for most of his life, and although he had finally decided that there was "a" god, he could not wrap his head around the literal truth of the Christian mythology espoused by his friends.

Until that one night.

They walked, and talked, and as Lewis later wrote to his friend Arthur Greeves, "I have just passed on from believing in God to definitely believing in Christ – in Christianity. I will try to explain this another time. My long night talk with Dyson and Tolkien had a good deal to do with it."

Considering how influential Lewis became as an advocate of Christianity, the chance to imagine possible events for my fictional Jack to experience, that might thematically fold into the real events of his life, was too good to resist.

I had a great starting point for the book with the most-asked question about the other books: Who is the Cartographer? I knew I wanted to tell his complete story, and I'd been careful about dropping hints in the other books. I also wanted to bring my history of the Archipelago into sharper focus, tying it as I have to Odysseus and the Trojan War.

We'd already established connections to Arthurian lore with the lineage of the Silver Throne – but I wanted to go back as far as I could, and it thrilled me beyond words to establish an origin and a pedigree for Arthur's sword, Caliburn. And once I got into it, I decided that I wanted to mess with the conventions of the tales everyone knows.

There are fathers and sons, and nephews and uncles, but they are not who you expect them to be. And the difference between good and evil is not always clear. Sometimes good people make bad choices, and vice versa. And that makes it harder to praise – or condemn them.

The history of the Cartographer is in many ways the history of cartography itself; and the history of the Caretakers is the history of the world. Geoffrey of Monmouth was the first great Arthurian scribe and the first "real" Caretaker. His Green Knight, Abelard, was a contemporary that suited the role I put him in.

As to Chaz, I wanted a way to address Charles Williams's very influential works, which had a great effect on Lewis in particular but are much less well known than either of his friends' tales. His theories of many dimensions gave me a means to create a "what if" story inside my own book.

Author's Note

And as for Hank Morgan, he was the first real time-travelling character from Mark Twain's *A Connecticut Yankee in King Arthur's Court*, and since I'd already earmarked Twain as Jules Verne's predecessor, Hank fit in nicely in several ways.

As to some of the other characters, Reynard the fox was a minor player in *Sir Gawain and the Green Knight*; Gwynhfar is, obviously, a nod to Arthur while giving me my Holy Grail connection; and as for Rose . . . Well, as Bert said, only time will tell.

James A. Owen
Silvertown, USA